DESCENDANTS
OF ANGELS
BOOK 1

Loss
of the
Unguarded

TRACY DALEY

Copyright © 2023 by Night Nook Publishing

All rights reserved.

All characters and events in this story are fictitious, and any similarities to persons living or dead are purely coincidental.

No part of this book may be reproduced in any form or by any electronic or mechanical means, including information storage and retrieval systems, without written permission from the author, except for the use of brief quotations in a book review.

For news about cover reveals, new releases, and exclusive content, sign up for the Night Nook Publishing newsletter at www.nightnookpublishing.com

Trade Paperback ISBN: 978-1-960617-05-7

eBook ISBN: 978-1-960617-03-3

Library of Congress Control Number: 2023946369

For my husband who can bend the universe to his will, with all my love.

PART One

One

August 14

It's been ten years since I made the biggest mistake of my life. I know I can't go back and change things, not even the original Angels could turn back time, but I can't help wondering, "What if?" Especially, on the anniversary of the night my family disappeared.

Tonight, the questions swirl with a new intensity. I couldn't keep my eyes closed without the unknown attacking me like a physical thing in the darkness. I'm too old to hide under the covers, and as nice as my new foster family is, I wouldn't interrupt their sleep. The Creator knows Pat needs hers. When my eyes refused to close and the whirling questions made my heart beat nearly out of my chest, I decided I had to get everything out of my head and down on paper. Maybe then I would have a fair chance at battling the terror inside me.

I pulled out this leather notebook, a gift from Pat when I first came to live here three months ago. She'd said that we all needed external storage space to help us process everything. I didn't think I'd need it. After all, I'm not an Ordinary, not a normal human girl. I'm a Descendant. I have the knowledge and energy of creation written into my DNA. I shouldn't need a paper and pen to help me sleep. But tonight, I'm desperate. I feel so alone.

What would my eighteenth birthday have looked like if I hadn't been afraid? If I'd stayed to face the future instead of running from it? How different would my life be? Both our lives? All our lives? Was it all my fault?

I don't have all the answers. The things I do know shouldn't be written down. They are the secrets of the Descendants and the war that will eventually tear the world apart, but I have to get all of this out of my head.

Treadon Nelson

Treadon caught the football as a half-ton of human mass surged toward him, a collective hive mind with one objective. To destroy him.

He avoided conflict as a rule, but the freedom he felt on the football field gave him a confidence that didn't exist anywhere else. When the leather hit his fingers and the defensive line surged forward, cleats digging into the ground, his mind echoed three words. "Bring it on."

He knew the left tackle would break through the line an instant before it happened. Treadon noticed the safety relax his stance as the crowd roared. The cornerback favored his right knee. Treadon saw it all, knew exactly how each player would move and why.

He pulled back his arm and let the ball fly. Jarren Calivan caught the ball and Rachel Sampaio made the block. Touchdown. Game over.

They'd won their first game of the year.

But as soon as the cheers went up and the stands emptied onto the field, Treadon's freedom disappeared. He pulled back into himself and kept his head down. There were too many people, and it wasn't the physical noise that bothered him, it was the constant messages being tossed around that he wasn't supposed to hear or see. The facial expressions and body movements and voice inflections created a language as clear as a podcast through noise cancelling headphones.

He understood things that no one meant for him to hear. He'd learned to hide it, bury it deep, ignore the language other people knew was there, but only he could speak fluently. He'd reacted to things people hadn't really said enough times to know that he was different.

Jarren caught up to him on the sidelines. "Where are you going, Hero?" Jarren asked, knocking his helmet against Treadon's. He wiped the sweat from his forehead. His voice barely carried over the noise of the crowd. "Take a bow."

"I'm not the hero," Treadon said, leaning in close and yelling so the words would carry. "That was Rachel. You would have been flattened by that guy if she hadn't made the block."

"Are you guys talking about me?" Rachel jogged up, pulling her helmet off, her long black ponytail swishing back and forth, her face split with a smile. There was nothing timid or petite about Rachel Sampaio and her confidence won her friends and admirers both on and off the field. "If not, you should be. You owe me seven laps for saving your ass today." She poked Jarren in the chest.

"You only bet laps?" Treadon asked. "His dad drives a Bentley. You should have bet six grand for every block. This guy's going to get bought out by Oregon because you make him look so good."

Rachel kept a smile on her face, but when Treadon mentioned Jarren's dad, she dropped her eyes and tightened her shoulders.

Don't read into it. Treadon turned his attention to Jarren to avoid the tension he felt from Rachel when it came to Xander Calivan. Treadon didn't think Jarren's dad was so bad. At least he showed up to the football games. That was more than Treadon could say for his mom and Gabe.

A couple of guys from the other team walked by, scowling after the loss. One of them saw Rachel and spit on the field. "I think you forgot your skirt."

Jarren's fists tightened on his helmet, his dark skin going light around the knuckles from the pressure. He stepped forward, but Rachel pulled him back as the other football players disappeared into the crowd.

"I don't need you to protect me. I'm your tight end, remember?" Rachel said, shoving Jarren playfully in the chest. "I block for you."

"Let me give you a ride home," Jarren said. "Just to make sure they don't bother you again."

Rachel paused, considering. Treadon kept his head down. He liked Rachel and Jarren, but they had this swirling, complicated relationship that gave Treadon a headache trying not to read all the message the two of them were sending. Even trying not to read into their private feelings, Treadon knew exactly why Rachel shook her head. Xander Calivan was at the game and would be driving Jarren home in the Bentley. Rachel didn't want anything to do with her best friend's dad.

"I've got a ride," Rachel said, giving them a wave with her helmet. "Senior year starts next week, and we've started with a win. Let's keep the streak going."

Jarren watched Rachel walk away. His normally straight posture sagged a little, his hands swinging at his side.

Treadon tried hard to ignore the noise. Everyone had a story. Everyone had things about themselves they didn't want other people to see. It wasn't fair that it felt like people were yelling those things at him all the time. He felt like he was watching the world through a one-sided mirror. He could see out, but no one could see him.

"Good game," Treadon said, needing to get away from the crowd and the people and the voices. "I'll see you next week."

"Can I pick you up?" Jarren asked. "I'm getting my own car and I want to show it off, but I don't think Rachel will appreciate it."

Treadon wanted to say no. He wanted to say that he didn't need a ride to school as a senior in high school, but they only had one car and his mom needed it for work. It would probably be a big help.

"Yeah, sure," Treadon said as he backed away. "I want to see this new car of yours."

Jarren nodded, waving as he joined the celebrating crowd.

Treadon headed toward the parking lot, keeping his head down. But something still caught his eye.

A trick in the flow of bodies. A disturbance in the normal ebb of traffic. His stomach flipped and he felt a wave of dizziness. The ground tilted like he was on a boat rocking on waves in a storm.

He closed his eyes for a second, trying to shake the feeling. When he opened his eyes again, his focus zeroed in on the anomaly.

A girl. Walking against the crowd. Treadon felt another wave of nausea, his mind fighting against him, telling him to look away. He fought the sensation. The crowd milled around him, people bumping into his shoulder, forcing their way past. Someone shoved him. "Watch where you're going."

The words were garbled like sound traveling through water.

Another bump on his shoulder and Treadon realized what was wrong. The girl should be experiencing the same thing. Anyone can walk the wrong way through a crowd, but not without getting bumped and jostled. This girl wasn't touching anyone. And no one was touching her. It was like she walked through the crowd with a bubble of protection around her.

Treadon moved forward, watching her. She kept her head down, studying a piece of paper. Not a single person seemed to notice her. She moved unheeded, untouched. The chaotic scramble of people parted unconsciously for her. She walked evenly, no break in her stride.

Then he saw a group of football players from the other team, shoving and joking as they headed toward their bus. One of the football players jumped on the shoulders of another, messing around, trying to pull the other to the ground. The girl was walking right into their path. They wouldn't see her. She couldn't see them.

She was only a few steps away from him.

"Watch out." Treadon said the words at the same time as he reacted. He jumped forward and grabbed her arm, pulling her out of the way.

He pressed her against the wall of the school, sheltering her from the crowd with his body as the football players ran into him.

"Watch it," they called. One of them flipped him off, but they kept moving toward their bus.

Treadon looked down at the girl to ask if she was okay, but the words caught in his throat. Her eyes were wide, her fists pulled up to her face, her shoulders arched in a boxer's stance like she'd just seen her worst nightmare and she wasn't going down without a fight.

Two

GABRIEL TUOER

Gabe studied a nondescript house from across a residential street. He stood in an older neighborhood, the cookie-cutter houses unique only in their state of dilapidation. The same color stucco chipped away in different places. The same shaped arches cracked and fading in different spots.

The house Gabe singled out had no numbers on the front. No mailbox. No identifying features. No cars in the driveway. No toys littering the front yard. No arrays of odds and ends sticking out from under the porch or piled against the fence. Every other house had at least one of these things. If no one was here, it meant he was too late.

Abigail had been worried. She'd told him to hurry.

The windows stared out at him, empty and lifeless, reminding Gabe of a taunting skull.

He walked across the street and up the porch steps which creaked under his weight. The small noise was thunder in the silence.

The front door stood open behind the screen and Gabe could see into the front room.

Spotless. Empty.

There was no sign anyone had ever lived here. He opened the screen door and stepped into the hall, tensed for any movement, listening for any noise. His footsteps echoed through the abandoned house.

This was the third empty house in a row. He and Abigail Nelson had been finding the Unguarded, taking them to safety, protecting them from a worse fate. But something had caught up to them. It had been a race for all these years, but now he knew he was losing.

Fighting an invisible enemy made him feel crazy. Losing to an invisible enemy made him feel powerless.

They were just children, Descendants of Angels barely coming into their knowledge. Abigail had the ability to see those auras even though she was neither Descendant nor Guardian. She had been his ally during the darkest times of his life, when all others had abandoned him.

Her voice came to him through the airwaves. She spoke into a CB radio over a hundred miles away. But Gabe could hear her voice with no special equipment, only the knowledge granted him when the Descendant Adura chose him as her Guardian. He was a Guardian of Descendants, and he couldn't even protect the children anymore.

He'd lost another one.

Maybe something had been left behind this time. A clue. An unlikely hope. He checked the house anyway. Each room was the same. Devoid of furniture. Floors wiped clean. Even the windowsills were clear of dust.

In the kitchen, the appliances had been removed, forlorn wires hanging from the wall.

Gabe opened the nearest cupboard, but stopped when he heard a sound. A deep rumble that reverberated through his bones.

He stilled, listening. Then he reached up for the leather handles of the two double-edged swords on his back. He pulled the swords from the sheaths and turned to face the back door.

His swords glowed a pale green, edged with the green hematite stone that burned a demon's essence. The green hematite could transfer a Descendant's or Guardian's energy to their weapon, making it harmless to humans, but deadly to the twisted creations that tried to feed off human misery.

There was a pause. No sound. No movement.

Then a shadow crossed over the window. Another growl. Louder. Closer.

Gabe tensed. His heart surged with a strangled hope. The creatures were still here. That meant he wasn't that far behind.

The snarls grew louder. A sound Gabe was familiar with—a guttural growl mixed with grinding stones and howling wind. The next instant, the windows shattered as four creatures burst into the house. Their heads were more mouth than face, the unnaturally large jaws snapping open and shut, spittle flying from sharp teeth.

Their front legs were small, most of the weight gathered in their rear haunches. Their bodies were covered with a thin layer of wet hair, slimy, sticking to their skin like the feathers of a chick recently hatched from an egg. Fenris. The demon's basic form. It was the shape they took when they were hungry, when they hadn't had a chance to feed on human essence for too long. Hunger drove them. Anger fueled them.

Gabe didn't wait for an invitation. He caught the closest animal with his sword, severing the head from its body. He turned as a second animal attacked from behind and a third dove at him from the side. Gabe stabbed his sword through the skull of one of the creatures, the green hematite crackling with electricity at the contact. He brought his other sword around in time to cut off the bottom half of another creature, shifting his shoulders so the claws barely missed the exposed skin on his neck.

He turned on the fourth creature and drove both his swords into its chest. The growl turned into a pained whine as it dropped to the floor. The creatures' bodies crumbled; the poor structure of their forms unable to hold together without the life force. They weren't dead. Nothing could kill a demon essence, but they would be scattered, taking weeks or months to reform.

Gabe stood in the middle of the kitchen, nothing left of the fenris except black dust swirling across the floor.

Three

August 15

 Mom used to tell me I was special, that I'd received more knowledge than most Descendants. I had a lot of responsibility to carry. She didn't tell me why, just made sure that I was prepared. Still, I used to have nightmares I couldn't remember and Mom couldn't explain. She'd crawl under the sheets with me and tell stories of the past with a flashlight bouncing off our cave of covers.

 Mom's hair would get staticky, standing up and sticking to the sheets. She'd make faces that would help me laugh the tears away. I'm not sure I can still hear her voice, but I remember the cadence, the rhythm of the stories as she would tell me about the beginning when Valde Novo made a world for his precious creations, human beings. He wanted to share his accomplishment with his son, Cado Fillius, but the son wanted to wield his father's power. Cado tried to imitate the creations of Valde Novo, but without the love and understanding his father had, the creatures Cado created were incomplete, empty souls that craved sorrow. Demons.

Mom's voice would go low when she talked about the demons. She'd come in close and wrap her arms around me like she would protect me from all the darkness in the world. I know now that there is far more darkness than even a mother's love can chase away.

When Valde Novo returned to earth to check on his creations, he found that the demons had run wild, corrupting humans, and magnifying sorrow, enhancing selfishness and cruelty. Valde Novo banished his son to the earth, leaving Cado Fillius with all the knowledge of creation, but none of his father's energy. No influence over the kingdoms he had once ruled.

Before leaving the earth, Valde Novo gave one final gift to humanity. He chose three of the purest souls and divided the knowledge and energy of creation between them, commanding them to bring hope and happiness through miracles. The Angels' single purpose was to defend humans against the hoard of demons directed by Cado Fillius.

Mom would stop, making sure my head was down on the pillow. She'd touch my eyelids with her fingertips, brushing my eyes closed. She'd whisper their names into my ear like she was counting sheep. Adeona, the Angel of Life. Samuil, the Angel of Elements, and Baldur, the Angel of Light.

I can hear Jake in the next room, fighting his own nightmares. My foster brother has his own pain, a pain I cannot take away. I think about telling him the story to help *him fall back asleep. It isn't a story for Ordinaries, but Jake can't tell anyone.*

TREADON NELSON

Treadon watched the girl's movements, feeling like he was an outside observer. He could read her intentions, saw the muscles flex, and knew her fingers were going to jab into his windpipe, cutting off his breath, leaving her free to run.

The part of Treadon that had always wanted to fit in, wanted to be normal, considered letting the hit land so she wouldn't know he could tell what she was about to do. But there was another part of him that won out, an unconscious impulse to protect, not just himself, but this girl in front of him.

His hand came up, knocking her fist aside. She used the moment to spin, lifting her leg to kick the side of his knee. She was fast, her movements fluid, her body balanced. He stepped back to avoid the kick, but she adjusted, landing on both feet, facing him, and went for three punches to his stomach. Treadon blocked with his left arm, then his right, pushing her arm aside. He could have blocked the third, could see what she planned to do and knew he had time to react, but for some reason, that was what this girl was expecting.

She thought she had to defend herself against him.

Treadon let the third punch land. There was strength behind her swing and the impact knocked the air out of him. He bent over and grabbed his stomach. Now she was surprised, and she hesitated. He had half a second.

"I'm not who you think I am." He looked up at her, reading her reaction. "I'm not what you think I am."

"And what do you think I think you are?" She remained tense, her hands raised in front of her, prepared for another offensive attack.

"An enemy." Treadon took a step back to give her space. To prove he wasn't a threat.

He looked around, expecting to see a crowd around them or someone yelling, "Fight."

No one had noticed a girl taking on a football player still wearing his uniform. He felt that wave of nausea again. It had nothing to do with the bruise he was sure to have on his stomach. "What's going on right now?"

"Why did you shove me?" The girl asked why, but Treadon read a different word. She wanted to know how he had been able to shove her.

"Someone was about to run into you. I thought I was helping you get out of the way."

"I don't need anyone's help," she said, eyes narrowing. She sucked in the corner of her lip.

"You don't believe that," Treadon said like he was reading a fact book. He wished he could suck the words back in.

"Are you reading my thoughts now?" The girl put her hands on her hips. "You think you know what I believe?"

"No," Treadon said, putting up his hands like he could wipe the words away. "I meant everyone needs help sometimes. My name is Treadon. Treadon Nelson." He turned and pointed to the last name stenciled across his uniform.

The girl lowered her hands. Her lips remained tight; her eyebrows pulled down in suspicion. "And you're really just a football player?" Her voice had an odd note—relief, but still an edge of concern. "And you noticed me?"

His curiosity warred with his commitment to hide what he could do. Curiosity won. He looked up at her.

"Why wouldn't I notice you? You're . . . different."

Her face tightened and he could see that her hatred of that word reflected his own. He never should have said it. He knew how much he hated being called different.

"I mean you look good, beautiful, and you walk nice, and people get out of your way, and you hit hard and so, yeah, I noticed you." He couldn't stop the words. He wanted to melt into the pavement.

"Don't. Don't do that again."

"What? Notice you?"

She sent him a sideways look, her muscles fighting a smile, but the real fear, whatever had set her on the defense from the beginning, still controlled her features. "Yes. I mean, right. Don't notice me."

"I don't know if I can help it."

"Don't worry. You won't see me again." She turned, flipping her hair over her shoulder like it was a final goodbye.

"Wait."

She paused.

"What are you afraid of?" he asked.

She turned around and stepped right up to him. She was shorter than him, but with her face turned up and his turned down, their noses almost touched. He caught a whiff of strawberry shampoo.

Her eyes bored into him, dark brown pools that could have pulled him in, but instead, dared him to look away, begged him to look away.

"I'm sorry." Treadon said. "I'll leave you alone. But I want to help if I can."

"How do you do that?" Her curiosity was genuine.

"I don't know." He felt like he was taking a flying leap off the edge of a cliff, but he didn't have a lot left to lose with this girl. Her closeness was more of a threat than an advance. "I've always been able to read people. It kind of sucks."

She stepped back and the way her shoulders fell, the way the fight drained away, spoke of disappointment. Not all of it was directed at him. "And you play football? That's it? Do you do anything else with it?"

"I'm not proud of it. It makes me weird."

"Different." She echoed the word he'd said to her earlier.

"Yeah."

She took another step back and it felt like a canyon opened between them. "You could see so much and choose to see nothing." Her full disappointment hit him in the middle with almost as much force as her punch.

There was a honk from the parking lot; Treadon turned to see his mom waving to him from the car.

When he turned back around, the girl was gone. He hadn't even asked her name.

Treadon picked up his duffle bag and jogged over to the blue Pontiac that was held together with duct tape and prayers. He threw his duffle bag in the back seat and climbed in the front.

"Thanks for picking me up, Mom." He avoided looking at her, keeping his eyes out his window. Being able to read people came as advantage on the football field, but he tried to ignore it the most at home. Even when he tried to close his eyes to it, he could read the unhappiness, worry, and overall unease in his mother's shoulders. Her smile always seemed to snag on something when she tried to pin it on.

The problem was Gabe. He slipped in and out of their lives, disappearing for weeks at a time, showing up like a wrecking ball. He wasn't drunk or abusive or anything Treadon could put his finger on. The guy was unreadable. Cold.

His mom worked. Gabe traveled. He never brought home a paycheck and the weight of the finances fell to his mom. Treadon was going to change that after this year.

"How was practice?" she asked. Abigail ran her hand to push back her hair. Her fingers paused on the long scar just along her hairline. A nervous habit. The memory of an injury from a long time ago.

"It was good." Treadon leaned back against the headrest, breathing in the pine air freshener that almost covered the slight smell of burning oil and old musty car smell. It was so hard to explain to her how he felt. Abigail would never be able to earn enough with her job to help him pay for college, but now, with the NIL, he could help support her the way Gabe never had.

Treadon needed to lead the team to an undefeated year if he wanted to make the kind of money that would really make a difference, to be able to help his mom move on, find happiness. He would do it for her.

But he couldn't fight the nagging feeling that he shouldn't leave her alone. A sense of protectiveness had always made it hard to imagine leaving his mom with only Gabe. The girl's words haunted him like she was sitting in the back seat. *And you choose to play football?*

Her words echoed the feeling he couldn't quite put a name to, this belief that he was meant to do something more important than win a football game.

Four

August 18

    I've been hiding for ten years, but it wasn't until two days ago that I had to face the reason why. I'm scared. I'm a coward. I'm afraid to face the consequence of my mistake and I'm afraid of the monsters in the dark, the ones Mom would tell me about under the blanket, the ones that made me run away that night. But when I bumped into a guy at school . . . no, that's not what happened . . . When that guy at school bumped into me, on purpose, it felt like being jolted awake from a dream where you've fallen off a cliff. That moment right before you hit the ground.

    Treadon. He said his name was Treadon and he had nice eyes and strong arms. He gets a dimple in his cheek when tries not to smile and he acted like he understood me, like he could see me. I haven't let anyone notice me, remember me, for almost ten years. My abilities as a Descendant have helped me stay hidden, wrapping my light up inside myself so I'm invisible to other Descendants and demons. I've isolated myself and I've done a good job.

But he noticed me. My concentration must have slipped, but somehow, I don't feel like I can push him away the same way I do others. He feels . . . slippery. That's not the right word, but I can't think of a better one. Still, I felt someone looking at me for the first time and it made my small world feel like a shrinking cage. There is a whole life out there and I've locked myself away. Maybe I deserve it, but he made a crack in my cage, and now I'm tempted to slip out and see what I've been missing.

Dad would have told me to get out there and live life. He was Mom's Guardian and helped tell the bedtime stories. Nothing brought Dad more joy than putting a record on an old record player and pulling Mom around the living room, dipping her behind the couch where my brother and I couldn't see and making loud kissing sounds for our benefit. It was Dad who told me about the daggers. He told the stories with his deep voice that vibrated through my soul like base speakers turned up too loud.

There were three original Angels against a whole race of demons. Where the demons brought darkness and despair, the Angels brought hope and light. Miracles as simple as lifting someone's eyes to the sunset. Miracles as impossible as bringing a loved one back to life. Angels moved among the children of Valde Novo and brought smiles and joy that protected the Ordinaries' life force from the hungry demon forms.

I remember Dad picking me up, tossing me high and

catching me as he told the next part. As he talked about Cado Fillius' jealousy of the Angels who had been given his father's energy when he'd been robbed of his birthright. With his knowledge, he discovered that by using an element of the earth, black hematite, he could steal the Angel's energy. Even writing those words made me shiver. I slipped out to the living room to grab an extra blanket. Pat always keeps extra bedding around, never knowing when the next foster kid will join us, always prepared to make this place a home for a displaced child. My parents would have liked Pat, an Ordinary bringing light to a dark world. Just like the Angels of the past.

But no matter how much you prepare or how much goodness there is, something always goes wrong, just like in the stories.

Cado Fillius found a way to capture Samuil, the Angel of Elements, and steal some of his energy. Baldur and Adeona rescued Samuil and scattered the black hematite to the ends of the earth, but not before Cado Fillius used the energy he'd absorbed to create a way to kill an immortal Angel.

My hand is shaking so bad I can hardly write this. The memory of my dad, his love for life, the way he helped my brother and I ride a bike and plant a garden. And now he's gone. Descendants are not immortal, not the way the original Angels were, but it's very hard to kill us. Someone must have found away. I can't bear the thought that it might have been me.

It's difficult to understand the consequences of an action. Just like Cado Fillius didn't understand that all things must *remain in balance. And when he tried to create a single dagger, he ended up with two.*

One black dagger.

One pure white.

The white one was the accident, a balance of all things to permanently scatter a demon essence.

The black dagger, made of hematite, could end the life of the immortal Angels.

Treadon Nelson

Treadon's moments between solemn slumber and wakeful awareness were torture. His fingers could almost grasp reality while his mind fought the pain, the crushing pressure, the lack of air, the dark void that pulled him toward the end.

He woke with a gasp. His room came into focus slowly, his dream slipping back into the shadows. He tried to close his eyes, but the sensation of drowning was too overwhelming, chasing away any chance of sleep. The clock read 3:30 am.

He stumbled into the hall to escape his room. He stopped as he entered the kitchen. The lights were on. His mom sat deflated at the kitchen table, her hands spread out over a map, a CB radio planted on the chair beside her. Her whole body said, *not again*. Treadon didn't know what Gabe did when he was gone or why he insisted on teasing Abigail by communicating through that stupid radio.

Treadon pushed away the urge to try and read more. Some things he'd decided to close his eyes to a long time ago.

Abigail looked up. Treadon read the pain etched on her face. Something lost. He wanted to change this for her, to fix everything.

She jumped slightly when she noticed him. She wiped away the emotion and put on her everything-is-fine face. Even if Treadon had wanted to read more, Abigail had a mask.

He walked past her to the sink.

She folded the map, her movements a little too fast. She put the map and the CB radio in a kitchen drawer. "You're up early. Did you have a nightmare?"

Treadon filled a cup of water but didn't take a drink. He didn't want his mom to see his hands shaking.

"Nope. Just thirsty." He paused. There was an unspoken history of Treadon's night terrors when he was younger, but he didn't tell her about them anymore. He wanted her to believe he'd grown out of them.

"Everything okay with Gabe?"

"Of course. He'll be home this weekend."

"Great." Treadon hadn't expected a real answer. There was so much left unsaid that the words could have filled a book.

"How about school?" She always had to turn the conversation back to him.

"I still feel different. Like I can't quite fit in."

"Treadon, the things that make us different . . ."

"I don't want to be special." Treadon started for his room, but Abigail touched his arm, stopping him with hardly any pressure at all.

"I was going to say, the things that make you different, are the things that make you important. Sometimes we don't get to choose our differences. But we can choose the impact we make."

He took the water back to his room and shut the door. He sat on the edge of his bed, holding the cup with both hands as he brought it up to his lips, the water sloshing back and forth.

It was just a dream. He wasn't a kid anymore. The water was a balm on his parched throat, and he gulped it down. He heard a cupboard shut and the shuffle of Abigail's feet across the floor. She came down the hallway. Her footsteps paused outside his room, and he imagined if she came in, wrapped him in her arms, and rocked him like she had when he was small, screaming and sobbing after a nightmare.

Her robe would smell of roses and mint and her voice would be soft, her touch warm. Treadon leaned toward the door, swallowing to keep himself from calling out to her, asking her to come in. He was the captain of the football team. A senior in high school. He was the one who needed to be strong for his mom, not the other way around.

Her footsteps moved on, and Treadon lay on top of the covers, keeping his eyes wide open, checking the clock every few minutes, willing the night to go faster.

He did not go back to sleep.

When Treadon came back out to the living room, the memories of the night brushed off in the shower, his hair combed, his backpack packed, Abigail was already on the couch. Maybe she hadn't slept either.

"I can drop you off on my way to work if you're ready."

Treadon shook his head. "Jarren's coming to pick me up. He wanted to show off the new car his dad bought him. I guess it's pretty fancy." Jarren's dad was an example of the power of money. Treadon wanted that, wanted to give his mom a fancy car, and enough gas to drive from California to New York just for fun.

Summoned by the musical sound of his own name, Jarren Calivan breezed through the front door without knocking. He entered with a confident swagger, moving as if the world conformed to support him. He wore a blue collared shirt and khaki pants. His skin was dark brown, teeth white and perfect, and his hair black with short tight curls.

Abigail stood; coffee mug balanced in one hand.

"Morning, Ms. Nelson." Jarren wrapped his arms around Abigail, giving her a full hug. Abigail relaxed, a few of the lines on her face smoothing out. Jarren stepped back.

"Are you ready for the ride of your life?" Jarren said. "The car came in last night. My dad special ordered it for all the work I did for him this summer. Kind of a bonus."

"I don't think a ride to school will be the ride of my life." Treadon tied his shoes, angry at himself for being too caught up in his own nightmare to think of giving his mom a hug. "Let's see this new car." He stood up and pushed Jarren toward the door.

Halfway out the door, Treadon stopped and stared. He let out a low whistle of admiration. A shiny, silver convertible was cradled in the driveway. The contrast between the immaculate vehicle radiating in front of the plain rambler house with a cracked, tilted driveway was painful.

"What is that?" Abigail had stepped up to the door behind them and was staring at Jarren's car.

"Aston Martin DB9 convertible with a V12." Jarren shrugged. "It's not the newest model, but she has less than fifty miles on her."

"There goes your last ounce of humility," Treadon said.

"Humility is overrated. Sometimes you got to make a statement."

"And what is your dad saying with this car?"

Treadon meant it as a joke, but he saw a shadow flicker across his friend's face. Treadon turned away before he could read it. The last thing he wanted this morning was to say something stupid in front of Jarren. He'd had enough stupid in front of that girl the other day. He'd hoped he could find her today and get a second chance.

Abigail bumped Treadon's arm as she moved out onto the porch. "That's a nice car. It's . . . interesting. Where did your dad get it?"

"Who knows. Some friend of a friend who buys cars, but never drives them."

"Let's go." Treadon felt a twinge of jealousy at the look on his mom's face. He wished he could get his mom nice things now, but he would be able to soon. Just on the other side of graduation.

Jarren jumped over his door and into the driver's seat. Treadon opened the passenger door and slipped in. He swallowed the nervous anticipation that rose in his throat. He had a fear of cars that left him sweaty and shaking, but he was pretty good at coving it up. His heart jumped into his throat when Jarren hit the ON button and the engine roared to life.

"Your mom's got good taste," Jarren said. "She really knows how to appreciate nice things—unlike some people I know."

"Yeah." Treadon gripped the handle on the door. They hadn't even started moving yet and he could feel the panic squeezing down on his chest. He focused on his mom watching them from the porch. He almost slipped and let himself read her. There was something more than admiration on her face. He could see disbelief. Confusion. Something about a secret.

Jarren put the car in reverse and accelerated with precision, controlling the car like he'd been driving race cars all his life. Treadon's stomach was left behind in his driveway. He swallowed, hoping Jarren wouldn't notice the pressure grip he had on the seat. He took a breath and tried to sound normal.

"This car will get stripped down for the headlights before you get out of homeroom."

"Don't worry about the car." Jarren flashed himself a smile in his rearview mirror. "It has a new security system developed by my dad's company."

"I thought your dad owned an energy company."

Jarren swerved around a garbage can, the wind turbulence throwing a plastic bag into the air and making the garbage can rock back and forth. Treadon turned his head so he could close his eyes without Jarren noticing.

"My dad's company does a lot of things: research, development, technology. We've got some exciting projects in the works."

Treadon didn't bother answering. He leaned back into his seat, opened his eyes, and focused on looking as relaxed as Jarren. The last thing he wanted was his friend to know about his illogical fear of cars, his anxiety when it came to driving. He was already different enough. He didn't need anything else that set him apart and made him look like a freak.

Five

August 21

    Pat's husband had a terrible accident a few weeks ago. This good family can't seem to catch a break. Besides me and Jake, there are the twins and she'd just taken in their new baby sister. Five foster kids and a serious incident that Pat hasn't reported yet. She doesn't want us to have to leave, especially Jake. He needs the stability, the time to heal.

    I overheard Pat praying in her room, asking for a miracle. I wonder if the original Angels could hear the prayers of Ordinaries. I wonder how they knew where they were needed. After Samuil was rescued and the daggers created, the Angels decided it was too dangerous for them to be alone, but the world was too large for the three of them to always be together. There was too much to do. So many demons bringing pain and darkness. The Angels decided to have children, to be able to pass their knowledge and energy on to their descendants so that they would not have to do the work alone.

But when Valde Novo created Angels to protect his creations, he had chosen them for their goodness and purity. And he had divided his knowledge and power into thirds so that no single being would be able to make the same mistake as his son.

Mistakes. So many mistakes. The Angels, in their fear, undid both of Valde Novo's carefully planned protections. Did the Angels make a mistake in breaking the rules of Valde Novo? They combined their knowledge and energy to rewrite the DNA of the Descendants, granting them the ability to choose a Guardian. Did they use that power as wisely as Valde Novo? Was it a mistake to give the energy and knowledge of creation to their Descendants, not knowing the purity and goodness of the souls who would inherit it? They had designed a system where Ordinaries would no longer be protected, but dragged into a war that was meant for immortals.

Pat's prayers are echoing in my head even as I'm writing these words. I haven't used my Descendant powers since I ran away because I'm afraid of making another mistake, but I don't know if I can listen to her cry herself to sleep for another night.

Treadon Nelson

. . .

Jarren parked the car. Treadon rolled out of the passenger side door. He had to lean against the car to catch his breath.

"My driving isn't that bad." Jarren brushed some invisible dust from his steering wheel.

"No. Nope. You're a great driver. I get a little car sick."

"My car has a firm 'No Vomit' policy. You should have warned me."

Treadon stood up and rolled out his shoulders. "Hey. I made it, didn't I? Let's see this new security system. Otherwise, me getting sick in your car is the least of your worries."

"Okay." Jarren jumped over his door, closed the roof, and pressed the lock button on his keys. He walked around the car to stand by Treadon. "There are motion sensors all around the car. If someone gets close it talks."

Jarren stepped closer to the car and a woman's voice emanated from the car. "Please back away from the vehicle. Please back away from the vehicle."

Treadon shook his head. "That's not going to stop someone from keying your car."

"Here." Jarren held out a traditional metal house key.

"You're joking."

"Nope. I wanted a different color, anyway. See what damage you can do."

Treadon took the key and held it out. He wouldn't really scratch it, but he was curious enough to see what would happen. He was still several inches away from the paint when he felt an electric shock hit his hand and travel up his arm.

"Ouch." Treadon dropped the keys. "What was that?"

"It's the new security system." Jarren had a little too much enthusiasm in his voice. "It has something to do with the metal getting too close to the car. And that was only level two! It goes up to ten. Do you want to find out what that feels like?"

"No. Do it yourself. That was my throwing arm." Treadon swung his arm up and around in a circle, testing the damage.

"Well, we could try it for freshman initiation. See what level ten feels like. Without actually feeling it."

"That would get us kicked off the team faster than you could say, 'daddy's boy.'" Treadon couldn't help laughing at the wounded look on Jarren's face. "Not saying it wouldn't be fun, but maybe not worth it."

They walked away from the car and joined the flow of kids walking toward the school. Treadon scanned the crowd, looking for the girl with the deep, brown eyes and the searing glare.

Her words came back to him. *Someone who could see so much but chooses to see nothing.*

His mom's words joined in. *What makes you different is what makes you important.*

He didn't want to be different. He didn't want to stand out. He did want to do something good for his mom, and he had a way to do that. By fitting in. By playing football. He didn't need anything more than that.

"Do you want to skip first period and hit the gym?" Jarren asked. "Coach Bracken will write us a note."

"You've got study hall first period. You skip ninety percent of the time."

"So?"

"So, I'm jealous. I've got math with Ashes-of-Hell Croft. I can't miss."

"Ooo." Jarren put his fist over his mouth like he just witnessed a painful tackle. "He is not a fan of athletes, football players specifically. Are you going to be able to stay eligible?"

"Not if I skip to go to gym."

"Sorry, man. I'll catch you on the other side." Jarren jogged off and Treadon trudged toward class.

He sat down in a desk in the back row where he could still see out the door, watching the students who passed, hoping to see her again. The girl who didn't want to be seen.

"Why don't you have your notebook out, Mr. Nelson?" A bony hand with a patch of hair growing on the back slammed down on his desk.

Treadon jumped. He hadn't been paying attention, but he was pretty sure the bell hadn't rung. Several kids slipped in the door and scurried to their seat. Students sitting near him pulled notebooks from their backpacks and placed them on their desk. He hadn't been the only student not ready.

"Math teaches reasoning skills and is a very important part of your education. Football can't give you that, Mr. Nelson. And I will not be giving free points just because you leave for school approved absences. I will expect all work to be made up and all material covered in class to be reviewed on your own time."

Treadon kept his hands under his desk so Mr. Ashcroft wouldn't see the fists he'd made. The anger surged up through him, but all he did was nod.

Mr. Ashcroft scowled and returned to the front of the room. The tardy bell rang.

He turned to his white board and started writing equations. Mr. Ashcroft was a short, skinny man with a receding hairline and unkempt curly hair. He had a long, pinched nose that created a nasal voice and a high-pitched noise when he breathed too hard. When Mr. Ashcroft got angry or excited his voice became so high Treadon was sure every dog within two blocks was going nuts.

"There will be a quiz each morning. I suggest you take notes and complete the assignments because quizzes will be forty percent of your grade." He locked Treadon with a stony stare as if the instruction had been only for him. Treadon didn't react, but he never let his eyes leave Mr. Ashcroft's murky, gray ones. He wasn't going to give Mr. Ashcroft the satisfaction.

Treadon pulled out his notebook and copied the numbers and letters Mr. Ashcroft wrote that seemed to appear without reason or explanation. By the time the bell rang he was thoroughly confused. If he had a gift for reading numbers instead of people, maybe he would be better at math than football, but he didn't. He couldn't let his grades get in the way of playing. Without a college scholarship and a NIL deal, he wouldn't have a way to get his mom away from Gabe. He wasn't going to let Mr. Ashcroft stand in the way of that. He just had to keep his grades above a C.

Somehow, that felt like an impossible task with that man as a teacher.

Six

September 4

My room feels cold tonight even though the fall weather is still warm. When the sun went down and the house got quiet, the temperature seemed to drop. I checked on the twins, the baby, and Jake. Their rooms seem fine.

I'm writing in the corner of my room, by the light of the full moon, with a dull pencil. Jake came in and handed me his ragged blanket, the one thing he brought with him when he came to this house. I was too afraid to say no and too afraid to take it from his hands. He set it on my knees and was about to back out of the room, but I couldn't let him leave without giving him something. I opened my dresser and came up with nothing. I've kept so little over the years, made sure not to get attached.

I only had one thing.

My Descendant amulet. I keep it on a chain around my

neck and I could see the circular scars that match the shape when I tugged my shirt down enough to pull the amulet out. I tucked my shirt back up to my chin as I held the amulet out for Jake to see. I can only offer him another story.

Jake eyed the amulet. The twirling circles and the white, green, and blue jewels are hypnotizing, even for me. I don't know how long we stared as it dangled between the two of us, but he didn't take it. He touched it for one instant, letting his finger still the spinning circles. And then he slipped back into the hall, leaving me staring at a piece of myself.

My compass.

The Angels wanted to keep their Descendants from being lost and alone. They rewrote their DNA to include the ability to create a compass. The compass is an amulet that points the way for a Bonded Guardian. Once the Guardian is Bonded, their DNA is tethered to the compass. The Guardian is always able to find their Descendant no matter where they are.

When the Guardian holds the compass in the palm of their hand, the jewels line up, directing the Guardian to their Descendant.

I almost put the amulet in Jakes palm, just to see, just to be sure. But it can't be him. Could it? Is it possible I made Jake the way he is? Or even if it is someone else, could I have hurt them as badly? I cannot bear the thought, so I'm holding my own amulet and Jake's blanket, knowing this compass will never be my Guardian's guide.

Gabriel Tuoer

Gabe sat silently in the kitchen, balanced on the edge of a chair. The legs creaked as he shifted his weight. Abigail Nelson worked quickly, with experienced hands. He could feel the cool brush of her fingers against his skin. He'd found the fenris a second time. There had been more; he'd let them get too close.

He had three long rips in his skin, stretching from his left shoulder blade down to his ribcage on the opposite side. The rips were black and swollen. The claws of the fenris were tipped with poison that slowed the healing process of a Descendant or Guardian.

"Tell me what happened," Abigail said softly. She pulled a blade from the flame on the gas stove and used it to remove the largest chunks of blackened skin. She moved without flinching.

Gabe hesitated. She deserved good news. The air left his lungs causing his shoulders to sag slightly. He brought no good news.

"It was empty." Gabe told the truth even though he could sense how it hurt her. "I don't know how they're finding them before us. Something's changed. I'm close behind them, but the fenris waiting for me." He meant the last sentence to encourage her, but her fingers tightened on his bare shoulder. She tried to cover it up by turning away from him.

"I saw when the light disappeared." Abigail spoke like the words didn't have the strength to come out. "I can see their aura, the light glowing bright white, but the shadows move in so quickly, I can't see where they come from. All I can do is watch."

She held the sharp blade over the burner again and turned back to finish cutting the dead skin from the lower parts of his wounds. His back flexed slightly at her touch. He leaned forward with his elbows on his knees, his fingers gripping hard enough to leave his knuckles white. The burning pain of the scratches was a relief compared to the nagging worry growing in his heart. If things were changing, if the work they did together had been compromised, he worried about the danger he might be putting her in. He worried he wouldn't have the ability to keep her safe.

Abigail held his arm, brushing softly against his bicep as she cleaned the wounds with a rag, warm water dripping over his shoulder and down his chest.

"I saw something today." Abigail dried his skin with a towel. Gabe could already feel the poison being leached out, his strength returning. "Something weird. Do you remember Treadon's friend, Jarren?"

Gabe cocked his head at the shift in the conversation. "Yes. They play football together, don't they?"

"Right. Jarren got a new car and came to pick Treadon up to show it off. But when I saw it, the car, it had an aura, a powerful one. Not white like a Descendant, but lighter yellow than an average person. And it was bright."

Abigail tapped him on the shoulder, signaling that she was ready for him to lift his arms for the bandages. She moved around to his front and pressed the white gauze against his ribs. "Have you ever heard of anything like that before? A machine with an aura?" Abigail asked as she wrapped the bandage around him, her arms encircling him.

"No." Gabe kept his arms up, letting her tighten the bandage. She paused as he knew she would. His throat went tight as she pressed her fingers against his chest, adding tape to hold the bandage in place.

She met his eyes and for a moment the world fell away. He let his arms drop and he let his fingers land on top of hers. They were shaking.

"If I had more to give." Gabe's sentence didn't speak half of what he was trying to say. "I still believe I will find my Descendant someday. I am pulled toward her still. I'm sorry." Abigail had worked with him since she saved him all those years ago. She had helped him deliver the visions of Adura. She now helped him find the Unguarded before they disappeared. But she'd always known that he was a Guardian. She knew he was Bonded to another.

"I know." She pulled her hands away, patted the bandage like that had been her only reason for touching him. "The changes worry me.

I'm worried about Treadon. I don't want him to get caught up in all of this. I want him to have a chance at a life . . ."

"A life you didn't have." Gabe finished for her.

Abigail opened her mouth to speak, but the roar of an engine cut her off.

"You could tell him," Gabe said.

He met Abigail's eyes. The firm set of her jaw and the steel look in her eyes told Gabe that nothing had changed. He did not argue or question, he simply moved into action along with her.

Abigail dropped the heated knife into a bowl of water in the sink with a sharp sizzling sound. Gabe grabbed a white t-shirt crumpled on the counter and pulled it over his head, covering the bandages. He used the towel to wipe up the floor around the chair, picking up the pieces of discarded dead skin. He wadded up the towel and forced it into the metal garbage can, closing the lid with a clank.

With a final flick, Abigail covered Gabe's upper body with a thin cloak of plastic used for cutting hair and pulled the cutters from a drawer. She turned the clippers on just as Treadon opened the front door. Gabe felt a stab of regret as Abigail wiped all emotion from her face.

Seven

September 5

 I'd accepted my loneliness, but I haven't stopped to look at the future. What does my future look like? The goal has been to stay hidden from the stories of hunters in the dark and punishments for my mistake, but even if I could stay hidden forever, I don't want to. One day, I will be ready to step into the light and take the consequences for my actions. I will fight off the shadows that haunt me in my dreams. I'm almost ready. But not quite.

 I've avoided the football player that ran into me the first day, but sometimes I catch a glimpse of him across the quad or out on the field for practice. I've seen him scanning the crowd, searching the faces of his classmates, and I know he's looking for me. The thought of him remembering me, of wanting to see me again, brought something to life in me that I thought had died a long time ago. There's a *sensation in my belly that makes me feel hungry. It makes me want to be seen again, but that line of thinking is dangerous. If I let one wall down, who knows how much of me I will expose. I might even forget why I started hiding in the first place.*

Like the Angels forgot their main purpose and were more concerned about their own future than the humans they were meant to protect. Or maybe, like me, they really believed that what they were doing was the only way to survive. For everyone.

I haven't worked up the courage to use my powers, to heal Nolan, Pat's husband, when they brought him home on a machine. I can heal. I used to practice on birds and our cat that liked to bother raccoons. I know I can heal, but Nolan's injury isn't in his body. It's a brain injury, and I'm afraid to make another mistake. Ruin another person's mind.

All I did was give Pat a hug and tell her she can do this. She's strong enough. I feel like an imposter.

Treadon Nelson

Treadon walked through the front door and was met with the smell of BBQ chicken, a little on the burnt side. There was a plate sitting on the counter. Abigail was by the sink cutting Gabe's hair.

He was back.

He always came back like an unwanted zit the day before Prom.

Gabe sat stiff under the hair cape, his head down, tilted slightly toward Treadon, but not enough to make eye contact. Abigail ran the cutter close to Gabe's ears, doing a final detail check.

"How was school?" Abigail asked.

Treadon sat down on the stool in front of the chicken. He picked up a leg and pulled a strip of meat off.

"Fine," he said through the piece of meat, sending the word forward like the white pawn in the first move of chess. Treadon chewed on the meat while his mom chewed on his response. He'd given her nothing and she was deciding if it was worth fighting for more.

Treadon studied the chicken in front of him. He could tell her more. He could also find out more than she was saying. If he tried to read her.

The girl he saw seemed to think he could do more. Treadon wasn't sure he wanted to go back to that kid who got beat up after school when he tried to read people. He didn't want his own mom to think he wasn't a normal teenage kid, even if it meant stupid answers like, "Fine."

Abigail turned off the razor and brushed a few hairs off the plastic cape with a swish. Gabe stood up before Abigail could take off the cape. He took a few steps, but then stopped at the edge of the hallway.

"How are your grades?" Even without trying to read Gabe, Treadon could hear the rusty gears in Gabe's brain turning, trying to remember how to have a normal conversation. He should buy the guy a book called *How to Sound Like a Dad for Dummies*.

"It's only the second week of school. Not failing anything yet."

Gabe gave a brief nod, formal. His shoulder was angled away from Treadon. Treadon couldn't help thinking he looked like a man on the edge of escape, wondering if he should continue to fight to think of things a father would say, or simply find solace in his office.

"You're capable of more than just not failing." Gabe pulled the hair cape off him like he'd just realized it was still around his neck.

"How would you know?" Treadon couldn't help biting back. "You don't know anything about me." He kept his eyes on his chicken because, even when he tried not to read Gabe, there was this constant message of disappointment. Gabe expected more from him. Which was a joke coming from the guy who was only around some of the time and couldn't hold down a job.

"Treadon." Abigail kept her voice even, but when Treadon looked up she saw Abigail give Gabe a look.

"Sorry." Gabe said. "I know you work hard. At football." He said the last two words like they were a piece of toilet paper caught on the back of his shoe.

Abigail picked up the empty plate of chicken. "Speaking of football, did Jarren tell you anymore about that new car of his?"

Master of subject change. Treadon appreciated it this time. He jumped on the lifeline like an acrobat grabs a trapeze and let it swing him away from Gabe's critical energy.

"Fancy, right? It has a high-tech security system."

"What kind of security system?" Gabe had unfortunately jumped on the same trapeze. Treadon wished he would take his escape down the hallway and leave them in peace. Without the hair cape, Gabe had on only a white t-shirt and his leather bike pants. The guy was a walking steroid add. His arms were thick, each muscle defined. He held his shoulders military straight and had a jaw that looked like it could take on a brick and win. Treadon resisted the urge to sit up straighter when he turned to answer Gabe's question.

"It's some kind of electronic paneling or something. I don't know how it works, but it shocks you if you get too close."

"Did Jarren say what it was designed to shock?" Gabe rolled up the hair cape and twisted it in his hands. Treadon imagined Gabe wringing the life out of an innocent animal the way he wrung the joy out of his mom. The image probably wasn't fair, but the thought was enough to make Treadon stand and head to his room. Gabe stayed, blocking the hallway.

"Not exactly." Treadon said as he waited for Gabe to move out of the way so he could slip down the hall. "Said something about metal, and freshman initiation."

Gabe didn't look entertained in the slightest.

"That's all I know," Treadon said. "I have some homework to do to keep from failing. Can I go?"

Gabe hesitated a second longer, then stepped to the side. Treadon pushed past.

He went into his room and shut the door with more force than necessary. He wanted them to hear it slam. He didn't want them to hear as he carefully turned the handle and pulled the door open a crack.

He pressed his ear to the opening. Getting catches of their soft conversation.

"He's getting older, Abigail. You should give him the chance to make his own decision. He deserves it."

"There's no need to involve him."

"There are two reasons. One, he has more potential than he's living up to. He could do more."

"And let you drag him into this the way you dragged me?"

Gabe was quiet for a moment. "Is that how you feel?"

"No. No, I chose this. You know I did, but not for him. I didn't choose this for him. I want him to be able to have a normal life. What's the second reason?"

Gabe's voice was even quieter now. Treadon imagined them standing close, their faces almost touching.

"If he knew, you wouldn't have such a burden to carry alone. He could be there for you when I can't."

Something clattered to the floor. Abigail must have pulled back and knocked something from the counter. "We have each other," she whispered.

"You know I can't be there for you, not the way you need. How long can you continue alone?"

Gabe saw the struggle in Abigail as well, but he didn't sound sympathetic. Treadon opened the door another fraction of an inch. He could step out, tell his mom that he didn't want her to be alone anymore. Tell her that he could be more than he was.

"Treadon is on track to get a scholarship, money that he needs for his future. I won't let him give that up."

Treadon let the door close again, a sinking feeling in him. If he stepped out there, he was afraid there was a chance he'd end up like

Gabe, unable to give his mom the life she deserved. But if he stayed with football, he could change things for her.

He opened his computer to start on an English paper, but he had to close his eyes for a moment. He was good at football. He had a real chance to make a difference.

So why did he feel like Gabe was right.

Eight

September 15

I remember Mom telling me how the Angels continued helping Ordinaries, creating miracles, spreading hope. They each had a few children who had a few children who had a few children, but in the fourth generation, one of the Descendants betrayed the Angels and helped Cado Fillius to find them. Cado used the black dagger to kill the Angels one at a time. Baldur was first. Samuil was next. Adeona, the Angel of Life, was last and she knew it. Instead of running and trying to hide, Adeona remembered her purpose had multiplied. She had children and grandchildren and great-grandchildren to protect as well as the human race.

Mom always spoke of Adeona, the Angel I'm descended from, as a hero. The one Angel that would not go into hiding to save her own life. My mother's words are like a dagger in my heart when I think of them.

Instead of hiding, Adeona created a trap for Cado Fillius in which she sacrificed her own body, ripping the daggers from Cado Fillius' fingers and plunging them into her own heart. She used her knowledge of life to absorb the daggers into her DNA, transferring them down through her Descendants as a recessive gene so Cado Fillius could not use the daggers against her Descendants anymore.

Cado Fillius swore he would find the Descendant and rip the daggers from their bones. Adeona promised with her last breath that the death of that Descendant would be Cado Fillius' undoing.

Not the best bedtime story for a seven-year-old, but Mom wanted me to know my heritage, know the courage of my ancestors, and know that there would be a future where we would have to fight Cado Fillius again. I don't know who the Descendant will be that will bring about the end of the eternal war, but I hope it's someone who is far braver than me.

Treadon Nelson

Treadon led his team to victory the next two weekends. After each game he waited for the thrill of the win, the excitement that he saw in the faces of his teammates. Instead, he only felt a strange sense of emptiness.

He tossed and turned at night, and tonight was particularly bad.

He stared into the blinding lights, his feet frozen to the pavement, but his mind processed everything at warp speed. Move. Pick up your feet. Run.

The words didn't register with his body. He fought with all his might to lift one foot. It started to respond—too late. Too late. The lights got brighter. Closer.

Treadon bolted into a sitting position, sucking in life-giving air. His room was dark and peaceful. A light breeze swayed his curtains playfully as he stumbled from his bed to lean against his dresser. It was a dream. Only a dream. He looked at the dark silhouette outlined in the mirror against the trickle of moonlight coming in through the window. He was whole.

There was a soft tapping, a knock. Not on his door. He heard Abigail's voice and Gabe's low rumble. A few minutes later, the roar of a motor signaled Gabe leaving on his motorcycle. He was gone again for who knew how long. Treadon flopped on his back and tried to fall asleep, but the nightmare was there, behind his eyes, the headlights appearing, bearing down on him. He lay still, staring at the ceiling, his breath coming in short gasps, unable to get out from under the weight of the fear that seemed to be crushing him.

He could do more.

He should be better.

Sees so much but chooses to see nothing.

The ceiling was shadowed, hardly visible, but her eyes seemed to look down on him, accusing him. Could he do more if he stopped pushing back? If he tried to understand the language that was always being spoken, but only he could hear?

"Fine." He spoke to the ceiling, but somehow, he felt approval in the deep brown eyes. Felt comforted. "I'll try. I'm not promising anything, but I'll choose to see more."

This time when he closed his eyes, the sleep was peaceful and deep.

But the next morning, as he lagged behind Jarren and approached the quad, students milling in different directions, standing in groups, talking and laughing, the calmness disappeared. He had done this for three years, walking onto the school grounds every day of the school year, but today felt different.

Today he wanted to see. He took a tiny breath and held it for a second before focusing on the sea of faces that surged past him.

Nothing. Kids walking. Friends talking.

He let out his breath in relief. He didn't know what he was expecting. Tortured, haunted souls that were crumbling without his touch. No. The world continued to spin without his interference. And he was glad. What had she expected him to see?

He studied a group of girls, giggling as they walked. One of them had just been asked out and one was madly jealous. Three of the girls simply enjoyed the gossip.

A boy walked alone with a terrified look in his eyes. Treadon looked. Quick steps. Nervous movements. A twitching glare at other students. Treadon knew as clearly as if the boy had told him: he forgot to study for a test. He'd be okay.

Another small group caught his attention. He could pick out the leader, the one at the front that the other boys used as a shield against the oncoming traffic. He could tell that there were two who felt confident in their place. The last boy struggled to keep step and the others seemed to stay slightly apart from him. There were other faces that looked worried, stressed, tired of the rat race, but none of them looked desperate or in need of some kind of self-appointed hero.

He felt ridiculous. He let his head drop and laughed at himself. What had he expected?

The first bell rang, and he turned toward the East Building, his home room class. He didn't realize he was still reading people when he felt a pull, a question. Just before he stepped into his classroom, he saw a girl wearing a purple sweater, jeans, tennis shoes. There was a hole in the elbow of her sweater that she kept hidden by holding her arm close to her body. She was embarrassed that her shoes were hand-me-downs. But it was her face. Desperate. Lonely.

He knew what she was looking for. He waited, knowing she'd look up when she passed, knowing she expected to be ignored. When they made eye contact, Treadon smiled, raising his chin. Acknowledgement. If Jarren were here, he would have used the line from Avatar. "I see you."

The effect was immediate. The girl's face flushed; her thin lips pulled tight by the energetic smile that enveloped her whole face. As the girl walked by, eyes straight ahead, chin held higher than before, he felt that rush of victory that he was sure he should feel after a football game.

That was a real win. One person. One smile. It felt better than all the touchdowns he'd thrown this year.

Maybe choosing to see wouldn't be so bad. If he could keep his mouth shut and didn't say stupid things. This could be fun.

He caught sight of Jarren walking with Rachel across the quad, too far away to hear. They walked with their heads close together, Jarren's hands moving with sharp, quick movements. Jarren was worried about something serious, and Rachel wanted nothing more than to take his pain away. Treadon moved to follow his friends, but a voice from inside the classroom caught him mid-step.

"Care to join us, Mr. Nelson? Class is starting."

Treadon would ask Jarren about it after school. Maybe he would finally be able to make a difference.

Nine

September 20

    Writing under a blanket on the floor of Jake's room, using my phone as a light reminds me of Mom. Jake fell asleep to another story about demons and Descendants. Pat is working a night shift and Nolan hasn't shown any improvement. I'm doing what I can to help the family out. Cooking dinners. Watching the twins. Holding the baby. Being with Jake. In the busy moments, I can almost pretend this is how things are supposed to be. That I'm a part of a family. My chest feels tight when I think about it. I want to smile and cry at the same time. Why couldn't I have made a better choice? Why did I let my fear get the best of me? And the sad part is, I haven't let go of the fear. It's part of me, like a huge cancer that's wrapped around my internal organs and if I try and pull it out, most of me will come with it.

    When I'm with Jake, I think about my brother and

what he'd be doing now. My brother wouldn't have been afraid even though he was younger by a year. He was better than me at all things Descendant related. He was always full of questions, a mind focused on science and discovery. If there was something he didn't understand, he'd take it as a personal challenge. He believed there was an answer for everything. I wonder what answer I would give him if he had a chance to ask me, "Why?"

He was most fascinated by Descendant weaponry. The science behind the hematite element that could be both our salvation and our undoing. Green hematite scatters a demon essence and is placed on Descendant weapons. Red hematite burns a demon essence and works better for containment. Red hematite can be used as an electrolyte for Descendants, strengthening our energy when we're running low. Good for us and bad for them.

My brother could never understand what made black hematite the opposite of the other forms. Red and green were good for us. Black hematite is our kryptonite. It weakens us. It absorbs the energy out of our very bones.

Treadon Nelson

Treadon spent the rest of day distracted by the thoughts that kept bombarding him from every direction. Not fun to hear a hundred conversations that people are having with themselves on top of the noise of actual voices in the classroom. By lunch,

Treadon was ready to bury his head in sand. His mom would have told him to find a balance. Look at things from both sides. He decided not to eat with anyone and spend the lunch hour in the locker room. It was generally empty during lunch.

As he walked toward the gym, he bumped shoulders with a girl walking with her head down.

"Sorry. My fault." Treadon let his hand rest on her arm for an instant, making sure she was balanced. She looked up and jerked her arm away from him. She didn't stop walking, but Treadon got a look at her eyes. Empty. Hopeless.

But she was gone, disappeared into the flow of students before he could read more.

He felt a slap on his back and turned to find Jarren smiling at him. The stress from this morning was buried deep, and Treadon couldn't see any evidence of what had been bothering his friend. Treadon wondered how often Jarren buried his feelings. Maybe more than he realized. He imagined he could see a switch that Jarren was able to flip when he was around people, a happy Jarren and the real Jarren.

"Where are you headed?" Jarren asked. "The food and the girls are that direction." He pointed toward the quad where students gathered in small groups, eating and laughing.

"I wanted to see Coach, talk about strategies for Friday's game." Treadon felt bad about the lie, but he wasn't about to tell Jarren he was going into the locker room to be alone. That had Jarren joke fodder written all over it.

"Sounds tempting. I'll skip food for some football talk." Jarren followed him to the locker room door where Coach Bracken pushed the door open just as Treadon reached for the handle.

He had a pile of papers on a clip board, his nose nearly touching the top sheet. He was mumbling to himself.

"Coach?"

Jack Bracken was a large, intimidating man with reddish-brown hair. His bristly mustache complimented a stern, oval face. He was middle-aged, silver streaks in his hair and mustache. He had once been an intimidating opponent, but his soggy middle showed years of telling people what to do instead of engaging in his own workouts. He jumped at the sound of Treadon's voice and then recovered with a genuine scowl. Treadon looked deeper, read deeper.

"You were looking for me?" Treadon felt the knot in his stomach as Coach reacted, twitching his face so his mustache moved like a broom across his top lip.

"Yes. Glad you're here. You're a real inspiration to the other boys, an example. The team looks up to you and they need their leader."

Treadon couldn't help it. He read the words that hadn't been spoken, that he'd been worried would come the minute he stepped into Mr. Ashcroft's classroom. "I'm in danger of being ineligible."

"That sucks." Jarren hadn't even stepped back to give them a private conversation. "I could pay a couple of brains to do your homework."

Coach Bracken shook his head. "We've got to do this right. And we have to fix it now before eligibility reports come through. And no cheating." He shot a look at Jarren.

Jarren put both hands in the air. "All my grades are legit, self-earned, and stable at solid C pluses."

Treadon felt his stomach clench. If he couldn't play, he wouldn't get the scholarships or the funding. There would go his chance of changing life for his mom. "What do you suggest, Coach?"

It was Coach Bracken's favorite thing, to be asked advice. Well, his actual favorite thing would be to give advice. Being asked was a close second.

"I've already signed you up with a tutor and you start today, right after practice."

"A tutor?"

"Oh, sh . . . snap," Jarren said after getting a look from Coach Bracken.

"I've signed you up with the best and the one that will stay late enough for you to make it to practices. Her name is Eleanor Agarwal."

"Eleanor?" Jarren asked. The guy just couldn't keep his mouth shut, but it kept Treadon from focusing on the rising panic. More time after school. More time trying to understand mathematical nonsense. "Isn't that a name from like King Arthur's time? Knights and jousting and things like that."

"Show some respect, Calivan. Eleanor is a perfectly common name. And she'll be able to help." Coach gave Treadon a fatherly nod. "Don't forget you start today."

He handed Treadon a piece of paper with Eleanor's name, a time, and a room number written on it and then walked away. Treadon looked up in time to see three other guys from the football team pass them and go into the locker room, carrying a duffle bag. Warnings blared in his head, though he couldn't quite identify why. He needed more practice at this whole reading people thing.

"Let's go find Rachel. She'll know more about this Eleanor girl. Rachel knows everyone and everything."

Treadon moved to follow Jarren and then stopped. Something about the guys that went into the locker room was bothering him. "Did something seem off to you about those guys?"

"You mean that new guy from Ventura? Is it weird that he has friends? A little. The guy's shaped like a refrigerator box and acts like his brain is on ice."

"I just want to say hi really quick. Make him feel welcome. Like Coach said. Let's be a leader."

Jarren raised one eyebrow. "You be the leader. I'm more of a check out the competition kind of guy." He motioned toward the locker room door. "After you, Cinderella."

They walked into the locker room and the three guys that were hovering over the duffle bag stood and turned. Guilty. Treadon saw annoyance flash across the new player's face. Bridger Michaels. That was his name. The other two were also from the team, Garcia and Daniels. Both Juniors. Both very large offensive lineman. They were the ones who kept the other team back long enough for Treadon to throw the ball.

The annoyance left as soon as Michaels saw Jarren. "Just the guys I wanted to see. We're having a party this weekend, big blow out at my house. Thought it would be a good chance to bond with the team, get to know some of the girls from school." Garcia and Daniels shared a look and laughed. Treadon felt a feeling of disgust settle in the pit of his stomach. Girls. Party. He could read way too much intention on their faces.

"You two should come. It will be the talk of the school." Michaels was inviting them, but Treadon could still see a trace of disgust under Michaels' demeanor. He didn't want them to come. Not really.

"You just need us to show up so girls will actually come," Jarren said. "You think they want a shot at the greatest football star this school has ever known." Jarren kissed his bicep.

Michaels' jaw tightened. Truth. Part of what Jarren had said was true, and Michaels hated the fact that it was.

"I already have plans this Saturday," Treadon said.

Michaels ignored Treadon's comment. It was Jarren he wanted to come. What girls would come just for Jarren? Then it hit him. Not girls. One girl. One amazing girl that played on the team and would never consider going to a party unless Jarren dragged her along as the designated driver.

"Rachel." Treadon said her name out loud, and Michaels flinched like he'd been jabbed with a needle. "You think you're going to make it with Rachel? You don't have a chance."

"What are you talking about?" Jarren had gone stiff, like he had his finger on that switch Treadon had noticed earlier. "Rachel doesn't go to those kinds of parties."

Rage flashed across Michaels' features for an instant and then it was gone. Buried. He looked at Treadon with mock pity, turning his head to address Garcia and Daniels.

"Poor Nelson. He's never seen how fun girls get after a couple of drinks. Or just one." Michaels' anger had spurred more words than he intended.

Michaels exchanged smirks with his friends. Treadon felt heat rush to his head, that desire to do something more, to make a difference.

"Where is it?" Treadon grabbed the front of Michaels' shirt. Michaels was solid and barely moved when Treadon tugged him forward. He probably should have thought this through before getting physical. Still, the question spurred a response, and Michaels glanced at the duffle bag. Barely a twitch, unintentional. But Treadon saw and understood.

He let go of Michaels' shirt and shoved him to the side. His shoulder hit Garcia in the chest and knocked him backward into the lockers. He was down the aisle, reaching for the duffle bag before Daniels could react.

"Stop him," Michaels yelled.

Treadon felt a jerk on the back of his shirt and was halted an inch from grabbing the duffle bag. He turned and barely missed a swing from Daniels. Daniels swung too hard, and his fist left a dent in the metal locker door. Daniels swore but didn't stop. He brought his elbow back, aiming for Treadon's jaw.

Treadon ducked again and Daniels leaped on top of him, trying to take him down with the sheer force of his weight. The guy was heavy. Treadon felt his knees bend, the locker room floor coming closer. But the weight was off center; Treadon could feel Daniels moving forward. Instead of trying to push Daniels' weight off him, Treadon straightened his legs and bent forward at the waist, reaching up at the same time to grab Daniels' head. He pulled down and bent forward at the same time, using the inertia of Daniels' attack to flip him over. Daniels landed on his back with a sharp crack of bone against concrete. Daniels' mouth opened, but the air had been forced from his lungs. He'd need a minute to recover.

Garcia stepped over Daniels. The space in the row between the lockers was limited as he took up most of the width. He was smarter, more patient. After a staring standoff, Treadon saw the moment Garcia decided to use his bulk and smash Treadon into the lockers at the end of the row. It would have been a good plan, since Treadon didn't have the ability to stop him.

Instead, when Garcia moved, Treadon stepped onto the bench, jumped over Garcia's head, and landed on his feet. He turned at the same time as Garcia did, but this time it was Treadon's elbow in the air, and it caught Garcia right in the mouth. Garcia rocked backward and slammed into the lockers. He held a hand over his bleeding mouth.

Treadon turned, ready. Michaels stepped toward him, his face suddenly twisting from anger to pain. Jarren, tall and scrawny, twisted Bridger Michaels' arm behind his back and pinned him to the lockers at the beginning of the row. The mass difference between the two boys didn't make a lot of sense, but Jarren didn't even seem to struggle holding the larger boy pinched against the metal, the grill of the locker cutting into Michaels' face.

"Tell me there's a reason," Jarren said.

There was a reason. A message in the way the boys had talked and moved. Treadon threw things out of Michaels duffle bag. Then he saw it. A plastic baggie full of round, white pills. He lifted the baggie and let it dangle in the air.

Jarren let out a low whistle. "That's a dirty way to get some action. Did you say he was going to use those on Rachel?" Jarren twisted up harder on Michaels' arm. Michaels grunted.

"Okay. Stop." Michael kept his voice calm, but his eyes were on the bag of white pills. "Rachel's out. She wouldn't have come anyway. Put the pills down." Michaels made a sudden lunge for the bag. Jarren slammed Michaels against the locker again.

Treadon turned to look at the others. Garcia still had his hand over his mouth, head down. Daniels groaned on the floor; air finally able to reach his lungs. "No way. No girl deserves this. You don't deserve any girl."

He walked to the stall and dumped the bag of pills down the toilet. He went back and helped the other two players to their feet. Then he gave a nod to Jarren.

Jarren shoved Michaels toward the exit, and Treadon gave Garcia and Daniels a helpful push toward the door. The two friends didn't hesitate to run out of the locker room, but Bridger stood there, seething.

"You have no idea how much that cost me." Michael was shaking, spitting the words. He locked eyes with Treadon, his face red and twisted with rage.

The door to the locker room slammed open and Coach came around the corner, reading a clipboard. He looked up and stopped.

"Is there a problem here, boys?" His scowl bounced between Jarren, Treadon, and Bridger. "Each of you has a good chance to play college ball. I'd hate to see a disagreement get anyone kicked off the team."

Slowly, Michaels body language changed. He flexed his fingers, unclenching his fists. His forehead smoothed out and his mouth thinned into a controlled smile. "No, sir."

"I'm not going to tell you guys how to solve a problem, but whatever this is, I want it left off the field. All three of you have a future in this sport and I don't want to see you throw it away." Coach Bracken focused on Treadon.

"Got it, Coach." Bridger took a breath, shot one last glare at Treadon, and then left the locker room with a calm swagger that made Treadon's skin crawl with concern.

"Treadon," Coach Bracken stepped closer to him. "I want you out there leading the team, but I won't hesitate to bench you if you're breaking us down. Stay out of trouble or the whole team will pay for it." He nodded like he'd solved world hunger and went into his office.

Jarren waited a beat and then slapped Treadon on the back. "When did you become guardian of the helpless, defender of the weak?"

"Knock it off. Rachel's anything but weak." Treadon tried to feel heroic, but the feeling wouldn't come. The sick anger still boiled in his stomach. His mind analyzed Bridger's parting look. A tingling warning crept up his spine. The calm, serene look on Michaels' face wasn't acceptance. It was patience. And a promise for revenge.

Ten

September 23

    I sat with Nolan for an hour after school. He's breathing on his own but surviving on a feeding tube. His eyes stayed closed. Pat came in while I was writing. I helped her shift Nolan so we could change the sheets and keep him from getting bed sores. The twins watched from the doorway and the baby started crying. Jake stayed in his room. I want to change things for them. I want to make everything better. Instead, I vacuumed the living room. Anything I can do to lighten Pat's load. We both know I only have a few months left. Things will be different when I turn eighteen, but I still don't know what that's going to look like.

    Eighteen is an exciting age for most Descendants. That's the age we gain the ability to choose a Guardian. The age where we begin our search for a companion to share our knowledge and energy, who will serve as a *protector and friend. Not all Guardian-Descendant relationships are romantic. There are some friendships and even some business partners, but choosing a Guardian and having a Guardian accept, creates a powerful bond that leaves little room for other relationships. I don't know of very many Descendant/Guardian duos who were able to maintain a significant relationship while Bonded to another.*

I won't have that choice to make when I turn eighteen. My birthday will only be a symbol of all I've lost and everything I destroyed.

Treadon Nelson

Tutoring. Getting a little help. No matter what Jarren said, this wasn't a big deal. Still, Treadon felt his nerves tingling with anxiety, a pressure constricting his chest. If he could fail at something as easy as High School math, he was worried he didn't stand a chance in college. Even if he wanted to do something besides football, this might be a sign he wasn't capable of anything more.

He bit his cheek as he approached the door to the tutoring room. If she could help him, he would take it. He was sure part of the problem was Mr. Ashcroft and blaming the teacher made it possible to bury the feeling of failure a little deeper.

With his hand on the door, he practiced a couple of different smiles. An awkward one. A scary one. No. A half smile. This was going to be embarrassing. Finally, he decided on a Jarren-style confident grin and opened the door.

The cool act lasted less than a second.

He was in a small room used for one-on-one tutoring sessions, speech therapy, or counseling sessions. A single rectangular table sat in the middle of the room taking up most of the floor space with a chair on either side. Occupying the chair opposite the door was a gorgeous dark-skinned girl with long black hair and stunning deep brown eyes.

"It's you." Treadon wished he could pull those words back out of the air. Instead, he watched her absorb his words with a mixture of disdain, surprise, and fear. It was less than an instant, but he watched her struggle with those emotions, like she was trying to pull an octopus into a ball. But then she won some sort of battle and sat back, arms crossed, eyebrows raised in expectation.

"It's you." She returned the words on a flat plate, devoid of emotion.

Treadon fiddled with the strap on his backpack. "I mean, I remember you. From the first game. When we bumped into each other. You hit me in the stomach. Do you remember?"

Realizing that he was spouting words without breathing, he sat in the chair on the opposite side of the table from her. He wanted to lean forward to add intensity to his excitement, but he saw her stiffen, his proximity making her uncomfortable. He scooted his chair back a few inches, as much as the room would allow, and leaned away from her.

Her shoulders softened a fraction.

"I've been looking for you," Treadon said. "I mean, that sounds worse than it is. I just wanted to see you again. Explain things."

"You wanted to explain why you attacked me?" Eleanor raised one eyebrow. Somehow the movement sucked the air from the room.

Treadon folded his arms. "I wasn't the one who attacked you. If I remember right, you're the one who swung first."

"You fought back."

"It was a reaction." Treadon shrugged his shoulders and put his hands out toward her. Not quite an apology. More of a justification. She understood, maybe even agreed, but she wasn't about to admit it.

"You couldn't find me because I didn't want you to find me," Eleanor said.

"And you always get what you want." He meant it as a joke, but the sudden flash of pain and sorrow that shadowed her face was the opposite of what he expected. "You don't always get what you want. Or you haven't. Yet."

Her head snapped back, and Treadon wished he could think through his words before they popped out of his mouth.

"Don't pretend like you know me." Eleanor slapped a notebook on the table in a way that said the conversation was closed. "What subject are we studying today?"

"Math. I'm struggling with my math teacher. I'm pretty sure he's from a different planet."

Eleanor swirled the notebook in a circle, one finger on the corner, spinning in a spiral. "Are you struggling with the subject or the teacher?"

"Teacher." Treadon didn't know why he answered so quickly. He should have thought about the question. Her withering stare told him she was unimpressed.

"I'm not sure the teacher is the problem," she said.

"It's not me," Treadon said, pointing to himself to punctuate his innocence. "I used to do fine in math. It's the way the guy talks and the way he looks at me and the way he has it in for me, like he expects me to fail just because of who I am. I stay focused and pay attention the whole time. He just doesn't make any sense."

"What do you focus on?" Eleanor asked.

"I focus on the teacher." Treadon spoke slowly, checking each word like he was running them over a scanner at the store to check the price.

"Not the lesson?"

Treadon felt the trap snap shut. She had meant to catch him on that one.

He thought back to class, to the way he watched Mr. Ashcroft, and even without trying, could read the man's judgement of him, his expectation of failure, his dismissal. Treadon blew air between his lips in frustration. "Okay. I do watch him. I try and predict what to do to stay out of trouble. He's got it in for me. He thinks I expect a free ride because I'm a football player."

"Do you?"

"What?"

"Expect a free ride?"

"No." Treadon felt like she'd snapped a rubber band at his chest. He felt offended and exposed at the same time. He shifted in his seat, leaning forward. "You sound like you agree with him."

Her blank stare was her only answer.

"I don't expect a free ride. I'm willing to work hard; I'm willing to fight for this. I need to pass my classes so I can play football. It's important."

She didn't answer for a moment. The silence was so complete that the sounds of teachers' muffled voices and shoes squeaking on tile leaked into the room.

"It sounds like you have a hill to climb to prove him wrong," Eleanor finally said. "I think the best thing you can do is focus on the lesson and stop trying to predict the teacher."

"But you told me I should."

"No, I didn't."

"Yes. After you hit me, which hurt by the way. You weren't pulling your punches. It was like you thought your life was in danger. But anyway, you said that I should try and see more."

"That's not exactly what I said."

"I know. But I did it. I did what you said." Treadon sat forward, resting his elbows on the table and this time she didn't pull back, she seemed more like she was resisting the pull to mirror him, to draw herself closer. "I tried to see more. I smiled at a girl in the hallway."

"Congratulations." Her voice was still flat, but he caught the lilt, so small. Amusement. Below her prickly protection of thorny bushes, she had a sense of humor.

"No. I mean, she needed a smile. I could tell. And then there was a girl who'd lost the light in her eyes. I didn't do anything about that, but I wanted to. And then those guys. I got in a fight in the locker room; Jarren called me a hero and it felt good, and I wanted to do more."

"I'm a little confused."

"No." Treadon didn't mean to say the word with so much confidence, but he could see she knew exactly what he was talking about. Not the details. Not the stories. But his excitement, the hunger he'd felt when doing good things. She reflected the hunger he felt multiplied by a thousand. "You're not confused," he said. "You know exactly what I'm talking about."

Treadon pushed everything else from his mind and focused on her eyes, let himself fall into them, letting her emotions, thoughts, energy swallow him up. Something shoved at him, tugging at his mind to look away, like the pressure in his lungs underwater when it's time to go up for air. He resisted and looked deeper.

For an eternal moment, Treadon found himself in an endless universe, the edge of impossibility within his reach, the intensity of the sun, the depth of the fathomless ocean, the eternal potential of a single soul filled him and drained him at the same time.

Eleanor jumped from her chair, knocking it back against the wall. "Never do that again."

He blinked several times. The shape of her eyes burned into the back of his vision, flashing white against the dark.

He stared at her—his mouth open. "What are you?"

"If I tell you, you won't believe me. And I'll have to kill you instead of just punch you."

"You don't want to kill me. But you do want to tell me," Treadon said.

"Are you always so aggravatingly arrogant?" She closed her eyes, pressing her back against the wall.

Treadon imagined her refortifying her defenses. He could see her struggling, trying to fix the wall of a sandcastle after an unexpected wave.

"No." Simple. Honest. "I'm usually very insecure."

Eleanor made a choking sound, but she wasn't actually choking. The breath jumped out of her in a laugh that threatened to turn into a sob. Twice. Three times. She let her shoulders shake and matched the rhythm with her head.

"I'm not supposed to do this," Eleanor said.

"What? Laugh? You need to work on it. You kind of sound like you're dying." Treadon still had the urge to lean over and pat her on the back to help her breathe. Instead, he let her laughter lighten the weight he felt on his own chest.

She took a deep breath. "I'm fine. And I know how to laugh. Just not like this. Not with you."

"Now I'm a little confused."

"No. You're right. I'm going to tell you and you're not going to believe me. And then you have to shut your mouth and let me tutor you in math."

"Okay." Treadon had a feeling he was going to regret this agreement.

"I'm a Descendant of Angels. I am descended from Adeona, the Angel of Life. And I'm supposed to make the world a better place."

Treadon leaned back in his chair, his shoulders sagging with the weight of his heart. He'd thought they were connecting, but she still didn't trust him with the truth. She couldn't really expect him to believe something like that, but the lift in her eyebrows, the slight twist at the side of her lip. Hope. She knew he'd never believe her, but there was a part of her that hoped he would. Did she think he was gullible or just plain stupid?

Eleven

September 26

I decided to try something this year that allowed me to make a difference without using my Descendant abilities. I guess I'm not surprised it backfired. I wanted to help people and make a little money to put away so signing up to be a tutor seemed like an easy exception to remaining invisible.

I never expected the one person who remembers me to sign up for after-school tutoring. What are the odds he'd get assigned to me? And why does he look at me like I'm the missing piece, the solution to his problems? I'm probably just the beginning of his problems because bad luck swirls around me like a rotten egg smell. And I told him. I told him I was a Descendant of Angels. His face was priceless. No one would believe such a crazy story, but it felt so good to be honest for once.

I didn't expect him to believe me, but it also hurt that he

didn't. There's something about Treadon and his intense gaze that goes past the shell I've created on the outside, that drills into my very soul, that made me feel like a weight had been lifted off my chest. I should probably walk away, but I want to see him again. Even if all we talk about is math. I guess it's up to him if he comes back.

I walked out of the school with the urge to hum a tune my dad used to sing. He had an amazing voice and used it to serenade my mom. I remember her smile creeping onto her face no matter how mad she tried to stay at him. Before he was a Guardian, my dad was a lead singer in a band. I could never imagine it, my dad, standing on stage with a microphone. But when he sang me to sleep, when he hummed a tune while washing the dishes, I could almost imagine the dreams he'd given up serving the cause of the Descendants.

But he chose that life. He chose my mom when they were both old enough to make that decision. I ran away before I learned everything. Imagine leaving home with only a second-grade education. There's no one to ask what happens if someone Bonds too early. Or is Bonded without a choice.

TREADON NELSON

Treadon worked through the next few days in a daze. She hadn't expected him to believe her. He didn't believe her. It was impossible. She was messing with him. There was no such thing as angels.

Unless there were.

And if there were, then he'd just found one.

Treadon let that sink in without letting himself fully believe it. If he had found her, and she really was what she said. Was it possible there were other people who knew? Who wanted to hurt or capture or use . . . angels? It was hard to even think the word.

He couldn't deny the fear he'd seen in her the first time he'd met her. Whether she was descended from angels or not, Eleanor Agarwal believed she was in danger.

Someone grabbed him from behind and Treadon whirled, fists up, ready for a fight.

"Woah." Jarren put his hands up. "Still wanting to fight someone? Thought you'd had enough of that in the locker room."

"Sorry. I'm a little jumpy."

"What happened in the locker room?" Rachel walked up behind Jarren, flipping her long ponytail behind her shoulder. She wore her school sweats and hoodie and still managed to walk like she'd stepped onto a fashion runway. Rachel Sampaio was the picture of believing in herself. Treadon felt a sting of jealousy. Apparently, believing in anything was a weakness of his.

"What are you two still doing here? It's late." Treadon walked with them to the parking lot. Normal people. Normal conversations. It felt good.

"Jarren was helping with some posters for student council. I made him paint all the letters," Rachel said.

"Yeah. I worked and she talked," Jarren said.

"That's what directors do. Besides, you have the best handwriting of anyone I know," Rachel teased.

Jarren stopped walking and wagged a finger in Rachel's face. "Don't ever say that again. I've got my manly reputation to maintain here."

Treadon let their friendly banter wash away the anxiety and adrenaline from the last few days. The fight in the locker room. Coach Bracken's threat to cut him for fighting. Eleanor and angels.

"How was tutoring?" Rachel asked. "You seem kind of distracted. Was she nice?"

"It was interesting. She was good at math."

"Uh oh. Haven't I warned you about tutor/client relationships?" Jarren joked.

"It was the girl I told you about after the first game."

"You mean the invisible one that hit you?"

"Yes, that one. She's my tutor, and she's not invisible, she just doesn't like people to notice her." And they didn't. Why? Was that proof that she was an angel? Or was it a weird coincidence?

"Good. I like her already," Rachel said.

"No. It's more than that. She's alone and wants to stay that way for some reason. But I bet you know her, Rachel. You know everybody. Her name is Eleanor Agarwal."

"Eleanor? That doesn't sound familiar, but I don't know everybody."

"Yes, she does." Jarren tossed his keys in the air and caught them. "You know I can get you a girlfriend that isn't imaginary, right?"

Before Treadon could respond, Jarren's phone rang with the ring tone of a song saying, "Money, Money, Money."

Jarren pulled his phone out of his pocket, and Treadon saw that the caller was labeled Dad.

"That's your dad's ringtone?" Treadon asked. "That song is from the eighties."

Jarren made an offended face as he retorted. "The eighties were amazing. I'm bringing them back." He touched the screen to answer.

Treadon realized he hadn't stopped reading people as Rachel's shift in demeanor left impressions on his mind. She was upset. No. She had a burning dislike for Xander Calivan. That seemed very opposite to Rachel's personality. She was accepting and kind to everyone. He glanced at Jarren. The personality switch Treadon had noticed earlier that day was all the way up. The facade he put on at school was a dress rehearsal. Even on the phone, Jarren put on a dazzling smile and lilted his voice for optimal casualness, a powerful smoke screen that hid something even Treadon couldn't see.

"Hey, Dad." Jarren turned away, putting distance between them while he talked.

Treadon glanced at Rachel. He wanted to ask, but her face had closed off. A wall going up that wasn't that different from Eleanor's. Two days ago, he never would have pushed, he would have been afraid of her reaction, afraid she'd think he was weird. But he wasn't happy sitting back and ignoring other people anymore.

"What's going on with Jarren's dad?"

"What are you talking about?"

"I saw you guys talking in the hall earlier. He seemed stressed. You seemed aggravated."

Rachel held his eyes for a few seconds. He saw the questions there, the concern that he was acting strange. But she shrugged and answered him.

"I've been working evenings at an online news station. We're always looking for stories, and they want to run one on XC Energy." Rachel paused. Her stance suggested excitement about the opportunity. The wrinkle between her eyes said she was conflicted. A concern for Jarren. And then that twitch in her jaw. Anger.

What good was being able to read people if it just left more questions?

"Is that good?" Treadon asked.

"I found some things from the past. Documents that had been redacted. Questions that were never answered. Some things that might cause problems for Jarren's dad."

Rachel's emotions teetered back and forth so quickly Treadon couldn't get a read on her. There was so much behind her simple statements that Treadon felt dizzy trying to work them out.

Jarren hung up the phone and came back over to them. "Great news. Calivan Senior has a free evening and wants to take us out for dinner. Are you both in?"

Rachel bit the inside of her cheek. "I wish I could, but I've got work." She glanced at Treadon. It was a question. A favor.

"Yeah. I'll go."

Treadon had never met the famous Xander Calivan, owner of XC Energy, business tycoon. Five years ago, he'd been featured on the cover of Money Magazine. Even with all the money and notoriety, Jarren chose to go to the same school as Rachel. There were layers inside layers between Rachel and Jarren's friendship Treadon had never chosen to try to see through. What would change if he tried to pry now? He wanted to help people, but seeing more than people wanted him to see, accidentally digging up private experiences? That wasn't the kind of person he wanted to be.

"I'll see you tomorrow. Let me know how it goes," Rachel whispered, touching Treadon's arm. "Take care of him. His father is a shark." She walked away.

She couldn't know about Treadon's ability to read people, but her steps showed her confidence in Treadon. She wanted him to learn more about XC Energy for her and protect Jarren from what he found.

"I still think that is a lame ringtone," Treadon said as they reached Jarren's car. Treadon waited for Jarren to push unlock. Jarren jumped over the door and settled in the front seat.

"Everyone has a perfect ringtone." Jarren fiddled with the fob, not pressing unlock yet.

"Oh yeah? What's mine?"

"When you call, I hear the theme song from Rudy. You know the movie about the kid that tried as hard as he could, but was never very good?" Jarren raised an eyebrow at him. Then he pressed unlock.

"You're lucky you're on the other side of an electrocuting car." Treadon opened the door and climbed in, hating that Jarren's words hit a little too close to home.

Twelve

TREADON NELSON

Treadon gripped the door handle as Jarren pulled his car through the valet parking.

He had to take several deep breaths to slow his heart rate and tried to hide the fact that his knees were shaking. It was just a car ride, but Treadon felt like he'd had some kind of brush with death. He tried to push away the shame and embarrassment. He didn't know why the most common form of transportation left him a quivering mess. How was he supposed to function in life he couldn't even handle driving a car? It was hard enough riding with his mom who was the master of defensive driving.

Not that Jarren was a bad driver. He just belonged on the racetrack at the Indy 500.

Jarren gave his keys to the white-gloved valet.

Other patrons entered through the rotating glass doors. The dress code called for suits, ties, dresses, jewelry, tuxes, and freshly shined shoes. One woman in a short gold dress with some kind of animal wrapped around her neck stopped to watch with an expression close to horror as Treadon and Jarren stepped into the lobby in their school clothes.

Jarren pressed the button for the elevator, hands in his pockets, tapping his foot. He seemed oblivious to the stares and whispers around them. The elevator chimed and the doors slipped open. They waited for the couple inside to skirt around them and then stepped into the elevator. Jarren held the door, but no one else joined them.

The doors slid shut. Treadon read the impressions of the other people. Disgust, revulsion, and a sense that their space had been violated. Money gave people power. Treadon understood that. He didn't understand the exclusivity of it. Jarren had never acted that way.

The elevator walls were covered in spotless mirrors, an intricate gold rail wrapped around the edges, offering support for its very wealthy inhabitants. Treadon was in jeans and a t-shirt. Comfort had always been more important than style. Jarren wore a blue collared shirt and khakis. He pressed the highest button labeled with a black twenty-two.

When they stepped out of the elevator on the top floor, Treadon stopped in amazement. The ceiling of the restaurant rose in an aesthetic dome shape with white, recessed squares patterned above the tables. The walls of the building were solid glass and provided a full 360-degree view of the city of Los Angeles.

An official looking man nodded at Jarren, grabbed two menus, and led them through the other tables. He took them to a private room. It wasn't technically a room, but a single table divided from the noise of the restaurant by glass walls.

Xander Calivan stood to greet them. His presence seemed to fill the restaurant. He was a tall black man, several inches taller than Treadon, square shoulders, confident stance. It wasn't his size but his demeanor that spoke of authority. A man who knew how to inspire the best out of people around him.

"Have a seat." Xander gave his son a hug with a business flare, gripping his hand and pulling him in for a slap on the back. He turned and shook Treadon's hand, and they all sat.

Another man in a pristine suit laid an artistic salad in front of each of them. Treadon awkwardly copied Xander's movements with his napkin.

"How was work today?" Jarren asked. "Did you sign the Haberly account?"

Xander laughed, wiping the corner of his mouth with a napkin. "Not even ten seconds into dinner and you're already talking about work." He winked at Treadon like they shared an inside joke about Jarren's passion for business. The truth was, Treadon had never noticed it before, but now that he was looking, he realized Jarren had been far more interested in talking about business than football. Maybe Treadon wasn't the only one feeling unfulfilled each time they won a football game. "I know you enjoyed the internship this summer, but maybe keep your focus on football a little longer."

"I'm ready to work for you," Jarren said. "I could start full time tomorrow."

"Slow down. Finish school. Your enthusiasm reminds me of me, but that doesn't mean your future is set." There was a nervous twitch at the side of Xander's mouth.

Rachel's parting look came back to Treadon. Something more going on.

"Jarren hasn't told me much about what you do," Treadon said. "What exactly is XC Energy?"

"That's obviously my favorite subject," Xander said, stabbing his fork into a long stalk of asparagus.

"Oh," Jarren broke in. "Rachel needs to get an interview with you. Do you have time to schedule that in?"

Another twitch. "Not this week. She'll have to call the secretary and get an appointment."

Jarren looked disappointed. "I told her I had connections. Can't you give her thirty minutes? You could tell her about how you have a fantastic intern that's learning how to run everything after his old man is gone."

"Not this week." Xander didn't lose his professionalism, but the skin around his eyes pulled tight, his smile stiffened. There was an awkward hesitation, and then a nod. "The business may not be everything you think it is."

"C'mon, it's Rachel." Jarren flipped his napkin onto his lap. "It's the least you could do for her."

"This is not the best time." Xander put his fork down and wrapped his fingers around his wine glass, his grip tight enough that the glass seemed in danger of cracking. "If you want to work with me, you'll have to learn not to mix business and personal relationships."

Jarren tossed his napkin back on the table. "I'll be back. Don't eat all my soup." He stood up and almost ran into another waiter who approached with a tray empty of food; a small, folded piece of paper sat in the center. Jarren pushed past him and headed for the bathroom.

"A note for you, sir," said the waiter.

"Thank you." Xander accepted the note as the waiter lowered the tray to table level. Xander unfolded the piece of paper.

Xander Calivan's business persona shifted almost imperceptibly. Treadon wasn't sure he would have noticed anything if he hadn't been trying to read people. But the small widening of his eyes, the tremor in his bottom lip, a shift in his shoulders. His confidence shifted into fear.

"Excuse me." He stood. Hesitated. Pulled his suit coat down and straightened his tie. Then he stepped out of the small private dining room.

Treadon watched him walk across the restaurant. He didn't stop at the elevator, but walked around the corner, probably to where there was an entrance to the emergency stairs.

Stay or go. Follow or wait. What was his role? Would he be betraying a friend or helping both Rachel and Jarren? It was the last look on Xander's face, the fear of a single piece of paper when he was the master of an empire, that made Treadon's decision for him.

Thirteen

September 27

Pat asked me what was wrong after I danced with the twins in the living room and made Jake his favorite desert and read an article from FishingNews Magazine to Nolan. It was a silly question. Nothing is wrong with me other than I'm a Descendant without connection and I can't stop thinking about Treadon. And this room feels so hot. I asked Pat to turn up the air conditioning, but she was busy bouncing the baby who had been crying for a few hours without stopping.

I took a turn holding her while Pat checked on Nolan.

I imagined Treadon looking at me. I remembered how I blamed him for ignoring his ability to read people when I'm the one ignoring what I can do. I'm the one who is afraid to face who I really am. I let myself touch the Descendant light in me. It was a tiny amount. The poor baby had a bad case of acid reflux and I let myself soothe her. I used my powers.

I've been sitting on the window seat, looking out at the yard, biting my nails, wondering if the sky is going to fall or the hunters are going to walk up the driveway. But nothing has happened, yet. And using my abilities felt good. It felt right. Now if I could only push away this nagging fear.

There is a safe place for Descendants, a gathering place called The Veil, but not everyone is welcome, and Mom said there was a division even among the Descendants. Some believed in coming together to create a place of safety. Others believed in being out among the people, doing their best to uplift and protect Ordinaries.

I don't know how to find The Veil, but I'm not sure about a place that creates division and declares itself judge and juror of the Descendant community. Still, it would be nice to have someone to ask my questions, to find out the truth about what happened.

Xander Calivan

Xander paused inside the door of the stairwell, twenty-two stories up. The lighting was dim compared to the brilliance of the restaurant with the sun setting in the west, the bright pinks and purples coloring the white of the restaurant tablecloths. In here the bare gray walls and concrete steps held no comfort. Xander took a calming breath and looked down at the note. Despite his best efforts to still his hand, the paper shook on the edge of his fingers.

The succinct note stood out clearly against the embossed paper.

Seventeenth floor. Stairs.

The words by themselves would have been easy to ignore, shrugged off as a prank by a desperate admirer, but the symbol at the bottom of the note was unmistakable. The hastily scrawled words were on a paper with the symbol pressed at the bottom. The official seal of the Triune. Xander had not dealt with the Triune for over seven years, not since Jarren's surgery. His son had always seemed healthy, but the Triune had insisted, if he wanted to keep the company and have a son to follow in his footsteps, Jarren needed brain surgery. It was nowhere on Jarren's medical records. No doctor knew about it. And it was before Xander decided that being a parent wasn't so bad.

Their symbol was a black triangle, each side failing to connect. The lines of the triangle shifted inside, curling into an intricate design in each corner of the triangle.

His hand flexed, nearly crumpling the paper.

He stopped, smoothed out the paper, and folded it. He tucked it into the breast pocket of his shirt. There was no reason to panic, no reason to assume. He forced himself to walk down the five flights of stairs with calm steps. He thought he heard a small click, maybe from the edge of his shoe. He checked the stairs up and down, but no one came into the stairwell this high in the building.

The last turn before the eighteenth floor, he stopped. Below him, a man leaned against the wall, casual, head down. Xander's footsteps on the concrete stairs were loud enough to alert the man to his presence, but there was no reaction.

The man wore an old, wide brimmed hat, pulled down low to cover his entire face. Although bulky, his tan trench coat stretched tight over his body and only showed the tips of dirty, steel-toed boots. He stood with his shoulders hunched, head down as if he thought he could disappear into the wall that supported him. This wasn't the Triune's normal type of messenger, but it had been quite a few years. Maybe the Triune had fallen on hard times.

"Do you have a message for me?" He started with his impatient business tone; get this over with. Authority, whether real or perceived was an asset. "What was so important that Mr. Bachman couldn't wait to contact me until tomorrow?"

There was a pause before the man turned. His head came up and his shoulders straightened. He tilted his head purposefully to one side, exposing his neck between his wide-brimmed hat and the collar of the trench coat. His neck had the stretched and thin skin of an old man. Clean. No tattoo. The Triune messengers all had the tattoo of a triangle on their neck.

"Who are you?" Xander's mind couldn't process who would dare to use the mark of the Triune, but not claim loyalty to the cause.

The man finally looked up with unexpectedly clear eyes: a light, washed out blue from age, but intelligent, piercing.

"It has been quite a few years, hasn't it, Mr. Calivan?" He nodded and smiled like they had met accidentally. He extended his hand as if he expected Xander to shake it. Xander remained halfway between the two landings, feet on two different stairs.

Xander stared at the hand. "We've met?"

"Once. We had a short interview about your company when you were a small start-up, struggling to get off the ground."

A small memory tugged at the back of Xander's mind. Then a sinking feeling as recognition set in. "Vox?"

"You remember." Vox's smile left and his eyes remained hard.

"He told me . . ." Xander began.

"That he took care of me? That I wouldn't be bothering you anymore?" Vox put one foot on the steps. Xander had to grip the handrail to keep from retreating, mirroring Vox's motion in reverse. He would not show intimidation. The man was not a ghost. But he should have been. "Did he tell you how? Did he tell you what he did to remove the 'annoyances' or did you plan it out together, sending his hounds out on their little missions?"

Xander shook his head. "No. I never knew. I didn't ask. I took care of my part of the business, and I let him . . . he took care of the rest." There was no excuse, no hiding his discomfort. It wasn't a past he was particularly proud of, but he'd moved on. Thought he'd put it behind him.

"And you trusted him. Good to have trust in a business relationship." Vox took one hand out of his pocket and studied his fingernails. "Do you trust him still?"

"Trust him?" Neither of them said his name. Vox probably didn't even know the man's name. Caden Bachman was the businessman who had given Xander the break he needed to become successful, had offered the services of the Triune to help him achieve his dreams. But was it trust?

Vox looked up the stairs and then down as if someone might be watching them. He even glanced left and right like it was possible for someone to see them through the concrete stairwell. Then he shrugged his shoulders as if deciding. "I've been watching you, Mr. Calivan. You aren't the same man I met nineteen years ago, are you?"

"What are you talking about?"

"You knew what was going on then, but you turned a blind eye. You thought you could succeed without sharing the guilt if you pretended you didn't know, but you knew, deep down, that something was wrong. But you refused to see past all the green."

"I . . ."

"That's why you came, isn't it? It was the sign. His calling card. You know what that means and so you came." Vox pointed a crooked finger at Xander. Xander hadn't even realized Vox had made it up three more steps until he poked the folded piece of paper in Xander's pocket. Xander brushed his hand away.

Vox continued. "I know why you're nervous, Mr. Calivan. Like I said, I've been watching you and I don't think you're the same man you were then. I don't think you'd sacrifice the same things."

"You don't know anything about me."

"You had nothing to lose before, but you got something now. And you know you can't have it both ways."

"We're done here." Xander straightened his shoulders like he could knock off the weight of guilt Vox had placed there. "You don't know what you're talking about. You're talking about things you have no understanding of. I'll give you five minutes to clear out before I call security." Xander turned to walk up the stairs. Vox's voice made him stop. The hairs on his neck stood up.

"I should kill you," Vox whispered. "Kill you for what you let them do, what you helped them do. But, like I said, I think you've changed, and I think we need each other. We're going to have to work together if either of us wants to win."

"What would I possibly need you for?"

"Because he's been calling in on his favors. He's been cashing out his investments and leaving a trail of smoldering businesses behind him."

Xander tried to not suck in a breath. He'd been watching the business news. He'd seen three other companies involved with the Triune go bankrupt this year alone. There could be others, but he hadn't dug that deep.

"The word is, he's headed here next," Vox said. "He's not going to bother leaving you anything to live for."

"I've put precautions in place." He had been smart. Put some money in offshore accounts. Kept his research and development team ahead of the curve to keep his business invaluable. He'd made his payment to Caden Bachman regularly, even with the increases.

Vox gave a derisive snort. "You think all the security in the world will be able to stop him? You know as well as I do that once he has a goal, or a target, there is nothing that keeps him from following through. He's got a plan. I don't know exactly what, but you're going to have to choose—again. And I don't think the choice will be so easy this time."

Xander flinched like the words were a gunshot echoing through the stairwell. He turned his head and looked at Vox through the corner of his eye. "How could you possibly know?"

"You may not remember, but digging up hidden information is what I do best." Vox's smile returned, his lips a curved line of steel. The expression gave Vox a strange, hysterical look. "I know what he's looking for and I can tell you when he finds it. I can give you a head start. You know how much that's worth."

Xander paused for a long time, his hand touching the note in his pocket. Then he let his arm swing to his side, two fingers rubbing together like they were trying to ignite a spark of hope.

"What do you need from me?" Xander finally asked.

Fourteen

TREADON NELSON

Treadon fumbled with his napkin as he sat back down at the table. Jarren was just coming back out of the bathroom and Xander Calivan almost ran into his son as they met in the hall outside the elevator. Treadon's seat was on the far side of the table, so he watched as they walked back across the restaurant together. The energy between them had changed. Jarren was quiet, almost sullen. Xander fidgeted with the single button on his suit coat.

The waiter placed a fourth course in front of him. A piece of meat drizzled in fancy sauce with some tiny basil leaves sprinkled on top. Treadon tucked the cloth napkin in the collar of his shirt and then took it out and laid it on his lap, then he folded it up and put it back by his plate. He didn't know how to hide his own nervousness. He shouldn't have followed Xander into the stairwell. He wondered if Xander saw him sneak out when the conversation stalled. But the conversation left him sweaty and a little shaken. Xander had people killed to start the company? No one had said it directly, but the guy called Vox had made it clear. If Xander knew he was listening, would he try to shut him up?

"Can we talk about it?" Jarren spoke as he entered the small glass room with his father. Treadon put his napkin back on his lap. He picked up his fork and knife to cut the piece of meat even though he could have eaten it in one bite.

"The discussion is over. My decision is final."

"What if I don't even want to play football?"

"I won't let you throw away your talent. There will always be business opportunities in the future, but not a chance like this, to play for a college, to experience the dorm life, to get an education."

Jarren hit the table, bouncing the silverware against the plates with a clang. Xander convulsed, jumping at the noise like it had been an explosion. Even Jarren noticed his dad's reaction. Some of his anger drained away.

Treadon felt like he'd been caught in the wrong place at the wrong time. He tried to keep his eyes on his food as he cut a second tiny bite, but his eyes kept glancing up, taking in the father and his son. The businessman and his employee. The man with secrets and the boy who thought he wanted more.

"I've sent some tapes to Oregon and the coach is impressed. He's coming to watch a game himself. You'll get signed on, no problem."

"Oregon? Are you kidding?"

"I've locked up a spot for you in one of the highest-ranking teams in the country. You should be grateful." Treadon wasn't even trying to read Xander when the unsaid words came through the way Xander shifted, the way he held his fork too tight. *And you should get as far away from me as you can.*

Rachel had wanted more information about XC Energy, but Treadon wasn't sure this was the kind of scoop she wanted. From the way Xander was acting, this might as well be the next Watergate. A kind of story that was dangerous. The kind of information that got you killed.

"I want to stay here," Jarren said, as close to desperate as Treadon has ever seen him. "I want you to hire me full time after I graduate. We talked about it all summer. XC Energy is at the top of technological advancements. I'll be out of touch if I go away for four years."

"Things have changed." Xander stood. He made the motion of

buttoning the suit coat that was already buttoned. "My decision is final. You'll play football or you'll be cut off. You'll do as I say, or you'll get nothing from me."

Xander looked at his son. His face was stone, but Treadon could see veins of weakness streaking through Xander's hard exterior. There was a strange note of pride, a strain of frustration, and an underlying smell of fear.

"Business is business," Xander said. "Technology only changes the media we use to conduct it. You're a natural. You won't miss a thing by going to college. It will be a great start, a great opportunity." He pushed back his chair and opened the glass door into the main restaurant. He paused for a moment before turning back.

"Jarren, I gave up *everything* for this business. I don't want you to have regrets twenty years down the road." He held Jarren's gaze for another moment and then left the restaurant.

They sat in silence; Jarren playing with his food, Treadon wondering if he should cut the last portion in half or eat the whole thing. He glanced at Jarren.

"Rachel's going to be disappointed," Treadon said, pulling his friend back to the present.

"What do you mean?" Jarren asked.

"I think she was hoping the shark climate of the business world would shrink your head down a few sizes. A college football star? They'll have to customize the helmet."

Jarren let the corner of his mouth tilt up. "He might change his mind. He has a habit of changing his mind." The last sentence held a note of bitterness. Broken promises. Jarren shoved his fork and plate away from him. "What just happened?"

Treadon thought of the way his mom had talked the other night, about pushing him to get the money, to go away for college. "No idea. My mom wants me to go to college, too. Isn't it supposed to be the other way around? You know, parents shedding tears of regret and worry while we fly from the nest with confidence and excitement. At least that's how it was in the eighties."

That got a full smile from Jarren, but it was extinguished as quickly as a candle being blown out. "You know what Rachel's going to say?"

"No."

"She's going to say, I told you so. She never trusted my dad; never thought he'd really turned a corner."

Treadon thought of the way Vox had said Xander changed. What did Rachel know about Xander's past?

"She's wrong," Jarren said, squeezing his napkin like a sponge. "He has changed. He may not know it, but he wants me to stay and work with him. I know he does."

From what Treadon read in Xander's face before he left, Jarren was right about part of it.

"He was talking about my mom, you know." Jarren tossed his napkin on his full plate.

"What?" Treadon hadn't heard Jarren talk about his mother in years. He mentioned once that she left them when he was still a baby, but that was it.

"When he said he gave up everything for the business, he was talking about my mom. He chose the business over her."

Treadon was at a loss for words. All he could do was nod and shake his head like a bobble-head.

"Let's get out of here." Jarren stood up and headed for the elevator. Treadon followed.

He didn't want to tell Jarren that he was wrong or explain his unfounded suspicions. It didn't make sense, but from the expressions and movements of Xander Calivan, Treadon was sure he'd read something different. Xander hadn't said those words mourning a woman he hadn't seen in seventeen years. Xander was mourning another loss, regretting the fact that he'd sacrificed everything for his business, including the son that was sitting right in front of him.

Fifteen

October 3

Our second tutoring session is tomorrow.

Part of me wants to run. Part of me is looking forward to it.

Part of me wants to change. Part of me wants to stay the same.

Which part of me is Descendant and which part is Ordinary?

Because we are all mixed up. Our DNA. Part of the reason for the division of The Veil is that, after thousands of years, the Angels' DNA had been diluted and mixed with the Ordinary population. It was bound to happen. Laws of evolution. There are those who were born from other Descendants and there are those who have Descendant abilities even though both their parents are Ordinary. About the age of twelve, their energy of creation begins to manifest, and their light is visible to other Descendants, demons, and even a few Ordinaries with the ability to see the energy. That's why I've been careful not to use my abilities and keep my light wrapped around myself. I don't know who would find me first, but I do know I wouldn't be welcome at The Veil.

The Veil of Descendants looks for Descendants with as much Angel DNA as possible. They claim to be preparing for the final battle when Cado Fillius finds the daggers and attacks the Descendants with an innumerable force. But they don't invite those who truly need protection: Descendants who have been born from Ordinaries. Or Descendants who refuse to follow the rules. Or Descendants like me, who've made mistakes. Life-changing, unalterable mistakes.

Mom believed that The Veil was unfair and should open its doors to all Descendants and Guardians. Mom believed in helping those who came into this world alone.

Would she have chosen differently if she knew she would leave her daughter in the very condition that she tried to save people from? It's not Mom's fault, it's my own. My own choices. As much as I want to change, I'm not ready. I won't let him get close to me. If I push him away, I can't hurt him.

Treadon Nelson

. . .

Treadon's nightmare pulled him from sleep, his sheets sticking to him, his face drenched in sweat. A light breeze swayed his curtains as he stumbled from his bed to lean against his dresser. It was a dream. Only a dream. He looked at the dark silhouette outlined in the mirror against the trickle of moonlight coming through the window. He placed his hands on his own chest and let his lungs fill and empty, rising and lowering. He was whole, but he couldn't figure out why he felt so broken.

He slumped back on his bed, checking to see if he could get away with getting up. The glaring red numbers read 1:45. Not the best time for a shower. He readjusted in the bed and forced his eyes closed. They popped back open, the dream still playing tricks behind his eyelids. He tossed and turned trying to find something else to concentrate on. He thought of the mystery of Xander's business. He had more questions than answers. He thought about Rachel and Jarren and the football team. There was a drop in his stomach as he thought about the fight in the locker room and Bridger Michaels' parting look. Michaels hadn't done anything, yet, but the wait might be worse than the revenge. He tried to change directions again and thought about his mom. She'd worked late again tonight and then spent the evening on that stupid CB radio with Gabe. His stomach twisted even tighter. He needed something relaxing, not stressful.

School wasn't any better. Tests and homework. Math. He almost groaned out loud, but then he thought of Eleanor Agarwal. The girl who claimed to be descended from angels. She had to be lying or teasing or delusional. But Treadon felt the knots in his stomach untwisting. His lungs relaxed. The weight lifted from his chest. He thought of her eyes, of getting lost in them, when the world had melted away.

His breathing returned to normal. He stopped twisting in his blankets. He lay on his back, arm behind his head, staring at the ceiling, but seeing her face, her eyes deep and intelligent and swirling with emotion. He sunk into a peaceful sleep, encased in a cocoon of warm comfort.

The next day, Treadon felt rested for the first time in months. He sat through math, focused on the math problems and not the teacher, reading the board and not the withering glances of Mr. Ashcroft. He understood two new formulas and by the end of the class, Mr. Ashcroft gave him a grudging compliment.

He went to lunch in an unusually good mood.

He found Rachel and Jarren standing together in the lunch line, heads close, words whispered. The good mood drained away as he remembered Xander Calivan facing the man in the heavy trench coat and wide-brimmed hat. Vox.

"Do you think he'll let me do an interview?" Rachel asked.

Treadon joined them in line.

Jarren shrugged. He hadn't switched all the way over to his charming school persona, but he still nodded at Treadon and bumped fists with a couple kids as they walked by. There was a wall to cover his pain, but it was raw, incomplete.

"I'll ask again," Jarren said. "He owes you. We'll head over after school and see if he'll do a quick impromptu one. He can't say no if we're standing in front of him." Jarren picked up a tray.

"I'll have the questions ready." Rachel scribbled some notes in the notebook she carried everywhere but onto the football field with her. "Maybe I'll send him an email beforehand so he can prepare the answers." Rachel turned to Treadon. "Did you learn anything about Xander Calivan last night or XC Energy? Would you like to make an official statement for the article?"

Treadon looked around, hoping for an escape or distraction. He really didn't have enough information to help Rachel with her paper. He didn't understand what the meeting was about and couldn't trust his weird ability to read people as material for an online article. Then he caught sight of Eleanor across the lunchroom.

She sat by herself, which was weird in the crowded room. There were several empty seats on either side of her and across from her. No one seemed to notice, even those who were looking for a seat. Her back was to him, head down, black hair spread across her back and hanging down on both sides of her face like a veil. Her shoulders stiffened. She knew he'd seen her.

"There she is," Treadon said, pointing. "The girl sitting over there by herself. You've got to come meet her."

Rachel's head came up. Her eyebrows came together like she recognized the ploy, but meeting new people was Rachel's tenth passion. "Who?" Her eleventh passion was making sure no one was alone. Rachel's ultimate weakness: Jarren.

"The girl I told you about," Treadon said. "She's tutoring me in math."

"You mean your imaginary girl friend?" Jarren gulped down the new subject like it was Gatorade at halftime. A moment of relief that let him flip his switch back on.

But then both Rachel and Jarren started acting weird. Treadon couldn't put his finger on it at first, but his sudden urgency to get through the lunch line seemed to make them move in slow motion.

Rachel studied the salad bar like she was picking out her words for an article.

"This isn't rocket science. Throw on some tomatoes and let's go." Treadon stayed behind Rachel since the salad line was the shortest, bumping her tray with his to get her moving. Jarren took the burger and fries line and started a conversation with the lunch lady.

Treadon checked over the heads of the other students in the cafeteria. Eleanor hadn't moved. She hadn't touched the brown lunch bag in front of her and she held a book open on the table, but Treadon didn't think she was reading.

Jarren stopped at the sauces, acting like he was shopping for a car. The choices were ketchup or ranch. Not a lot of options.

Treadon pointed to the ketchup. "Go with door number one."

"Calm down, Hero. You're acting like there's a fire," Jarren said as he reached for the ketchup and then changed his mind and grabbed the ladle in the ranch.

Treadon wanted to pull Rachel's arm and kick Jarren in the rear end. He took a deep breath. There was still time before lunch ended.

While he waited for Jarren and Rachel to pay, Treadon glanced again at Eleanor. She was bent over her book, hair falling over her face. Nothing out of the ordinary. She wasn't flying. She didn't have wings. She didn't even seem to have friends. There was no extra glow about her or markings that set her apart.

So why did he feel such an incredible pull towards her? Why was there a nagging doubt in his mind that she might have told the truth just so he wouldn't believe it? Descended from angels? Impossible.

Treadon took three determined steps before realizing that Jarren and Rachel weren't behind him. He turned and found them two tables away, sitting with a group of kids Treadon had never talked to before. Hadn't really noticed before. Rachel squeezed in between a boy wearing rose lipstick, guillotine earrings, and fingerless gloves and a girl with short hair, finger tattoos, and a blank stare. Rachel got a smile out of the boy, but the girl stirred an almost empty cup of coffee with a straw and gave Rachel no reaction.

The two people Jarren sat between stared at Jarren, faces frozen in disbelief. They wore bull nose rings, black lipstick, chokers, and knee-high platform boots. Treadon could read their confusion and disbelief, but he also felt the same way. Rachel and Jarren had completely brushed him off, ignored him. Sat with a group of people that they'd never interacted with before. Even though Treadon was sure he had a few of them in a couple of his classes.

Jarren reached across the table, grabbing fries from the tray of a girl with a diamond stud glittering below her lower lip. Her eyes followed the path of her fries from Jarren's fingers to his mouth. He took a bite and Treadon heard Jarren ask about her favorite music.

Someone bumped Treadon, almost knocking the tray from his hands. Another person passed, hitting his elbow. He had stopped in the middle of the main path between the tables. People were trying to move by, get on with their lives. Treadon felt as if everything had paused.

Treadon looked at Rachel and Jarren, casually making friends like they'd forgotten all about him, all about Xander Calivan, and all about their normal social behavior.

Eleanor stood, grabbing her lunch bag and her book. She didn't look at him, but everything in her stance reflected her effort not to. She turned to walk around the table, and Treadon caught her profile: saw the slight twitch of her mouth, a blink that was too slow, her shoulder shrug like she was putting on a coat. She thought something was funny. He could almost hear her taunting him, *better luck next time*.

Sixteen

October 4

I only meant to avoid him, keep him away, but I think I may have started some kind of game. What is even more strange, is I think I'm enjoying it. The look on his face. The way he watched me walk out of the room. I almost felt . . . happy.

After hiding for so long. After being afraid for so long, I forgot what that felt like. But it doesn't change things. Pat keeps going to work. Nolan doesn't wake up. I spend time taking care of the kids. And Jake watches from the edges of the room like a shadowed guardian. I have a routine. Nothing's changed at school, but there is a pressing fear, a growing sense of foreboding. And I wonder, "What is the source of my fear?" There seems to be some gaps in my memories, stories that Mom told me. Something I've forgotten, but that has left an impression of impending danger.

When it's time to put the kids to bed, I stay in Jake's room, not because he's having nightmares, but because the fear squeezing my chest is so much worse when I'm alone in my room. I tell him about how the abilities of Descendants manifest. I'm able to influence minds and increase the speed of healing in a physical body. Mom's words come back to me again. *You've inherited more than most. You have a great responsibility.* Maybe it's because I can do two different things. There are Descendants that can influence waves of light, touch the elements of the earth, combine elements on an atomic level, think as fast as a computer, control the elements of the air, increase the strength of sound waves, and even bend light particles around time.

I'm sure there are more. I was only seven when I left, and my brother was the smart one. He liked to develop new technology with his knowledge. He would have changed the world.

If he hadn't disappeared with the rest of my family.

Xander Calivan

Xander Calivan sat rigid in his chair, staring straight ahead. His secretary, Miss Littleton, stood in front of him reading off the meeting schedule for the day. He adjusted the frame on his desk that contained a picture of Jarren in his football uniform, a smile as big as the sky. Only two papers remained from his search, sitting in front of Xander now, lined on the edge of his desk with precision.

"Mr. Calivan?" Miss Littleton had her pen poised over her clipboard.

Xander pulled his hand away from Jarren's picture and re-straightened the papers on his desk. "Can you repeat the last question?"

Miss Littleton didn't answer right away. She stared at Xander with a look of perplexed concern. "Would you like me to reschedule the governor for your lunch hour or ask him to wait until next week?"

Xander shrugged off his momentary lack of focus. The meeting with Vox had shaken him, but his research into Caden Bachman's four other holdings had chilled him to the core. No one knew the vast empire of Caden Bachman, but three of the four declared bankruptcy in the last year. His contacts with the other companies had not returned calls or emails. Crickets.

"Tell him it took some doing, but we can fit him in today," Xander said, folding his hands to keep from fiddling with anything. He'd learned to cover his nerves after so many years.

Another voice broke in. "Cancel it." The voice was quiet, full of authority, and sent a chill of fear down Xander's spine. He closed his eyes for an instant; the news article of a CEO's gruesome death flashed through his mind. "Clear Mr. Calivan's schedule for the day."

"Excuse me?" Miss Littleton said in her no-nonsense sixth grade teacher voice. She could inspire obedience from the most self-aggrandized business tycoon, but this was above even her skill level.

"That's all right, Miss Littleton." Xander interrupted her before she could go on. "Please clear my schedule for the day. That will be all." He dismissed her with a curt nod. Miss Littleton fluffed up like ruffled rooster, but then she took stock of herself.

"Yes, sir." She turned on the heel of her shoe and left the office.

Xander let out a small breath of relief. Miss Littleton closed the door behind her and Xander was left facing the very man he'd been thinking about. Caden Bachman stood just inside the door. A second man stood at Caden Bachman's shoulder, like a wingman or an overanxious intern. They both wore business suits, custom tailored, made of the smoothest material. The second man looked plain enough, too plain. The man's features showed no emotion, almost like his face was made of wax. His hair lay perfectly on his head like each strand had been intentionally placed.

"Please, have a seat." Xander motioned to the two chairs on the far side of his desk. Neither man moved to take a chair. Xander remained standing.

"I've come to collect on your contract," said Caden Bachman.

"My contract?" Xander lifted the papers he'd lined up on his desk. "You received a quarterly payout of thirty percent of our profits above and beyond your initial investment into the company. We are the number one profiting company in your holdings and have produced all your private technology on time and without cost. I am the best investment you've ever made. I am in no way in breach of contract."

He held the papers out, one a list of numbers, amounts in the millions of dollars that Caden Bachman received from XC Energy. The second, a list of privately requested items that the technology department had produced and handed over to Caden Bachman for patents. He had yet to see any of the technological marvels hit the public sector.

Xander thought Caden would ignore the papers he held out, but after a moment, Caden stepped forward and took the paper with the list of projects from Xander's hand.

"These have proven very successful," Caden said. "In fact, it is because of the WWAR that your contract is being called in for fulfillment."

"You mean the satellite that was sensitive enough to pick up the electromagnetic field around a human being from the upper atmosphere?" Xander remembered that project. He'd had to do some clever bookkeeping to keep that project from showing on his quarterly reports. He'd donated over 100 million dollars to a non-profit charity he'd created. They'd had to install extra software on the satellite that analyzed the data on population growth and the effect on climate to keep the non-profit legit. He hadn't told Caden Bachman about the extra software, but it was insignificant, sending the smallest number of ones and zeros down to his personal computer. Only several megabytes of data that would hardly be noticed compared to the rest of the satellite and specifications Caden Bachman had requested.

"Yes." Caden ran his finger along the edge of Xander's desk. Xander resisted an urge to slap his hand away. "We've found it most useful in our search and are ready to move to the next phase."

"And this next phase includes me." Xander felt himself relax. He'd been so worried Caden Bachman had come to shut him down, destroy his life's work like with the other companies, but Caden needed him, understood his value. "If you give me the specifications, I'll get working on it right away."

"This project is going to require more involvement from someone more . . . dedicated."

The sudden shift from calm to panicked left Xander breathless. "There is no one more dedicated to this business than me."

"I remember your competitive spirit and business sense, but I think you mistake those qualities for the quality that made me choose you over others."

In his attempt to remain professional, to keep from showing the swirling chaos rising in him, Xander thought of what his son would say.

"Perhaps you picked me for my good looks and hypnotic charm," Xander said, pushing his lapels up and shrugging his shoulders. The thought of his son snapped his senses into sharp relief like smelling salts had been passed beneath his nose. He had to focus like he did in every business meeting. Find the chink. Find the opportunity.

"Money," Caden said, the word clipped with finality.

"Excuse me?" Xander asked, raising an eyebrow.

"Your passion . . . for money. Very few would go to the lengths you did to succeed. But you've forgotten the original deal." Bachman lifted the picture of Jarren from the desk. "Or perhaps you've become distracted."

Xander stepped around the desk and took the picture from Caden's hands. He set it carefully back down. He faced Caden, meeting his eyes.

"I'm more focused than ever before," Xander said.

Bachman placed his thumb under Xander's collar bone and squeezed the back of his neck with his fingers. It could have almost looked like a friendly squeeze on the shoulder if it wasn't for the pain that flashed through Xander's mind and forced him to his knees. Caden leaned over him, pupils expanding until the eyes were like black pits. Xander felt the sensation of falling.

He heard voices swirling in the darkness, saw a younger version of himself, an ageless version of Caden standing across a smaller desk in a smaller office. He saw the words in fine print on a document in front of his younger self as he raised the pen to sign. Xander wanted to yell at himself not to do it, take it back, but he couldn't speak. He could only watch as the vision grew blurry, his focus on the document, the tiny print growing bigger until it was all he could see.

In exchange for the investment, Xander Calivan forfeits his soul.

It was impossible. Those words couldn't have been there. Xander had read through it. Surely, he would have read every word in that contract, memorized it before making the agreement. He would now, for sure, but had he been that ambitious back then?

Bachman released his grip on Xander's shoulder as well as his hold on his mind. Xander scrambled backward, rubbing his shoulder. He knocked over his office chair and had to use his desk to stabilize himself as he rose to his feet.

"You can't be serious." Xander spit the words despite the fear that gripped him. "I've done everything you've asked. I am the reason for your success. If you kill me, your precious satellite will go offline. I've seen what you've been doing to the others, and I've put some precautions in place." The favor for Vox seemed like they had been more of a favor to himself.

"You've already sold your soul to me," Caden said. "I've come to collect."

"My soul is not for sale."

"Everyone's soul has a price," Caden said. "It seems that yours has changed. I will leave Pravus to watch over you until the time is right." Caden motioned to his wax-faced assistant.

Xander's mouth was dry, and he tried to swallow against the rising panic.

"Why must we wait?" The assistant's voice grew in frustration, sounding more like the whispered screams of tortured prisoners.

Xander wanted to cover his ears and cower behind his desk. He kept his back straight.

Caden Bachman looked into Xander's eyes, and Xander felt the weakness in his knees. He kept his fist planted against the desk to keep from collapsing.

"He must choose to serve me," Caden said, leaning in closer, the darkness swirling behind his eyes.

"He will never choose it," Pravus said, a desperate whining that made the hairs rise on Xander's arm. "Let me free and I will weaken him. He will come to you begging for relief."

Xander stood taller. Despite the fear, he would go through hell if it meant denying this creature the satisfaction of touching his soul.

"No." Bachman opened the door. The shift of pressure created a wind strong enough to knock the picture of Jarren off the edge of Xander's desk. "He already has a weakness. The love of a son."

Seventeen

TREADON NELSON

Treadon sat down across the table from Eleanor in the small room. She smiled with professional accuracy and pulled out her notebook and pen.

"Do you have your assignment from today?" she asked. "Let's work through some of those problems and see where you're struggling."

"How did you do that?" Treadon put a hand on the notebook so she couldn't open it.

Her pencil hovered above the notebook, her head remained tilted down, her hair covering the expression on her face.

"Do what?" she asked.

"You made Jarren and Rachel ignore you. You make everyone in this school act like you don't exist. How?" Treadon realized what she was going to say before she said it. He slipped in the real question before she could answer. "Why?"

Eleanor looked up at him, clicking the top of the pen twice. "I think you're confused. Rachel sat down with some new friends. Jarren would follow her anywhere. Why do you think I had anything to do with Jarren sitting with a new crowd?"

Treadon felt a pressure in his mind, like he was sleepy. He leaned away from her. "Don't try to make me doubt myself. I know what I saw. Wait." He watched her, read her, the twitch of her pen, the tilt of her shoulders, the vein in her neck. "Are you doing it right now? Are you trying to make me do something?"

She sat back, a line of guilt between her eyebrows. "Why would you think that?" she asked, folding her arms tight across her chest.

Treadon sat straight in his chair. A familiar weight pressed down on his chest, like when he woke up after a nightmare. No air. No way to breathe. He fought to push the panic down. He felt like he was on the edge of a cliff deciding whether to jump.

"Because I can feel it," Treadon said, standing up and pacing the room. "But I don't understand it."

"You don't believe it," Eleanor said, raising one eyebrow. "I've told you that I'm a Descendant, so why are you asking something you already know the answer to?"

"I know," Treadon said, pressing his hands against the wall. "I know you told me, but I wasn't ready to believe. What I saw was real. You made Jarren do something he wouldn't normally do. If I accept the fact that you tried to do something to me, that you have that ability, that means . . ."

She kept her eyes on him. Cool. Calm. Expectant. She was content to let this play out. Consequences be damned.

Treadon turned to face her. "Maybe you were telling the truth—"

"I never lie."

"That you're a Descendant. Of . . . Angels." He paused, but he didn't choke on the word. It felt right. It felt true.

He was surprised when an emotion spread across her face. Acceptance. Relief. She covered her mouth with the hand holding the pen. The pen quivered for a moment as she fought down the smile.

"You wanted me to believe you?" Treadon asked.

"I wasn't sure," she said, opening the notebook. "But now that you do, we can focus on math."

"You're joking. I have so many questions."

"Good. Do you want to start with the Pythagorean theorem or how to fix your order of operations."

There was no distracting her. Fine. He'd play this game. Let her teach him some math. He took out his phone and showed her the assignment. She nodded and wrote a few things down. He followed her explanations until he was able to get three problems right on his own.

Treadon leaned back. "That's pretty impressive."

"What? My ability to explain the laws of math?"

"No." Treadon rubbed his chin in exaggerated thoughtfulness. "That you can influence people, everyone. Except me, of course. You should have seen Jarren's face after you left the lunchroom. He nearly choked on that girl's fries."

Eleanor didn't bring her hand up in time to hide the smile. He saw her shoulders shake with quiet laughter. The movement lifted something inside of him, like a lid off a steak dinner that makes your mouth water when you smell the aroma. Her happiness sent a craving through him, to see her smile again.

"You really believe me?" she asked, looking straight into his eyes.

Treadon hesitated. What did he believe? "Can you fly?"

"No."

"Do you grow wings?"

"Seriously?"

"Are there others?"

A pause. "Yes."

"Here at this school?"

"No. I don't think so."

"Is that who you're hiding from? Other Descendants?"

Her pen slipped and left a deep gash across the paper. Treadon read two answers. A Yes and a No. Confusion. Uncertainty.

He put his hand out to touch her, but she pulled back like she'd been burned.

"I'm sorry. I do believe you." He let the words sink in. He wanted them to feel truer. "I don't understand everything. But I can't deny what I saw or how you make me feel."

One eyebrow rose. Treadon felt heat rush to his face.

"Not exactly." Treadon shifted, clearing his throat. He couldn't meet her eyes as he stumbled over his words. "I mean, how you try to influence me, make me look away or ignore you. I can feel that. I didn't mean it in any creepy or romantic way."

She held her eyes closed like her eyelids could hold back her laughter.

"I'll stop talking," he said, rubbing his face.

"You did great today. I think you're making progress." She didn't clarify if she was talking about math or his terrible social skills.

They stood up and Treadon held the door open for her. "I still can't get over the way the rest of lunch went. When I sat next to Dillan, he wondered if someone slipped him bad shrooms."

She walked down the hall, turning slightly with surprise. "You sat down too?"

"Sure." Treadon caught up with her, shouldering his backpack. "Had to help Jarren save face. We had a good time. I think everyone kind of got a kick out of it. Except for one girl. I'd seen her before outside the locker room. Her eyes were . . . empty." It was the best word he could think of to describe what he'd seen.

Eleanor had a peculiar look on her face, a mixture of shock and disbelief. She had labeled him, and he'd broken her expectations. Maybe he understood some of Gabe's disappointment with him. Did he really act so shallow that talking to kids at lunch seemed weird? Did he work so hard to fit in and not stand out that he'd isolated himself from other people?

"Do you know the girl's name?" Eleanor asked.

Treadon thought for a minute. "Yeah. Meagan. She's in my math class. Meagan Shores."

"Thanks."

He opened the front door to the school. "I'll see you next week, Eleanor."

She stopped at the sound of her name. Treadon realized with regret that it was the first time he'd said it.

"You can call me Ellie."

Treadon was about to follow her, but he heard someone call his name. Jarren ran down the hall to catch up to him.

"Rachel and I have been doing some research. I'm taking Rachel to interview my dad. Do you want to come?"

"Sure." Treadon turned, trying to get one last glimpse of Ellie, but a commotion by the stairs caught his attention. Some boys across the quad were yelling.

"C'mon on," said one guy wearing a black t-shirt and ripped jeans. He held a skateboard under one arm. "Jess did it. Now you try."

A small skinny kid, probably a freshman, stood at the top of the steps looking nervous. He glanced around like there was something nearby he could hide under. When he found no way out, he picked up his skateboard and took a few steps back. He put one foot on his board and pushed off hard. He angled toward the railing that led down the stairs and jumped his board into the air. He made the jump and the bottom of his board balanced on the railing as he slid down.

There was a flash of a triumphant smile, and then the kid lost his balance.

He wobbled. He tried to bail, but the board tipped the wrong way and he crumpled onto the bar. He hit the concrete with a sharp crack, like two football helmets smacking together at full speed.

Both Treadon and Jarren flinched at the sound even though they were half of a football field away. Treadon turned to see if he could get help from the office, but the front doors were already locked for the night. He and Jarren ran across the quad, approaching the group of skaters that had gathered around the kid. Then, the group pulled back, spreading out. The kid who had fallen stood up, stretching his arm like he expected pain and was surprised there was none.

No way. Treadon saw that landing; he saw the arm hit and bend at an unnatural angle.

A flash of black hair caught his eye. Ellie was slipping away from the scene, turning the corner at the top of the stairs.

If she really was an Angel, he'd just seen a miracle.

Eighteen

October 7

I want to cheer and cry and wail and shout all at the same time. All the emotions swirling in me are fighting to find a way out. I used my powers again today. Something about meeting Treadon is changing me and making me want to do more. It was a simple bone break. Something I'd practiced as a child. But it felt amazing. This freedom.

But it comes with so much fear.

He's a football player. An Ordinary. A hook that has embedded himself in my brain like a foxtail weed in a wool sock. A boy who sees so much and chose to see so little. But he's changing, too. And I can't help but think that we make a good team. I can't help thinking I could do so much more.

The feeling didn't last. It never does. On the way home today, a car rolling too slowly followed me for a block. I put my head down like a turtle and tucked myself into my shell.

Despite my newfound joy, I cannot shake the feeling that something bad is about to happen. Like the thing I've been hiding from is getting closer. Like that night, when I listened at the door when I was supposed to be in bed, and I knew things were about to change. I didn't want things to change.

I loved the house and the surrounding forest and the warm fire that crackled in the fireplace. That was my home. My safe place. I never believed anything bad would happen to me there.

But when a stranger knocked on the door a few minutes after bedtime and spoke in low tones with my mom and dad, I crept to the door and listened to what the messenger had to say.

Abigail Nelson

Abigail Nelson drove past the high school every day on her way home from work. It was usually too late to pick up Treadon from school, but she always glanced across the parking lot, imagining so many moments of her son's life. He'd been a quiet kindergartener, hanging on to her leg, begging her to stay with him a little longer. She'd loved those days of being needed, of being his whole world. She wished that she'd been able to do better. Every parent wanted to do more for their child, but she'd put so much on him. Raising him without a father. Expecting him to accept Gabe as some kind of roommate without explanation. Keeping so many secrets from him. He didn't deserve the life she'd forced on him.

Abigail kept her eyes on the school for a moment too long and swerved slightly when she saw her tires drifted toward the center lane. A car honked, but she straightened out before there was any damage.

Then, from the corner of her eye, she saw a bright light. A white flash. She glanced again, but she was almost past the school. She caught sight of a group of kids at the far side of the quad, but then the building blocked her view. There was nothing after the flash. Even in the glimpse she'd had before passing the school, she could tell there were no Unguarded among the kids she'd seen.

But that light. She saw it on her map every evening as she and Gabe scoured the world for Unguarded who were just coming into their own. When their light turned on, she could see it.

She used to think she was the only one who could see the lights, that she was special and the only one who could help Gabe, but now she knew there were others finding the Unguarded before she could. She tightened her grip on the steering wheel. She didn't want to fail these children. She didn't want to lose any more.

Abigail pulled into her driveway and hurried up the porch steps. She didn't know what she'd seen, but she would check her map, see if she could find an explanation. She walked into the house.

"Treadon?" It was late, but Treadon didn't answer. Maybe tutoring was going long. She'd pushed him too hard to focus on football, but it seemed like such an easy solution to push him away from the dangers she felt coming closer, always just a shadow away.

She pulled out her map and laid it out on the table. She used her fingers to look closer at the school and the area around it.

Nothing. No aura. No white light of an Unguarded.

A hand came down on her back and she whirled, using her palm to snap up into the attacker's jaw the way Gabe had taught her.

Gabe caught her wrist, stopping her hand a whisker away from his chin.

"I'm sorry I startled you," he said, gently checking her arm where he'd stopped her from hitting him.

Abigail pulled away, her heart fluttering, her words a little breathless. "I didn't know you were back."

"I wanted to investigate Jarren's car a little more with you," Gabe said, folding his arms across his chest. "I got some information about some movement in the Triune, and I think it's connected to Los Angeles somehow."

Abigail had to turn away to keep her throat from closing. Whenever he was so close, she couldn't quite catch her breath. "Do you think they've found you? Are we in danger?"

"No. Nothing like that." Gabe took a step back. "Just a few whispers I wanted to clarify. What were you doing with the map?"

"I thought I saw an Unguarded aura today. At Treadon's school."

"Here? Why didn't you call me?"

"I . . . I'm not sure what it was. It only lasted for an instant and then it was gone."

"That's strange. You sure you weren't seeing Jarren's car again?"

Abigail paused, trying not to let her emotions show. He held his in an iron box. It wasn't fair that hers bled out onto the floor. "Maybe. Maybe you're right. I was driving past the school and if the car was there, I might have mistaken it for an aura. It really does shine bright, but it doesn't show up on the map because it isn't a living aura."

"I'll look into it."

"Did you find the last one?" She knew the answer by the drawn look on his face. She'd sent him after an Unguarded aura near Dallas, Texas. He'd gone as soon as she'd seen it but had found another empty house.

"No." Gabe leaned his arm against the door frame, his head lowered.

"How are they finding them before us?" Abigail asked. She brushed back a stray strand of hair, letting her fingers linger on the scar along her hairline. "I'm watching as often as I can."

"I don't know. But I will find out what is happening to them if it's the last thing I do." Gabe straightened, his hands coming to his side, fingers curled into fists.

Abigail turned to face him again. "Even if you lead them here?"

Gabe's eyes dropped; his jaw flexed. He didn't answer.

Nineteen

JARREN CALIVAN

Jarren gave the familiar security guard a knuckle bump through the front of the entrance gate to XC Energy. He swiped his access card and the gate rolled sideways. Jarren glanced at Rachel sitting in the passenger seat. She always managed to be appropriately unimpressed by the wealth of Xander Calivan. She grew up with it, but in a different way than Jarren had. Until she'd gotten sick, Rachel's mom had been Jarren's nanny, as much as he hated to think that word. Nannies were women who watched spoiled children in Europe and flew on pixie dust or umbrellas.

He'd gone to public schools with Rachel instead of private institutions for rich kids. He'd spent far more time with Rachel and her mom at skate parks and farmers' markets and cheap amusement parks than golf courses and rotary clubs. It was Rachel's mom who signed him up for football, who'd picked him up from the hospital when he'd needed brain surgery at seven years old. No one was allowed in the hospital with him. Jarren remembered peeling paint on the walls, orderlies with prison tattoos, and a doctor with terrible bedside manners with a kid about to go under the knife without his dad around to hold his hand.

Rachel glanced at him and then up at the open gate.

He was hesitating. He was nervous. But that wasn't something he wanted Rachel to see.

He lifted his foot from the brake and the car rolled through the ornamental iron gate that stood fifteen feet high. The gate closed behind them, and Jarren watched it through his rearview mirror. The center of the gate had a cursive XC surrounded by a circle of intricate vine patterns. The edges were lined with black, twisted, three-inch bars. The thick top bar was curved from one side of the gate to the other. In the top center of the curve was a large black triangle with pointed ends and sides that never seemed to touch but twisted into intricate swirling shapes within the triangle itself.

Jarren had spent time trying to follow the lines of the triangle with his eyes, never quite being able to find where the bars began, ended, or connected. He used to think if he could solve the puzzle behind the triangle, he would be able to solve the puzzle of his life.

He drove to the front of the parking lot and found the usual open spot right next to his father's tan Bentley. This was a spot he'd gotten used to over the summer, one he'd started to think of as his. Rachel got out of the car, but Jarren closed his eyes for a second in the driver's seat. He needed to visualize, picture the way he wanted things to go in his head. It worked for football. He could see the ball, visualize it in his hands, and it would happen—just like he saw it. Now, if he could only work the same technique on his dad.

Sure. You can work for me. We'll be business partners, father and son. I love you.

Jarren popped his eyes back open and jumped out of the car. Rachel was taking pictures of the front of the building for her article, so hopefully she hadn't noticed anything. He'd let his visualization get a little out of hand. His dad didn't say the word love, but in the last two years, Jarren was sure he'd heard it in his voice. Once or twice.

Jarren led Rachel through the front doors and into the lobby. Rachel paused, lifting her camera again. The entrance lobby was designed to impress. The walls were made of black granite, flecks of gold that glittered in the light and had the appearance of motion, like they had once been part of a flowing source that dried up a millennia ago.

"This is beautiful." Rachel ran her fingers through a fountain of LED lights in the center of the room. "At least the designer had good taste."

"I know you're angry with him," Jarren said, "but just give him a chance to change his mind. Maybe you could get a job here too. We could work together."

Rachel huffed. "Xander has some explaining to do before I stop looking into XC Energy. A public company like his should be more open book. And his non-profits seem like a joke. Almost nothing except a single page website that claims he's using a satellite to counteract global warming. And that's it. You can't say you're combating global warming without telling us how."

"I'm sure he has to balance things. He can't have people stealing his prototypes and research. Technology is full of pirates and hackers that sell the information to the highest bidder."

The elevator door opened, and Rachel and Jarren stepped inside. "Yeah, but there's things you need to make public, especially when you have shares and claim to serve the people. I hope he'll answer my questions."

Jarren straightened his tie as the doors closed, then scanned his key card and hit the number five. Top level. Restricted access. The rest of the employees worked on the lower levels, but Xander Calivan's office was the top story of the building. Jarren wore the Gucci suit his dad purchased for him over the summer. "Tactful, yet impressive," Xander had told him as he'd handed the cashier his credit card.

The elevator dinged and Rachel stepped out first. Jarren followed.

Miss Littleton was hunched over her desk, phone to her ear, speaking in a hoarse whisper. Jarren flopped onto one of the waiting couches and eyed his dad's closed office doors.

"Excuse me," Rachel said, approaching the desk.

Miss Littleton startled at Rachel's voice, almost dropping the phone before catching it and putting her hand to her heart.

"I'm sorry," Rachel said. "I didn't mean to startle you. I'm here to interview Mr. Xander Calivan about XC Energy for an article. I'm a student and I have an official press pass."

Miss Littleton's head was shaking before Rachel finished. "This is not a good time, young lady. Not a good time at all. You'll have to come back. Or pick another company for your school project." Miss Littleton put the phone back up to her ear.

A tingling sensation crawled up Jarren's spine at the sound of Miss Littleton's voice. She'd worked for Xander for as long as Jarren could remember and was every bit a professional. Her dismissal of Rachel was clipped and distracted. Miss Littleton had run this office with white-glove professionalism and could calm a businessman about to lose his investment. But today she seemed rattled.

"What's going on?" Jarren stood up and Miss Littleton jumped a second time. This time her attempts to catch her phone didn't work and it fell beneath her desk.

"Jarren," Miss Littleton said, gathering up papers on her desk and closing her appointment book. "I didn't see you back there. Nothing's going on. It's just not a good time for an interview. You know how your dad gets when he's in one of his moods. He's got a bee in his bonnet and won't do anything else until he gets it settled. I'm sure you can find plenty of information on the internet to write your essay."

"This isn't an essay," Rachel said, placing both hands on the counter like she was planting roots. "This is an official news article."

Miss Littleton was trying to find her phone on the floor while keeping her eyes on them. "Not today, sweetie. I'm sorry Mr. Calivan's schedule is full." She gave up her blind floor sweep with her hand. She stood and came around the front counter, arms wide to herd them toward the elevator doors.

Rachel didn't move. Jarren pushed past Miss Littleton, unable to keep the panic he felt in his stomach from rising into his throat. Why would Miss Littleton try to keep him away from his dad?

"He's asked not to be disturbed," said Miss Littleton as she turned, one hand out like she could pull him back with the power of her mind. Jarren waved her off and pushed open the double door. Xander Calivan's office was usually the picture of minimalism and taste. But today there were several file boxes on the floor and two more on his desk.

Folders and papers were scattered on the surface. Xander flipped through one as he sat on the edge of his chair, muttering.

For a moment, Jarren stopped; he found it hard to swallow. He didn't know why the sight of his dad shuffling through a mess of paperwork would trigger fear. He tried to shake it off.

"Looks like we're getting audited. Did you forget to file your taxes?" He laughed but it sounded as hollow as it felt.

Xander slammed the file closed and stood too quickly. He knocked one of the boxes from his desk and the files slid across the floor, creating a line to the window.

Rachel pushed Jarren to the side so she could see in.

Miss Littleton came up behind them clucking her tongue. "No. No. You need to leave. I told you it's not a good time."

"It's all right, Miss Littleton. I can take care of this." Xander put up his hand and straighten his shoulders, fighting an invisible weight that cramped his usually perfect posture.

"What can I do for you, Rachel, Jarren?" Xander folded his arms, but not before Jarren saw a slight tremor in his father's hands.

"I'm doing an article on XC Energy," Rachel said, "and wondered if you'd be willing to answer a few questions for me. There are a lot of things about the company that doesn't add up and you haven't published any useful information. It's all marketing mumbo jumbo."

"An article?" Xander's eye twitched, his neck tensed, a vein bulging. "You're researching XC Energy? Now?"

"Yes, sir," Rachel said. She wrapped her arms around the notebook she was carrying like an official reporter, upping her intimidation two levels. Jarren would have admired the strength in her stance if he hadn't been so baffled by his dad's reaction.

"What's going on?" Jarren asked for the second time. "Is the business in some kind of trouble?"

Xander came around the desk and shut the door, leaning against it as he turned to face them. "Listen. I can't give you any details. I can't answer any questions. All you need to know is that you need to be careful."

"Careful of what?" Rachel's fingers twitched, and Jarren could tell she was resisting the urge to start writing.

"I will only give you one warning and then I am not responsible for what happens." Xander stepped forward, forcing Rachel to take a step back. "Clear your browser history. Don't ask any more questions. Don't write the article. It's not a good time."

Jarren had never seen his dad like this. He'd seen the football fan version, the business tycoon version, even the aloof father that couldn't give him the time of day version. But this was something different.

"But Mr. Calivan—" Rachel started. Jarren interrupted her.

"Fine." Jarren gave Rachel big eyes, trying to communicate without saying anything. "She won't. She'll stop. But if you're overwhelmed, I could come in after school, do some extra work." He walked over to the toppled box of files and started picking up the papers. "If you need me to go through some old files from . . ." Jarren looked at the dates on the papers. "From fifteen years ago, I'm sure I could help you out."

"No." Xander's voice was hard, cold, and breeched no argument. He glanced at the door like he expected the Grimm Reaper to walk in. "Get out. Both of you. Get out now or I'll call security and have you escorted out."

"I have a press—"

"I don't give a damn!" Xander pounded his fist against the desk, making papers hop and a pen roll off and land on the floor. Jarren froze as he reached for another file. He couldn't imagine a pressure that would make his dad lose his cool. Jarren's gut twisted.

"Get out," Xander said, his words going soft, but no less scary. "Don't come back here. It's too dangerous and I don't want either of you getting hurt." He ripped the papers from Jarren's hands and shoved Jarren toward the door.

Rachel's fingers tightened on her notebook. "You've never given a damn about anyone or anything. I know better than anyone you could care less who you hurt." She turned with a flip of her hair.

"Don't let her dig any deeper," Xander's voice was almost a whisper this time. Not a command. It was a plea.

"I don't understand," Jarren said. "I want to be a part of your business. I want to work with you."

"This business isn't for you." Xander checked the doorway again, but Rachel was already over by the elevator. He glanced around the room like he was looking for hidden cameras. His fingers drummed on the desk. Then his eyes landed fully on Jarren for the first time since they'd walked in the room. His fingers stopped moving. The tightness in his face loosened, the stress draining from him as he made a decision. "I'm cutting you off. No inheritance. No shares. I built this company from the ground up with my energy, my blood, my life." Xander's voice caught for an instant. "You have to make your own way in life."

Jarren's throat constricted. His lungs felt on fire. A sharp pain started at the base of his skull, but he ignored it.

"You can't—"

"I can. And I just did. Now leave." Xander took a step toward him, and Jarren stumbled back.

Jarren wanted to argue, but there was a sting in his eyes that he was struggling to blink away. He didn't cry, ever. Xander had taught him that.

Jarren turned sharply and moved into the waiting area.

"Wait."

Jarren stopped.

He glanced back at his dad. Xander's entire frame seemed to melt as the stiffness drained from his body. He leaned forward supporting himself with his palms flat against the desk. "Jarren. Accept the scholarship to play football. Things have changed and this is not the best future for you. There is no future at all. I want you to get as far away as you can. Please."

Miss Littleton closed the doors to the office and stood with her back to them, her head shaking.

There was a ding as the elevator doors opened and Jarren followed Rachel inside. The image of his dad's hunched shoulders remained burned into his vision as the elevator doors closed. He'd seen that look before, but never from his dad, never in that office, and never so complete.

It was the look of defeat.

Twenty

October 8

Jake interrupted my writing last night. He came in and sat on my floor, like he sensed my unease, like he wanted to comfort me instead of the other way around. He didn't look at me or touch anything in my room. He sat in the middle of the floor, cross-legged, shoulders hunched, head down. And the strange thing was, I did feel comforted. Just by having him there.

The voice of the stranger as he spoke to my mother has been haunting me. He told her that there was a Descendant named Adura that could bend light to see around time. And she'd seen me. She'd seen what my future held. He'd told my mom that he wanted to take me away with him. That Adura had seen my future and it wasn't good, but I was important. The stranger told my parents that he wanted to keep me safe.

I had waited for Mom to tell him no. That she and Dad would protect me, but I peeked out the door and saw her face fall as she read from an old-fashioned scroll. She showed Dad and he went pale. I couldn't see the stranger through the small crack of light, but I saw my mom nod and my dad put an arm around her.

They were going to send me away. And I was afraid.

I climbed out the window of my bedroom and ran.

The baby is crying again, and Pat is calling for help. I will have to finish my story later, but I need to write it out. I need to remember exactly what happened so that these shadows in the dark step into the light. Even if I have to die fighting them.

Treadon Nelson

"48, 36, 15, HIKE." Treadon caught the football and backpedaled a few steps. He waited two heartbeats as the line surged forward. Jarren ran his route out to the side and back to the middle. Treadon let the ball fly. Jarren wrapped up the ball and barreled into the end zone. The play was perfect. The crowd rose to their feet. Another victory.

Refs with their black and white striped shirts raised their hands, signaling the end of the game. A flood of high school students poured onto the field. The mad rush resembled a destructive wave of orange and blue, waving flags, painted faces, dyed hair. The deafening sound of victory filled the air as the other team retreated with their head down, skittering off the field.

Treadon moved slowly back to the bench, enduring the back pounds, chest bumps, and butt slaps that erupted out of the milling melee of bodies at random from unknown sources. Jarren and another player managed to drench Coach Meyers in a shower of orange liquid from the cooler. Bridger Michaels went out of his way to hit Treadon with his shoulder as he headed for the locker room. If that was the most revenge Bridger had planned, Treadon could handle it. So far, Bridger and his friends had played their hardest on the field; they played like they wanted to win.

Two men dressed in suits made their way across the football field. They stopped in front of Jarren and put their hands out. Jarren shook their hands half-heartedly. One waved Treadon over.

"You two played well. Good game. We'll be in touch." And then they walked away.

"What was that about?" Rachel asked, helmet in hand. She squirted water into her mouth from her bottle, swishing it around.

"Those were scouts from Oregon," Jarren said, his eyes on the ground, no excitement in his voice. "My dad sent them."

Treadon didn't think he needed his extra ability to see the disappointment in his friend. He found his mind wandering as he thought about the benefits of playing for Oregon. A scholarship. Possibly a contract for advertisements. But it was so far away. And the plane tickets were expensive. He'd be leaving his mom alone.

They cleaned up in the locker room and met back out on the field. Jarren moved slow, and they were the last people left as they walked back out on the field. Jarren sat on the bleachers. Rachel approached, cleaned up in her school sweater and jeans. She took one look at Jarren and sat down beside him.

"Do you want to go out for ice cream to celebrate the win?" Rachel's words seemed to be taken by the wind and flopped across the field like the wrappers left over from the game. They sat in silence, Treadon leaning against the railing.

"I thought he saw me as more than a football player," Jarren said, looking up into the stadium lights. "I thought he was really starting to see me for who I am." Jarren kicked at an empty soda can. "People really should clean up after themselves."

"I think Xander Calivan should clean up after himself." Rachel paused. "I found a lead. A guy who asked a lot of questions when XC Energy started up. He fell off the face of the earth for a while, but I think I found him."

It was a statement and a question. Treadon wasn't sure why there was a question behind it. Some kind of understanding between them. A threat?

Jarren stared out at the field. There was a chorus of resounding booms as the lights shut off in sections around the field. "Are you being careful?"

Careful? That wasn't a word Treadon expected from Jarren.

"Yeah. I'll be careful. I'll let you know if I can get him to respond." Rachel stood; her energy renewed. "You're better than he is. You'll figure this out." She stretched and offered her hand to help Jarren up. "I better get home. I don't think my ice cream excuse will last much longer."

They walked out of the stadium and down the sidewalk toward the parking lot. At the corner of the school, four men stood outside the reach of the closest streetlamp. They stood close together, talking quietly. Each man wore high-collared jackets that covered their necks and part of their chins. They were too shadowed for Treadon to read anything, but he made sure they walked Rachel to her car.

Treadon glanced back but couldn't see the men anymore. He followed Jarren to his Aston Martin. Jarren scuffed his foot along the ground before unlocking the car.

"Do you want to go for a drive?" Jarren asked. "I don't really feel like going home."

A drive. Just for fun. Treadon felt his anxiety skyrocket. It was just a drive. No reason to be afraid. He was inside the car—not in front of it. He tried to push the memory of his nightmare to the back of his mind. "Sure." He sounded far more casual than he felt.

He checked the time on the dashboard. After midnight. Abigail would already be in bed, and he didn't want to wake her. He'd be home before she woke up, but for some reason, he felt the urge to text his mom an "I love you." That was silly. He wasn't saying goodbye.

He opened the door and climbed in the passenger seat. He grabbed the seatbelt, but before he clicked it, Jarren accelerated with unnecessary roughness. Treadon's heart clambered up into his throat and clung there like a clog in a chimney. He tried not to panic as he jammed the seatbelt into the latch, the comforting click allowing him a quick, shallow breath.

Before Treadon could get up the courage to tell Jarren he'd changed his mind, he noticed four sets of lights turn on simultaneously at the far end of the parking lot.

Jarren noticed too. Treadon saw his eyebrows come down as he glanced in the rearview mirror. Jarren drove through the neighborhood and then out onto a main street. They stopped at a red light. A red truck sped by with people hanging out the windows and standing in the bed. A police car drove through the intersection, lights flashing. There was a collective groan loud enough to reach them from a block away.

"Maybe this isn't the best time to go for a drive." Treadon hoped the words didn't squeak out the way they felt in his mind.

Jarren let out a sigh. "You want me to take you home?"

The disappointment in Jarren's voice tugged on the heart stuck in Treadon's throat. "You could crash at my house for the night. Gabe's out of town so we have the extra futon."

Jarren tapped the steering wheel. The light turned green at the same time as a couple SUVs reached the intersection. One pulled up to the side of Jarren's car and two lined up behind them. There was a second where it felt like no one breathed. The windows were tinted on all the vehicles and their license plates weren't visible.

Treadon and Jarren shared a look. Well, Jarren shared a look with Treadon and Treadon could read the words loud and clear.

Hold on.

Oh no.

The tires squealed and they hit forty before they'd reached the other side of the intersection. Treadon was pressed back against his seat and gripped the seatbelt like a lifeline. His vision went dark and then flashed white as fear ripped through him. Maybe he would die tonight. He wished he'd texted his mom.

The car beside them tried to keep pace, but another car in the other lane got in the way. The driver had to swerve while the car behind them stayed on their bumper.

Jarren ran a stop sign as another SUV came from a side street and pulled even with the car still tailing them. Jarren took a left. The SUVs followed.

Treadon's normal panic from riding in a car was multiplied a thousand times. His vision blurred, and his breath came in short gasps. He had to swallow the nausea as Jarren swerved onto another street.

Jarren swore. "Are they cops?"

"They would have their lights on by now." Treadon felt paralyzed. Streetlamps flashed overhead like a spinning disco ball.

"Who the hell are these guys?" Jarren's head was tucked low. His movements were smooth and unpanicked. The only thing that kept Treadon from a full-fledged panic attack was the confidence in Jarren's driving. Jarren was welcoming the chase, enjoying it. Like it gave him something else to focus on other than the problems with his dad.

Jarren took a sharp turn into a parking lot and pulled behind a semi-truck before the following SUVs came around the corner. They watched through the wheels of the semi-truck. The SUVs passed them, but one stopped on the side of the road and idled.

"Not cops." Jarren backed up, snapping Treadon forward so that he had to put his hands against the dashboard. Jarren spun the Aston Martin in a full donut, shooting smoke out from the squealing tires. He pulled out of the parking lot and passed the parked SUV. Treadon could just make out the shape of a man through the tinted window—same high-collared jacket.

"They followed us from the school," Treadon managed to gasp out. Talking helped him ground himself. He pushed the panic down.

Another SUV ran a stop sign in front of them. "Look out!" Treadon said.

Jarren swerved to avoid a collision. Another SUV came out of nowhere and Jarren had to drive up on a sidewalk, knocking over a street sign. The SUV drove up next to them as Jarren swerved back and forth on the sidewalk. The window rolled down and the man driving the vehicle tilted his head to the side. An instant before Jarren swerved away, Treadon saw a black triangle tattoo on the man's neck just above where the collar pulled away.

"Who are these guys?" Jarren asked. "What the hell do they want?"

Treadon didn't have an answer.

Jarren swore under his breath and pulled into a completely deserted parking lot with an exit on the opposite side. He sped through and came out onto a one-way road. Before he could make it a block, two more SUVs were behind them. A third was coming up another street. Jarren was too fast. He turned before the SUV reached them and all three vehicles had to swerve, squealing tires as they tried to intercept the fleeing Aston Martin.

The next little while was a blur. Treadon lost track of time and direction. All he could do was cling to his seatbelt and yell out any time he saw another SUV coming at them. The fear was constant, his heart thundering like a crowd stomping in rhythm in a football stadium. Somehow, his mind continued to function, and he started to notice patterns in the SUV's movements.

Despite Jarren's excellent driving skills, the SUV's remained consistent, never getting too close, never losing track of the car. They weren't being forced into an accident. They were being herded—like sheep. Jarren was going exactly where they wanted him to.

"Screw this," Jarren said as he floored the pedal and hit the on-ramp without slowing down.

Treadon was too late to warn against it, but he knew this had been the SUV drivers' intention all along. Jarren accelerated onto the highway, his fingers tight on the steering wheel.

Once they were on the highway, one SUV stayed less than a car length behind. A second SUV pulled up on the right side of the car with a sudden burst of acceleration. As they rounded a curve, they found themselves behind another SUV, driving in front of them.

Waiting for them.

The front SUV controlled the pace. The SUV to the side made it impossible for Jarren to change lanes. The one behind kept them from slowing down. The SUV beside them towered over the Aston Martin on Treadon's side, making him feel painfully exposed without the roof of the car for protection. They were trapped between the entourage of

SUVs and the cement medium. Treadon's stomach dropped as the rear SUV sped up and rammed into the back of the convertible. Jarren's string of profanity evaporated into the air as the wind sucked the last bit of oxygen from Treadon's lungs.

The panic overwhelmed him. He could hear the sounds from his nightmare, could feel the crushing pressure, could see the headlights swimming behind his vision. He could feel himself dying even though they were still driving ninety miles an hour on a dark freeway.

Jarren managed to keep control of the car and sped up to prevent another attack from the rear, but now they were inches from the SUV in front. Jarren's hands gripped his steering wheel, his eyes locked forward, a look of concentration carved into his features. The SUV in front increased their speed and Jarren maintained the distance between them. The speedometer climbed past 150 miles per hour. Terror filled Treadon's mind.

The unnatural escort extended for several rigid minutes. Jarren continued to control the steering wheel with a steel grip, his knuckles colorless, the veins in his forearms protruding like dark webs of pulsing energy. The scenery changed as they headed north on the 405, away from the city and into the hills north of Los Angeles. The suburban houses gave way to industrial warehouses and those were swallowed up by greenery, fields, and then shrubs and trees. The ground rose on both sides as they entered the canyon.

The SUV on Treadon's side of the car moved in closer, leaving only inches between Treadon and the black, reflective door paneling. Treadon turned his head away as the noise of the air being sucked between the two vehicles rose to a deafening scream. Jarren's face transformed. His concentration melted away, replaced by a frightening calm. His hands and arms remained flexed, but his face showed no strain as he closed his eyes.

While driving.

Treadon could only look at his own frightened reflection in the door of the SUV as it closed the gap and made contact, lights and colors swirling in the black paint.

A deep, rumbling came from below the car as the SUVs squeezed the Aston Martin toward the cement medium. The roar of the rumble strip was over-powered with the sound of crunching metal and screaming tires.

The SUV fell back and Treadon saw the edge of the road approaching, the mountain rising to greet them. The SUV on the right hit one more time. Jarren jerked the wheel sharply, and Treadon's stomach lurched and dropped. The tires left the road. The car flipped up and over the guard rail. Silence engulfed Treadon's senses as the car rotated and he found himself looking out into the deep darkness of the sky.

Xander Calivan

Fifteen miles away, Xander locked up the front doors on the XC Energy building. He found the information on the girl that Vox had requested. It took a lot of digging, and he didn't even remember his company doing the research, but he'd finally found it. He just needed to give it to Vox and the two of them could work out a plan to get Caden Bachman to back off.

His cell phone buzzed in his pocket. It was probably Jarren. He'd had a game tonight and it was the first one Xander had missed this year. It was better for him to move on, to not get caught up in this blood sport of business. Jarren would be disappointed, but it would be for the best.

Xander pulled out the phone and touched the screen.

He dropped his phone in horror.

He stood stiff, his heart in his throat.

I was too late, he thought. *Too late.*

Xander picked up his phone with unsteady hands and looked at the screen again. The light from the phone threw an eerie glow onto Xander's taut face as he looked at the picture of a black triangle, three points where no side seemed to touch. Each line getting lost in intricate, swirling patterns.

Twenty-Two

October 9

This weekend left the whole family rattled. Nolan's heart rate dropped, and Foster and Mike had a supervised visit with their father. By Sunday night, Pat was frazzled, the twins were out of control, and Jake wouldn't even come out of his room. If only I could do more.

If only. If only. If only.

I'm so sick of those words. I want to scratch them out until I put a hole in the paper. I want to change them, rewrite my past, present, and future. I want to write a thousand times, no more. No more mistakes. No more regrets. No more hiding. No more shame.

I strengthened Nolan's heart, gave him a shot of the energy of creation. His body responded. But he still didn't wake up. His brain is damaged from the head injury. I've had no training and the brain is so complicated. I am not ready to risk Nolan's life to experiment on him. I'll have to try other things first, build up to this, even if it means I risk being seen.

Is that what I'm really afraid of?

Was that what I was afraid of the night I ran away? Afraid that if Mom saw me crying, she'd be disappointed? Afraid to look into the face of a stranger that wanted to take me away?

I don't remember. There are several pieces missing in my memory. But I do remember running, the feel of the branches against my cheek, the wet dew soaking through my slippers.

I ran all the way to the road between the forest and the park where my brother and I used to play. I never crossed the road without him and so when I reached the last tree before the asphalt, I stopped. I leaned against the trunk and sunk down to the ground. The cold seeped through my thin pajamas and I shivered, wrapping my arms around myself.

All I could think about was being taken away, Mom and Dad giving up on me. Was it my fault? Hadn't I trained hard enough? Hadn't I learned their lessons and listened to the stories? It was all so unfair.

I remember the dark night feeling deeper than usual. The wind picked up and the branches began to sway, reaching out for me. There were movements in the shadows and, even though I was a Descendant, with the knowledge and energy of creation, I was only seven. And I was afraid and confused and angry all at the same time.

I started to cry before I realized I wasn't alone.

Gabriel Tuoer

Gabe leaned against his motorcycle on a deserted dirt road. His headlight revealed a field of drying hay with a single gnarled tree as the only distinguishing landmark. Everything else along the road looked exactly the same: row after row of freshly cut hay occasionally interrupted by a barbed-wire fence. Now he waited.

Abigail's voice reached him again, repeating the directions. He nodded once, sending his reply. He climbed back on his motorcycle and shot down the road. The roar of his engine shook the lone tree as he whipped by.

He followed her directions precisely, turning on a single tire trail nearly hidden between two barbed-wire fences. He followed the trail for several minutes and began to worry he was on the wrong path. Then he saw a single light in the distance. A porch light that shone from a very remote farmhouse.

It was on. A good sign.

He pushed the throttle, and the motorcycle approached a dangerous speed. Poles in the barbed-wire fence passed by less than an inch from his handlebars, blurred until they looked like a solid wall.

The fences dropped away. He entered a very pleasant looking backyard. He hit his brakes, his wheel tearing up grass as he turned around a swing set and drove through a homemade volleyball court. When he passed the back patio, he hit the brakes again and skidded to a stop in a gravel driveway, throwing up a spray of rocks.

The rocks peppered a dark car, a man emerging from the passenger side. He was a tall man, dressed in a black business suit. He was unusually thin, and his boney fingers flew up to protect his face from the flying rocks. The rocks stopped and disintegrated before hitting the man while the others plinked against the car and ground all around him.

Gabe shut off the bike and stepped off, facing Caden Bachman: the man who stole everything from him. Gabe pulled his two double-edged swords from their sheaths on his back and held them out in front of him.

"You've been waiting a long time for this, haven't you?" Caden didn't move into a defensive position. Instead, he raised his arms, palms up in front of him. "But I'm afraid you'll have to wait a little longer."

Gabe bent his knees, preparing to spring, when Abigail's voice penetrated his mind. "They are there. Hundreds of them. Get out! Get out!"

Caden Bachman paused as he turned to open his car door. He stopped to watch Gabe with a renewed interest. "You have a watcher." It was a statement.

His hungry stare chilled Gabe's insides. He knew what he had to do, but the hate filled his mouth with a bitter taste. He couldn't just walk away. He'd been searching for this man for twenty years and his goal was standing less than five feet away. He had to finish this now. Gabe raised his swords, but Abigail's voice cut through.

"The Unguarded is still there. I can see them. Do you have them? There are so many, it's like a black blob on the map. Why aren't you moving?"

They hadn't taken the Unguarded. It was either Caden or the girl he'd come for. He couldn't leave another one to disappear. He swallowed his anger with difficulty and turned to bound up the front steps. The car door shut behind him and he heard the car pull away, wheels crunching on the gravel like mocking laughter in his ears.

He grabbed the door handle at the same time as he heard the creatures approaching. Abigail was right. There were more than four. It sounded like a hundred. He turned as the snarling creatures gathered around the circle of driveway the porch light illuminated. Their primal growls and the sound of their claws scratching the ground filled the air with a horrible noise. He heard a sound from behind the door, but he couldn't bring an Unguarded out into this. They were safer in the house.

He turned and walked back down the porch steps, standing in the center of the manic hoard, his swords extended to either side.

The first foolish creature jumped at him, mouth distorted, jaw hanging agape, exposing long sharp teeth. Its shorter front legs were equipped with blackened claws, dripping with poison. Its rear legs were beefy, designed for power, and it used these to propel its slimy body at Gabe.

He beheaded the creature with a single swipe of his sword, stepping to the side in the same motion. The momentum of the beast carried its body past him. The fenris skidded, headless, to a stop at the feet of his numerous companions. The growls fell silent—the moment marked by an eerie stillness as the fenris regarded their disintegrating counterpart.

Using the distraction to his advantage, Gabe drew both hands together, swords pointed to the sky, and with a cry of anger, he crouched down, smashing both handles of his swords into the ground. Gabe fed the impact wave with his energy. The ground sunk under his swords and then bulged upward, rippling out from the impact point.

The driveway surged like a wave toward the creatures surrounding him. By the time the ripple reached the deformed animals, it was over a foot high. The fenris were thrown off their feet, landing in heaps, scrambling to regain control. Gabe attacked after the second wave. He dropped four more heads to the ground and proceeded to swing both his swords in a blur of deadly metal that glowed green in the dark night.

The creatures attacked as they regained their balance. Gabe sent one creature flying with an elbow to its chin. He brought down the sword in the same hand to cut another creature in half. His other sword arm twisted in a low arc, cutting off the paws of three creatures in succession. He spun away from the reaching claws of another fenris while thrusting his sword through the belly of one of the creatures that had climbed on top of its companions, attempting an aerial assault. The creature fell to the ground with a shrill cry, whining bark, and then dissipated into black dust.

Fenris were not smart; they attacked and fed on instinct. Strategy usually won the day, unless the fenris attacked with overwhelming force. Each time Gabe disintegrated one warped demon essence, three more fenris replaced it. One darted low along the ground and Gabe knew that he would be too late. The long, poisoned claws managed to rip into his calf before he could bring his sword straight down, piercing through the skull and into its brain.

He continued to fight, not for victory, but with a manic passion to bring down as many as possible before he was overwhelmed. He would die without ever finding his lost Descendant. His frustration gave him a burst of energy and he cut through several more creatures, spinning his swords with blurring speed. A fenris jumped at his back and left three dark streaks across his cheek as he turned to destroy it. Gabe could feel the burning as the poison ate at his skin and the blood began to run down his neck. He knocked the creature off his back and stabbed it through the heart.

It was a useless battle. He looked up and saw an extra-large fenris flying through the air, straight at his face. *I've failed.* The thought was familiar to him, and the acceptance came with sadness and relief. At least the war would be over for him. The constant grief and consuming guilt would finally be gone.

He pulled his sword from the disintegrating body and swung it up toward the pouncing creature, knowing it would not save him. He noticed a movement to his side but remained focused on his doom.

Just before the creature reached him, there was a loud thud, and the fenris stopped mid-air, its face smashed up against an invisible surface. There was a cracking sound as the rest of the fenris' momentum carried the creature's powerful haunches into its head, snapping its neck. The fenris dissipated as it slid down an apparently smooth surface.

Gabe paused mid-swing as his mind tried to understand the unexplained phenomenon. He turned to see a young girl, maybe eleven or twelve, standing beside him. Her arms were stretched out to either side, trembling under some invisible pressure. Her long, blond hair was pulled into a single braid down her back, the bangs plastered to her head with sweat. She looked up at him with an excited grin, despite her obvious strain.

"They promised you would come," she said.

They were surrounded by a very small perimeter, a circular area with the two of them on the inside and the fenris snarling and growling on the outside, meeting an invisible, solid surface whenever they tried to attack. Gabe's ears rang with the dull thuds of their bodies against the barrier. He looked to the girl for an explanation.

"I'm an elemental." She had a strong southern twang. "I can rearrange atoms at an atomic level, so I made bullet-proof glass." Her face shone with pride.

"Where are your parents?"

Her smile faded. "My parents are both Ordinaries. I had a feeling and asked them to go to the store for me so they would be out of the way. At least they aren't around to see what these dogs are doing to their yard."

One fenris tired of banging its head against the glass. It jumped in a high arc and hit the glass several feet above Gabe's head. A long, thin crack appeared.

"It gets weaker the farther away I am from it. It doesn't go much higher than that." She shrugged apologetically.

"Can you move it?" They only had a few precious seconds left.

She nodded.

"Walk that way. We need to get to the bike."

Another creature jumped. This time the crack spread out in a web pattern reaching halfway around the circle of glass.

"Move."

The girl obeyed, walking as if she carried a great weight. Gabe sheathed one of his swords and placed a hand on her back for support. He could see his bike three creatures away. He tried not to push her, but it was difficult to be patient with their slow progress.

A third fenris jumped, hitting the other side of the circle. The weakened glass shattered at the top, sending a shower of glittering shards down on their heads. They were almost there.

"Drop the glass. Can you cut it in pieces and push it out?"

She nodded again. Gabe saw vertical cuts form, dividing the circle into four parts. The pieces fell outward, landing on top of the closest creatures. He picked up the girl and jumped on top of the glass in front of them. The curved glass created a path over the last two creatures to his bike. He jumped on, setting the girl in front of him while slicing through the belly of a creature with the sword in his left hand.

He sheathed the sword and started the engine. The bike roared to life. The back tire peeled out and then gripped the ground, sending the bike flying forward. One last creature made a jump for the girl. Gabe leaned forward to protect her and received a deep cut in his upper shoulder.

Then they were free, leaving the fenris snarling behind them in frustration.

"How far to the nearest city?" He spoke the words and manipulated the sound waves to reach her ear.

She yelled back. The words would have been drowned out by the sound of the engine, but he concentrated on the sound waves and redirected them toward his ear.

"Forty-five minutes to Atchison by truck, but that isn't quite a city. My family thought it would be safer if we stayed off the beaten track."

There was nothing around them but farmland. No more porch lights. No other sign of civilization. Many Descendants who hadn't joined the Veil thought finding a low population area would make them safer. It was about as effective as hiding in a sea of people.

"I guess it didn't work." The girl's shoulders deflated slightly.

"It worked well enough. I have a safe place for you."

There was a moment where the only sound was the motor thundering its way through the dark, but the sound felt strange, almost silent. Then he realized why. He hadn't heard from Abigail since before the attack. He sent a pulse. There was no response. When the second attempt was left unanswered, he said her name out loud.

"Abigail."

She responded a few seconds later, her voice shaking. "You're alive. You made it out." Her voice resonated with an unusually high pitch.

"What is it?"

He heard her break down into sobs.

"Something's happened to Treadon."

Twenty-Three

TREADON NELSON

Treadon surfaced slowly, surrounded by pain. It was the only sensation. He fought to come out of it, like swimming up from a deep dive. The pain began to localize. His neck. His back and shoulder. Most of the pain was coming from his shoulder.

His right shoulder.

He forced his eyes open. The dim light of an approaching dawn silhouetted an uneven skyline, everything cast in grays and darker grays. The blurry surrounding came into focus. Expensive leather, sleek dashboard: Jarren's car.

There was a layer of dust on his arms and chest. He pushed the airbag off to the side and tried to dust himself off. His shoulder screamed in protest. He touched the side of his face and felt where the airbag had left a burn.

The driver's side seat was empty. Treadon felt a surge of panic. The deflated airbag hung lifelessly from the steering wheel. Treadon tried to look around, but a stab of pain stopped him from sitting forward.

He looked down and tested his shoulder with his left hand. The seat belt had dug deep into his skin, leaving a large red gash bleeding through his shirt. He unlocked his seatbelt and wrestled to open the door. A short tree with a mass of winding branches blocked the door from opening. He stood up to climb out on the driver's side and caught sight of Jarren.

Treadon climbed across the seat, bumping his knee on the steering wheel, and catching his foot on the deflated airbag. He used the door for balance and flopped his body over the side. He straightened up too quickly and had to lean heavily on the door as a wave of dizziness threatened to send him back into unconsciousness.

He took several deep breaths to clear his head and then stumbled over to where Jarren balanced on his hands and knees.

The sound of a car driving past echoed between the hills. They were a hundred yards from the highway, the car half-buried in the hill. No one had stopped or noticed the accident. And the nice men in the SUVs didn't appear to have called 911.

Treadon leaned down and put a hand on Jarren's back. "You okay?"

Jarren swallowed, holding still for a full minute. Then he sat back on his heels.

"That was close," Jarren said. "I almost puked in my car."

"You were worried about the inside of your car? That thing has got to be totaled."

Jarren's face took on a look of panic and he struggled to his feet. He swayed dangerously, grabbing his head with both hands. Treadon reached out, but Jarren waved him off.

"I got this." Jarren dropped his hands and looked up at the sky. "It just feels like someone jabbed a nail into the base of my skull." He pointed to a spot on the back of his head, a few inches above his collar line where a scar had kept his hair from growing.

He rolled his head around, cracking his neck. Then he walked unsteadily back to his car and began a detailed inspection, rubbing both hands along the outside of the driver's side door. Treadon waited for the groan at the sight of damage, but it didn't come. Treadon took a better look at the car.

It was covered by a layer of dirt, but there wasn't a scratch or dent anywhere on this side. Treadon walked around the back of the Aston Martin, disbelief welling up in him. The back was undamaged. The side showed no scratches. Either the car was made of some material that didn't scratch, or he'd dreamed the whole chase. He could still see his reflection in the side of the black SUV. It couldn't have been a dream.

"Oh no. This is terrible."

Jarren pointed at a crack in the headlight he'd uncovered at the front of the car. It was the only damage Treadon could see. Impossible.

Deep tire marks were gouged into the ground from where the Aston Martin had hit and skidded into the side of the mountain. The ground had wave marks in the rocks and dirt all around the landing point, like a ripple moving out from where the car had hit.

"What happened?" Treadon asked. "How are we still alive?"

Jarren shook his head. "I don't know. We must have got lucky, I guess. I kind of blacked out there for a little bit. I feel super weird, like my head is going to explode." Treadon read his friend's posture, facial expression, and the way his left hand moved from his hip to his side to his face like it couldn't find a comfortable landing place. Jarren wasn't lying, exactly, but Treadon could read that his friend felt responsible for both the accident and their survival.

A movement near the overpass at the bottom of the hill caught his attention. A familiar blue Pontiac, his mom's profile visible, hair wild like she'd been driving with the window down.

"It's your mom," Jarren said. "How'd she know we were here?"

"I don't know. No one even called the police."

Before Abigail reached the road that hit a T at the bottom of the hill, a second familiar car took the exit. A Bentley, immaculate, with rims that flashed as the first rays of the sun climbed over the mountain.

"Word travels fast," Jarren muttered.

"How did your dad find us?"

"He probably bugged my car, but that doesn't really explain why he came. Since he's so adamant that I'm on my own now." They shared a look, shrugged, and climbed gingerly down toward the road. It was steep; dust kicked up whenever they slipped a few inches.

Abigail was out of her car, parked haphazardly on the side of the road, and climbing over a short crash barrier when Jarren and Treadon reached her. Abigail stumbled forward and pulled Treadon into a hug. Pain flashed from his shoulder, white filling his vision. He flinched away from her.

"You're hurt." She said the words with so much relief, Treadon felt bad. There was a note in her voice, like a part of her thought he'd died. She touched his face and arms like she was checking to see he wasn't a ghost.

"I'm okay," Treadon said. "Really. Just a seatbelt bruise and an airbag burn."

She pulled her hand away to see the blood from his shoulder. He expected a worse reaction, but for some reason, she handled it like she dealt with wounds all the time.

Xander pulled up and stepped out of his Bentley. He held the handle of the door with a white-knuckle grip. Jarren stopped a few feet away from his dad, hands in his pockets.

"Were you drinking?" Xander asked.

Abigail's nails dug into Treadon's forearms at the mention of alcohol. Even before reading people, Treadon could tell his mom hated alcohol with a passion. Her internal fear left Treadon avoiding getting drunk for more reasons than athletics.

"No," Jarren said.

"Are you hurt?" Xander's tone was crisp and careful, but not unkind.

"No."

Xander let go of the handle and stepped forward, pulling Jarren into a full hug, pinning Jarren's arms to his side, clinging with a desperate pressure. When he pushed Jarren back, he took a moment to look into his son's face.

"What happened?" Abigail asked.

Xander's mouth opened, but before he could answer, the roar of a loud engine overpowered the conversation. The deep, guttural roar of a motorcycle echoed through the valley, making it difficult to tell which direction it came from. All four of them turned to look where the sun created a halo of light, blinding them for a moment. Then as if it had come straight out of the sun, a motorcycle burst into view, cresting the top of the mountain, and then driving straight down the side, leaving a trail of dust blowing up behind the back tire.

Treadon blinked and the motorcycle was on the road, driving toward them from the east. The bike came to a stop an inch from Xander's Bentley.

"Careful," Xander started, but cut off when Gabe stepped off the motorcycle.

Gabe had a wild look in his eyes, two blackened streaks across his cheek, both of which still oozed. Darkened blood trailed down his thick neck. He wore all black, long leather coat and riding gear. His clothes were torn and dirty. A rip in his sleeve revealed more blackened skin.

"Woah. You look worse than Treadon," Jarren said.

Gabe threw his kickstand out, jumped off the bike and stepped across the barrier without breaking stride. He stopped in front of Treadon, looking him up and down. There was a moment when Gabe blinked, two seconds too long, and the muscles on his face relaxed slightly. Relief. When he glanced at Abigail, his expression changed, his eyes widening slightly. Treadon read an apology in the look.

That's when he noticed his mom's face. Abigail was livid. The locked stare and the tension that squeezed the corners of her mouth spoke of anger, a secret exposed. No. Treadon looked again. Underneath Abigail's anger, another emotion played with the light in her eyes. Concern. Not just for Treadon, but sincere concern for Gabe. And from the looks of it, Treadon wasn't the only one that had got in an accident last night.

"I had to know if he was hurt," Gabe said.

"We'll talk about it later." Abigail shook her head like she could shake away the images in her mind.

Gabe turned back to Treadon. "A bit dirty, but he's up and walking, so that's a good sign." He clapped Treadon on the shoulder.

Pain sent a wave of blackness, red sparks flashing behind his eyes. Treadon couldn't keep in the yelp of pain, the dizziness sending him down to one knee.

"Careful." Abigail came down to Treadon's level, checking the wound on his shoulder a little closer.

"If there are any injuries, I'll cover it," Xander said. "No questions asked. All medical bills paid if we could avoid any legal paperwork. I'd like to keep Jarren's record clean for his future. I'm sure you understand that."

Gabe and Abigail exchanged glances. It wasn't so much that the request was odd, it was that both Abigail and Gabe wanted to avoid the police as much as Xander did. Maybe the reason for Gabe's appearance wasn't exactly legal either.

Gabe nodded. "No police. No report. Agreed."

"I'll call Miss Littleton and she'll make sure the car gets taken care of." Xander cleared his throat. "I have one more favor to ask."

There was an awkward pause.

"Would you take Jarren home with you, let him stay for a few days? I've got some business I need to wrap up, something I need to take care of, and I don't want him home. Alone."

"I don't need a babysitter," Jarren said, arms folded over his chest.

"I'm not worried about you making your own meals. I need you away from the estate for a few days. A precaution."

"Dad." Jarren took a step closer to Xander. "Tell me what's going on. I can help."

Xander looked his son straight in the eyes. "Remember our agreement. You're going to play football." Xander put a hand on Jarren's shoulder. "Don't be like me. Don't let greed take everything that's truly important."

Then he stepped back, straightening his jacket as if he were about to step into a business meeting. "If you would allow him to stay, as a favor to me." He addressed Abigail like the last moment with his son hadn't happened.

"Of course. He's welcome. Always." Abigail stood and put her hand on Jarren's arm.

Xander walked to his Bentley and climbed inside without looking back.

Jarren's face was steel, every muscle taut. Finally, Jarren walked to the Pontiac and climbed inside, slamming the door. Treadon watched Xander's car pull out onto the highway and disappear. Treadon hoped he was wrong, but there was little doubt in his mind that Xander Calivan had just said his final goodbye.

Twenty-Four

October 11

I am on the rise before the fall. The part of the roller-coaster that takes you higher and higher and it would be fun except for the anticipation of the breath-taking drop at the top of the hill. Things have been going too well and I keep waiting for the drop, for something bad to happen. I'm not the kind of girl that sits with a group of friends at lunch. Or am I? Who would I be if things had been different? I'm not the kind of girl that feels giddy over a boy and melts on the inside when he smiles at me. Am I? I didn't realize that hiding from others kept me hidden from myself. I never stopped to figure out who I was and what I liked and what I wanted. What I really, really want is to stop being as afraid as I was when I was seven years old.

I remember holding my breath when the boy called out to me from across the road. He'd been playing at the park, in the *dark, all alone. But he didn't sound afraid. He sounded brave. He sounded like he wanted to help. I remember his words.*

"Is someone there? Are you okay?" he asked.

I was hidden in the shadow of a tree. He couldn't possibly see me. I held in my sobs and sat as still as the tree trunk so that he would think no one was there. Instead, he stepped onto the road.

I remember the image of the boy, red tennis shoes, a light jean jacket, and brown hair that was tousled from the wind. Every detail is burned into my memory as the boy was caught in a beam of light. I thought maybe he was a Descendant like me.

But then I heard the sound of an engine. The light shifted as headlights bore down on the boy. The car was driving too fast for a winding road in the dark.

And the boy was moving too slow.

TREADON NELSON

Sunday was a blur of pain and sleep and unanswerable questions. Abigail pulled a mattress into Treadon's room for Jarren. He didn't have any injuries from the accident except for a headache.

"I don't see any signs of a concussion." Abigail had just finished stitching up the gash in Treadon's shoulder. She'd sewn the wound like she was a veteran nurse in a war zone. Her ease with the needle and thread was as strange as the looks she and Gabe kept sharing.

Treadon could hear the back and forth.

Tell him.

Don't tell him.

He's ready.

I'm not ready.

"Stop." Treadon couldn't take it any longer. His shoulder throbbed, his stomach was queasy, and nothing made sense about what had happened.

"I'm done." Abigail lifted the needle and thread into the air, showing she'd finished sewing him up. That wasn't what Treadon had been talking about.

"No. I mean stop keeping things from me. Stop acting like I can't see you two talking about me over my head. What don't you want to tell me? What am I not ready for?"

Jarren sat up; eyes squinted from the headache. "And how did you guys know about the accident so fast?"

Abigail and Gabe shared a glance again. They were only going to give a partial truth, but it was better than nothing. Treadon knew if he pushed, he'd get more lies.

Abigail answered. "Gabe and I work together to help people who can't help themselves. I can see things, find people, when they need to be found. And Gabe goes to help them. That's why he is gone so much. Helping people."

She said the words like she was convincing herself. Treadon shifted in his seat. He tried to pull his shirt back over his head, but the stitches pulled, and his muscles locked up. Abigail took the shirt and helped him.

Jarren leaned back on the kitchen stool, balancing on the back two legs like gravity had no claim on him. "You see things." He sounded skeptical. "Like the accident."

"No. I didn't see the accident." Abigail looked to Gabe for help.

"There are somethings in this world that can't be detected with the basic five senses—like the energy your body gives off—" Gabe said.

"Like heat you can see through infrared cameras," said Jarren, coming back to all four legs of the stool.

"Yes, similar to that," Gabe said. "There is an energy given off by the soul, an aura. Abigail can sense those who have a special aura."

Again, a glance. They were not telling him everything, but still, the information they were sharing gave him chills. His mom was special, gifted. And she used it for good.

Treadon might have rejected the idea a week ago, but believing his mom could see a glowing light around people wasn't as far-fetched as Ellie being Descended from Angels.

"This doesn't explain anything about the accident." Jarren shrugged.

"You're taking this very well," Gabe said, looking at Jarren with lowered eyebrows. Suspicion. Both Abigail and Gabe seemed more interested in Jarren's reactions to their story than his own. Treadon tried not to feel a twist of jealousy. He couldn't imagine why Jarren had captured their attention.

"There's been plenty of research into auras and energy, people with extra-sensitive sensory receptors," Jarren said. "There were a couple projects at my dad's company, like a satellite that could help track the population for global warming, but I didn't get to look very close at those. It isn't hard to believe that there are people who can see auras. It's rare, but I believe it."

"Did your dad's company build your car too?" Abigail asked.

Jarren nodded in answer and pushed a question of his own. "Sensing auras doesn't explain how you knew about the accident."

Abigail looked down. "I like to keep track, like every mom, and I usually know where Treadon is. Like a parent app on your cell phone. Except he doesn't have to have his cell phone with him."

"Then you knew he was okay." Jarren had a Rachel-like intensity about him. Interrogation mode. "Why did you come so fast?"

It was Gabe's turn again. "There are bad people who would want to stop me from doing what I do. Even hurt someone close to me. I was afraid . . . we were afraid that the people who drove you off the road were there because of us."

Treadon's mind skipped to Ellie. Her fear. Her secrets.

"But we won't let it happen again." Abigail kept her eyes on Gabe for a long second, and then turned to Treadon. "I know you have a lot of questions. I know we haven't given you a lot of details. But it was for this reason. I don't want you to have to suffer for our mistakes or be collateral damage for a cause you never signed up for."

Abigail closed the drawer where she kept the needle and thread. It was the sign of the conversations closing as well.

"Get some rest," Abigail said, kissing Treadon on the forehead. "We'll talk more in the morning."

But sleeping wasn't as easy as his mom made it sound.

His shoulder ached and he tossed and turned each time the pain pulled him from sleep. Jarren hit the mattress and didn't move, the pillow pulled over his head like he could block out the world. Treadon was jealous of his soundless sleep each time he checked the clock and another ten minutes had crept by. He fell into a fitful sleep about three, but something pulled him back out of the darkness only two and a half hours later.

It was a sound. A sound that didn't belong in his house, but one he recognized immediately. The noise was low and muted, not meant for his ears, but close enough that it was unmistakable.

Football.

Not the sound that comes from a professionally recorded game on ESPN. It was the chaotic noise of personal game tapes.

Treadon's breathing came a little faster. The low murmur of voices floated in through the hall. No one in this house had ever watched his game tapes. Abigail worked too hard. Gabe wasn't always around and when he was, football was not the subject of conversation. So why now?

Maybe pining for the time lost with a son who'd almost died.

Maybe the near-death experience had made them want to be more supportive.

Maybe they suddenly saw value in what he did.

Instead of Gabe's constant disappointment in him.

Treadon rolled out of bed, but the stabbing pain from his shoulders made him pause, kneeling on the ground in the small space between his bed and the mattress Jarren slept on. He waited for the crippling pain to subside. He stood up and slipped into the hallway, careful to hold the door so the hinges didn't squeak. If his mom was taking a moment to appreciate his skill on the football field, he wanted to witness it unobserved.

He tried not to think of the consequence of having a hurt shoulder. They had a game this weekend and he wasn't sure he'd be able to throw the ball. How bad would that hurt his chances at an offer?

Gabe's office door stood slightly ajar. Gabe watching his game tapes. A strange, almost embarrassing, excitement rose in him.

He could see the office through the slit in the door, Gabe sitting in his office chair, Abigail standing behind him, both of their eyes glued to the computer monitor. He couldn't see what was on the screen. The only other thing visible was the Perpetual Motion device that had been there as long as Treadon could remember. Even now, the constant spinning motion of the circles, spinning around and inside of each other, a couple of small marbles that added weight to the circles and kept them spinning.

When Treadon was little, he used to watch it, trying to see how they managed to spin without bumping into each other and how they continued their rotation, where each circle began and the next one ended. They moved too fast for him to make any conclusive discoveries, and he'd never seen it stopped.

The motion device had captured his attention for a moment, and it took him a second to remember why he was standing in the hall. Proud parents. Watching football game tapes. He almost laughed. It wasn't a life he'd ever had, as much as he loved his mom, she had only pushed football when she realized it would make him money and take him far away.

Even though he couldn't see the front of the monitor, the looks on their faces weren't what he'd hoped for anyway. Instead of awe or pride or whatever he'd been hoping for, there was a look of deep concentration, like they were looking for something beyond the monitor's screen.

He'd come too far now. He pushed the door open and stepped inside. The screen was turned enough that he could see the football field and the jerseys moving around. The number that streaked across the screen was not his. The name across the shoulder read Calivan. Number seven.

They were watching game tapes of Jarren. Not him. Jarren caught a smeared bullet arching through the sky and ran it in for a touchdown. Then another shot. Jarren, juking a defender, running center field, making a catch, and dancing out of the way of three more guys before spiking the ball in the end zone.

Black screen.

Jarren's jersey front and center. A defender illegally grabbed his jersey and held him back. The ball flew overhead, out of reach. Jarren knocked the defender off him and dashed across the field. He shouldn't have made the catch, he'd been too far behind, but he did, diving forward to grab the ball with the tips of his fingers.

Gabe noticed Treadon, a small glance out of the corner of his eye, but he kept his focus on the screen.

"He's fast." Gabe clicked the mouse, replaying the last shot. "Almost like the ground moves him."

"His aura is normal, not like his car," Abigail said, leaning on the back of Gabe's chair.

"What are you looking for?" Treadon couldn't keep quiet any longer. "You think his aura should be brighter? Because he's good at football?"

Abigail jumped at his voice. Gabe closed the video and turned to face him.

There was a pause, a breath like something more was going to be said, like the answer was a hair's breadth away.

They were interrupted by a loud knocking on the front door.

Abigail looked at her phone. "It's 5:30 in the morning. Who would be here this early?"

Treadon saw Gabe glance at the blank wall of his office, like he was considering something on the far side. "Let me check first."

Abigail and Treadon followed Gabe down the hallway and into the living room. Gabe checked through the peep hole.

"It's a woman. I don't know her."

Abigail stepped forward and checked. "Normal." Abigail glanced at Treadon. "Nothing strange about her aura."

"Do you really do that all the time?" Treadon asked.

Jarren wandered out of the bedroom, scratching his head. "What's going on? Who's pounding on my skull before the sun is even up?"

Gabe answered. "There's a woman at the door. She's a stranger, but after what happened, it's better to be cautious."

The knocking continued, not like a friendly neighbor visit, but a persistent sound.

Jarren pushed past Abigail and looked through the peep hole.

"It's Miss Littleton. My father's secretary." Jarren twisted the three dead bolts and turned the lock. "You know there are better security systems than this one."

Miss Littleton nearly fell forward as she continued pounding without the door in the way. Jarren caught her by the shoulders and helped her stand up.

"Your father told me to bring your car and give you this." She handed him the keys. "And turn on the news." She looked up and down the street. "I can't say anything else but stay here until things settle down."

She pulled the door shut and Treadon saw her hustle down the stairs and out to a car parked on the street. There was another driver waiting for her. Treadon leaned out onto the porch and saw the Aston Martin in all its glory parked in their driveway. Clean as a whistle. No sign of damage.

He heard a click behind him and saw Abigail, remote in hand. The sound of a news report filled the room.

"LA was shocked this morning with the news of the closure of the business giant, XC Energy. There have been no warnings that the business was in trouble, and a thousand local employees have been laid off. The company assures a smooth transition for those who depend on electricity, but the layoff came without warning, without severance, and without any kind of explanation."

The news feed switched to the clip of a man being interviewed. "They didn't tell us anything. A lot of people are out of work and over a million people have less than twenty-four hours to switch energy companies. We deserve some answers."

"A press conference is scheduled for 4 pm this afternoon, but that hasn't stopped protestors from marching on the Calivan mansion. Xander Calivan is the owner of XC Energy and has yet to give a statement."

The clip changed to drone footage of the Calivan estate. The words PROTEST AT CALIVAN MANSION scrolled across the screen.

"Looks like I need to change my last name." Jarren was frozen in place, fists clenched, but his voice sounded the same. Sarcastic, like nothing could touch him.

Abigail hit the power button and the screen went blank.

"We better move the car into the garage," Gabe said. He opened his hand toward Jarren.

"I can do it," Jarren said.

"I'll move our car." Treadon jumped up, grateful to have something to do. His shoulder hurt, a burning sensation, but he couldn't imagine what Jarren was going through right now.

"I'll make some breakfast." Abigail tossed the remote on the couch, as the three of them headed out to play Tetris with the cars and motorcycle.

It only took a few minutes. As they sat down to breakfast, Jarren's cell phone broke the silence with the original chorus to Beat It.

Jarren pulled his phone out of his pocket and smiled. "Only one person I know who is crazy enough to be up watching the six o'clock news."

He pressed the screen.

"Where are you?" Rachel's voice had a sharp panicked pitch and was loud enough to be heard by everyone in the room.

"In the kitchen." Jarren had a slight smirk as if the idea of Rachel panicking over him was his own idea of a prank.

"Are you at home?" Rachel asked. "I just saw the news. I'll come pick you up."

"What are you going to do? Drive through the crowd like a bowling ball?"

"This isn't funny. You shouldn't be there if the protests get out of control." Rachel's voice was dead serious, determined yet on the edge of hysteria. Treadon could picture her driving straight through a crowd to get to Jarren.

Jarren must have believed it, too. "I'm not there. I'm at Treadon's."

"Thank God." Rachel let out an audible breath into her phone's speakers. "I'm not far. Don't move."

"Where do you think I'm going to go?"

Rachel had already hung up.

Jarren stared at the phone. "Does she think I'm going to go talk down the mob?"

Abigail put her hand on Jarren's shoulder. "You're welcome here as long as you need."

"Thank you, Ms. Nelson. I really appreciate it."

They had each dished up a plate when Rachel walked in without knocking. Gabe was halfway across the room with his hands up for a fight before Rachel had a full foot inside the door. Gabe pulled up short and turned around, hiding a look that made Treadon go cold.

Gabe's face was hard and emotionless. Treadon had no doubt that if it had been an enemy, the person stepping through the door would be dead.

"What happened to you?" Rachel asked, pointing at the bandages across Treadon's shoulder.

"We had a couple friends run us off the road," Jarren answered.

"What?" Rachel stepped forward, her notebook coming up in a reflexive motion. "Who were they? When did this happen? Was anyone else hurt?"

"Good to see you too," Jarren said, his mouth full of scrambled eggs.

Gabe cleared his throat. "It's possible that those people who chased you off the road wanted revenge for things I've done. I may have put you all in danger."

Treadon thought about the accident, the shutdown, Xander's last goodbye.

"I think you're wrong," Treadon said to Gabe.

There was more to Gabe than Treadon knew, more than they said last night, but the accident didn't have anything to do with Gabe's secret life.

"Why would you say that?" Gabe asked.

"Those people who ran us off the road—that wasn't about whatever you two do in your spare time," Treadon said. "It was about XC Energy. It was to scare Xander into selling out his company."

Gabe's eyebrows came together. A question. But Treadon could also see relief that there was another reason for the accident.

Rachel walked right up to Jarren. "We need to find out what's going on. I'm calling that source whether it's dangerous or not. You deserve some answers."

Twenty-Five

TREADON NELSON

Treadon had to sit out at practice. His shoulder locked up even lifting it an inch. Coach Bracken pointed him to the bench, thin-lipped, and silent. Treadon held his shoulder as he watched practice, his stomach twisting as he thought about what his injury might do to the team. To his own future.

Jarren was completely distracted and when Coach Bracken caught him checking his cell phone at a drink break, he benched him, too.

"Sampaio, you're in as running back. Calivan needs some time to get his head in the game."

Jarren threw his helmet under the bench and sat, content to watch practice with his eyes on the horizon. Treadon could tell his mind was on what had happened: his dad's business, the accident, everywhere except football.

Treadon watched the second-string quarterback jog out onto the field. The guy called for a sweep pass right. Bridger lined up on defense. With his mind distracted, Treadon thought about Gabe and Abigail. They were part of some kind of crusade to save kids from human trafficking or something. He'd misjudged Gabe, that was for sure, but it didn't seem like the kind of job that needed to be kept a secret from him. Sure, there might be drug lords or something that would like to get revenge for messing up their business. Was that all this was, protection from repercussions? Something from the way his mom reacted made him feel like there was a lot more.

He came back to the present when the ball was snapped. He watched as his replacement caught the pitch and backpedaled. Everyone was wound tight after coach's lecture and the defense came in fast and hard. The guy panicked and threw the ball to Rachel, but it went wide.

Rachel twisted, jumping into the air.

Bridger Michaels went in for the tackle, hitting Rachel in the hip and flipping her up over his body, feet in the air, helmet hitting the ground with spine-crushing force.

The world seemed to freeze, the movement on the field paused. Rachel didn't move.

Then everyone did. Jarren was first and fastest, leaping from the bench and sprinting across the field. He knelt beside her, fists clenched, jaw muscle flexing. The rest of the team made a tight circle. Coach Bracken pushed his way into the circle, yelling at people to back up and give her some space, but even he hesitated to touch her. She lay in a way that any movement might tip the scales in the wrong direction.

A shift at the edge of the circle caught Treadon's eyes. He realized that everyone in the circle had stopped moving, even Coach Bracken. A slender girl in a dark blue hoodie stepped through the tight huddle, not even having to push anyone aside. They parted for her. She kept her head down, but Treadon knew he would recognize the deep, brown eyes if she looked up.

Ellie knelt next to Rachel, touching an exposed part of her neck with a single finger. Then she pulled the helmet off Rachel's head and pressed her hands on either side of her cheeks. Everyone watched, but no one seemed to see. Ellie stood, her head purposefully turned away, like she knew Treadon was watching but wouldn't acknowledge him.

She walked through the huddle. His attention was pulled back when someone spoke. "She's moving. I think she's okay."

Rachel's hand moved up to her face and she let out a low groan. She rolled over on her elbows and knees, her ponytail cascading over her face. The movement broke Jarren from his stone prison. He was by her side, hand hovering an inch from her back. "Are you okay? I shouldn't have let you play for me. I should have protected you."

She shook her head as she pushed herself up onto her knees, shooting Jarren her back-off look. "I don't need you to protect—"

Jarren cut her off by wrapping his arms around her waist and lifting her to her feet. He kissed her on the mouth, full, passionate. Rachel stood shocked for a moment and then returned his kiss wholeheartedly, wrapping her fingers around the back of his head.

"Cut it out and get your heads back in the game." Coach Bracken's voice was a little weak. He rubbed his eyes like he had gotten some dust in them.

Treadon tried to find Ellie, but she was already gone.

Miracle number two. And this time she'd saved his friend.

At lunch, Treadon got his food quickly. He was going to sit by Ellie whether he could get Rachel and Jarren across the lunchroom or not. He scanned the lunchroom, looking over the heads of the milling students.

He was surprised when he saw she wasn't sitting alone. A girl with a nose ring sat next to Ellie. No. Not any girl. The girl he'd seen before. Megan. And across from Ellie was a group of skaters, the skaters he'd seen earlier. The one in the middle was the kid that should have had a broken arm. Her lunch group was expanding.

Treadon didn't mean to feel the heavy disappointment that settled in his belly. He should be glad she had friends, but the part of him that felt disappointed liked the idea of being special, of being the one who could see an angel when no one else could. And there was another, deeper part of him, that wanted to shove everyone away, make sure she was safe. Protect her. The way Jarren wanted to protect Rachel. It was wrong, but it was an impulse he struggled to suppress. Rachel could protect herself. Ellie was stronger than he would ever be, but neither of them deserved to be alone.

Jarren followed him through the line, quiet and distracted. Treadon was about to leave Jarren to sit wherever Ellie made him, when he caught sight of Rachel's head bobbing through the lunchroom, making a b-line for Ellie's table.

"Are you going to sit by Rachel?" Treadon asked. He wondered if Ellie was strong enough to keep Jarren away from Rachel. That would be a feat.

Jarren groaned. "One kiss. One kiss in front of a hundred people and you're automatically labeled as a couple." He exaggerated the last word, but there was a quirk to his lips and an excitement in his eyes that had been missing the last few days.

Rachel sat down across from Megan and Ellie as the skaters got up to leave. Jarren led the way. No distractions or deviations. Jarren sat next to Rachel. Treadon hovered, standing next to Megan. He cleared his throat, but Ellie didn't look up from her food.

Jarren tried to keep from touching Rachel, coolly ignoring her. An extreme feat with the lunch stools so close together. Rachel shared her normal acknowledging smile and introduced Jarren to Ellie.

Megan looked up at Treadon; her eyes narrowed. "Are you going to sit?"

Treadon sat down and tried to get a glimpse of Ellie's reaction, but she just took another bite of yogurt. Rachel continued the conversation, perfectly happy to pretend the kiss hadn't happened. Rachel understood Jarren. He didn't need a girl who begged for attention, to suffocate him. He needed someone to play his game.

"So, what is it like tutoring the best football player in the school?" Rachel addressed the question to Ellie while sending a barb toward Jarren in the same breath.

She was good.

Treadon tried to hide his smile as Jarren digested the meaning of what Rachel had said. Jarren's face twisted into a grimace as he fought the urge to defend his status as the better football player while remaining aloof to Rachel's presence.

Ellie smiled. Treadon could tell she was aware of the game between the two of them as well. "No. My foster parents don't care about football, and they don't care who I tutor as long as I get home safe."

There was an awkward silence. Rachel lost some of her game, really focusing on Ellie.

"Where are your real parents?" Rachel asked.

Treadon read the pain before Ellie spoke. "They died. When I was little. It was a long time ago."

"I'm sorry." Megan and Rachel spoke at the same time. Treadon could tell each person was looking for a way to change the subject without making it awkward.

"Do you remember them?" Treadon blurted. He regretted the question when he saw the look on her face.

"Yes." Her voice was soft, barely loud enough to hear over the din of the lunchroom. "I was eight."

"I lost my dad, too," Treadon said, "but it was before I can remember."

Megan dropped her fork and leaned over to pick it up. Ellie's and Treadon's eyes met for a moment. A small nod from Ellie, an acknowledgement of shared pain. She stood up. "I'll see you later."

Megan sat back up, twirling her fork between her fingers. She rested her elbows on the table, head turned obviously in Treadon's direction, staring, calculating. Treadon met her gaze, somehow feeling like he'd been drenched with cold water in too thin of a shirt.

Her face was calm, but different than before. Her eyes shone with a new light. Her nose ring was slim, highlighting the freckles along her cheeks. She wore fingerless gloves, exposing her bitten fingernails. She tilted her head.

"She saved my life." Megan spoke low, the general hum of the cafeteria almost drowning out her words. Jarren and Rachel were both engaged in conversations with people on either side of them, conveniently ignoring each other. They weren't paying attention to Treadon and Megan.

"What?" It wasn't the information Treadon expected, but he saw how much it meant to her.

"I was going to end it." Her voice was deep, smooth. "I'd already made up my mind when she showed up at my door. I wasn't going to let her in, but she came in anyway, kind of pushed through without stopping. So, I let her talk. Figured another few minutes of life couldn't hurt. She stayed all night. She talked. Then she listened. She made me laugh and then she let me cry. For hours. Somehow, she knew I needed help, and she came. When the sun rose, it was like the world was different." Megan stopped, chewing on the inside of her cheek. "No. The world was the same. I was different."

Treadon held his breath while she talked. He let out the air when she finished and looked at the empty seat Ellie had left behind.

Miracle number three. Once she helped someone, they noticed her, felt drawn to her. He remembered her fear from the first day. Was doing these things putting her in danger?

"I've seen you look at her," Megan said. "She's different than you and me. If you jerk around with her, I will personally kill you."

She said it like a fact. She meant it as a fact.

"I believe you," Treadon said.

"Good." She picked up her tray and stood, stopping to shoot Treadon one last appraising look. "She needs somebody. I'm just not sure it's you."

Megan walked away. The sound of the lunchroom grew louder and Treadon turned his attention back to Rachel and Jarren. Rachel grabbed her backpack from under the table. She and Jarren still hadn't spoken a word. She caved first but made it look casual, she gave Jarren a chance to win, but lose at the same time.

"They're doing a press conference this afternoon. Do you want to go with me?" Rachel asked Jarren.

"As long as I get to drive." Jarren picked up his tray. "And we keep it G rated."

Rachel leaned forward, letting her breath hit Jarren's ear. "You're not that hard to resist."

Jarren shot up. "Good. I want to see what's going on with my company."

Jarren walked away, his shoulders tight. Rachel watched him go.

"What is with you two?" Treadon asked. "You make out on the field in the morning and then he ignores you at lunch. You can't be okay with that."

Rachel shrugged. "I've known Jarren a long time. He plays his game, but he hides a lot—too much. I'm worried about this stuff with the company and his dad. Jarren shouldn't have gotten his hopes up. I always knew things would go back."

"Back to what?"

"His dad used to be different, when Jarren was little."

Rachel glanced at the door. Treadon could read her consideration to whether she was betraying Jarren's trust or not. She wanted to keep Jarren's confidence. Treadon respected that. She bit her lip and twisted her sweater zipper. She wanted something else from him, something she was nervous to ask for.

"How can I help?" Treadon realized he'd answered a question she hadn't said out loud. Rachel glanced at him. "I mean, what was his dad like, before?"

Rachel looked down. "He didn't used to treat Jarren like a human being. He acted like Jarren was a prop or a problem. Something in the way. Xander hired my mom as a nanny when I was a baby and we've known each other for as long as I can remember. He used to disappear inside that gigantic house of his, hiding and refusing to come out. My mom would freak out."

"He thought his dad would care if he disappeared." Treadon wished he could stop saying things at the wrong time.

Rachel just nodded. "Jarren always wanted to impress his dad, but Mr. Calivan never cared. He would come through the front door. Jarren would run to him, jumping up and down, trying to show him something. A coloring page, a ball, a frog. He just wanted his dad to notice him. His dad would brush past him, shove him aside without a word, tell my mom to get him out of the way. Xander never cared if his son was dead or alive."

There was anger in Rachel's voice.

"So, what changed?"

"My mom convinced Jarren to go out for football our last year of middle school," Rachel said. "She took him to tryouts, but for some reason, Xander Calivan showed up, said something about surgery and company property. He was angry. But then Jarren made this play out on the field, something incredible. I don't even remember what, but it must have been pretty amazing because his dad stopped and watched."

"That doesn't seem like something that would change years of neglect." Treadon twisted his fork against his tray.

"It wasn't just football," Rachel said. "It was like he'd taken off blinders. Like his eyes had been closed until that moment. It was like . . ." she paused.

"He saw Jarren for the first time."

Rachel let out a breath of air, lowering her head with slight embarrassment. "I don't know what it was, but Xander Calivan changed. He suddenly wanted to be a dad—after all the hard work was over. But he never really changed."

Treadon heard the venom in Rachel's voice. Rachel had been waiting for this to happen, for Xander Calivan to turn away from Jarren—again.

"You want me to watch out for him."

"You know, you're sensitive for a guy," Rachel said. "In the best sense of the word. But yeah, I'm worried. Xander never deserved to have Jarren for a son." She turned away with a shrug.

Treadon sat alone, thinking about all that had happened and the look on Xander's face as he walked away from the crash. The accident hadn't just convinced Xander to give up the company. Whatever threat Xander had received, it was enough to give up his son a second time.

Twenty-Six

Treadon Nelson

Ellie stood outside the room where she usually tutored him. Her head was down, her focus on her phone as she typed out a text.

"What's going on?" Treadon asked. He could tell she was going to cancel, but he had a big test. Between his grades and his injured arm, Treadon was worried he wouldn't be able to get an offer. He wouldn't be able to help his mom.

"Sorry," Ellie said. "I have to cancel today. I just got a call from Pat, and she got called into work. I have to go watch the kids."

"Can I help?" The words slipped out before he could pull them back. He tried to cover the fact that he'd read something different, that she needed a different kind of help, but he wasn't sure what it was. "I mean, I have a test tomorrow and I'm still a little shaky on the concepts. Maybe I could come help you with the kids and then you tutor me at your house."

It sounded like a lame excuse, but for some reason, she was considering it. She played with a thin chain around her neck.

"It's not exactly a good environment for studying."

"I'll take the risk," Treadon said, gesturing for her to walk in front of him.

She nodded with her eyebrows raised. "You better ace that test and then I want a five-star review for my tutoring services."

"Five and a half."

Treadon followed her out to the parking lot. She led him to a small green Gremlin. Dents, dings, and scratches marred most of the exterior. She manually unlocked the driver's side door and then reached across to unlock his side. He turned to put his bag in the back, but felt the tug on his stitches, and settled with his bag on his lap. He had to grit his teeth to pull the seat belt over his shoulder and click it into place.

Ellie kept both hands on the steering wheel. She hadn't started the car. Her back was rigid, and she blinked several times like she was restarting a conversation in her mind.

"Do you want me to get out?" Treadon put his hand on the door handle.

"No." The response was immediate. Truth. "I'm not sure I'm doing the right thing. I'm afraid I'm putting other people in danger."

"The people at lunch who can notice you now. Is it because you helped them?"

"Not exactly, but it is nice to have people to sit with at lunch." She closed her eyes. "I just don't want to be the reason any of them get hurt."

"Maybe my mom's friend could help. He helps save people in bad situations. Maybe not people exactly like you."

"Like me?" She took her hands off the steering wheel and turned to glare at him.

"You know. A Descendant. An Angel." Treadon tried to shrug like it was no big deal, but his stitches pulled tight. "But he might have a safe place for you to help you hide from whatever you're running from."

"You haven't told him? You haven't told anyone, right?" Ellie was alert, looking at him, boring into him with those dark brown eyes.

"No. No." Treadon shook his hands in the air. "I promise, no one else knows."

She let out a sigh of relief. "Thank you for the offer, but he can't help me. Sometimes I'm not even sure I need help." She paused and looked at him again, this time with something else in her eyes. "Thank you. It is so nice to have one person who believes."

She started the car and drove in silence. Treadon had to look away as the fear gripped him, stole his breath. He tried to breathe through the panic of being in a moving vehicle, even at normal speeds.

He was grateful when they pulled into the driveway of a small home a couple blocks from the school. It was a clean neighborhood, a few flags on flag poles, flower gardens, and trimmed lawns. Ellie smiled at him as she shut off the car.

"Are you ready for this?"

"For what?"

"Pat and her husband have several foster kids. It's a good home but there's always a little bit of chaos."

"I was born ready."

She smiled and led him up to the front porch. When she opened the door, Treadon was met with the earsplitting wail of something that sounded like a foghorn, yelling from another room, and the shatter of a plate being dropped on the floor.

Ellie shrugged as she shut the door.

Two small bodies piled into the entry way to pounce on Ellie with hugs and kisses. A third person, a boy that looked to be about twelve, hung back, almost like he could hide in the shadows of the hallway.

A middle-aged woman came around the corner, a crying baby in her arms. She had silver roots beneath her brown hair that was pulled back into a ponytail. Several strands had escaped, swaying freely with every bob of her head. She wore a pantsuit with dress shoes and a large purse hung over her shoulder.

"Ellie, thank goodness." She handed the baby over to Ellie.

"I came as soon as I could," Ellie said. "Treadon, this is Pat Greyson. Pat this is Treadon." Ellie made a quick introduction over the howling baby. "How is Nolan?"

Pat wiped a finger across her eye, quick and subtle, like she could hide the tear that had almost escaped. "Same. He hasn't spoken and I had to adjust his oxygen level today."

"I'll check in on him, too," Ellie said, shifting the baby to one arm as it wailed.

"I've got to run," Pat said. "Thank you so much, and it was so nice to meet you." She sent Treadon a wave as she slipped out the door.

The two boys circled Treadon. The first one pulled on his sleeve. "I'm Foster." He had short hair and a freckled nose. Intelligent eyes that held plenty of mischief.

The second boy was almost identical in appearance, but he kept his distance. "I'm Mike Jenkins."

"Hi." Treadon smiled. "I'm Treadon. I'm a friend of Ellie's from school."

"You're really tall," said Foster, leaning his head way back as if to prove his point. "Are you a giant?"

Mike pushed his brother back. "He's not a giant. He's just really old."

The boys were practically yelling to be heard over the crying baby Ellie bounced in her arms.

"Everyone to the kitchen," Ellie said, tugging Foster away from Treadon with one hand. The baby only wailed louder. Ellie closed her eyes for a moment. She pulled the baby closer and put a finger to her cheek. The crying slowly subsided until the baby was taking small gasps of air.

Treadon couldn't pull his eyes away from Ellie. He knew she could feel his eyes on her, but she kept her focus on the baby. An angel. A girl descended from Angels. It was unreal. Unbelievable. And yet, he believed. He believed that there was a world just beyond his knowledge and she was the key to understanding it.

Ellie stepped down the hall, bouncing the now calm baby in her arms. Mike and Foster followed close behind. She stuck her head into a small room off the side of the entry. Treadon could make out some medical equipment and a man on a bed hooked up to some tubes.

"Who is that?" Treadon asked.

"That's Pat's husband," Ellie answered. "He had an accident at work and hit his head. They think he may have permanent brain damage, but Pat is praying for a full recovery. She doesn't want to lose the kids, but she's struggling to make ends meet right now. I do what I can to help out."

Treadon paused outside the door. He tried to read more behind Ellie's words. "Can't you help him? I mean, the way you did Rachel?"

Ellie looked down. "It's brain damage. I can't fix the mind. It's too complicated. I won't do that again."

She shut the door too quickly, shaking her head. There was more behind what she was saying, but it was buried beneath an avalanche of pain. Regret.

"I'm sorry," Treadon said.

"Come on." She waved her hand away, like emotions as deep as the ocean could be ignored like a gnat. She went around the corner with the twins, leaving Treadon in the hall with a tall, skinny boy.

"What's your name?" Treadon asked him.

The boy stared at him through dark eyes shadowed with circles. His shirt hung loosely on his shoulder, collarbone protruding from where the stretched-out neck of the shirt exposed his upper shoulder. He wasn't the kind of skinny you see when a kid hits a growth spurt. He looked as if he'd been denied too many meals. His hair was shaggy and unkempt.

Treadon met the boy's glare and tried to get a read on what he was thinking. There was a single emotion with no words behind it. Distrust. The boy's face held a firm determination that no matter what physical pain was inflicted on him, his emotions lay dormant, untouchable, protected.

"I see you've met Jake." Ellie led Jake to the kitchen and Treadon followed.

Dinner was a blur of spaghetti, sauce, and the twin's voices. After dinner, Ellie got the kids ready for bed and Treadon stood in the doorway, watching.

"Can Treadon tell the story?" Foster asked.

"I don't know if he can tell a good story," Ellie said, a challenge in her voice.

"I think I can handle it." Treadon stepped into the room and took Ellie's place on a stool.

"Turn the lights off when you're done. I'll get the table cleaned off so we can study."

"Uh," Treadon started. "Once there was this awesome football player."

"Noooo." Mike rolled his eyes and bent his head back. "You have to start with once upon a time," he said, punching his fist into his bed.

"Okay. Once upon a time there was a really good-looking football star. He saw a girl."

"I want him to fight a dragon." Foster sat up, pushing his covers off.

"I want him to be a ninja." Mike punched both fists in the air.

"Okay. Okay. Only if you lay back down." He helped Foster pull his covers back up.

"Once upon a time there was a great ninja dragon fighter and he had to rescue a princess. He jumped in an awesome car and drove to the dragon's cave."

"What if the princess doesn't want to be rescued?" Mike asked.

"Why wouldn't the princess want to be rescued?" Treadon couldn't help the question.

"Lots of reasons. She can probably take care of the dragon herself."

"Or she doesn't want the knight to get killed."

"Or she broke the law, and the dragon is keeping her in jail like my dad."

Both boys had risen to their knees, out of their covers again. This was harder than he thought.

He folded his arms. "Do you guys want me to tell the story or not?"

"We want a story. We want a story."

"Lay down."

They grumbled but finally got their heads back on their pillows.

"A ninja went and fought a dragon. The princess came to help him. She was better with a sword. They rescued everyone from the prison because they all promised to be good and go to bed. The end."

"Ellie was right," Foster said, glaring at Treadon.

"Uh-huh, bad story," Mike agreed.

"Well, go to sleep before the dragon comes back." Treadon stood up and shut off the light. He couldn't help glancing back as the two boys rolled over. Why wouldn't a princess want to be rescued? The question was left hanging in the air, unanswered.

He went back into the living room and sat down next to Ellie. He checked his phone.

"It's pretty late," he said to her. "You don't have to do this."

Ellie opened her mouth just as the tall skinny boy walked back into the room. She jumped up.

"Jake, are you still hungry?"

Jake shook his head, his brooding eyes scanning the room. Ellie set a plate of spaghetti in front of him. He sat down at the table but didn't move to eat.

"Why doesn't he talk?" Treadon asked.

"He's had a very difficult life. A part of him shut down due to abuse." Ellie looked at Treadon.

He leaned closer to her. The set to her jaw, a crease in her eyebrow, lines near her eyes, all spoke of a deep pain. He felt lost in her eyes—a swirl of sorrow, guilt, and loneliness.

Ellie pulled back and raised her palm between them. "Stop."

Jake jumped from his chair and reared over Treadon, a small growl coming from his throat. He pushed himself between Treadon and Ellie.

"Oh, no." Ellie stood. "Jake, it's okay. He's a friend. He wasn't hurting me."

Everything seemed frozen in time as Jake's eyes bored into Treadon. Jake refused to look at Ellie.

"Let's get you to bed," Ellie said. "Everything is okay."

She touched Jake lightly on the shoulder. Jake's arm jerked up catching Ellie across her cheek. His whole body shuddered. He grabbed his head in both hands and grunted as he doubled over. He looked at Treadon with tortured eyes and ran from the room.

Ellie stood stunned, her hand over her cheek where Jake had slapped her.

"Are you okay?" Treadon wanted to reach out and take her fingers away from her cheek, but she looked as wound up as Jake had been. He kept his hands down by his side.

"He was protecting me." Ellie sucked in a breath and blinked back tears. "I've been telling him about Descendants and their Guardians.

He must have taken it to heart, thought he could protect me like he was my Guardian."

"Descendants and Guardians?" Treadon asked. He'd seen her working miracles but was only just beginning to comprehend what she could do, what she really was.

Ellie looked away. "Descendants choose someone to be their companion, to help fight the evil in the world. So that they are never alone." She looked out the window, her gaze far away, a deep line of sorrow etched into her forehead.

Treadon reached out to her, unable to hold it back, but he chose the wrong arm. His shoulder, tight from sitting so still, protested at the movement with an intense wave of pain. He grunted and grabbed his shoulder.

"You're hurt."

"It's nothing. We got in an accident this weekend."

"I can feel it. Your pain." Her eyes were pleading. "Let me do one thing right today. I can't fix Pat's husband. I can't help Jake. But I can do this one thing."

Treadon hesitated. He wanted to help her, he wanted to take her pain away, but she was leaning toward him, begging him with her eyes. He couldn't say no. He nodded and lifted his shirt up over his head, exposing his torso and the stitched gash along his shoulder and chest. She reached up and traced her finger around the red, irritated stitches that stretched across the center of his bruise.

"That looks like it hurt."

Treadon blushed as she examined his chest.

"No need to blush. It's not that impressive." Her small smile and slight dip of her head told Treadon she wasn't that unimpressed, either.

"If you heal this, I'll be able to find you at lunch with your other fans. Are you sure you want that?"

Her finger was cool and hot at the same time. It sent a burst of cold that went straight to his bone and then spread from the center outward. He let out a sigh of relief. Her hand spread out and she leaned into him. "I couldn't stop you from finding me at lunch, anyway."

The pain in his shoulder was gone. He could move. He could play football again. The relief was overwhelming.

He put his own hand over hers. "Go out with me."

She raised an eyebrow as she looked up at him. "I don't make long-term commitments."

"One date. Come out with me Wednesday night. I'll take you to dinner."

"Restaurants make me nervous."

"Okay. I'll take you somewhere else. Somewhere beautiful."

"Why Wednesday?"

"We have an away game this weekend. State Championships, and now thanks to you, we have a chance. We leave Thursday morning."

She paused and then pulled her hand away.

"I'll pick you up at five." Treadon held his breath. The pain in his shoulder was gone, but his pull toward her felt like a rubber band that only she could snap.

Ellie let out a breath. "Okay. It's just one time. No promises."

"No expectations."

The corner of her mouth lifted as she ducked her head. "You still have to pass your test tomorrow so we better study."

Twenty-Seven

October 12

I messed up with Jake last night. I've been working so hard to gain his trust and build a connection with him that I didn't stop to think. I didn't think how he would react to a stranger in the house. I didn't think he would try to protect me, that he wants to keep me safe.

I can hardly see the page, even when I wipe the tears away. Sweet Jake. After all the stories I've told him about Descendants and Guardians and heroes and demons, he's taken them to heart. Just because his mind is keeping him from communicating right now, doesn't mean he didn't understand more. I'm so stupid for not thinking of how much he would understand and that he'd want to be the one to help protect me.

I'm too upset to talk to him right now, but I will apologize to him soon. I will try to reach him without hurting him again. Does that mean staying away from Treadon? Maybe. I need to stop playing like a child and grow up. I've said yes to the date, but I need to cut it off. I can't lead him on like this. Not when I can't give him all of me. Not when I've already been torn in half.

Like the boy on the road. The accident happened so fast. In a blink. I didn't even have time to call out, to warn him, before the car slammed into him, tossing his body off the road and into the forest.

The car didn't slow down. Hit-and-run. Or maybe it was so dark and the boy so small that they didn't even realize they'd hit something. I don't really believe that, but I will never know. I want to give the benefit of the doubt, believe that Ordinaries are better than that, than leaving a boy crushed and bleeding on the side of the road. I know that most of them are better and that some of them are not. I've seen the darkness they're capable of since then.

I crawled over to the boy's body. He'd landed on his back, blood coming from a gash in his head. His chest had taken most of the impact and was crushed, ribs broken, two bad enough to have punctured his lungs. The boy held his hands against the open wounds in his chest, like he was trying to hold himself together.

There was blood on the ground and blood rushing through my ears. There was no time to get help. No time left before the boy's energy would be gone and there would be nothing for me to increase. I couldn't heal him after he was dead.

I had only healed small things, a bird's wing, a papercut on my brother's finger, a nosebleed.

This was none of those things. But I couldn't sit there and watch him die. It wasn't who I was.

As terrified as I was, I reached out and touched the boy's bloodied hand.

Abigail Nelson

"What do you see?" The deep baritone of Gabe's voice sent familiar chills down Abigail's spine. She crossed her arms to cover an involuntary shiver. She turned from the map to face him. He wore his black biking leathers, and his chin sported a rough shadow of a beard. His blue eyes were soft as he watched her wipe the tears from her cheeks.

"There's a light, a bright one, only a few hours away," Abigail said, voice steady like she could pretend everything away.

"Tell me where."

Abigail turned away, unable to meet his gaze. "What if it doesn't do any good? I haven't been much use lately."

"You saved Paige and dozens of children before her. We can't stop trying just because we've lost a few." His large frame filled the doorway, his voice too low and tender to come from his warrior's frame. But it was something she loved about him. Another thing that broke her heart when she thought of his Bonding to another. Her deep yearning was a pain so deeply embedded that she thought of it as part of her now.

"Someone is beating us to them," Abigail said. "And they know who I am."

"No." Gabe shook his head and took a half-step toward her. "They know there is a watcher, but not who or where."

"What if they find us?"

"I will never let that happen." Gabe's eyes hardened, his fists clenched, the tender moment gone.

"You know you can't promise that." She saw the truth of her words slam into Gabe, his breath catching, his shoulders hunching a fraction of an inch. "And you owe me more than a promise."

Abigail felt her resolve weaken. Gabe had always been her weakness.

She turned to the pictures hanging on the wall, tracing a frame with one finger. It was a picture of Gabe and Treadon next to the ocean. Gabe held Treadon's hand as they jumped over the waves. It was from the early days, before the Unguarded started disappearing, when they delivered messages and took Treadon with them. Abigail didn't always understand the messages they were delivering, but it was a time when Gabe was lighter and Treadon was younger.

"He's almost a man now. He doesn't need your protection anymore," Gabe said. "You need to let him make a choice."

"And ask him to die for a cause that was never his?" Abigail let the unspoken part fall to the floor between them. The way she was asked. The way she gave up everything for a cause that was never hers. When Gabe could never be hers.

"He needs to know who you are, what you've fought for all these years."

Abigail turned, back straight. "I will not let him be dragged into the life that destroyed his father."

Gabe's face registered pain. He looked down.

"Go. Maybe we can save this one. If you hurry." Abigail looked away as the tears started again. She felt like she was being torn in half each time they risked being discovered, potentially leading the hunters to their own front door.

She felt his presence behind her. He had stepped closer, close enough to touch, but his hands remained pressed against his side.

"I'm scared." She pressed her fingers against the sides of her head. She could feel some kind of pressure there, growing. "I'm scared that we are going to be swept away in the darkness. I can feel it. And it will be my fault."

"I will find the ones taking the Unguarded," Gabe said. "I will stop this."

"And you will find her," Abigail said. Gabe wasn't just looking for the Unguarded. He still had a lost Descendant to find. He hoped each time a new light appeared, that somehow, it would be her. It chipped a piece off Abigail's heart each time. "Promise you'll keep Treadon safe if something happens to me."

"Nothing will happen to you." He was close enough that she could feel his shadow, feel the absence of his touch.

Abigail turned, their faces close, his body stiff as if he pressed up against a wall. The tears dried on her cheeks. She waited.

"I will protect Treadon with my life."

Abigail nodded. "Then go. North of Bakersfield. Hurry."

Gabe paused and for a moment, Abigail thought he might break through the wall he'd built, lean toward her and reach out a hand. Instead, he turned on his heel and left the room.

Abigail leaned against Gabe's desk, smoothing out the map that was already perfectly smooth. She watched Gabe's light leave the garage and head toward the white light half-way across the state. Her eyes wandered to the perpetual motion device as it twisted in the air, three circles with marbles, blue, yellow, and green, twisting intricately, eternally, to remind her there would be no end to the pain.

Less than forty-five minutes later, Abigail watched Gabe's light approach the outskirts of Bakersfield. The map was a high-tech gadget that one of the first Unguarded they'd rescued made for her. Abigail had always been able to perceive the aura around people, each person pulsing in their own unique signature. When she met Gabe, she'd been fascinated by his aura. It was brighter than any human being she'd ever met, even though he was on the verge of collapse. He was lost and alone and her heart was drawn to him, even back then. She brought him home out of curiosity and charity.

That decision changed everything.

She used two fingers against the map and pulled them apart, zooming in the view. It was a screen of sorts, but as thin as a piece of paper with the ability to let her use her vision from a birds-eye view. It allowed her to help Gabe from a distance instead of traveling everywhere with him. It gave Treadon more of a life.

The front door slammed open, and she heard voices in the living room. Abigail jumped, running to the wall that held Gabe's weapons.

It was too late. They were already in the house. She crept to the door and peaked into the living room.

She let out a sigh of relief. It was Jarren and Rachel, sitting down at the kitchen table, opening a laptop.

Treadon walked in just as Rachel and Jarren settled at the kitchen table. Abigail turned back and checked the map. Gabe was a few minutes away and the light still shone from the image on the desk.

"Mom?"

Abigail bit her lip, not wanting to leave, not wanting Treadon to come in. She quickly went out into the living room.

"Is everything okay?" She stopped when she saw the look on Treadon's face. His smile lit his face and filled her son with a joy that pulsed out of his aura. Treadon crossed the room and wrapped her up, a hug and a spin that left her dizzy. How long had it been since she had seen Treadon this happy?

"You're great, you know that?" Treadon set her back down, hands dropping back to his side like he'd just realized they had an audience.

"You're shoulder?" Abigail asked.

"So much better," Treadon's smile widened. "I just needed to rest it for a day. I'm going to be able to play this weekend."

Treadon slapped Jarren on the shoulder and grabbed a soda from the refrigerator, tossing one around to each person. Abigail caught hers and held it against her chest, the warmth of the hug still humming through her.

"What's gotten into you?" Jarren asked.

"Nothing's up with me," Treadon said. "How's the investigation?"

Rachel crossed her arms. "We've got a guy willing to meet us about XC Energy, but he's very secretive. He's got no history, no social media, no records. It's like he doesn't exist. But as interesting as that is, you need to spill. What's going on?"

Treadon leaned back on his chair balancing on two legs as he popped his soda open.

"I've got a date with an Angel."

Abigail's fingers went numb, and her soda slipped before she could catch it. It hit the floor with a pop, and she bent over to hide the color that she knew had filled her face. It was a normal comment—a boy with a crush. It should fill her with joy instead of this dread, but she couldn't help it.

She checked to see if the three of them had noticed her reaction. No one was looking at her.

Jarren stared at Treadon with his mouth open, shaking his head. "No wonder you're still a virgin."

Abigail let them laugh as she slipped back into the office and touched the map.

"Oh no."

The light was gone.

Gabe's light was still there, moving at impossible speeds, but the bright white light of the Unguarded was already gone. She scrolled the image around and zoomed in, knowing it was too late. Knowing exactly where the light should have been and that it was no longer there.

Abigail didn't realize she was crying until a drop fell off her chin and splashed onto the map between her fingers. She finally lifted her hands and let the map snap back into place. She took a deep breath and reached for the CB radio.

"It's too late. They've taken them." She released the button.

Crackling static came through the speakers and then Gabe's voice. "When?"

She'd lost another one. This time she didn't even watch the light disappear.

That's what the man had called her. A watcher. And maybe that's all she would ever be.

Twenty-Eight

JARREN CALIVAN

Rachel and Jarren stepped into the small cafe. There was no sign on the street, and they'd passed it twice before noticing the small stencil on the door.

"I think that's him." Rachel motioned to a man in the corner, sitting on the edge of the stool at a tall table. He wore a long trench coat, large and heavy, and a large-brimmed hat that was pulled down to shade his face. There were two people in line and the guy taking their order. Jarren took a step back toward the door.

He didn't know what this guy was going to tell him about his dad's company, but he knew it wasn't going to be good. He wasn't sure he was ready for more disappointment. But if he wanted to find out why XC Energy had shut down, why his dad told him not to come home, and what he could do to show his dad he was worthy of a place beside him, he had to go through with this.

He told himself to move, but it was like there was a brick wall in front of him. Rachel broke the wall by pulling him forward. They stood across the table from the man.

There was no movement and for a moment, Jarren thought maybe the man had fallen asleep. Then the hat tilted, exposing pale, washed-out eyes. The guy was as old as a dinosaur.

"Jarren Calivan. I've wanted to meet you."

"At least one of us has a name." Jarren didn't see another stool, so he leaned forward, elbows on the tall table.

"You must be Rachel," the man said. "You've been asking dangerous questions. Are you sure you want to go through with this?"

"Yes, I'm not going to be intimidated if there's a truth that needs to be told."

"I wasn't talking about her name." Jarren pressed his palms flat against the table. "Who are you? How do we know you aren't the one making this dangerous?"

The man's eyes studied Jarren, and he felt like a little kid in front of his dad again. "You can call me Vox. The only way you can know I'm not the one making things dangerous is that you've already met them. And they came with a tattoo." Vox tilted his head and exposed a neck, loose skin, but clear. No tattoo.

Jarren remembered the neck tattoo of the men who had chased down his car.

"That doesn't mean you aren't dangerous," Jarren said.

"Spoken like a true Calivan," Vox responded, a cold smile painting his lips. "Always weighing the risks. People close to me have been hurt in the past. I can't say I'm not dangerous. What I'm asking you, is how bad do you want to know?"

The ache rose inside him, the hunger that made him chase down every ball, the desire that pushed him harder and faster and was never enough. He met Rachel's eyes and she nodded.

"We want to know everything," Jarren said.

Vox cleared his throat and leaned forward. "XC Energy was funded by a society known among some circles as the Triune. They are untouchable, untraceable, except for their contributions to companies that provide power, technology, and information. There are dozens of companies all over the world that create a great front, but underneath, they only release partial truths. I started researching the Triune when XC Energy was first created."

"What did you find out?" Rachel asked.

"I was only able to discover that XC Energy provided power that shouldn't exist, they couldn't explain where it was coming from, and no one was asking questions. No permits. No safety inspections. Just a dead-end trail of engineering reports that didn't make sense."

"Why didn't you report them? Dig deeper?"

Vox lowered his head, his hat covering his eyes again. Jarren could barely hear the words.

"I was a coward. I cut my losses and ran."

"Why?" Jarren asked.

"They came to my house the day after I ran my first story in the LA Times. They tracked down all my sources, anyone who gave me leads, tips, information. They sat me down, sticky-sweet and professional, and told me to drop the story."

"You were a journalist." Rachel leaned in, sucking up his story like soda through a straw.

"I was an investigative reporter, but the meaning of the word has changed. We dug deep and found the truth when people still cared about the truth. Now there is so much empty entertainment out there, people don't even know how to find the truth. Most people don't even want it. It's easier to have instant access to millions of useless bytes of information than to accept one grain of truth into your soul."

Maybe this guy was a nutcase, an embittered crackpot.

"Did you agree to stop the story?" Rachel asked.

"Hell no," Vox said, his head snapping back up. "I told those boys they were welcome to borrow my fire poker and stick it where the sun doesn't shine."

"And then?"

Vox showed agitation for the first time. He tried to rub his hands together to cover the shaking as he searched the restaurant from beneath his hat.

"I was a family man. Had the sweetest wife, three boys, just like their dad, and a little one on the way. We were having a girl."

He paused to take a breath, and Jarren wondered if his dad had feelings as deep as Vox. Was there excitement when Xander Calivan found out he was having a son?

"I'll never forget the way the tall visitor touched my wife's hair on the way out the door. He reached out and took a handful with his filthy hands. He smelled it like some perfume strip out of a magazine. Then he looked at me. His face empty, lifeless, that black tattoo sticking out on his neck like a brand on a cow. He smiled." An involuntary shiver ran through Vox. "I've never seen a look like that—like an animal right before it feasts. He pulled a card from his pocket and flipped it across the room."

Vox paused now, his hands shaking uncontrollably. He moved them under the table to place them on his knees.

"What was on the card?" Rachel gripped the table like she was pulling back against the string that was trying to pull her right into Vox's story.

"That black triangle with three points and the edges that never quite seem to touch, the lines getting lost as they twist their way into the center. That same symbol on your father's gate. The same symbol on the necks of the men who chased you."

"How did you know?"

"I know more than any man should." Vox took a drink from the cup that had been sitting on the table in front of him. The cup wobbled, his hands unsteady.

"The card was a warning?" Rachel asked.

"A promise. My wife and unborn baby girl were killed the next day, burned to death when their car caught fire in a roll-over accident. My two older boys were taken less than a week later. The oldest drowned in a local swimming pool. The other was caught in the crossfire of a drive-by shooting." Vox leaned forward as if the memory of his family weighed him down with physical pain. "I was there. Each time they made sure I was there to watch, helpless to save them."

"That's awful," Rachel said, one hand to her mouth.

Jarren wanted to turn away, feeling sick, but he'd found himself lost in the old man's eyes.

"They left that damned symbol as a mark each time so there would be no doubt it was them. When they moved the remains of the burnt car, the black, twisted triangle was scorched into the ground. Beneath the body of my oldest, in the concrete soaked with water, the triangle stayed dry." Vox fell silent, the emotion causing his voice to crack at the last word.

"And the other?" Rachel pressed softly.

"Formed with my son's own blood on the street."

"You had three boys?" Jarren asked. "What happened to the last one?"

"They left me the youngest, not out of mercy, but as insurance, leverage, to force me to keep my mouth shut. And it worked. I had to. For my son's sake. I took him and ran. Disappeared for the last twenty years."

"Where is he now?" Rachel asked.

"He was taken a year ago, natural causes. Now it's just me. There's nothing left they can take."

"Are you saying my dad did those terrible things so he could be rich?" Jarren wanted to take Vox's water and swallow the terrible taste in his mouth.

"Xander was a pawn, an ambitious man with the right skills, motivations, and connections. He knew what was happening to keep his company clear, but he ignored it. I don't know if I'll ever forgive him for that, but I was running short on allies and some of the things Xander had been doing, well, I took a chance."

"What are you saying?" Jarren asked.

"Before the shutdown, Xander agreed to help me, get me information about the Triune. See if there was a way to stop them."

Jarren shifted his weight to his other foot. He wiped the table like he could clean off a stain that wasn't there. "He was helping you?"

"Your father isn't the same man that started XC Energy. Something changed him. For the better. But that was before the shutdown. I haven't been able to get in touch with him since Sunday."

"Since the accident," Rachel said.

Vox checked his watch. "We only have a few more minutes. They've been following me." He reached into the oversized overcoat and pulled out a manilla envelope. "This is all Xander was able to get out to me. He said he had more. He said that he believed the entire purpose of the Triune was to find one person. Twenty years developing technology and equipment was all for one purpose. And he thought they were close. He was supposed to get me some information on Monday, but he didn't come through. Something about a key and a girl.

"I can't get close to XC Energy right now, but maybe you can. See if you can find out who they're looking for. If we find this person first, we have a chance."

Vox stood, looking past the glass door into the crowd of people. "I have to go. Take the back exit through the kitchen."

He was out the door before Jarren could take a breath, before he could say yes or no or anything.

"He's crazy," Jarren said.

"With grief." Rachel tugged his arm. "Let get out of here."

Jarren tucked the manilla envelope into the front of his pants, pulling his shirt down to cover it. They slipped out the back door of the cafe into an alley between two buildings. At the end of the alley, Jarren saw a bald man, smooth face. A small end of a triangle tattoo visible above his collar.

Jarren grabbed Rachel and pulled her back against the wall. He kissed her. He didn't plan it. Hadn't really thought it through, but his lips pressed against hers like it was the most natural thing in the world. Like he wasn't doing this to look like a normal couple making out in the alley so the Triune would look past them. It was like this was the message he'd always wanted to send to her. His kiss was real, passionate, and she returned it, wrapping her hands around his head as his fingers lifted her shirt, brushing against the skin of her back.

"You two." The voice was deep, flat. "How long have you been here?"

Jarren didn't want to let go, didn't want to turn around. He pressed his head against hers for an instant, wondering for the first time what he would do if she wasn't there. She'd been his constant. His everything.

He turned to face the man holding a pistol with a silencer on the end. Jarren raised his hands and stepped in front of Rachel. "Woah. No need for that. We'll find another spot."

"Did you see anyone else come out that door?"

Rachel pulled Jarren back and stepped forward so they stood side by side. The man moved the gun back and forth, like he was debating which one to take out first.

"No, sir. Just the two of us and we've been here for a while." Rachel smiled as she ran a finger up Jarren's spine. If it wasn't for the gun in their face, Jarren would have given up his father's entire fortune to push her up against the wall again. "If you need this spot, we'll leave. No worries."

"Sorry," the man said. "Wrong place. Wrong time." He kept the gun aimed at Jarren's chest. Rachel jumped in front just as they heard a dull thud. Jarren flinched before his mind registered that it wasn't the sound of a gun. The bald man's eyes went wide, his mouth dropping open as if in protest. Instead of words, a gurgling sound came out, followed by a red trickle of blood out of the corner of his mouth.

He fell forward.

Vox stood behind where the man fell. A pleased smile pulled his face into a maze of wrinkles. A crowbar jutted out of the man's back, the straight end penetrating the clothing and buried several inches into the ribs. The curved end of the bar still vibrated from the impact of the body.

Jarren couldn't stop the question. "A crowbar?"

"Household tools are under-appreciated." Vox brushed his hands against each other. "They have a variety of uses."

"I don't know if a crowbar counts as a household tool." Rachel poked her toe against the guy's arm. No reaction. "But it was effective."

Vox walked them back to Rachel's car. "I had a brother who thought he was a hero. Always saving people, trying to get them to see a brighter future. I went into journalism thinking I could make a difference by taking a different path than him. He taught me a lot, but now I'm out to prove I can be just as big a hero as him, without all the special abilities. Make up for who I left behind when I ran."

"The Triune didn't kill your brother?" Rachel asked, pulling her keys from her pocket.

"I'm sure he's on the top of their most wanted list," Vox said with a huff for a laugh, "but he's a hard one to kill."

Vox handed Jarren a card with a number on it. "You can call me there if you find out anything. Xander was going to get the information to me. Maybe he has it ready somewhere, and you just have to find it."

He stepped back and disappeared into the crowd. They both climbed into the car, Jarren flipping the card between his fingers.

"That was some kiss." Rachel started the car and pulled onto the street. "It almost felt serious."

Jarren knew this was going to be hard, but he couldn't shake the image of a burning car with a woman and a baby trapped inside.

"You know I don't get serious. I thought it was a good cover story, making out in an alley."

"That's fair," Rachel said, keeping her eyes on the road. "Just wanted to make sure. What time do you want to go to your dad's office?"

"Not we," Jarren said. "Just me. This is way too dangerous."

"I'm not some girl that needs to be protected. One of these days, you're going to realize you're the one who needs me."

"I've always needed you," Jarren said, his throat feeling tight. "That's why I need you to back off. Stay away. This relationship is . . . is . . . over." He turned, unable to look at her. He folded his arms and tried to imitate his dad's stance when he fired a client. Cold. Aloof. Instead, he had to swallow hard and blink back the doubt.

A sad half-smile lifted the corner of Rachel's mouth. She didn't argue.

"You have to promise me one thing."

"Technically, I don't have to promise anything. I just broke up with you."

Rachel put a hand over his mouth as she pulled up to a stop sign. She leaned into him, the smell of her coconut lotion filling him with longing and a stabbing regret. "Promise me you won't go to your father's office alone."

Twenty-Nine

TREADON NELSON

Treadon knocked on Ellie's door. He wished he'd had time to grab some flowers, but there was a part of him that knew he needed to take smaller steps, let her take her time.

He could hear the Jenkins twins, Mike and Foster, fighting over the door handle. Foster won the tug-of-war and opened the door a crack.

"What's the password?" Foster asked.

"Ninjas?" Treadon took an educated guess when he saw the costume Foster wore.

"Yep. You can come in."

The door opened wide. Ellie stood there in a loose, black turtleneck and high-waisted pants. It took Treadon a moment to catch his breath.

"Are you ready?" Treadon asked.

"Yes. I think it's time." She turned and kissed both the boys on the head and then carefully shut the door, backing up to make sure they didn't try to put their fingers in the way.

"Cute kids," Treadon said, noticing the intentional way she kept him from going into the house.

"They are, aren't they. I imagine you used to be adorable once." Ellie kept her eyes forward, her mouth quirked as she led the way to the old Pontiac in the driveway.

"I was actually a very ugly child."

Ellie gasped. "You can't call children ugly. They're all beautiful."

"So ugly I was irresistible. These cheeks are naturally rosy from all the old women who used to pinch them." He quickened his step and beat her to the door in time to open it for her.

She paused, lips pressed together. "Thank you."

Treadon waited for her to settle into the seat and then shut the door. He tried to read her, but there were too many messages. She liked the attention. She liked that he'd opened her door, but there was a hesitation, like she was doing something she'd promised herself she'd never do. But not letting a guy open a door for her seemed like a weird promise to make as a child.

He started the car and pulled out onto the street. He gripped the wheel tight so that his fingers didn't shake. He could push down his fear of cars when he had control of the wheel as long as he didn't take his eyes off the road. Keeping his eyes straight ahead made it hard for him to gauge Ellie's reactions to his questions.

"Are you okay with eating outdoors?" Treadon asked.

"Yes."

"Any allergies?"

He stopped at a red light and could see Ellie turn her face toward him, head to one side, eyebrow raised. Treadon risked a glance at her, feeling his pulse race even though the light was still red.

"Okay, dumb question. You're an Angel. You can heal, so no allergies. Spring must be great for you."

Ellie let out a huff. Not quite a laugh. "We're technically all allergic to black hematite. But fortunately, I don't think we'll run into any of that on an outdoor patio."

"That's good. I don't exactly have a patio for us, though."

"Where are we going?"

"It's a surprise."

Treadon took them up into the hills on the 405 until they were out of the city, past the suburbs. Past where he and Jarren had the accident.

He took an exit and pulled off onto a dirt road that was barely two tire tracks wide. The road was steep, and the Pontiac roared with effort.

"I don't suppose you can heal a car if anything happens out here?" It was a joke, but his anxiety was growing, and he questioned his decision. Maybe they should have just eaten in his backyard.

Ellie pressed her hand against the dashboard as the car hit a large rock.

He drove slowly. There was no conversation as they struggled to keep from bumping their head against the window or against each other.

Rachel recommended the lookout and had given him instructions. She'd shared her advice on a way to a girl's heart, but she hadn't said exactly how many times she'd been up here, or with whom.

Treadon finally saw the tree that marked the destination. The car rolled to a stop.

"Here we are." He watched the reaction on Ellie's face. She wasn't impressed yet. The two tire tracks disappeared a few feet in front of the car into short brush and patches of long yellow grass. The churned-up dust caught up to them, giving the air a polluted appearance.

"Charming." Ellie tried to open her door, but it caught on a thick, prickly bush.

"Wait for it." He popped the trunk and pulled out the picnic basket. Rachel had offered to help him pack it, but he wanted to do that part himself. He shut the trunk and pushed the bush's branches aside. Ellie's door opened a little wider but stuck on the edge of the rut so that Ellie had to squeeze out of the door sideways.

She turned in a slow circle. "Not exactly where I pictured our first date, but you did hit the population criteria. No one around. Just the two of us. Did you say something about dinner?"

Treadon lifted the picnic basket. "Right here. Come this way. There's a spot on the other side of the tree."

The tree was an anomaly in the area. Its height of twelve feet towered over the surrounding plants. The crooked branches sported sharp pine needles growing in protective bunches. The trunk leaned pathetically to one side, depicting its constant battle with the wind.

The barely visible rabbit trail snaked around tufts of grass until the tree was behind them and the ground dropped away unexpectedly in front of them. Ellie let out a squeak of surprise as they reached the crest of the hill. Los Angeles played out in front of them and in the distance, the Pacific Ocean sparkled with the reflection of the setting sun.

Ellie walked closer to the edge. Treadon set down the picnic basket and spread out a blanket on the ground. He tried to keep his eyes down, but he couldn't help glancing at her silhouette against the sky. Her shoulders were back, her head up, the air playing with her hair. He moved to stand beside her, watching the light reflect off her skin, her eyes closed.

"It's beautiful." Ellie put her hand out, touching his arm. Her eyes still didn't open. "I needed this. I haven't opened my eyes to see, not for a really long time. It's good to see the light in the world when I was so busy hiding in the shadows." She opened her eyes. "What's for dinner?"

"Do you like grape or strawberry?" He led her back to the blanket and pulled out two sandwiches that had somehow gotten smashed in the basket. The jelly had soaked through the bread, leaving a stain in the center of each sandwich.

Ellie covered her mouth, a laugh escaping through her fingertips.

"I didn't say anything about a five-star dinner." He tossed her the least squished sandwich and then pulled out a bag of potato chips.

"It's perfect." She daintily pulled her jelly encrusted sandwich from the sticky bag and took a bite. "Strawberry is my favorite."

"Lucky guess."

"Is grape your favorite?"

Treadon took a bite and chewed slowly, exaggerating his thoughtfulness. "No. I should have made myself a ham and cheese. Swiss."

Ellie laughed, rocking back a little. "Tell me more about you."

Treadon shrugged. "I wouldn't say I have a lot of deep layers. I play football so that I can support myself in college, maybe even earn enough to take some pressure off my mom. She's always working so hard."

"I thought you had a dad that saved people. Doesn't he help?"

Treadon took another bite of his sandwich and regretted it. The peanut butter balled up with the white bread and refused to go down his throat. He swallowed hard, forcing the entire lump down. His eyes watered from the pain.

"Gabe isn't my father. He isn't even my stepdad. He's just a negative presence that brings my mom down. I guess he's trying to do good, but he doesn't make any money and he's gone more than he's around. I just think my mom deserves better than that."

"And what about Gabe and you?" Ellie took another bite of sandwich, a bit of red jelly squeezing out the back.

Treadon looked out at the ocean, wondering how he would answer that question. "He's always disappointed. I can tell in the way he stands when I'm around, how he's always on edge, like I should be doing something more and he's waiting for me to step up. I guess football isn't enough for him."

Ellie took her last bite of sandwich. She stared at her fingers covered with excess jelly. Treadon reached into the basket and pulled out the two napkins and the soda he'd brought. She took the napkin with her sticky hand and wrapped her fingers around the can. Their fingers interlocked; their eyes met. The pull increased until he thought his heart might burst from his chest. He leaned closer, but she pulled the soda away and dropped her gaze.

But not before Treadon saw that she felt it too. That she wanted, needed, to not be alone anymore. He couldn't tell what was holding her back.

Ellie became absorbed in cleaning her fingers with the dry napkin. Small pieces of torn napkin stuck to the jelly on her fingers. She wiped harder, rubbing her hands together, spreading the jelly and the napkin bits. She dropped her hands into her lap in defeat.

"I'm sorry," Treadon said. "I didn't mean to ruin the dinner."

She turned, facing the cliff and the ocean and the edge of the sky. A tear fell down her cheek. "You didn't ruin the dinner. This was perfect. A moment out of time. An instant where I could believe there was more for me, that I could have happiness like a normal girl."

"I know what it's like to want to be normal, but I've seen what you can do. I believe in what you are." Treadon scooted closer to her, wrapping one arm around her shivering shoulders. The temperature was dropping and the wind coming in from the coast was cold. She leaned into him, hands in fists, like she was fighting against an invisible force.

"I know you believe me," Ellie said.

"But there's more you're not telling me."

Ellie sighed. "The original Angels were killed, but not before they left their Descendants the ability to never be alone. To choose another person to be their companion, their Guardian."

Treadon's breath caught. "You mentioned that before. The other night." He could feel his blood running hot, the desire in him to be by her side, to protect her, filled his mind, squeezed his chest. If this was real, if all she was waiting for was someone to choose her, he would be the one. Gladly. "What does that mean?"

"It means that the Angels never wanted their Descendants to be alone, but every Descendant must choose, and every Guardian must accept, or the Bond will be incomplete. Ineffective."

"Is that what you've been afraid of? That you won't find a Guardian?"

"No. No, there's something else, something more."

Treadon shifted their bodies so she leaned with her shoulder against his chest, their faces close together. "What?"

"I was never meant to have that happiness. I don't deserve it."

He pulled her closer, arms wrapped around, their lips a hair's breadth apart. "Everyone deserves happiness."

She closed the distance, pressed her lips into his, warmth and heat and desire spread through him in a way that made him feel complete. Whole. Her hands came up and touched his chest, their bodies curled in perfect harmony. And then she shoved him back.

She pushed him away hard enough to make him fall back as she jumped to her feet. She brushed the tears from her cheeks and put her back to him.

"I'm sorry." He was sure he hadn't misread that. He was sure he'd let her accept the kiss. Had he wanted it so bad that he'd ignored her body language?

Ellie shook her head. "No. I wanted it too."

Treadon stood up and matched her posture, crossed his arms, but let his shoulder brush hers, letting her know he was here, that she was all he wanted. "You said you get to choose a Guardian." Treadon swallowed. "What if it was me? I could be yours." He said the words and the idea filled him with all the energy and passion he'd been missing. This was his purpose. There was nothing he wanted more. "Let me be your Guardian."

Ellie turned, her face flat, her body sagging. "I can't. You can't. It's too late."

"What do mean?"

"I already have a Guardian. I've already chosen, and we only get one chance."

Treadon's chest went cold. He reached out for her, but she stepped back. "I'm sorry. I never should have led you on, let you believe there was a chance. That was wrong."

He wanted to take her into his arms again, tell her he didn't care. But she was gone. She'd put up a wall that even he couldn't break through.

His phone buzzed in his pocket, followed by a song claiming an irresistible sexiness. He fumbled the phone out of his pocket and silenced it. Jarren's name flashed across the screen.

"Jarren messes with my ring tones." He tried to smile, tried to reach her across the chasm she'd created. "He does think he's pretty sexy."

Ellie looked at the last rays of the setting sun. She had a strange calm acceptance that broke Treadon's heart.

"You should answer that. And then I want you to take me home."

Thirty

October 13

Is it possible for a Descendant's heart to break? I feel like mine has been ripped into a million pieces. He offered to be my Guardian. The one thing he cannot be. The one thing I can never have. Because of my mistake. He knows I'm a Descendant of Angels. He believes me. And instead of asking me to be his girlfriend and pretend to be an Ordinary, he was willing to rise to my side and be bigger and better for me.

I want to sink into my covers and disappear, never to be seen again. I can feel the scars on my chest, my skin puckered and white like an old burn. I had been afraid to leave my home, but that night, I was willing to give my life for a stranger.

Even the best of intentions can have unintended consequences. Ripple effects that you can't control or pull back once the stone has entered the water. I still don't know how many lives I've ruined by what I did to that little boy.

Touching him wasn't enough. I didn't have enough energy to heal such life-threatening wounds. He was slipping away, his light fading. He squeezed my fingers, his eyes wide, his lungs unable to get air out to form words. His lips moved without sound, but I knew what he was trying to say.

"Help me," he said.

His grip on my fingers reminded me of when I held my brother's hand when he was scared of the dark. Even with all his brains and ability with technology, the shadows of the unknown haunted him after the sun went down.

I wouldn't let this boy die. I leaned over the boy's broken body and wrapped my arms around his neck. I pressed myself against him, held my cheek against his cheek. The warm blood was sticky against my face. His eyelashes tickled my skin as he closed his eyes.

It wasn't enough. I wasn't enough.

I threw myself on top of him, pressing my body against his shattered chest, knowing the pain I was causing him, knowing this was the only chance. His last breath passed my ear.

I pushed all my energy into him with a single thought.

"Take it. Take it all and live."

TREADON NELSON

. . .

Treadon slammed the door on Jarren's Aston Martin, shaking the whole car.

"Careful with my baby." Jarren patted the steering wheel. "What did she do to you?"

"Sorry." Treadon leaned forward and put his head against the dashboard. "Just had a bad night."

"You didn't make it with your angel?" Jarren asked sarcastically, but there was a change to his voice. Less confidence than normal.

Treadon looked at his friend for the first time since they got in the car. "Yeah. I guess you could say that."

"Rejection hurts." Jarren held the wheel with both hands, eyes on the road like he was concentrating on staying between the lines, but the car wasn't moving, yet. "Did she say it wasn't you, it was her?"

Treadon chuckled. "Okay. I get it. My relationship problems are lame, and you've got a real problem. This just felt, different. Like she needed me. Like she was special, but I was too late." He had to take a deep breath and push Ellie out of his mind, her face as she said she'd chosen another Guardian, that she wouldn't, couldn't, be with him. He didn't want to believe it. But she walked away, put up an impenetrable wall. There was more she wasn't saying, something that made the future seem short and eternal at the same time. "Tell me what's going on with your dad."

Jarren flinched.

"That bad?" Treadon asked.

Jarren took one hand off the steering wheel and rubbed his eyes. "It sounds like my dad might have been using technology to spy on people, not just spy, but make them disappear. I helped my dad work on a prototype this summer. He called it the WWAR. A satellite that tracks energy, not just a heat signature, but an energy wave given off by living things. He said it was for non-profit climate change and population research."

"Your dad has a satellite that tracks people by their energy?" Treadon thought of Ellie, hiding in plain sight. She could distract people, but he doubted she could distract a satellite. The odds would be astronomical, though. One satellite for eight billion people.

"We met with Rachel's source, some guy who tried to dig into XC Energy when it first started up." Jarren paused. "They killed his family." He hit the steering wheel. "They killed his entire family to shut him up, some secret behind my dad's company was worth killing people to protect. And now I have to find out what it was."

"You think it has something to do with the satellite?"

"No. I'm going to use the satellite to do a favor for Vox. It's the least I can do after what those guys did to him. He needs us to find someone before they do. I was going to see if you wanted to come."

Treadon understood why they hadn't started moving. Jarren was waiting for his permission, making sure Treadon understood that there were risks, that people had died, and that this was his choice. Ellie hadn't had a choice. Treadon did.

"Yeah. I'll come," Treadon said. "Just drive careful this time."

Jarren's shoulders dropped like a weight had been lifted. A smile crawled onto his face.

The last two words were lost in the roar as Jarren accelerated out onto the street, leaving black tire marks on the road. Treadon closed his eyes and squeezed the door handle, nothing to hide his fear as he felt like his soul had been ripped out and left behind on the sidewalk.

By the time Jarren pulled into the parking lot, Treadon's pulse was in a drum-off with his head. It took him a moment to refill his lungs. Another minute to realize Jarren was bent over the steering wheel, forehead pressed against the leather.

"Are you okay?' Treadon pushed past his own panic attack. Jarren looked like he was in pain.

"I'm good. Ever since the accident, I've had this sharp, stabbing pain in the back of my skull." He rolled his head around, cracking his neck. "In the alley today, some guy threatened Rachel and for a minute, I wanted to open the earth to swallow the guy. I thought my head was going to explode."

"Are you sure you want to do this?"

"Yeah. I'm fine. Just give me a minute."

They both got out of the car and looked up at the five-story glass building. Several windows were broken, discarded furniture littered the lawn and parking lot. Loose pages fluttered in a light breeze.

Broken glass glittered in the three street lamps that were still working.

"They trashed the place." Treadon wished he didn't always speak the obvious, but he couldn't help it.

Jarren's hands were balled into fists. "I guess we'll find out if he deserved it."

"I don't think there's going to be anything left to find in there. I think the place was cleaned out."

"We're not looking up there."

Jarren led Treadon around the left side of the building to a steel door. Jarren pulled a key card from his pocket and held it against a gray keypad. The scanner buzzed as a red light flashed.

"He locked you out."

"He tried."

Jarren pulled a manilla envelope out from under his shirt. The envelope only held a few pieces of paper, but when Jarren dug down to the bottom, he pulled out a blank white card. An access card.

"You got that from Rachel's source?" Treadon asked. "How did he get an access card that works? Do you trust him?"

The light flashed green with a friendly beep when Jarren held the key card against the pad. "He says he was working with my dad, that he was going to get some information out to him before the company shut down. I guess my dad trusted him more than he trusted me."

Treadon didn't have a response.

Jarren opened the door, and Treadon followed him inside. They stood in a stairwell with dim lights. A security door leading up. The glass in the door had a crack in it like someone had tried to get through but failed. On the left was a solid steel door labeled, Lower Level: Restricted Access. On the wall beside the door was another small gray card scanner.

The card worked, again, the light flashing green, but this time instead of a friendly beep, the green light was followed by a loud buzzing sound and a metallic clank that Treadon associated with prison doors being unlocked. The queasiness in his stomach increased after his car ride. If the people who wanted this company were willing to kill to keep the secrets safe, what would they do to a couple of football players sneaking around in the middle of the night?

Jarren held his phone light under his chin causing dark shadows to dance under his eyes and mouth. "Welcome to the lower levels, where secrets come in, but never come out." He let out a maniacal burst of laughter.

"You deserve whatever happens to you down there." Treadon couldn't suppress the panic that climbed into his throat. He turned on his own phone light and forced himself to lead the way down the stairs. At the bottom of the stairs was another door, this one with a keypad. Jarren flipped the key card over and there was a number written on the back. He keyed the number into the pad and the door unlocked.

"It's like your dad wanted this guy to come down here and do this himself. Do you think Xander would want you doing this?"

"No."

That ended the discussion as they stepped into a server room from a science fiction movie. There were server towers on both sides of the room organized into rows, each row with its own meshed sliding gate. The towers glowed with blue LED lights, lined up twenty tall and maybe a hundred deep. The amount of information that could be stored here had to rival a government spy center.

"What are we looking for?" Treadon asked.

"Vox said we were looking for a person."

"I think we're in the wrong place unless the person we're looking for is in the Matrix."

"That wasn't an eighties movie," Jarren said. "You'll have to use Blade Runner or Deadly Friend."

"Yeah, we're in one of those movies."

They stared around the room, phones acting like pathetic points of light against the room of glowing information.

"Where do we start?" Treadon asked.

Before Jarren could answer, a loud buzzing followed by the metallic clank of a lock disengaging echoed through the room.

"Someone's here."

"Thanks, Sherlock."

"What are we going to do?"

"Hide."

Jarren chose a row three isles down and pulled open the mesh gate. They both slipped inside, and Jarren pulled it shut.

"Turn off your light," Treadon hissed just as the lower door opened and Xander Calivan stepped inside.

Treadon knew he needed to step back, get out of sight. Even in the shadows there had to be some blue light bouncing off them, but he couldn't take his eyes off the man.

It was like he was looking at a completely different person than the father he'd met at dinner. The features on his face were the same. His height and build. The suit shouted Xander Calivan. But nothing else worked. The muscles on his face were frozen like he'd had a Botox injection that went wrong. There was no expression at all. The strong, confident posture was gone. Xander was hunched, his neck arched low. He held a laptop, but the way the fingers kept tapping across the edges, it was like it was taking all his concentration not to crush it.

Jarren pulled him back and they both covered their own mouths to try and hide the sound of their breathing. Treadon's sneaker squeaked on the floor. They waited.

Xander walked past their row, not turning to look, and set the laptop on a docking station across the aisle, his back to them. If Treadon leaned to the right, he could see the screen as Xander typed on the keyboard.

A cell phone rang. Xander pulled a phone from his front pocket and both Jarren and Treadon fumbled to make sure their phones were powered off. Nothing like getting caught because of a phone vibration from a text.

"It's been confirmed. Start the process. Destroy everything." The voice was tiny through the speaker that Xander held away from his ear, like the cell phone was painful against his skin.

"I will," Xander said.

Xander hit a few more keys on the laptop. Pressed enter. He walked to the end of the room. There was the sound of breaking glass and when Treadon peeked out, he saw that Xander had pulled an axe from the emergency fire case. Xander opened the grate to the farthest row of servers. Jarren's face was slack with shock. "What is he doing?" he whispered. "This is his life's work. There's enough information in these things to make him a God."

Then they heard it. The crunch of metal. The whoosh as the axe fell again and again. The shower of sparks that splashed out of the aisle.

"We have to get out of here." Treadon pulled back the mesh. The swing of the axe was rhythmic. He could measure the distance and movement of Xander from the sounds of destruction.

"Give me one second." Jarren stepped into the main aisle and pressed a key on the keyboard.

"We're totally exposed."

Jarren shrugged him off as he turned his phone back on. The time it took for the phone to load up felt like an eternity. Treadon kept his eyes on the last row, counting the axe strokes, watching pieces of destroyed servers shoot into the aisle.

Jarren took a picture of the screen, pressed a key, took another picture.

"He's coming." They didn't have time to get to the door. Treadon opened the nearest grate and pulled Jarren inside, shutting the gate just as Xander came out of the farthest row.

Smoke started to fill the air along with the sound of a crackling flame. Once the crunching of metal started again, Jarren slipped back out to the computer. "What are you doing? He's started a fire. We need to go." Treadon punctuated his words. "Just take the computer and let's go."

"I don't know the password. And the information we're plugged into will be gone."

Xander was almost done with another row. He was moving at inhuman speed, unbelievable strength.

"Times up." Treadon pulled Jarren behind the first row, farthest from the fire and Xander's axe-wielding chaos. "How are we going to get out of here without him noticing?"

Jarren paced to the end of the row and back as they heard Xander start in on a third row of servers. He stopped and punched the nearest wall in time with Xander's swings. "I knew there were secrets, but I wouldn't believe he would go this far." He punched again.

"We can deal with that later." The smoke was bad enough that Treadon had to lift his shirt up and breathe through the fabric. "What are we going to do?"

"We can't leave before him. He'll hear the door. They'll know someone was down here." Jarren rubbed his knuckles. Treadon was sure they hurt, but the motion looked more like he was thinking. "We have to get him to leave."

"How are you going to do that?"

Jarren pulled out his phone again.

"Are you calling the police? If the police come, we'll be on the morning news. Everyone will know we were here."

"No. I'm texting my dad."

An instant later, a short ding signaled that someone received a text. The hammering paused.

Treadon mouthed the words. "What did you say?"

Jarren held up his screen. *I want to talk. I'm here and I'm coming in.*

He'd lured his dad outside by telling him exactly where he was. Well, not exactly.

They both held their breath. Xander cursed and the axe clanged to the floor. Xander Calivan stalked past the row they hid in. There was a crunch and a smash and then the upper door buzzed.

"Let's go." Treadon pulled open the grate and ran for the door. He paused when he saw that the door was gone, the opening ripped apart like Xander had pulled the door off the hinges rather than taking the time to turn the door handle.

He turned and saw Jarren facing the other direction, watching the room fill with smoke. His body was stiff and angry, pulled between facing his father and trying to save the remaining servers.

Treadon got right in Jarren's face, coughing on the smoke that had a bitter chemical taste. "There's nothing you can do."

"I know." There was no emotion. The switch that turned on and off had short circuited.

They ran up the stairs and out the side door. Jarren ran around the building faster than Treadon could keep up. By the time Treadon came around to the front door, Jarren and Xander stood almost toe to toe in a fierce staring contest.

"There is nothing left for you here." Xander's voice was the same, but different at the same time. The wrong inflections. No emotions.

"I need you to tell me why you shut the company down. You can tell me. I'm your son." The last words were soft.

"Not anymore. Leave before I have you arrested for trespassing." Xander turned away. Treadon caught up to Jarren just in time to catch his shoulder and stop him from going after Xander.

The front doors swung shut and they could see Xander's frame against the glowing fountain of light.

"Tell me that's not my dad," Jarren said.

Treadon kept his hand on Jarren's shoulder as he watched Xander step into the elevator. "You're right. I don't know what that was, but that's not Xander Calivan."

Thirty-One

October 14

There was an unmarked SUV parked at the end of the block. When I walked toward the mailbox, the driver pulled out and drove away. The foster care office is requesting a meeting with both Nolan and Pat. A follow-up. A check-in. Pat's not sure how long she can put them off without letting them know about Nolan's condition. I help get the kids off to school every morning and help with the baby in the evening, but it doesn't feel like enough. There's a pressure in my head like I've climbed a mountain and can't get my ears to pop.

Something bad is coming. I can feel the change, but all I can think about is telling Treadon the truth, explaining to him why I can't Bond, why I can't even give him the chance.

I succeeded that night, alone, seven years old, scared of the dark. I saved the boy. I felt the change, knew I had won. I felt my energy go into the boy, felt his heart start beating again. I was special. I was powerful. I wasn't in danger. I didn't have to leave my family.

But when the boy shifted beneath me. Alive. Awake. I felt strange. Our eyes met. He saw right into me. My chest burned like a hot coal was being pressed into my ribs from the inside, a searing pain that made me want to scream. I rolled off the boy and touched the center of my chest. My fingers traced the circles that were rising from under my skin, burning through, growing out of my own bones, and ripping their way to the surface. My back arched, the pain blinding me as I saw flashes of light.

When it finally stopped, the boy held me in his arms, asking me if I was all right.

I wasn't. He was alive, but he had taken a part of me I wasn't supposed to give. In my hand, covered in my own blood, was an amulet made of Descendant DNA, three circles and three marbles, blue, green, and yellow.

I held my own compass.

I lay stunned for a few seconds, looking down at the compass in my hands, the blood seeping from my chest onto my shirt, the smell of my burnt skin, my chest branded from the way my compass was ripped out of me. The boy saw my hand with the compass. He knew I had healed him. But I was terrified. Even though I was young, I knew I had done something wrong. Like any terrified child, I tried to hide it, cover it up and pretend it didn't happen. The boy was the only witness. I reached up to the boy's head and told him to forget. Not with words, not in a way he could choose. I rewired his mind. I erased his memories.

I was so young, so inexperienced. I have thought back to that moment a thousand times, wondering if I damaged his brain, left him broken like Jake. Because of my fear.

Whoever you are, however I hurt you, boy, I am sorry.

The ironic part is that after that moment, my own memory becomes blurry. I remember running back to my house. I remember empty rooms. Tables tipped over. Chairs shattered. Black dust covering everything. Burn marks on the wall.

Everyone was gone. My house was empty. And all I could think was that I'd done that to them when I'd Bonded. I'd burned them all.

TREADON NELSON

"You two need a shower," Coach Bracken waved a hand in front of his face as Jarren and Treadon stepped off the bus. "Did you stay up all night at a bonfire? I hope neither of you were drinking. This is the big game. All the cards. Win or lose."

"We're ready, Coach." That was the furthest thing from the truth, but they had to play. After what they'd seen, they couldn't let anything seem out of the ordinary. They had to act like they hadn't just watched someone who wasn't Xander Calivan destroy fifteen years of technological advancements with an axe and a bad temper.

Treadon felt dizzy with exhaustion and probably some smoke inhalation, but he jogged out to the center of the field when the refs called for team captain. The world moved forward. The fans cheered or booed. The other players stretched and jogged up and down the field to warm up. It felt so normal and so out of place at the same time. No one knew something was wrong. No one knew they had almost died.

This game was the pinnacle of everything they had worked for. It felt insignificant and essential at the same time.

He wasn't going to lose this game, not because of Xander, not because he'd been rejected by a girl, not because he wanted to fix things for his mom. Treadon wanted to win this game to see for himself how strong he was. He sensed that what he'd seen at XC Energy was the beginning of something bigger, something that was on the edge of his life and pressing in, coming for him. If he won today, he would show himself that he was strong enough for what was coming.

"I guess we won't be seeing my dad here today," Jarren said. "We lost a fan last night."

Treadon watched his friend. "Jarren, I don't know exactly what it was, but that wasn't your dad. It was his body, it was part of him, but he wasn't the same."

Jarren leaned his head back and looked up at the lights that flooded the football field. "It was him and it wasn't him. He was a murderer, but he'd turned a corner. He was helping Vox, but he betrayed him. I don't know who my father is. I may never know."

"He was fighting." Treadon wasn't sure why he said that, but he'd seen it somehow. "That's why we were able to get out. There were two different people in one body. I know that sounds crazy."

Jarren nodded. "Everything about this is crazy. I can't make sense of it." Jarren looked to the other end of the field. "My dad was right. There's nothing for me here. No business. No future. No parents. Maybe football is all I have."

"Not true, but after last night, we could both use a win."

"You mean you want to play?"

"I want to bury these guys six feet under."

They stood up and joined the huddle, jumping with the rest of the team. Treadon saw the weight lift from Jarren's face, saw the excitement of the game push away the unknown. The unexplained. This was something they understood. This was something they could control.

He believed that until he noticed Bridger Michaels glance at the other team, nod slightly with his helmet, pull his gloves on a little too hard. Bridger had been waiting all season for his chance at revenge. Treadon had been so distracted he'd forgotten about the fight, forgotten that Michaels was planning something.

Coach Bracken called everyone in for the huddle, laying out the line-up and the initial strategies. Treadon barely heard him. Michaels made eye contact with Treadon and winked. Michaels had played hard all season. He'd gotten a scholarship with the Oregon coach that Xander had brought down to see Jarren. Now that Michaels had secured his future, there was nothing stopping him.

From throwing the game.

Special teams came off the field and the offensive line ran out, huddling up. Treadon made the call Coach wanted. "Pass back to Phillips, fake run down the middle. Break." He barked the play and the team clapped as one before heading to their position. Treadon grabbed Jarren by the arm.

"Go for a Hail Mary."

"It's the first play of the game."

"I think it's the only one I'm going to get."

Jarren shot him a confused look but nodded.

Treadon bent over, hands open and ready for the football. He looked both ways to check positions. Michaels had three guys on his side. He could tell by the way they shifted. They were going to let the defensive line through. Treadon was prepared. If he could make it through this first drive, maybe he could convince Coach to take Michaels out. Put in a different offensive line.

"Hike." Treadon felt the firm pressure as the football entered his hands and he backpedaled as fast as he could.

There wasn't even a pause. The defense came straight through as Michaels and the others stepped to the side. The first defender bore down on him, spittle flying from his mouth guard. Treadon faked a step to the right, spun left. The defender couldn't adjust and dove past him. Treadon planted his foot and threw the ball as hard as he could. He couldn't see Jarren over the heads of the next two defenders, but he knew he would be there.

Treadon planted his foot to spin out of the next tackle, but something seized control of his mind. His body felt paralyzed, and all sound became muffled. Other noise filled his mind, shooting painfully through his skull. Children crying, yelling. The sound of something smashing, a plate, a glass, the crunch of wood, a door slamming. A single scream, high and piercing that ricocheted around Treadon's skull.

Ellie's face filled his vision. Treadon felt as if the sounds were severing him in half, ripping him apart from the inside.

He knew the late hit was coming, was even aware when the helmet crashed directly into his lower back. There was no pain, only the reverberating echoes of terror as he was swallowed up in welcome unconsciousness.

PART Two

Thirty-Two

TREADON NELSON

Treadon stepped onto campus Monday morning, feeling strange. He'd been cleared health-wise Sunday evening. No concussion. No paralysis. The doctors said he was lucky. The helmet hit close to his spine, but the main impact missed by a centimeter. He escaped with whiplash and a large bruise. They'd warned him to come back if he felt any nausea or dizziness. The truth was he felt both, but he wanted to be at school today. Wanted to tell Ellie there had to be another way. As bad as losing the football game should have hurt, wanting to be with Ellie was more raw, real, than anything that had to do with football.

The usual crowd of students flowed onto campus. He felt bumps and shoves as people moved past him. He was moving too slow, feeling like he was in a fog. He received a few intentional pats on the back.

"Bad luck."

"Sorry about the loss."

"Last year. Bummer."

The pep rally banners on the wall inside his first class seemed to know they had lost the game. The top corner had come loose and flopped over some of the letters. The poster read OD LUCK, WILD CATS.

The only thing that had pulled him out of bed this morning was wanting to see Ellie. He slumped into his desk. Mr. Ashcroft walked in with a pile of graded papers in his hand. Treadon closed his eyes, not sure he could handle the gloating that was sure to come. A piece of paper slid onto his desk as he studied the wood grain. There was a grade marked at the top in red pen. A capital B followed by a plus sign.

Mr. Ashcroft stood next to his desk. Treadon looked up in resignation, waiting for the jibes about the loss, about the pointless purpose of sports and the damaging egos it gave people. That wasn't the message Treadon read on Mr. Ashcroft's face.

There was no contempt, none of his usual distain. He shuffled the papers nervously.

"Sorry about the game." Mr. Ashcroft's nasally voice was offset with a note of humility. "You didn't deserve that ending. You worked hard. Not all of them do."

Worked hard. For what? What was a grade on a math test? What was a win in a football game? Things that should be important, that had always been important, seemed insignificant next to his pull to be with Ellie. To be part of something bigger.

The morning dragged by, but when lunch finally came, he skipped the food line and went straight to the table. He imagined what he would say if Ellie tried to ignore him, if she kept her head turned away and pretended he didn't exist. If he could only explain that he didn't care about another Guardian, he didn't care if she didn't have all of herself to give to him. He didn't need that. She could be who she was, and he could be a part of that. Whatever she needed to be.

Treadon stopped as he approached the table. Ellie wasn't beside Megan. The skaters were eating together, glancing at Ellie's seat. Jarren and Rachel came over and found their chairs, the one Ellie usually sat in stayed empty. Treadon squeezed in on the far side of Megan. He leaned over to talk to Jarren but spoke loud enough for everyone to know they were included in the question.

"Have you seen Ellie?"

Several heads shook in the negative.

"She's probably going out of her way to avoid you." Jarren bit four fries in half. "I mean, she did tell you she wasn't interested last week."

"I know, but she should still be at school, even if she is avoiding me." The dizziness increased and he had trouble focusing on the conversation around him. The nausea was bad enough that he thought he might throw up.

Rachel and Jarren were in their own world. Treadon could tell Jarren had filled Rachel in on the office, the ruined servers, his father's rejection. The mystery behind XC Energy was important, but Treadon couldn't seem to get himself to care. Ellie wasn't here. That was priority number one.

Megan turned toward him. She had a new blue streak in her hair that brought out the light in her eyes. She watched him expectantly, not saying anything.

"Do you know where she is?" Treadon asked her.

"No," Megan said in a flat voice. "I only know where she isn't."

Treadon leaned back. "What's that supposed to mean?"

"A lot of our understanding about life comes from what is absent. Especially when that thing is usually present, then an absence feels physical. Absence feels as real as a presence."

Treadon could only nod. Ellie's absence felt physical at this table, like everyone was avoiding looking at something because it wasn't there and it should be. She should be there.

"She'll be back." Treadon said the words for himself because he couldn't imagine a permanent hole.

"It's possible." Megan's tone implied the opposite. She must have seen the distressed look on Treadon's face. "Ellie helped me see that life is full of better tomorrows. We're never really alone."

Treadon felt a flash of anger and slammed his fists on the table, rattling lunch trays. "You're saying that like she's already gone."

Megan stared at him; her face unreadable. "Because she's just home with a cold."

Treadon stood up, pulling the table and everyone sitting on it three feet to the side. He didn't know if Megan understood what she was saying, that a Descendant of Angels wouldn't get sick with a cold when she could heal broken bones and wipe away wounds. Somehow, Megan understood that if Ellie wasn't here, something was wrong, and she stared at him like she expected him to do something about it.

He remembered her words to him a few days before. *She needs someone, I'm just not sure it's you.*

Treadon turned and pushed away from the table, fighting his way across the lunchroom, barely making it to the men's bathroom before he puked in the toilet. The nausea and dizziness coming to a head as he thought of the possibilities. Ellie was missing. After all her fear, hiding, secrets, and finally learning to trust him.

She couldn't be gone.

He stumbled to the sink, washed his hands, and splashed cold water on his face. He leaned against the porcelain basin to try and clear his head. The door opened and when Treadon looked in the mirror, he saw Jarren leaning casually against the wall.

"What are you doing here?" Treadon asked, his voice scratchy.

"You ditched me at lunch. I was going to give you a swirly, but it looks like you already took care of that."

Treadon shook his head. "I didn't give myself a swirly."

"Seriously, man. Do you need to go back to the hospital?"

Treadon shook his head. They couldn't help him at the hospital. He needed to find Ellie. "I need a favor. Can you give me a ride?"

Thirty-Three

TREADON NELSON

"Are you sure this is the right house?" Jarren pulled into Ellie's driveway. The house number was the same. The street was the same. The neighbor's house looked the same with the large fence and beware of dog sign. Everything else was right, but the house in front of them looked like a strange photoshopped version of the house Treadon visited last week. Only one week and the world felt like it had tipped up and started walking on its hands.

"Yes," Treadon said. "It's the right house, but it looks like someone mowed the lawn and picked up the kid's toys. They might have even painted the door."

"It does look staged to sell," Jarren said. "Are they planning on moving?"

"No. I was here a couple days ago and there were no packing boxes. There's no way."

They both stepped out of the car and saw the For Sale sign at the same time. The breeze picked up and sent the sign knocking against the post with an eerily rhythmic thud, thud, thud.

"She didn't tell me they were moving," Treadon said. "This is weird. I just want to check in on her, make sure she's okay."

"You said she made it pretty clear she didn't want to be serious with you. Don't cross the line into stalking mode."

"I'm not here to ask her out again or pressure her. I'm worried about her, that's all. A friend can worry. What do you know about stalking, anyway."

"Absolutely nothing. I worry more about breaking hearts when they come begging."

"Shut up."

"Shutting up," Jarren said, raising both hands in the air.

Treadon stepped up to the door. Jarren pushed a bush aside and peaked through the front room window.

"What are you doing?"

"There's no one home," Jarren said, hand over his eyes as he pressed his face up to the glass. "Look. They've already moved out the furniture. And cleaned the windows. Look at this thing. I left a smudge with my breath." Jarren rubbed his sleeve against the spotless window. These weren't details Treadon would normally notice, but he was almost a hundred percent sure there had at least been some hard water stains on the outside of the window. These ones were spotless.

Checking the neighborhood to make sure there weren't any nosy neighbors watching, Treadon joined Jarren at the window. Jarren was right. There was no furniture. The house was empty. He could see from the window seat to the kitchen, where he'd sat at the table eating spaghetti with the kids. He'd picked up Ellie for a date on Wednesday. Now it was Monday. Barely four days. An entire household picked up and moved with a husband on life support and kids in foster care and a mom working two jobs. It was impossible.

"She would have at least told me she was leaving." Treadon pulled out his phone to check for texts, like there would be a new one from her because he willed it.

"Would she?" Jarren raised his eyebrows, a sympathetic invite to accept reality.

Treadon jumped back onto the porch and knocked. Hard. The door swung open. The latch had barely been resting against the door frame.

The entry hall was immaculate. The rack that had been loaded with kids coats and backpacks was gone. The shoes from the floor. Gone. There weren't even any holes in the wall from where the rack had been hanging.

Treadon felt a wave of dizziness, the hall warping and waving in his vision, looking twice as long and half as wide. He leaned against the door frame and closed his eyes. He felt pressure on his arm.

"Take it easy," Jarren said. "Deep breaths. Breakups are hard."

Treadon felt a surge of anger that cleared his head. "This isn't a breakup. Something is wrong. People are missing. This whole family could be in danger. Ellie was scared of something since I met her—maybe they finally caught up with her."

"Who?"

"I don't know." Treadon pushed off the wall. "Maybe they left a ransom note or a clue or something."

"This isn't an episode of Unsolved Crimes. They really could have moved."

Treadon whirled around. Jarren still hadn't stepped inside. "And your dad could totally be himself and set fire to his own business."

Jarren gripped the railing on the porch and a muscle flexed in his jaw. "Don't bring my dad into this."

"I'm sorry." Treadon rubbed his eyes, trying to get them to focus. He swallowed to push the nausea back. "I shouldn't have said that."

"I've tossed and turned about it all weekend while you were in the hospital. I didn't want to believe you. But I saw it too. My dad never acted like that, never lost his temper like that, even before when he was a bad dad. But that has nothing to do with this, with a girl who moved away with her family. It's totally normal."

Treadon shook his head. "No. No, this isn't normal. And Ellie wasn't normal. She was special."

"Every girl is special."

"No. I mean she was different than us." Treadon had promised not to tell, but that was to protect her. If she was already gone, then he needed Jarren's help to find her. "She was a Descendent of Angels. She could do things. Make people ignore her. She's the one who healed Rachel when she landed on her neck."

"You've lost your mind," Jarren said, backing up on the porch. "Let me take you back to the hospital because you're delusional."

"Wait." Treadon reached out and pulled Jarren into the house. He shut the door behind them before Jarren could leave, before a neighbor noticed them standing in the doorway. "Let's walk through this. Rachel got hurt, do you remember?"

Again, Jarren had to turn his head to get his emotions under control. "It was close, I admit. I thought she'd broken her neck. But she got right up. She wasn't hurt."

"She was," Treadon said, squeezing Jarren's arm. "I saw Ellie touch her, but no one else paid attention because she can do that thing with people's energy. Make them not notice her. But I saw her. She healed Rachel. It's because of Ellie that Rachel is okay. We owe it to Ellie to make sure she's okay."

"Look at me." Jarren took Treadon's face in both his hands. "I want you to listen to what you're saying. There is a girl at school that is an angel and can heal people. Come on, dude. This is the real world."

Treadon didn't knock Jarren's hands away like he wanted to. He reached out and grabbed Jarren's shirt, pulling the fabric into his fist and lifting. Both of them were breathing hard, tensed. Treadon could see Jarren getting ready to fight back.

"Do it." Treadon pushed Jarren against the wall. "Hit me. See if it wakes me up. See if it makes the world make sense because it doesn't anymore. Don't you get it? Nothing makes sense anymore. If we can agree that your dad isn't your dad. If we believe he was possessed or taken over by something completely different, then how far of a stretch is it to believe there is the opposite of that evil? If there are things that possess people, then maybe there is something out there that can fight it. If there is sorrow, there can be joy. If there is water, somewhere there's fire. If there are demons out there with a triangle on their neck that can murder children and leave them lying in their own blood, maybe, just maybe, there are angels."

Jarren's fingers tightened, his thumbs digging into Treadon's neck. For a moment, Treadon was worried he'd really have to fight his friend. But then Jarren sagged. He dropped his hands from Treadon's face and neck. He grabbed Treadon's wrists and shoved his hands off his shirt. Treadon let go and put his palms forward in a gesture of peace.

"I've always believed that I was in control," Jarren said. "That I could figure things out on my own if I needed to, but in a world that is that messed up, if there are these greater powers fighting over our head, what's the point? What are we fighting for?"

Treadon put his hand on Jarren's shoulder. He could read his friend's pain, how long he had been fighting to impress his dad, what this failure felt like for him. And now his dad was gone, somehow, in a way they didn't understand. In a way that left them helpless to know what to do.

"Maybe our job is to save an angel. Keep the world a little brighter, one girl at a time."

Jarren rolled his eyes. Treadon could tell it was as much to hide his emotions as it was to make fun of him. It still helped break the tension that had twisted up between them. "You really are a hopeless romantic."

"I have to have some hope, or I wouldn't be here."

"Have you thought about the consequences of stalking someone descended from angels? They might have a higher court if she presses charges."

"I'm not stalking," Treadon said. "If we find her and she's fine, I'll back off. I promise."

"You don't have to promise me."

There was a pause, but there didn't seem to be a lot more to say.

"I'll check the bedrooms." Jarren moved through the living room and down the other hallway. Treadon opened the bedroom where Nolan Greyson had been. There was no medical equipment, no bed. An empty room.

Jarren came back. "I want to get a number for their cleaning company. There isn't a speck of dust anywhere. Not even a smudge on the glass in the bathroom. It's too clean. Like cleaning up before the cops sweep for evidence."

"That's a dark twist to your doubt."

"Let's just say," Jarren said, running his finger across the windowsill in a white glove check. "I'm starting to come around to your way of thinking. This doesn't feel like the normal state of a house after a frantic move."

A wave of nausea hit Treadon again. He thought about Ellie, somewhere in the dark, alone. He saw her eyes when he closed his and imagined her facing down a powerful enemy. One he couldn't see or even imagine.

"Woah," Jarren said. "You're looking pale. I mean even for a white guy. You better sit down before you fall and get your blood all over this clean crime scene."

Treadon stumbled over to the window seat. Jarren sat down beside him.

"Let's walk through this logically," Jarren said. "Where could we get information about Ellie and the family she was living with? Did you say Gabe helps people, saves lost kids or something?"

"I think he's out of town. Besides, I don't think he'll believe us."

Jarren scoffed. "I'm not sure I believe us."

"Maybe we can track down the rest of the family," Treadon said. "They're in the system. Let's try the foster care office. They can't have just disappeared."

Thirty-Four

ABIGAIL NELSON

Abigail heard the phone ringing inside as she fit her key into the doorknob, her other hand full of groceries. She turned the key and pushed the door open. She dropped the groceries on the table and pulled her phone from her purse.

"Hello?"

She listened silently as a monotone voice repeated a recorded message.

Gabe walked into the room as she lowered the phone from her ear and stared at the screen.

Abigail jumped, pressing her phone to her chest. "I didn't know you were back."

"I didn't mean to startle you," Gabe said. "Who was that?"

"It was the school," Abigail said. She tried to keep her voice even. Ever since Treadon's accident, ever since the Unguarded started disappearing, she felt like there were moments when the slightest movement would push her over the edge, and she would sink into a corner and let the pressure crush her. "Treadon's missed a class. I know he left for school this morning." Abigail pulled her stress inside, fighting to hide her physical symptoms. She set her phone down, proud that her fingers weren't shaking.

"I used to play hooky with my brother," Gabe said with a small shrug. Abigail tried to talk herself through this logically. It wasn't unheard of for a teacher to accidentally mark someone absent. Or for a senior to skip a class. Nothing unusual. Everything was normal.

She still couldn't shake the feeling.

"Treadon doesn't skip class," Abigail said. "And with all the weird things going on, I'm worried. Maybe he's feeling sick and had to go back to the hospital."

"I think you would have got more than a recorded message." Gabe moved closer to her, one hand out as if he meant to comfort her. Touch her. Their eyes met as they realized it at the same time. He took a breath and changed directions. Reaching for the groceries instead. He pulled a block of cheese from one of the plastic bags and held it in his large hands. He studied the cheese like it held the secrets of the universe.

"I know you've been worried about him." Gabe turned the cheese over. "I worry about you too. You need to know that. That I do care."

Abigail didn't know what hurt worse, when he was cold and aloof, pretending that it was easy for him to have this wall between them, or when he tried to make her feel better by acknowledging it was hard for him. So many years of walking side by side, unable to lean on each other, unable to get closer. A missing Descendant creating an impenetrable wall between them. How long would he hold out? How long would the bond demand his full devotion?

"You're right. It was probably a mistake. Treadon's fine." Abigail took the cheese from Gabe's hand and put it in the fridge, keeping her back straight, a fake smile on her lips.

"You could check the map," Gabe said. "Just to be sure."

It was a peace offering. Gabe would never suggest using the Descendant technology casually in the middle of the day, but he wanted her to know he cared. And she heard the message.

They cleared the table and Abigail pulled the map out of the hidden compartment. She rolled it out and spread it across the clean surface. Gabe leaned closer, their shoulders an inch from touching. She placed her thumb in the small square in the bottom corner of the map. The surface flashed beneath her hand and began to glow. The map looked like a satellite picture taken from space, the earth's surface cast in its own shadow. The light array was not limited to modern electrical lights that were lit with technology.

The countries with the largest populations glowed the brightest.

Abigail put a finger on the map and turned the earth until the shape of the western coast of North America was centered. She placed her pointer fingers close together and then pulled them apart, dragging them toward the outside of the image. The map shifted, zooming in.

"Do you see him?" Gabe asked. Too quickly. He paced away from the map and then paced back again, exhaling his breath next to her while she looked. Like he did care, and he was not immune to the anxiety that constantly sat on her chest, that the forces they fought would someday come too close to home. He was usually better at covering his emotions, but his clear vulnerability in this moment wedged into the already weak cracks in her heart. She let her fingers slide closer, almost touching his hand, when she noticed something weird.

The map zoomed into Southern California, but the lights were missing in a large area. Abigail used her fingers to spin the map and zoom in closer. She wasn't wrong. There were no lights. A good part of Northern Los Angeles was blank. Not the dark, energy-absorbing emptiness she saw when the fenris were present, but the blank emptiness that engulfed the map where life failed to thrive. An entire section of the city looked completely deserted, lifeless, like the middle of the Sahara Desert.

"Something's wrong," Abigail said. "There's no one here." She placed her hand on Gabe's, not in the comforting way she had intended a moment before, but with a desperate pressure, wanting him to be able to see what she saw.

Gabe leaned closer. "How is this possible?"

"I don't know," Abigail answered. She pulled her hand away, the heat from his skin beginning to seep deeper. Gabe paced back and forth again, his body stiff with tension. She wished she could calm him, reassure him. He knew how to fight an enemy, but how would he protect them from something he didn't understand?

"Is it an evacuation?" Gabe asked.

"No. It's moving. Spreading out." Abigail zoomed in with her fingers until houses and streets became clear, until she saw the familiar shape of her own neighborhood, the outline of her own house dark and shadowed. "And it's coming closer, towards us."

Gabe took three long steps to the front door and threw it open. He stepped out and looked up at the sky like he expected the sun to be blotted out. He moved like an animal, graceful and powerful, pent up, always ready to spring.

On the map, Gabe's light burned a golden orange, the aura of a Guardian. Her aura pulsed a soft yellow, the same as an average human. Abigail watched as the emptiness approached them on the map, until it was right over them. She stared with her eyes wide as their own auras were engulfed and disappeared.

Nothing happened. She felt no sensation or loss. She could still breathe. She studied the map. They were gone.

No light. Not her own. Not even Gabe's.

Abigail watched the map for another moment and then moved to the porch with Gabe.

"Do you see anything, feel anything?" Gabe asked, the confusion on his face caused deep wrinkles in his forehead as he stared at the sky. Abigail wanted to reach up and smooth them out. Instead, she took a step back.

"No." Abigail shrugged. "There's nothing." She watched an old man walk by with his dog on a leash. She could see his yellow energy pulsing from his core. She looked at Gabe, his orange aura waving powerfully around his solid frame. "I can see your aura out here, just not on the map. Maybe the map has a glitch. Maybe it's broken."

"In only one place?" Gabe asked, shaking his head. "No, no, your vision is being blocked. He's preventing you from watching."

"Who?" She knew the answer. The demon who stole Gabe's Descendant all those years ago. The man who was taking the children out from under them now. "The leader of the Triune."

"Yes. He knows I work with a watcher. He knows you're out there."

"Even if he knows exactly where I am, why would he block me from seeing myself? What good would that do?"

Gabe pressed his lips together. His arms lifted slightly, like he was ready to sweep her off her feet and carry her away from here. Then his fingers tightened into fists. "He doesn't know you're here."

"But he's blocking me from seeing myself."

"He's not. He doesn't know."

Abigail's worry boiled over and she had to brush an angry tear from her cheek. "What doesn't he know? What are you talking about?"

"He doesn't know where *you* are, just that you exist."

"Okay. Why is he blocking me from seeing Los Angeles?"

Gabe's mouth opened slightly, a look somewhere between excitement and terror.

"You need to find Treadon," Gabe said. "Call him. Get him home now. I want both of you here, safe, together."

Abigail rocked back in surprise. "Tell me what's going on. What does Treadon have to do with this?"

Gabe took a deep breath. "If Caden Bachman is trying to hide something from you, but he doesn't know where you are, then he can only block your vision of what he's doing, from where he is. Don't you see? It means he's here, Abigail. After chasing leads from Mexico to Indonesia, the leader of the Triune is right here."

Thirty-Five

TREADON NELSON

Treadon read the last direction off Jarren's phone. "Turn left on Green Street. The office should be a few buildings down," he said.

He pointed to a two-story stucco building with a street address on the door, but no business sign. Jarren swerved across the lane to get into the parking lot, cutting off a purple minivan. He received an angry honk for his trouble. He pulled into a badly finished parking lot and drove to the far side with an empty space on either side of his car.

"You know this car is indestructible, right?" Treadon said. "You could park in the middle of the street, and it would probably be sitting pristine in the middle of a twenty-car pile-up."

"Just because it doesn't scratch, doesn't mean I want people bashing their doors into my baby." Jarren got a thoughtful look on his face. "I still haven't seen what happens when I turn the security system up to level ten. Maybe I should park closer to someone."

"Seriously? You'd test your car's security system on unsuspecting foster parents?"

"You were the one complaining about where I parked."

"Let's go." Treadon exaggerated speed walking to get across the entire parking lot faster. Despite the jokes, Treadon felt an increasing urgency to find Ellie, to know that she was safe, even if that meant knowing she didn't want to see him again. They stepped inside the front doors. He heard a buzzing. He reached for his phone, but his back pocket was empty.

"I left my phone in your car." Treadon groaned.

"Do you want to go back for it?" Jarren shifted from foot to foot. Treadon could read his impatience. Jarren had his own worries with his dad, but Treadon was grateful he'd come with him.

"Forget it," Treadon said. "I want to see if we can learn anything here. I'll check my messages when we're done."

On the second floor they found the door labeled "Los Angeles County Field Office." The door opened toward them right as Jarren reached for the handle. An exhausted-looking man in a suit escorted two young children with a hand on each of their backs. A boy with bangs covering his eyes, and the other, a girl with brown curls, each carried a black garbage bag held tight against their chest. Treadon could read a feeling of fear, of confusion. He thought of Ellie—unsure of what the future held for her. He squeezed the door handle too tight as he held the door open for the trio.

Jarren followed him into a large room divided into offices by temporary walls that were solid on the bottom, top half made of glass. Ahead of him, down the hallway created by the office dividers, stood a tall counter with two attendants staring at computers. One attendant was a middle-aged man, his hair slicked back against his head. He had a long nose and a weak chin. The other was an older woman wearing bifocals. She had age spots up her neck and the extra skin there hung in tandem with the chain holding her bifocals in place.

Treadon approached the man and waited for him to look up. He didn't.

"Excuse me, sir?" Treadon said, trying to remain as polite as possible. He could already read the stiff way the man sat, his focus on his current task, and the annoyance at having someone in front of him that he couldn't immediately guess the reason for their visit. This guy liked efficiency and very short interactions with other human beings.

The man sighed and looked up. "What can I do for you?"

"I'm looking for someone in your system." Treadon tried to speak slowly, but the rising anxiousness in his chest made the words come out louder than he intended. He repeated himself, softer, leaning forward. Several heads inside the office dividers swiveled to see who had raised their voice. The office was way too quiet. The tick of a clock. The brush of a file folder being shifted on a desk. Every sound echoed through the room. His raised voice seemed like some kind of code violation. "I know she was in a foster home, but she's gone. The whole family is gone."

"Are you next of kin?" Flat. Checklist question, like he hadn't registered the fact that a family was missing. Or he didn't care if it didn't fall under his jurisdiction.

"No."

"Do you have written permission from the legal guardians or foster parents to access personal records?"

"No. How would I have gotten written permission if they're missing?" This time Treadon didn't keep his voice down.

"Do you have legal court papers signed by a judge?"

"Please."

The man softened enough to shake his head.

"Has she been missing for twenty-four hours? At that point, you would need to call the police and file an official missing person report. I'm sorry I can't help you here unless you're interested in becoming a foster parent."

The man lifted a stamp and slammed it down on something behind the counter. "If you'll excuse me."

He picked up a pile of papers and stepped into a back room. Treadon's fingers curled around the edge of the counter. Anger raced through him, competing against the raging anxiety. He flexed his knees, ready to jump over the counter and corner the man in the back room. If civility couldn't help him find Ellie, he wasn't above threats.

"My friend here loves cats." Treadon felt a hand on his arm, a squeeze. He turned a little too quickly and knocked Jarren's hand off his arm. Jarren sent him a look. A condemning and begging glance that told Treadon everything he needed to know. He should have let Jarren talk first, work his magic with people. Now they only had one option left and the woman liked cats.

"I used to have a cat," Treadon said, trying to follow Jarren's lead. "When I was little. It ran away." Three short sentences. He felt like a robot. He had no idea how Jarren acted so natural under stress.

"I have three," the woman said with a smile. "A tabby, a hairless, and a Persian. They're all spoiled rotten, but they know who their mommy is."

"We're doing a report in English," Jarren said. "And we were wondering if you could tell us more about the foster system."

The woman leaned back and laced her fingers together. This was a subject closer to her heart than cats.

"There are over sixty thousand children in the foster system in the state of California. There are too many children and not enough resources. Each child deserves a chance for the brightest future we can offer them, but trauma at an early age can be detrimental. They say the single most powerful factor for a child is having one trusted adult in their lives. That can make fostering a child literally life changing."

"You really care about them, don't you?" Treadon stepped closer to the woman's side of the counter. Jarren had gone quiet, stepping back, and looking down at his feet. One trusted adult. Something Jarren hadn't got from his mom or his dad.

"Of course," the woman said. "Every child is important and there is always hope for the future."

"I met some great kids the other day," Treadon said. "I played with them, and they meant a lot to me. They had a great future." He emphasized the word *had* and lowered his eyes. He shook his head back and forth.

The woman took the bait. "Had?" She leaned forward so Treadon could see her eyes over the top of her glasses. "What do you mean?"

"It looks like the family up and moved in the middle of the night. Without a word. Just whoosh and nothing."

The strings on her glasses waggled back and forth as she shook her head. "They aren't allowed to move while caring for foster children without the appropriate paperwork. We would know if they had moved."

"Is there a way you can make sure? I know the dad was sick. I would hate to think anything had happened to them."

"I can't give you any information."

Treadon waved his hand. "You don't have to give me any information, but if I told you their names and the address, could you confirm that they filled out the paperwork and only moved. Their house looked like something bad might have happened." That was a bit of a stretch since the house looking mysteriously clean hardly meant something bad had happened.

The woman shifted, not convinced.

"Please. I only want to know if they're okay."

She sagged and then glanced around.

"What were the names of the children?"

Treadon thought for a second. He started with the twins. "Mike and Foster Jenkins."

"And the names of the foster parents?"

"Pat." Treadon thought back to the night Ellie had introduced them. He could hear her voice in his mind as clearly as if she was speaking next to him. "Pat and Nolan Grayson."

The woman tapped on the keyboard for a few minutes, while clicking her mouse and squinting at the screen. Each click seemed to increase a shadow of concern over her face. She glanced at Treadon.

"When did you say you played with these kids?"

"Last week. I saw them on Wednesday."

The woman shook her head. "You must be mistaken. Mike and Foster Jenkins were never placed with the Graysons, and the Graysons haven't had foster children for over a year."

Treadon was shaking his head before she finished speaking. "That's wrong." He leaned over the counter to try and see the screen, but she turned it away from him. He reached up and twisted his fingers into his hair. The ache in his head and the nausea from this morning returned full force. He felt dizzy and confused. This couldn't be right. Had Ellie lied? Treadon was sure he would have been able to tell. Were the records wrong? A twisting dread wound around his chest making it hard to breathe.

If someone went to all that effort to clean the house spotless, how much harder would it be to change some numbers in a computer?

"No. Listen, there were more. There was a baby." Treadon couldn't remember the baby's name. "There was a boy. Jake. His name was Jake and he needed Ellie. He needed her." He couldn't keep the desperation from his voice, and he found himself leaning too far over the counter.

The woman's eyes grew large, and she leaned back in her chair like she could get away from him. He was losing his chance. He tried to calm down. He straightened, placing his hands on the counter like anchors to hold himself back and took a deep breath. "Can you check on one more person for me? Eleanor Agarwal. Can you just let me know if she's safe?"

She tapped a few more keys. Treadon could see that curiosity was pulling her forward even though she had no intention of giving him anymore information.

"I'm sorry. We have no record of an Eleanor Agarwal in the system."

"That's impossible." This time the anxiety and dizziness came out as anger. He slammed both fists on the counter. "I was with her Wednesday. I talked to her and drove her home and she walked in the door."

The woman reached for a radio. "You need to leave now, before I call security."

Treadon stepped closer, ready to reach across the counter and pull the computer screen to face him. Jarren pulled him back.

"Let's go," Jarren said in a low voice. "There's got to be another way."

"I'm not giving up," Treadon said. "You heard her. She's as important as every other person, maybe more. Maybe a lot more." The other attendant came back through the door with two uniformed officers. A commotion at the entrance made them all turn.

The door slammed open and a man in a disheveled suit dragged in a boy who was flopping and flailing wildly. Jake. His sweater sleeve was ripped, and he twisted in the man's grip, but his arms were tight to his side, his fists buried in the front pocket of his sweater.

"Can I get some help over here?" the man called, trying not to lose his grip on Jake's flailing form.

The two uniformed officers glanced at Treadon and Jarren and decided that the other problem was more immediate. They quickly made their way around the desk and down the hallway.

Even with three grown men, they struggled to get Jake through the door and into one of the partitioned offices. Treadon could see the group through the clear wall as they tried to get the boy to sit in a chair.

"Now's our chance. Let's get out of here." Jarren pulled Treadon toward the exit. Treadon stumbled forward. It was Jake. Ellie's Jake.

"Stop," Treadon yelled. "Stop touching him." He darted into the office and shoved one of the officers into the wall. He pulled the other man away from the boy, and the other officer turned to face Treadon.

Without the pressure of the hands on him, Jake turned into a rag doll and collapsed into the chair. His head rolled back against the seat. The only movement was the quick rising and falling of his chest as he gasped for air.

"He doesn't like to be touched." Treadon stepped back, hands raised. They weren't armed, but all three of the men looked like they were ready to tackle him to the ground. "I'm sorry, but I needed you to let go of him."

"What's going on?" The man with the greasy hair demanded from the hall.

"The kid tried to run," said the man who dragged Jake through the door. He tucked in his shirt and straightened his tie. "The foster parents called me, and I caught him a couple blocks from their house. It's the third time he's run."

Treadon stepped toward Jake. "Can you hear me? Are you okay?"

Jake gave no response. He continued to stare blankly at the ceiling, his head lolled back against the chair.

"Buddy. Jake. Can you tell me what happened? Where is your family?" Treadon leaned back although every nerve in his body wanted to take the boy by the shoulders and shake him. Jake showed no signs of awareness.

Treadon knelt next to the chair, careful to only let his fingers touch the armrest.

"Jake," Treadon whispered softly. "Where is Ellie?"

At the sound of her name, Jake blinked for the first time.

Treadon hated that he could read the emotions. Jake didn't trust him or anyone. Jake wanted to do this himself, but he couldn't. He needed help and Treadon was the closest thing he had.

Jake continued to stare at the ceiling, his lips twisting like he was fighting his own impulses. An internal wrestle warred on his face. Jake slowly pulled his arms away from his body, slipping his hands out of the pocket of his hoodie. One hand had a journal gripped so tightly that the pages were bent. The other hand was held in a tight fist. The fingers uncurled slowly to reveal a pendant. Three different sized circles, one inside of the other.

Jake held the items out to Treadon, jaw flexed, a muscle standing out under his skin. A single tear slipped from the corner of Jake's eye and ran down his cheek.

Thirty-Six

TREADON NELSON

Treadon stared at the necklace gripped in his fist as he sat in the passenger seat of the Aston Martin. Jarren hadn't started the car yet. Treadon felt like he was an expanding balloon, stretched so thin he would pop. The security guards had physically ejected Jarren and Treadon from the building. Jake had stopped fighting and Treadon's last view of him was the sagging form in the office chair.

"What next?" Jarren asked.

"I've seen this before, this shape, but it was moving. Always moving." He let the necklace slip through his hand until the chain dangled from the tips of his fingers.

"Where?" Jarren asked. "Claire's?"

Treadon closed his eyes. "No. I've seen this almost every day since I was a little kid. In Gabe's office."

"You think your stepdad took Ellie?" Jarren looked back and forth between the twisting necklace charm and Treadon's face.

"He's not my stepdad." The response was immediate, automatic. "But maybe it is time to ask for some answers."

"Home it is." Jarren pushed the start button and the car roared to life. They sped out of the parking lot. Jarren shifted gears as he took the on-ramp to the 405. The wind roared past the car and created a bubble of pressure around Treadon's ears. He could almost see the black SUVs pulling closer, forcing them faster. It was in his head. There were dozens of cars around them, driving like normal people on a normal day, but Treadon felt like his lungs had collapsed. He couldn't pull in air. He leaned forward and pressed his arms against his chest, crossed, like he was preparing to be laid in a casket.

"Calm down." Jarren slapped Treadon on the back like he had a chicken bone caught in his throat. "Just breathe."

"Keep your hands on the wheel." Treadon managed to choke out. "I'm fine."

"And I'm a college graduate with loving parents," Jarren said. "I've seen it before. It's a panic attack and it can feel like you're dying. Just keep breathing. I'll get you home." Jarren changed lanes and sped up. That did nothing to help the increasing pressure on Treadon's chest, but his friend's hand on his back made it feel like there were two of them holding up the weight of an elephant.

When they pulled into the garage at Treadon's house, they both sat for a moment while the garage door closed. Treadon took as deep of breaths as he could, but he felt like he was breathing through a straw.

"Give it time. You got this." Jarren sounded like he was prepping Treadon for a football play.

"How would you know?" Treadon didn't mean to sound angry. It took a lot of force to get the words out.

"I used to get them when I was younger. At night. When Rachel and her mom were gone. I remember thinking I was going to die alone in the dark from an invisible boa constrictor."

Treadon could feel his heart rate coming back down. The pressure on his chest backed off, but the ache remained. Ellie was missing and all he had was a journal and a necklace. His only lead was that Gabe had the same charm.

He turned to his friend. "I'm sorry. I didn't know about the panic attacks."

"It was a long time ago," Jarren said. "I had them for a few years after the brain surgery. And I couldn't go running to my dad, so I learned to talk myself through them. Learned that the sun always rose no matter how long the night seemed to last."

Treadon nodded, breathing as deep as the tension in his chest would allow, thinking of Jarren facing this pain alone as a little kid. "I'm sorry, man. That sucks."

"You suck. Are you good enough to face the music and ask Conan the Barbarian what he does in his spare time?"

Treadon laughed in forced huffs of air. "Conan wasn't from the eighties."

"There was a remake."

"No, there wasn't."

"Don't judge me."

Treadon nodded, not ready, but not willing to wait any longer. "Let's go."

They got out of the car and entered the house through the garage door.

Gabe was on his feet before they'd crossed the threshold. He and Abigail had been sitting close, heads nearly touching as they bent over a map. Abigail jumped up from the table and came across the room. She wrapped both arms around Treadon's shoulders and pressed her face against his shirt. Her eyes were swollen from rubbing.

"What's going on? Are you okay?" Treadon asked her.

"Where have you been? You skipped school. I didn't know where you were, and you didn't answer your phone."

Treadon felt a stab of guilt. He hadn't thought to check his phone after they left the foster care office. He'd been too distracted, too sick, but his anger was able to make him push his guilt aside. "I was busy." He pushed past Abigail and marched down the hall, throwing open the door to Gabe's office. The perpetual motion device moved at its constant rate on its pedestal, three circles, three marbles, rotating around each other. "What is that? And where did you get it?"

Gabe and Abigail had followed him halfway down the hall. Jarren flopped down, his head at the end of the couch that let him see down the hall. He gave Treadon an encouraging nod.

"It's nothing," Abigail said. "A decoration. Why are you asking this now?"

Treadon could see the lie in his mom's face, saw the hesitation in Gabe.

"I need help finding someone that went missing and she has something to do with this," Treadon said, jabbing his finger in the direction of Gabe's ornament. "I need to know where this comes from."

"Who's missing?" Gabe asked.

"A girl from school. She didn't come today, and she's never missed before, and when I went to her house it was abandoned. I'm worried about her, and I thought, since you said you help people, that you could help her."

Gabe's face didn't show any emotion, but the way his muscles tensed, his fingers flexed, made him look like he'd been caught in a trap. Like he felt any way he answered this question would get him in trouble.

He and Abigail shared a look and Treadon read an apology that didn't make sense. That made him angry before they had even answered.

"What could be more important than someone who has gone missing," Treadon asked. "What else is going on that you're not telling me? That you're keeping from me?"

Treadon saw all those things, their distraction by something bigger, their secrets that had always been there, but he'd chosen to ignore. He wasn't going to take this anymore, not if it affected Ellie, not if there was a chance he could do something.

Jarren lifted a magazine from the coffee table, acting like this was a normal family discussion and he was just a fly on the wall, but his posture said he was listening to every word.

"What are you talking about?" Abigail stepped back, but a shadow of guilt crossed her face. "Why would you say something like that?"

"Because I can see it," Treadon said, exhaustion pulling his arms to his side. "I can see it in the way you look at each other and the way you talk to me and the way your eyes never land where they're supposed to. Something is going on, and if you are going to use it as an excuse to not help me, I want to know what it is. I deserve to know."

"We never said we wouldn't help," Abigail said.

"But you were thinking it."

"Abigail." Gabe kept his voice low, but firm. "I think he's right, and you know we are out of time. The best way to protect him is with understanding. He needs to know."

Abigail sagged, gripping Treadon's arm for a minute with an intensity that could stop the turn of the earth. Then she nodded. "You start."

Gabe turned to Treadon, straightening his shoulders like he was trying to impress the jury at his own trial. "I am not who you think I am. Sixty years ago I was chosen by a woman to be her Guardian. She was not an average human. She was descended from powerful beings, three beings that were called angels. With the commitment I made to protect her, I was given abilities, strength, knowledge, that allow me to live longer, heal faster. The amulet on the desk is a symbol of what I am."

There was silence for a moment, a moment that should have been filled with doubt and disbelief, but there was too much, too many things that clicked into place. Treadon could see the truth in Gabe's statement, could see the relief flow through him as he released a secret he had been holding for too long. Treadon felt the amulet in his pocket and thought of Ellie's fear. She was being hunted. And Gabe had been hunting people like her. Had Ellie been hiding from Gabe? Or someone like Gabe?

"I knew you couldn't get those arms without steroids." Jarren waved his hand in the air when everyone turned and looked at him. "Or something supernatural. Just so everyone knows I was right about that."

"Where is your Descendant now?" Treadon glanced at his mom. Could she be a Descendant this whole time without him knowing?

Abigail saw his look and shook her head. "Not me. We met later, after..."

"After I'd lost my Descendant. She disappeared almost twenty years ago, and I've spent those years searching. Not just for her, but for other Descendants. Descendants who are too young to have chosen a

Guardian. We call them Unguarded, and they're being hunted. Abigail and I have been trying to save them before they get taken."

"Let me get this straight," Treadon said. "You're not normal. I guess I always knew that, and you are?" He pointed at Abigail. "You aren't a part of this world and Gabe still stays here and acts like one of us? Why?"

Abigail answered. "I'm an Ordinary, but I can see. I can see the light that every living thing on earth puts off. I can see when an Unguarded inherits their knowledge, when they're ready to be trained. I've helped Gabe with his search all these years. It felt like the right thing to do."

"And you never told me because?"

"It's dangerous," Abigail took a step closer. "There was always a chance that they would try to stop me, that they would try to stop Gabe. And if that happened, if I led them here, to you, and anything happened to you, it would be my fault."

"Who would try and stop you?" Jarren asked. His eyes were wide; his fists gripped the corner of the couch.

"The Triune," Gabe said. "The demons who are trying to eradicate the Descendants of Angels from the earth."

Jarren swallowed. "The Triune. Angels and Demons. You know this is all really wild. Totally far-fetched."

He said the words, but Treadon could see that his friend had clung to this reality because of his dad. Treadon believed in Angels. He'd told Ellie he did. He'd believed who Ellie was, but this? The idea that his own mother had been involved and never told him was harder to swallow than the fact that Ellie could heal broken bones.

"If there are demons and angels," Jarren asked, studying his nails like he was debating whether to get a manicure or not, "does that mean sometimes a demon could take over someone, change them?"

"Yes," Gabe answered. "We call them Possessed."

"Creative. Someone dug deep for that one." Jarren pushed up off the couch and stretched like he didn't care, like he was slightly bored, but every muscle was tensed, telling Treadon the opposite. "What do you do for someone that is Possessed?"

"There is nothing to do," Gabe said. "Possession is a contracted choice, although coerced sometimes. Once an Ordinary agrees to a possession, it cannot be undone. They're as good as dead. Worse than dead. There is a special prison where we hold them until the physical body gives out and the demon essence is forced to leave."

"You mean until they die?" Jarren asked. "You can't help the person? Even if they were forced or threatened?"

"Possession is an agreement, a contractual binding," Gabe said. "The soul agreed to the exchange, even when it is coerced, it would require the demon essence to be destroyed and we haven't had the power to do that since the twin daggers were lost."

"How do you protect people then, what good are you if you can't save people after they're possessed?" Jarren asked.

"We bring light and hope to mankind so that they have their own willpower to resist."

"You're failing!" Jarren threw a pillow from the couch. Gabe caught it. "There's so much darkness that a thousand angels couldn't hold it back, let alone a pathetic Guardian." He was breathing hard, fists clenched, jaw muscles flexed. Treadon felt a shifting beneath his feet like he was losing his balance, a wave of dizziness washed over him.

Jarren believed that his dad was Possessed. It would explain a lot of things, but Jarren wasn't about to tell Gabe so he could drag him away to a prison to die. And Treadon wasn't about to betray his friend.

Jarren closed his eyes, like he was physically pushing something down inside of him. He let out a fake laugh. "Do you know what this is? You're all one toy short of a happy meal. I've got a few errands to run and I'm going to let you work out this family drama in privacy." He picked up his phone that he'd set on the coffee table and came around the couch to pat Gabe on his large deltoids. "Still, I'd like to know your real secret behind these babies."

Gabe gave Jarren a deadpan stare. Jarren just smiled bigger. Treadon was amazed that his friend could cover his fear so completely and turn it into a joke, face down a coiled rattle snake by patting it on the head. Before Gabe could respond, Jarren left in a cloud of festering silence.

Treadon wrestled with his promise and the need to break it. Ellie had been hiding and Abigail had admitted she could see them. If

Abigail and Gabe were the very people Ellie had been hiding from, this could be pure betrayal.

"I believe you," Treadon said. "I know that the Descendants of Angels exist. I've met one."

"What?" Abigail asked.

"The girl that I need you to help me find. She's a Descendant. And now she's missing."

"What do you mean she's missing?" Gabe asked.

"I went to her house, and it was empty like they'd never lived there. I went to the foster care office, and they said they didn't have any record of her. I was with her last Wednesday and now she's gone."

Gabe and Abigail shared another look. This one was different but said the same thing. Instead of communicating that they wouldn't help him, now they both believed they couldn't help him.

"Stop doing that," Treadon said. "Just tell me what's going on? Why can't you help me?"

"We're not sure how you met a Descendant, how you know about her, but I rescue Unguarded before they go missing, not after."

"I don't understand." He had a sinking feeling he did.

"Tell me where she lived," Gabe said. "I'll go check it out, but, Treadon, you have to understand, we've never recovered an Unguarded after they've been taken. Once they are gone, it's a complete loss."

The news hit Treadon in the gut and he had to run to the bathroom as his body tried to empty a stomach as hollow as his heart.

Thirty-Seven

JARREN CALIVAN

J arren drove up the steep hill, noting how the houses around him changed from crumbling ramblers from the sixties to newer larger homes. The higher the elevation, the fancier the houses. His destination was the very top, where the steep hill flattened out into a twelve-acre plateau, fully fenced to create the Calivan Estate.

Even from outside the property, the mansion itself rose into the sky, casting its shadow over the surrounding landscape and dwarfing the surrounding homes. Jarren didn't approach the front gate. He parked on the opposite side of the road and got out. He walked down the road, casually. With a quick glance, he saw the familiar red light of a hidden camera at the corner of the house. The security system was up and running. That meant the cameras would pick him up if he crossed closer to the black iron fence. He felt a strange surge of hope. If the security system was on, maybe his father was staying here. Maybe he could find him and convince him to go back on the contract.

He didn't really have a plan, but if his dad was here, he wanted to try and do something. He couldn't give up like Gabe. The guy acted like some kind of hero, but brushed off Possessed like they didn't even matter. Jarren was better than that. He had to try and get his dad back.

And the first step was to get inside without setting off the security system.

And he already knew how to do that. This was his home. The house and yard his very own playground.

He followed the sidewalk around the far side of the estate where the sidewalk ends and an abandoned walking trail disappears into tall foliage, an area outside of the estate that Xander Calivan prevented from being developed. Several yards down the trail, Jarren found the spot he was looking for. He looked both ways, checking for any signs of life through the fence. No security guards, no maintenance staff. The grass was yellowed from lack of water. Bushes hung limp like overgrown hair on a chimpanzee. Broken glass and garbage were strewn about the ground. No one had bothered to clean up after the protests. It didn't look like anyone had been around the mansion for several weeks.

The place looked forlorn. He felt a twinge of sadness that such a beautiful place had gone to hell. But he was looking for a demon, so maybe hell was the right place to be.

Jarren lined himself up with a giant tree growing between the fence and the mansion. Next to Rachel, this tree had been his best friend growing up. Not only was it excellent for climbing, but it sat in exactly the right location to create a blind spot in the security feed. Jarren and Rachel had spent weeks analyzing and testing the security system one summer. They found this gap and kept it a secret, pretending that one day the blind spot would come in handy. He never expected that day to come.

Keeping the tree lined up with the main window on the mansion, Jarren approached the fence. He gripped two of the square bars in front of him and wedged a foot in the gap between. His foot had grown since the last time he'd climbed this fence. It made the fit tighter, the climb easier. He alternated jamming his foot in between the bars and grabbing the fence a little higher. The fourteen-foot fence seemed smaller than he remembered. He made it to the top and stepped between the pointed rods. He pushed off, propelling himself into the air.

He landed lightly as a cat, knees bent to absorb the shock. He stayed in that position, crouched low with his hands brushing the brittle grass. No alarm. No shouts. He thought he heard a noise and the hair rose on the back of his neck. He thought of the crazy old guy, Vox, and his crowbar assassination. He saw the blank, emotional look of the guy with the triangle tattoo.

Possessed. He hadn't made the connection before, but that wax look was what had made his dad look so wrong when he confronted him outside of XC Energy. Jarren didn't know a lot about Possessed. He probably should have asked more questions, but Gabe had sounded so final, so sure. As good as dead. Worse than dead.

He clenched his teeth. He didn't know what he would be facing, but it had to be better than giving up, than letting something run around with his dad's body. He'd told Gabe that he was delusional, but deep down, Jarren believed it. Was glad to believe it. At least he had some sort of explanation about what had happened to Xander Calivan. At least his dad wasn't brushing him off like when he was little.

He heard no more sounds except for the creaking of the branches above him. He stayed crouching low and moved toward the tree, smelling autumn as he brushed his hands along the crisp leaves on the ground. It was an old tree. Probably the oldest tree in LA. Most of its branches were thicker than Jarren's body, the trunk challenging the length of a small car. Jarren climbed easily, his heart pumping with adrenaline. He must face his father, but he couldn't give him any warning: no time to call for wax figure backups.

The branches higher up were only as thick as his upper thigh and had grown long, reaching out toward the mansion like fingers trying to grip the windowsills. He shimmied out onto the limb stretching over the grounds and reaching all the way to the roof of the mansion. Jarren's weight started to bend the branch lower as he scooted forward. The branch touched down on the roof, creating a solid bridge right above the balcony he needed. He swung down, grabbing the branch with both hands and letting the momentum of his weight carry him around and up in an arc. He let go and landed on the balcony.

The window was unlocked. He'd expected to have to short the security alarm on the window, but it was already done. The screen already removed. The window slid open. The smell hit him, followed by a burst of hot, rancid air. He pulled his shirt up to cover his nose to keep from gagging. Mold and rotten water, broken sewer pipes. Stale air like it might come out of a tomb. His heart fell as his feet touched down onto thick carpet.

His father wasn't here. Even in his Possessed form, the guy wouldn't have let the mansion sit like this, not even cleaning up the inside after the riot, leaving the broken pipes. The water must have been turned off, but the dry pee-trap smell told Jarren no one had used the sinks or toilets. Damn. He'd hoped his father was here. He'd been dreaming of a reconciliation, a hero's journey, where he confronted his dad and found a way to get him to turn back. His dad was stronger than any contract, his soul was stronger than some wax-figured demon. It must be.

Despite feeling the emptiness of the house, Jarren started his search. When he moved down to the second floor, he heard noises. A shuffling sound. A drawer shutting. He froze on the last step, his foot hovering an inch from the floor. He had to fight an urge to run back up the stairs or hide in a corner, but he didn't come here to hide. Someone else was here. They hadn't bothered to turn on any lights. Could it be his dad? Or was it another member of the Triune? Would Jarren die in his own home? Would they leave the triangle as a message, the carpet soaked in his own blood? The hairs rose on the back of his neck. His fingers gripped the handrail, nails biting into the wood.

Jarren backtracked to his own room and grabbed a baseball bat from his closet. He'd tried to be a baseball player when he was younger, but standing out in the field waiting nine innings for someone to hit a ball his way was too slow paced. Still, a baseball bat worked in every eighties action film, so he might as well go out in his fan-era style.

He slipped back along the dark hallway. When he got closer to his father's office, he heard the sounds again; he saw an inconsistent light flash under the closed door. He stepped forward, shifted his grip on the handle of the bat to one hand and reached forward to turn the door handle.

The door swung open. Jarren swung the bat and heard a cling of metal as the bat connected.

With a sword.

In the hands of Rachel Sampaio.

"What are you doing here?" Jarren tried to pull the bat back, but the sword had embedded into the wood and Rachel wasn't relinquishing the sword.

"What am I doing here? What are you doing here? Sneaking around your own house with a bat?" Rachel took the bat and wedged it into the door frame so she could pull the sword free.

"Where did you get a sword?"

"It's been hanging in your dad's office since we were kids. It's not real. Just a display, but when I heard that board in the hall creek, I got freaked out."

"You got freaked out? I thought you were Possessed."

"Possessed?"

"Never mind. It's a long story."

"Maybe it's story time. I came here to get some answers, but it looks like most of the stuff got taken in the riots."

Jarren pulled Rachel down the hall, into the library, and around the back of the last row of books. He felt the small crevasse behind the bookshelf, slipped his fingers into it, and slid the bookcase sideways a couple feet.

"We can talk in here, who knows who might be listening to my dad's office."

"You used to hide in here all the time," Rachel said, ducking into the small opening. "I can't believe your dad never found you."

"I don't think he ever looked."

The room was only a few feet in diameter. The dim light filtered in through a small square skylight at the peak of the roof. The walls and slanting roof were covered in crayon drawings like hieroglyphics in an ancient cave. These were Jarren's dreams, each image created from his own hand, expanding, and transforming as he grew older. He'd drawn images of daring rescues, catching a bus falling off a bridge, punching an eight-legged creature attacking a group of children. He was the protagonist, the hero, a stick-figure drawn in black, fighting the world. Beating up his own fears.

One of the drawings stood out from the others, larger and protected by a bubble of blank wall, as if the sacredness of the drawing prevented the others from encroaching in on its space. It was a drawing of a family. A tall stick figure in a grey suit and tie. A smaller figure drawn in black crayon with an identical suit. Beside the shorter boy, a third figure was etched on the wall. The details were missing, and the figure was scribbled out.

Rachel reached out and touched it. "A mom you never knew," she whispered. "We could never take the place of someone who had never been there."

"She probably left after she found out what kind of man my father really was."

"You don't know what happened."

"And I'll never find out. Gabe said my dad was gone. As good as dead."

"Why?"

Jarren told her what Gabe had said about Possessed, about angels and demons, about trying to protect the world from darkness.

"He sounds like your kind of guy." Rachel motioned to the other pictures on the wall.

"He's no hero. He won't even try to help my dad."

"And you came here to try."

Jarren turned away from Rachel. He couldn't look at her because it felt like his failure was written all over his face. He'd failed to make his dad proud. He'd failed to get his dad to choose him over his business. And now he was going to fail to bring his dad back.

Rachel stepped closer. Her head brushed the ceiling. Jarren was hunched over, unable to stand up straight. She tilted her head back, looking up at him.

"You spent too much time in here," Rachel said. "All these drawings. All this talent wasted. You'd think with all this practice, you'd be on your way to becoming a professional artist." She walked her fingers along his waist to his back, wrapping her arms around him. He leaned into her. She had a way of making him feel whole, even while he was cracking into a million pieces. She held him together. He couldn't imagine losing her.

He bent his neck and Rachel went up on her toes. Their lips touched, a pause, the excitement building. The she squeezed her arms, pulling him into her, pressing up so that his head hit the ceiling, pinning him as their mouths moved together, opening, touching, tasting. He felt her smooth teeth, her warm breath, her fingers against his skin under his shirt.

A kiss for the ages.

A kiss that could take him away.

A kiss that could make him forget.

Rachel pulled back for a breath, but when she leaned toward him again, Jarren stopped her. "I came to find my dad, to see if I could help, but I don't want to drag you any deeper. I don't want to risk seeing you get hurt."

"You know it's too late for that. You think you're the only one your dad has hurt? You think by keeping me safe now you can erase everything your dad has done?" Rachel's fingers flexed against Jarren's back.

"Why would you come here without me?" Jarren asked. "I would have helped you."

Rachel shook her head. "You cut me out. It was more important to keep me safe than to let me battle my own demons. He let my mom die. He ignored her when she got sick. He didn't lift a finger when his insurance company refused to cover the hospital costs. You forgave your dad too easily when he opened his arms to you, and you deserved that. You deserved a dad that cared." Rachel took a deep breath. "But I never could."

Jarren's mouth was dry, his throat felt swollen. He reached out for her, but she put up her hand. Rachel's mom had been the closest thing he'd had for a mother, but he hadn't known his father's role. Hadn't realized Xander had refused to help.

"It's too late for my mom, but I want answers. I can't ignore the chance to find the truth. Too many things don't fit: the timing, the company, the press releases. Everything feels purposeful and planned, but none of it is translating into money. When a business does shady things, you expect a money trail where someone somewhere is gaining while everyone else loses."

"Are you sure you want to be part of this?" Jarren asked. "After what Vox told us? About what could happen to you?"

Rachel leaned forward, the flashlight creating dark shadows around her eyes. "If anyone tried to come for me right now, they're the ones who would need to worry."

Jarren felt a thrill at Rachel's intensity, a lightness in his chest. Rachel was on his side, and he wouldn't want her anywhere else.

"Okay. Let's look at everything again. Are you sure there's no money trail. There's always money."

"Nothing that raises a red flag." Rachel straightened and began to pace.

"What about influence?" Jarren asked. "Anyone using this as a political advantage? Start a war?"

"I can't find anything like that," Rachel said, tapping her chin with her finger. "No big fall out, no fingers in the wrong pie. It looks like a simple company shut down and rearrangement of resources. Other than the basement fire that destroyed most of the company's information, there was no other suspicious activity. But who knows what was being covered up by the fire. There would have been so much to go through, but now there's very little information."

Jarren pulled his phone from his pocket. He hadn't looked at the pictures he'd taken in the basement with everything else going on. And he still had the manilla envelope Vox had given him. Maybe Rachel could make more of the information than he could.

"This is all that I could recover before the fire took everything. And I still have the manilla envelop from Vox."

"You haven't looked at it yet?"

"I took a picture of them, but they don't show us a lot." Jarren showed her a screen shot of the two pieces of paper in the manilla envelope. The first looked like a criminal file. There was a square on the left for a mug shot. It didn't contain a photo, only a generic silhouette of a person's head.

The man's information was only partially filled in.

"Caden Bachman," Rachel read out loud. "Age: Unknown. Address: Unknown. Phone number: Unknown. Wow, this is really helpful."

"He's managed to stay anonymous while being one of the largest business tycoons in the industry. He guards his privacy more carefully than he does his money. He has funded the start-ups of eight of the largest companies in the world, but all his business is done through his lawyers and CEOs. Vox was trying to connect him to several criminal lawsuits, but there's no way to stick anything to him."

"Look at this." Rachel pointed to the background section. "It says he is suspected of espionage, money laundering, missing persons, arsenal, and genocide. How do we not know more about this guy?"

"Here's the next page." Jarren swiped on his phone. He enlarged the images and both he and Rachel leaned closer.

The three grainy pictures on the phone looked as if they'd been set crooked on a black and white copy machine. The first picture was the back of a man walking alone down a deserted street. The second picture captured a profile of the same man in an identical suit. He had on a hat and wore it low. His head was tilted toward the camera so only the bottom half of his face was visible. The last picture was black with a few blurred white streaks through the center.

"How is that even a picture?" Rachel asked with disgust. "How can this be all the information even an investigative reporter like Vox could have on such a bad guy."

"He's thriving off other people's money. His suit is not just off the rack at Gucci. That's a made-to-measure Fioravanti."

Rachel gave Jarren a flat look.

"Okay. Maybe not that helpful, but I do spend a lot of time around expensive suits."

Jarren flipped to the next picture.

"What's this?" Rachel asked.

"It's a screen shot of the last information my dad looked up before he destroyed the servers. I took a picture of the computer before the fire destroyed everything."

Rachel took the phone and squinted. "It doesn't look very important. Just a list of random names. You should have held still when you took the shot. It's blurry."

"Excuse me. I was running for my life from a demon-possessed man with an axe."

"They aren't names I recognize from my research." She read them out loud. "Foster Jenkins. Mike Jenkins. Could be anyone. Pat Greyson. Jake . . ."

Jarren sat up. He grabbed the phone from Rachel. "I didn't recognize them, but I've heard these names before."

"Who are they?"

"It's the names from the family, the foster family Treadon was looking for today. The names of the missing kids were on the screen in XC Energy's basement."

"You think it's connected? You think this guy might have something to do with Ellie?"

"We need to tell Treadon."

Thirty-Eight

TREADON NELSON

The murmuring voices from the kitchen grated on Treadon's already raw nerves. Abigail checked on him once, but they seemed so distracted, even after the news of the missing girl and Jarren's sudden exit. It was like they only had time to nod at the fact that they'd finally told Treadon about Gabe's true identity and Abigail's role. What could be more important than finding a missing Descendant?

Treadon sat back against the bathtub. He'd stayed close to the toilet in case another wave of nausea took him down. He didn't even feel like he had the strength to get up off the floor, but he felt that constant pressure in the back of his mind, the pull in his chest that pulsed painfully. Find her. Find her. He pulled his legs up and rested his forehead on his knees. Something in his pocket jabbed painfully into his thigh.

He felt the lump. With so much going on, he'd almost forgotten. He pulled the small journal and the amulet from his pocket, letting the amulet twist on the end of the chain as he held it in the air. He set the amulet on the edge of the bathtub. He held the journal in front of him, afraid to open it, afraid to leave it closed. The voices from the kitchen raised in intensity, but not volume. Treadon wanted to block out the sound, but curiosity pulled him to the door. He cracked the door and listened.

"I'll go to the house Treadon mentioned," Gabe said. "I need to at least look."

"Fine. I know we have to try," Abigail said, "but it feels so hopeless with the veil over the city. Why would they try to block me when they are already beating me to the Unguarded? They've never tried to shield what they were doing before."

"And look at the large area," Gabe said. "They must be hiding something bigger than one child, something so bright it couldn't be missed."

"What shines brighter than an Unguarded coming into their aura?" Abigail asked.

"There are a few things. The most common would be a Bonding between a Descendant and their new Guardian. The Bonding creates an explosion of energy, but it couldn't be that."

"Why not?"

"It wouldn't make any sense. A Bonding scatters all demon essence within its reach, a cleansing of the area. It's powerful. But the Triune would have no reason to hide a Bonding. They would want to stop it at all costs."

"What else?"

"The only recorded event that created a pulse larger than a Bonding was when Adeona absorbed the daggers."

"Maybe they're moving the Unguarded," Abigail said. "All the ones they've taken. That would create a large aura. And they wouldn't want me tracking where they were taking them."

"It's possible," Gabe said, drumming his fingers as he thought. "Keep an eye on the map. I'll check out the girl's house that Treadon was talking about. Maybe I can find some clues as to where they have taken the others."

There was no hope in Gabe's comment and the sound of his surety of failure made Treadon shut the door. Ellie was missing and no one could help him find her. There had to be more, something she'd told him. Something she wrote down.

Treadon opened the journal with shaky fingers. He felt another wave of nausea threatening but he swallowed it down. The words were blurry. He blinked hard and made his eyes focus on the first words written in Ellie's tight print. *It's been ten years since I made the biggest mistake of my life.*

He read slowly, absorbing every word, hearing her voice in his head, speaking to him, calling out to him for help. He read about the history of the Angels, the twin daggers that had been created to destroy them, and the brave act of Adeona that Gabe had just talked about. Absorbing the blades into the DNA of her descendants.

He learned more about Guardians. About the weapons they used to keep demons at bay. He came to an entry about the amulet. The Compass.

The compass is an amulet that points the way for a bonded Guardian. Once the Guardian is bonded, their DNA is tethered to the compass. The Guardian is always able to find their Descendant no matter where they are.

He had the compass. All he needed was the Guardian. He picked up the Compass and held it in his palm. It raised, spinning in a beautiful display. It didn't stop. Of course it didn't point the way to Ellie. He would need to be the one who was Bonded.

But he wasn't.

He knew what this meant. The journal had laid it out for him. There would be no room for another relationship. If Treadon helped find Ellie's Guardian, he'd be giving up his chance. There would be no room for another commitment. But Ellie had already made that clear. Despite the pounding in his chest, the desperate pull toward her he'd felt since he met her, he would walk away, knowing she was happy. Knowing she was safe.

For the first time, Treadon understood his mom. He understood why Abigail had stood by Gabe all this time, even without his returned affection. She would do anything for him and Treadon felt the same. He would help find the Guardian Ellie had lost, have him find her, make sure she was safe, and then he would let her go. But not before. Not before he was absolutely sure.

Treadon pushed himself off the floor, closing the book and putting the amulet and journal back in his pocket. He stumbled out into the hallway and shoved the door open to Gabe's office.

The perpetual motion device rotated on its platform like it had every day since Treadon could remember. Abigail came down the hall. "Are you okay?"

"Why can't Gabe find his Angel? If he has the Compass, why doesn't it work?"

Before Abigail could answer, the front door opened and closed, and Gabe stepped into the hallway. He shook his head at both their expectant looks. "There was nothing. Just like you said."

"I have another idea of how to find Ellie." Treadon pointed at Gabe's perpetual motion device. No. It had never been that. It was a Compass. "Her compass will point to her if I can find her Guardian. You said you can see auras, that Descendants and Guardians have a different light. Maybe you can find her Guardian and he can use the compass to find her."

Gabe shook his head. "That compass is tied to my DNA. It will only point to the Descendant I'm bonded to."

"Then why don't you use it?"

Gabe stepped over to his desk and touched the rotating circles. They stilled and stopped, but the marbled jewels didn't line up. He closed his eyes, swallowing like the lump in his throat was a constant companion. "It can't find her." He lifted his finger and the Compass continued to spin. "I had some of my DNA put into this base so if there was even a moment where her aura could be found, I would know, but they've found a way to keep her hidden. It has been twenty years." Gabe turned back to Treadon. "This Compass would not help find your friend. It would only point to my Descendant, even if it was working."

"Not yours, her Compass."

"She's Unguarded," Gabe said. "She wouldn't have a compass yet. That's why we can't find the Unguarded once they're taken."

"She does. She already chose a Guardian. She told me."

Gabe shook his head. "That's impossible."

Treadon pulled the amulet from his pocket, letting it dangle in front of Gabe and Abigail's faces. "She has a guardian. We just need to find them and let this lead us to Ellie."

Abigail reached out and held the amulet in her fingers. "How is this possible? And how did you get this?"

"She left it behind when she was taken. She gave it to a very brave boy."

The crease between Gabe's eyebrows was a mountain of confusion. Treadon didn't like their reactions. He'd thought he'd found the solution, but both were acting like he'd added to the problem.

"Why would they take her? If she wasn't Unguarded." Abigail let the amulet drop and hang from the chain again. She didn't look at Gabe's Compass.

"Why are only Unguarded taken?" Treadon asked.

"We aren't sure, but we think they're looking for ways to eradicate the Descendants. Find a way to wipe out what's left of the Angels' DNA. A genocide, a destruction of a species, starting with the unprotected."

"How?"

"We're not sure. There's a substance called hematite that can weaken a Descendant's knowledge and energy, but it's very rare. And we aren't sure how they're using it."

"Can we try to find her Guardian?" Treadon asked. "Can't you at least look?" He was begging now. "Her disappearance was planned with the intention of trying to hurt, not just her, but the entire race of the Descendants of Angels. Maybe if we find her, we can find the others."

They both looked doubtful, but Abigail nodded. "I can try."

Treadon led the way out to the kitchen table, but before he sat down, the front door burst open again.

"The names are the same." Jarren didn't even wait until he was all the way through the door.

"What names?" Treadon asked.

"From the computer screen in the basement." Jarren stepped inside and made room for Rachel. She stepped in and shut the door behind her.

"The same as what?" Treadon asked.

"What basement?" Abigail said.

"What computer?" Gabe asked.

Jarren threw his hands up in the air. "They don't get it."

"I can't imagine why," Rachel said, walking in and taking a seat at the table. "You explained it so clearly. I think you should slow down and add a few details."

"The names on the computer screen in the basement that my dad was looking at before he started the fire, the last search my dad did at XC Energy came up with the names of the kids you listed at the foster care office today."

Abigail's mouth dropped open at the mention of the fire, but Gabe's hand came up and she bit the question back.

Jarren continued. "I think your missing angel and my dad getting possessed and the company shutting down could all be connected."

"I thought you didn't believe." Treadon was trying to process the new information, a buzzing in his head like a hive of bees that needed to be calmed down with smoke. "We are all crazy, remember?"

"If you can't beat 'em, join 'em." Jarren shrugged. "Besides, you saw my dad. When the most illogical explanation is the only one you've got, you go with it."

"XC Energy has something to do with Ellie's foster family disappearing?" Treadon gripped the back of the chair.

"The whole family didn't disappear," Jarren said. "They were relocated. But Ellie is missing and, yes, I think my dad's company has something to do with it. Those guys with the triangle tattoos make people disappear. That's their job."

Gabe leaned forward, fingers pressed into the countertop. Treadon thought the granite might buckle under the pressure. "The triangle tattoos. You didn't tell me about the tattoos."

"A small detail when you're getting run off the road," Jarren said.

"The accident was caused by the Triune?" Abigail asked.

"You know about the Triune?" Rachel asked. "That will save a lot of time. Vox had to explain who they were."

"Vox?" Gabe's eyes were squinted into small slits. "When did he come back?"

"It can't be Vox. Not after all these years." Abigail had a hand to her mouth, her eyes wide.

"What did Vox tell you?" Gabe asked.

"He said that XC Energy was looking for someone," Rachel explained, "through a satellite meant to research climate and population called WWAR, but it was all made for one purpose. To find someone who was the key to their plans."

"It's been in front of us this whole time." Gabe straightened his shoulders. He went into his office and when he stepped back out, he was strapping two double-sided swords to his back. "Everything has been related. The missing Unguarded. They were using a satellite. The accident. The company shutdown. And now the way they are blocking your vision."

Gabe turned to Jarren, standing tall, swords sticking out above each shoulder, face as dark and serious as Treadon had ever seen it. He looked every inch a Guardian of Angels

"Where is your father now?" Gabe asked.

"He's not at the house," Jarren said, shrugging, his hands buried in his pockets, his head hanging low. "We were just there."

"Show me where he works," Gabe said.

"Only on one condition," Jarren said, pushing his shoulders back and lifting his head so his eyes met Gabe's. "You don't touch my dad. You don't take him to a prison. You try to save him."

Gabe shut his eyes with the new realization. "Xander Calivan is Possessed. That's why you asked about it earlier." He nodded. "I will do what I can for Xander, but a Possessed being is not someone to underestimate. They have inhuman strength and speed and there is nothing left of the person who had been inhabited."

Abigail cleared her throat and lay her hand on the corner of the paper. The white surface shimmered like a desert mirage. A two-dimensional view appeared and then shifted, parts sinking down, others rising off the surface, creating a topographical map, a three-dimensional diorama.

She brushed her fingers along the image, and Treadon felt the sensation of movement even though he was standing still. The feeling he got when a car beside him rolled forward, but the car he was in hadn't moved yet. She zoomed in. The ocean met the land in an unmistakable curve, the buildings growing bigger and more familiar in an aerial view of Los Angeles.

"Is this your dad's office?" Abigail asked Jarren, pointing to the map.

Jarren stepped up to the table, examining the map with eyes that danced with excitement, like a child distracted from a tantrum by a new toy. "This thing makes google earth look like an amateur sketch. Have you thought about production and distribution? You could make a fortune."

Gabe and Abigail stared at Jarren without blinking.

"Like father, like son," Rachel murmured under her breath.

"Right, probably not the best time. My dad's office is right here." Jarren pointed to a tall building in an obscure industrial area.

Abigail touched the map again, but this time it didn't move. She moved her fingers like she was measuring something Treadon couldn't see. "It's at the center of where I can't see. They're blocking me from seeing anywhere near XC Energy."

"I'll go check it out," Gabe said. "I'll let you know what I find." Gabe grabbed his helmet and moved toward the door.

Jarren stepped in front of him. Again, Treadon couldn't believe his friend's courage in the face of Gabe's stare down. "You're not going to my office without me."

"I cannot put an Ordinary in danger," Gabe said, waving his hand by his side in refusal.

Treadon saw the quick glance at Abigail, Gabe's eyes lowering quickly with guilt. "I've made that mistake too many times in the past. I must go alone."

"It will be easier to get into the building with the key." Jarren pulled the key card from his pocket and moved it out of Gabe's reach when he put his hand out for it.

"I'm coming, too," Treadon said. "If Ellie's there, I want to help get her out. And I have her Compass. Maybe it can help us."

"What about us?" Rachel hadn't stood up from the table. "I suppose you want us to wait here in case Lassie comes home."

Gabe's fingers flexed. "I would appreciate if you could stay with

Abigail. I don't know what will happen or what the Triune knows. I don't want her to be alone."

Treadon barely registered Rachel nodding out of the corner of his eye. He stared at Gabe, almost scared to blink. Gabe was going to let him come. Gabe must believe he could serve a purpose. Treadon had never felt so shocked, or so happy. He'd been waiting his whole life to impress this guy and now he had a chance.

"You both have to promise to do exactly as I say as soon as I say it," Gabe said, turning to look at Jarren and Treadon.

Jarren gave a sarcastic salute. Treadon gripped the Compass in his pocket feeling the circles against his palm. He was doing something. It felt so good to be moving.

Rachel and Abigail were silent as they headed out the door. Treadon knew they both hated to be left behind, but he didn't want to read their feelings right now. He kept his head down, not wanting to blow his chance to go with Gabe and followed Jarren out the door.

Thirty-Nine

Abigail Nelson

Abigail rubbed her own arms as she watched the lights disappear around the corner at the end of the street. Her heart felt weighed down with a thousand pounds of worry. After all her efforts to keep Treadon out of this, he was diving in head-first. He'd discovered a Descendant on his own. He'd known about this world and hadn't thought to tell her. She'd taught her son to keep his own secrets.

But she wasn't about to let him go face whatever was underneath the fog covering the city, covering her mind. She would not sit here. She would not wait in this house like a helpless watcher anymore.

She turned. Rachel had stayed. Hadn't even argued. Abigail was that way once, but she wished she'd been stronger throughout her life. Rachel looked strong; the way Abigail wished she felt. Rachel also looked perfectly calm as she stood up from the table.

"I'm going after them." Abigail was glad to have someone to tell, to say it out loud so she wouldn't question her decision any longer. "You can't stop me."

"You think I'm planning on sitting here, waiting?"

"You don't seem like the kind of girl that would sit on the sidelines."

"Damn right. I'm a starter." Rachel smiled. "I just wanted to make sure you had a choice. Sometimes it's easier to let the overprotective types think they've done their job and then take care of business with them out of the way. But it looks like you want to come with me. The difference is, I'd like to go in a little better prepared. Maybe a little more than a key card and necklace. Based on what I've heard, we've passed the investigative stage. This might be a fight."

"Gabe is always ready for a fight."

"Good. Let's be like Gabe. Does he have any weapons we could borrow, or does he only have those two killer blades on his back? We might have to find some of our own."

Abigail felt lighter than she had in eighteen years. "Yes, he has more weapons. And I know where they are."

Forty

TREADON NELSON

The ride to XC Energy was a new level of terror for Treadon. Gabe had pulled out of the driveway on his motorcycle and something about the deep rumble of another engine brought out Jarren's competitive streak. Jarren and Gabe drove recklessly fast, glancing at each other at the stop lights, tires squealing when the lights turned green.

By the time they reached the off-ramp to the XC Energy building, Treadon was sure his skin was the same color as the green light.

"Not bad." Jarren slowed and let the engine idle at the stop sign, letting Gabe roll his bike beside the car.

"That's a nice machine." Gabe examined the car. "With a little more control behind the wheel, you could really move."

Jarren blustered. "I'll show you control, Old Man."

Treadon closed his eyes and gripped the door handle as the roar of engines and Jarren's laughter rolled over him. The acceleration threw him back against the seat, but the nightmare only lasted a few seconds.

The car stopped with a wrenching jerk, the seatbelt digging into his shoulder, his head whipping forward. He opened one eye.

They'd made it to their destination.

In front of them was the large, black iron gate with the XC in the middle. Behind the gate, the building rose into the night sky, but it wasn't the dark, abandoned building Treadon expected.

Every window glowed with an unnatural light, a moving shifting light that danced in the glass and created moving shadows in the parking lot.

"Looks like a party," Jarren said, still inside the car. "My invitation must have gotten lost in the mail."

The rattling of Gabe's engine shook Treadon's teeth as the bike pulled next to the car, Gabe's hand clamping down on Treadon's door like a vice. "This isn't what I was expecting. You two need to get out of here before you're seen. Give me the key to the building and get back to the house."

"What?" Jarren yelled over the noise of the motors even though Gabe's voice hadn't been drowned out. "Use the key now? Sure thing."

Jarren moved fast, swiping his key card across the pad and pulling forward as the gate swung open.

Gabe revved his engine like a swear word, being forced to wait until Jarren was through. As soon as the gate was wide enough, Jarren shifted gears and pressed the gas, the Aston Martin shooting forward, leaving Treadon's stomach behind.

Gabe was faster, passing them on the bike, pulling in front of them with a 180 turn on the back wheel, and coming to a dead stop in front of them. Jarren slammed on the brakes. The tires hissed as they skidded across the pavement, searching for purchase. The seatbelt was the only thing that kept Treadon from flying over the windshield onto to Gabe's lap.

"Fast bike. I think he was taking it easy on me on the way here." Despite the joke, Jarren's voice was as tight as a calf-muscle cramp.

Gabe got off his bike, his knees an inch from the bumper. He crossed his arms and glared at them. The muscles in his arms bulged under his black shirt, his face a chiseled mask of determination.

He took a breath, his lungs filling, making his chest even larger.

"Wait here." Gabe's command reached them with a physical force. Treadon felt like the words slammed into him and pushed him back against his seat. Jarren's only reaction was a tightening of his fingers on the steering wheel.

Treadon tried to sit forward but felt like Gabe's words still held him back. Gabe turned, and Treadon could see his confidence that his orders would be obeyed. Treadon wasn't so sure. Jarren leaned forward, fighting whatever force held them pinned.

Gabe seemed to sense the struggle and turned, but then a deep laughter echoed around the parking lot. The thrumming of the laughter reverberated off the lamp posts and emanated from the ground. Jarren looked up. Gabe froze in his tracks. Treadon listened. It wasn't the laughter of amusement or irony or even an intimidation factor. The laugher was full of the raucous joy of a victor standing over his opponent.

The sound ended as abruptly as it had begun, as if the sound had been recalled, all echoes sucked back into the mouth that gave them birth. Beyond Gabe's still form, Treadon could make out the silhouette of a man standing in front of the brightly lit doors over fifty yards away. He was only a shadow against the dancing light, but Treadon could feel an energy, a power, emanating from the man. The body type was tall, broad shoulders, oval head. It wasn't Xander Calivan.

"I was hoping you'd make it, Gabriel Tuoer. You've been missing for so long; I was worried you'd miss the beginning of the end."

Gabe didn't respond, but his hands lifted, reaching for the swords strapped to his back.

"Your long quest should end with a hero's welcome." The silhouetted man raised his arms out in front of him, head tilted back. Gabe moved, faster than Treadon's eyes could register. Gabe's swords were in his hands as he sprinted across the parking lot toward the front doors. The man waited, unmoving.

Treadon felt a strange rumbling. His reflection quivered in the rearview mirror. When he looked toward the building, the lights from the first-story windows were blocked out as a moving mass rose out of the ground.

Gabe skidded to a stop as the blackness converged on him. Treadon could make out the shape of animals, sick-looking creatures with sharp teeth and long claws on their stubby front legs.

Treadon unbuckled his seatbelt and pushed the door open. He had no plan, no weapon, but he wasn't about to sit here and watch those creatures tear Gabe apart.

"Shut the door." Jarren's voice was calm, his fingers loose, one hand relaxed on the steering wheel, the other on the gear stick, his face a mask of confidence. "You've never seen me *really* drive, have you?"

His choice between the hoard of animals and Jarren's driving made him pause for a moment. He'd faced Jarren's driving before, and he could face it again. And if it meant getting to Gabe faster, Treadon wasn't even going to let himself close his eyes.

Treadon closed the door and put his seatbelt back on, surprised when Jarren pulled his seatbelt on as well. Jarren pushed a button on his dashboard and the roof closed over their heads. The first wave of creatures attacked Gabe. The double-edged swords flashed in the silver light and deformed creatures fell to the ground, dissipating into black dust.

There was a sudden pull of momentum as Jarren put the car into gear and pressed the accelerator. They approached the mass of creatures, going from zero to sixty in two seconds. The creatures became more defined, slimy black hair slicked back against their bodies, white foam dripping from their teeth and sides of their mouths.

The front of the car smashed into the line of beasts with a crunching sound, followed by a blinding flash of light. Treadon heard loud hissing sounds and smelled burned flesh, smoke, and rancid air. Streaks of light shot from all sides of the Aston Martin, catching the deformed, dog-like creatures in its brilliant flares.

Another streak of light connected to the skull of a creature right next to Treadon's window. The entire animal turned gray and then disintegrated into the air.

The car broke through the pack of beasts and Jarren slammed the breaks, jerking the wheel sharply so the car spun in a circle, leaving four crescent-shaped tire marks on the pavement.

"What was that?" Treadon gripped the handle and side of the seat like lifesavers in a stormy ocean.

Jarren smiled wide, showing teeth. "That was level ten. I guess we don't have to test it on freshman after all."

The animals turned at the sight of the car spewing lightning. Their attention only seemed to encourage Jarren and he forced his foot down on the gas again. White smoke billowed from the tires. The smell of burnt rubber filled the air. A few brave creatures advanced from the pack and when they were only a few feet away, Jarren slipped the car into gear, launching them forward.

The first two creatures flew up and over the top of the car, the streak of electricity catching both dog-like beasts in the air. They disintegrated before they hit the ground. Then the electrifying Aston Martin was in the heart of the horde again. Jarren didn't slow down, speeding from one end of the parking lot to the other, spinning in dizzying patterns and chasing down confused creatures that got separated from the main group.

Treadon found himself leaning forward, adjusting his body to the shifting force of the car, pointing out where the fenris were regrouping so Jarren could scatter them again. His fear, his anxiety, seemed buried in the moment of this battle. He could almost forget he'd ever been afraid.

It only took Jarren and his car a few minutes to purge the parking lot of the devilish forms. The last three creatures seemed disoriented as the headlights bore down on them. They each headed in a different direction and ended up running into each other. Jarren jerked the wheel at the last minute and caught two of the creatures with the side paneling right below Treadon's window. The third looked ready to launch itself at the car when a sword swiped through the creature's neck.

Gabe stood there half bent, swords held in front of him like some kind of superhero that had dropped from the sky.

"That was insane." Treadon took deep breaths.

"Are you okay?" Jarren asked.

Treadon couldn't stop the smile from spreading across his face. "That was awesome."

"See? I knew you'd come around. Now we can get you on Puff the

Magic Dragon kiddy ride at the theme park. You know how bad I've been wanting to ride that with you."

Treadon laughed and opened his door. Gabe approached the side of the car before Treadon could get out, sheathing his swords.

"I thought I told you two to go home."

"I practically lived here when I was growing up. It's home to me," Jarren said, shrugging.

"Where did you learn to drive like that?" Gabe placed a finger and ran it along the edge of the door.

"I wouldn't touch that." Treadon's warning went unheeded. The car didn't electrocute Gabe. Nothing happened. Except for a small glow on the paneling where Gabe's finger made contact.

"Where did you learn to drive like that?" Gabe asked Jarren, again.

"Driver's Ed," Jarren said flatly.

Gabe opened his mouth to say something else, but the sound of squealing tires made them all turn to look at the building. A black sedan came around the parking lot, speeding toward the gate, turning with enough force to put the car up on two wheels.

"That's him," Gabe said. "I have to follow him. Don't go in the building without me."

"Sure thing." Jarren gave Gabe a salute and leaned back in the driver's seat like he was ready to listen to a podcast on a relaxing drive to the beach.

Treadon could see how torn Gabe was between staying and making sure they followed directions or following that man who was behind the fenris. There was a deep yearning in Gabe's eyes that was more than a desire for revenge. He'd been waiting for this moment for years.

"Go. I'll keep him in line." Treadon nodded.

Gabe closed his eyes. They both knew it wasn't the promise Gabe wanted. But the car was approaching the gate. Gabe squared his shoulders and turned. He took three steps, bounding, almost like he was walking on the moon, and then he jumped, pushing off the ground with incredible force. He flew up through the dark night, pulling his swords from their scabbards in mid-air. He landed on the speeding car, knocking the car back onto all four tires, slamming one sword down through the roof. He held the protruding sword, leaning against it for leverage. His relaxed stance made him look like he was riding a snowboard across a black expanse. His face turned toward Treadon. His mouth didn't move, but Treadon heard the words on the wind.

"Wait for me."

The car approached the gates at break-neck speed. The gate had only partially opened, but the driver didn't even tap the breaks. The car scraped through the small opening, sparks flying from the friction between the car and opening iron gates.

Then the car, with Gabe still riding on top, disappeared into the darkness, leaving Jarren and Treadon staring after them with a glowing building behind them in a parking lot that smelled of burning rubber and scorched flesh, ash drifting around their feet.

PART Three

Forty-One

TREADON NELSON

Jarren stood outside the car, his hands on his hips. "Wait for me? Sounds like lyrics from an eighty's country song."

"More like soul. No one's dog has died yet."

"Unless you count all those things I just fried with my car. And your girl's missing."

"Good point. We're in a country song."

They both nodded, their jokes feeling hollow as they turned and surveyed the scene in front of them. Gabe's bike lay on its side where it had been abandoned. The engine on Jarren's car was smoking, two of the tires had gone flat, the rubber worn bald. The parking lot was covered with the swirling black ash left over from the disintegrated creatures.

The building still danced with light, creating shadows that stretched and twisted like beckoning fingers reaching out for them.

"I'm going in." Jarren spoke, but his feet didn't move.

"You know we have no idea what we're facing. We know almost

nothing about angels and demons except for a two-minute conversation."

"Do what your daddy said. Wait here." Jarren took a step this time.

"He's not my dad. And I never said I was going to wait. I just wanted to make sure we were clear on the decision."

"You think too much."

"It's one of my better qualities."

"That's sad," Jarren said, taking another step. "But I vote for action. Because you're right, we know nothing. Which means we could stand here all day trying to decide or we could walk in there and find out what we don't know. My dad could be in there."

Treadon looked up at the lighted windows. He thought he saw a shadow move across the fifth story window, but it was hard to tell with all the shifting light. "And he could help us find Ellie."

"That's more like it." Jarren slapped Treadon on the back, using extra force so that Treadon had to step forward to keep from falling over. He hadn't realized he'd been frozen in place until Jarren made him move. "Let's go find your missing angel."

They approached the front door. Jarren opened it. "It not even locked."

Treadon took a second to glance back at the road where Gabe had disappeared. He heard his mom's voice in his head. *Gabe is capable of things you can't even imagine.*

What kind of enemy did Gabe fight? What kind of enemy would they face? Would their abilities be equal to Gabe's?

They stepped through the doors and stared at the changes. The walls contained a fluid stream of golden specks, flowing from the ceiling to the floor, alive with a current that shifted and changed. No wonder the windows glowed.

The laser light display in the center of the room was now a solid pillar of the same black material as the walls, with more glowing specks falling down the tiers, pooling at the bottom of the fountain. Treadon felt like he'd entered a different dimension. Jarren brushed his fingers along the wall, unable to touch the specks through a clear layer of rock, but the flecks shifted beneath his fingertips.

"I thought I saw something on the top floor," Treadon said.

"My father's office. In an emergency, take the stairs."

A loud explosion outside rocked the building. Treadon turned just as a second explosion sounded, red flames visible through the glass. Smoke billowed up a few blocks away. A flash of light echoed in his vision each time he blinked.

"What was that?" Jarren asked.

"I don't know." Treadon felt a sinking feeling in his stomach. The explosion came from the direction the car had gone with Gabe riding on top. If the car crashed, if Gabe got caught in the explosion, that meant they were on their own, facing an enemy they knew nothing about.

"He'll be okay," Jarren said as he opened the door to the stairwell. "He's got that leather biker's jacket. He's probably fireproof. You'll see the dude again."

"Should we go see if he's okay?"

Before Jarren could answer, an echoing scream resounded down the stairwell. Goosebumps rose on Treadon's arms, his chest tightened, and his vision blurred. He gripped the railing.

"That was Ellie," Treadon said, trying to catch a breath.

"Looks like we're going up," Jarren said, cracking his knuckles like eighties wrestler before a match. Treadon didn't miss the slight tremor in Jarren's voice or the dip in his Adam's apple.

Treadon pushed past Jarren and ran up the stairs feeling like he was moving in slow motion. It was the same scream he'd heard during the final football game. It was a scream that scraped his nerves and left him raw. Ellie was here and he was moving too slow.

Forty-Two

GABRIEL TUOER

Blue fire engulfed the dark sedan. A blackened skull rested on the steering wheel. Not Caden Bachman. But Gabe was sure he'd been in the car.

The flames licked at the leather on the seats and the remaining flesh on the driver's back. It was too late to save him. Gabe felt a sting of regret. Another soul he'd failed to save.

Gabe tightened his grip on the handles of his sword. Caden Bachman was still here somewhere. Gabe had managed to pull his sword free and jump from the car as it slammed into a propane tank. The explosion was bigger than it should have been, like it had been rigged. But he'd seen the shadow of a man slipping away from the scene; he was gone before Gabe landed.

Gabe focused on the sound waves around him, pulling them toward his ears. He ignored the sounds of sizzling flesh, the crackling flames, the creaking metal.

There it was.

The soft sound of a man's breathing came from behind the burning car and around the side of a small building.

Bachman wasn't running. His breaths came easy and even. There were no sounds of footsteps. He was waiting. Gabe ground his teeth. He wasn't going to let Bachman get away again. He would end this tonight or die trying. He built up compression waves under his feet, releasing the pressure and letting the rebounding effect propel him over the burning car. Before he landed, he saw Bachman step out from behind the building. Gabe landed on his feet, immediately dropping into a roll.

He felt two darts, slivers of black hematite, pass above his ear. He jumped to his feet and sprinted toward Bachman. Bachman flicked his wrist and Gabe dove to the side. He saw the darts pass just inches from his nose. He landed hard on his side but didn't stop moving.

He used his momentum to rock back onto his feet. Bachman was only a car length away. Gabe tried to hit the ground as a third round of darts flew from Bachman's fingers. Four darts flew over Gabe's right shoulder, but the fifth hit its mark. The hematite shard buried itself several inches into Gabe's deltoid muscle, leaving a small sliver visible through his leather jacket. Gabe could feel the effects immediately, his energy sucked from the rest of his body, pooling into the small dart buried in his shoulder.

He stumbled forward, but Bachman had already moved. Gabe slammed into the wall of on old industrial building, old enough to be made of brick and mortar. He slipped around the corner of the building to put a wall between him and Caden Bachman. He sheathed one of his swords and used his fingers to dig into the wound deep enough to get a grip on the shard. He pulled with a sudden jerk and the shard ripped free. It was five inches long, a pointed crystal shape, the flecks of gold shifting through the black hematite with the energy it had absorbed from Gabe's body.

Gabe felt as if a piece of him was ripped out, trapped in the hematite. He threw the shard on the ground and retrieved his sword. He climbed to his feet, moving slower now, with more intention, and stepped around the building.

Bachman watched him with a dark grin.

"What are you?" Gabe had never seen a Possessed who was able to manipulate black hematite like that. He'd never seen hematite used as a disposable weapon.

"I am exactly who you think I am. The one you've been searching for. I am the answer."

"Where is she?" Gabe threw the words at Bachman with all the force he could create.

Bachman raised an eyebrow. "You think I'd give you that? Lead you to her after all this time? Of course, we are talking about your Descendant, the one that has been missing for almost twenty years, the one you could never save. You waste your time chasing a shadow. You always were a pathetic Guardian."

The pain of his words struck Gabe as firmly as the hematite dart. He hadn't been able to save her, even with all her knowledge, even with the visions and prophecies and preparations—she was gone. And he'd let it blind him.

That didn't mean he would let this man get away with what he had done. He pushed himself forward, the ground rebounding from the force of his jump. Bachman stepped calmly to the side and raised his hand toward Gabe's flying form. Gabe felt the pressure hit his chest like a metal fist. He flew backward until he hit the wall of the building. He struggled against the invisible force, but it was formless. He could only grip desperately to his swords and focus on drawing air into his restricted lungs.

"Pathetic." Bachman spat at Gabe. "You are all insignificant things, poor excuses for the power of creation. Can you feel this power? This gift that always should have been mine? It has been lost for too long, but my triumph is at hand."

Bachman stepped closer to Gabe. The force against Gabe's chest increased, cutting off the air. Stars swam in his vision. The cool bricks pressed against him, the inconsistencies in the grout digging into his back.

"Don't worry about your watcher," Bachman said. "She and her son will learn the truth about you soon enough, but they won't live long enough to hate you."

Gabe concentrated on the brick wall. He sensed its weakness, the natural vibration that flowed through the brick and mortar. He had no air left. The blackness started to overtake his vision. Gabe scraped the edge of his sword along the rough surface of the building. The resulting sound created a resonance that Gabe concentrated on, feeding it, making it grow. He matched the waves to the vibration he felt against his back and threw the sound waves against the wall. Bachman raised his other hand and Gabe prepared for the extra force that smashed into him.

The wall met its elastic limit and exploded inward, the structural integrity failing under the vibrations from Gabe's sword and the pressure Bachman put on it. Without the wall to create the opposing force, Gabe flew backward and was released from the pressure. He sucked in fresh air. Gabe twisted his body to the side and landed in a crouch inside an old, abandoned warehouse.

Bachman lost his balance when the wall collapsed and stumbled forward. He landed on one knee, throwing his hands over his head as bricks rained down on him. Gabe lost sight of Bachman as bricks piled on top of him. The last brick fell with a clunk on top of the pile. Gabe took a tentative step forward.

The bricks flew outward. Gabe dove for cover behind a dividing wall as bricks collided with the front. Gabe looked up and saw a rear exit door in front of him. Crunching footsteps approached as Bachman walked through the rubble toward him. Gabe dashed for the door and slammed his shoulder into it, breaking a chain that held it closed, escaping to the outside. He circled the building in a sprint and didn't slow down when he came to the gaping hole in the wall. He jumped through the hole, knowing exactly where Bachman stood from the sounds he channeled to his ears.

Gabe lifted his swords and brought them together, slicing down through air. His own momentum carried him forward and he had to tuck and roll to keep from falling on his face. He jumped and whirled around, baffled at how he could have missed his target. Bachman stood facing him, undisturbed, a few inches to the side of where Gabe had calculated. *He moves too fast,* thought Gabe. *I should have been able to react to that.*

His chest squeezed tight, his heart thumping in fear. He spun away, ducking behind a steel column, keeping the column between them as Bachman paced in a wide circle.

"Fear," Bachman said. "A new emotion for you. You've experienced guilt, sorrow, anger, pain, but fear? I want you to feel that in the deepest crevice of your soul. You have been a sliver in my palm for too long, slowing my progress, throwing a wrench into my plans. I thought stopping her would be enough, but you've proved to be an infection just as severe. But as hard as you've been to find, I've had plenty of time to prepare. I am ready. And I need you out of the way."

Out of the way. Had this been a trick? To pull him away from Jarren and Treadon? Gabe's heart dropped. Not again.

"That's right. You failed once and you have already failed again. And you keep dragging the poor souls of others down with you," Bachman said.

Bachman spoke with a slow steady cadence. Gabe could feel the hope draining from him. Bachman was right. Gabe was a failure. What hope did he have at standing against the Triune when he couldn't even beat a single Possessed?

"You will lose all that you have fought for. But you should be grateful. I am about to spare you the sorrow of watching me destroy all who trusted you."

Gabe's shoulder ached where the dart had pierced him. It shouldn't be hurting so much. It should be healing. It was such as small wound, but the spot still seemed to be draining him. His legs felt weak; his head pounded from exhaustion. Gabe pushed the pain from his mind and focused all his hatred on Bachman. One more battle, even if it ended for him here—he would take this man down with him.

"You'll never get to see the disappointment on the face of the boy you thought to raise as your own. Never get to see the pain of betrayal on the woman who gave you her heart and received nothing in return. You won't hear them curse you from their graves."

Abigail didn't deserve this. Treadon never had a chance. And it was his fault. Gabe's anger blocked out the other emotions, blocked out all other sensations. Gabe waited for Bachman to step into view and then he pushed off the column, running forward, anticipating the five shards that shot straight from the end of Bachman's fingertips. He hit the ground at the last second, sliding along the concrete floor, shredding his jacket as the darts flew over his head. He was back up, moving so quickly he was a blur. He drew back his swords and aimed them at Bachman's heart. He thrust the swords forward, the gleaming tips of the swords an inch from his enemy's chest.

Bachman lifted his hands. The tips of Gabe's swords hit what should have been the fleshy center of Bachman's palms, but the sword hit something solid. The impact drove the swords from Gabe's grip. They landed at the feet of Bachman.

Bachman took a small step to the side as Gabe toppled over, unable to stop. He landed on his back beyond the reach of his blades. Bachman stepped over the swords to stand above Gabe, his hands out, fingers pointed down toward Gabe's chest. Gabe rolled out of the way as five more darts shot down at him. One shard cut through the top of his ear, grazing his head before penetrating the concrete floor. Another caught him in the ribs. The other three hit the ground behind him, shooting up puffs of concrete dust as they hit the floor.

Gabe jumped to his feet, but the crushing force hit him again. The wind was knocked from his lungs as he hit the ground, pinned on his back. Bachman held one hand toward him, controlling the force that held Gabe to the ground, while bending over to pick up one of Gabe's double-edged swords.

The pressure was intense. The floor beneath him solid, no chance of breaking the floor for relief. Hope pressed out of him, just as effectively as life-giving oxygen. The pressure increased. A normal man would have been crushed. Even Gabe, with the strength of a Guardian, knew his was reaching his limit. He followed the blade of his own sword as Bachman approached, dragging the tip along the ground. What kind of Possessed had a demon this powerful? With the knowledge to control gravity itself? Gabe's view of Bachman faded in and out as his vision grew fuzzy.

"You went off on your own, a vigilante, trying to save the world to make up for your sins. You deserve to die. You deserve to know your failure is complete. Your angel is alive, waiting for you, waiting for the Guardian who will never come. Even she couldn't foresee this ending."

Gabe refused to close his eyes as Bachman drew back his own blade, aiming it at his chest.

Forty-Three

TREADON NELSON

J arren and Treadon burst through the door to Xander Calivan's office at the same time. Treadon's heart pounded so hard he could feel it knocking against his ribs. Jarren wasn't even breathing hard. He stood with his back straight, taking in the scene in front of him.

There was a black table in the middle of the office, the floor cracked and broken around the solid slab like it had risen straight through the floor. It was made of the same black stone as the foyer, golden flecks swirling down and away from the form that was tied to the top of the stone slab like a sacrifice on an old-fashioned alter.

Ellie lay bound by her ankles and wrists, pinned down to the slab. She fought against the restraints, lifting her head to spit at the man standing over her.

Xander Calivan looked like a different person. His face was emotionless, the wax impression they'd seen earlier, but now it looked like the wax had been kept in a hot room. His features had sagged, one eye drooping almost to his cheek bone. One of Xander's hands hovered over Ellie's left forearm, her skin there was boiling, bubbling like a pot over high heat. She screamed again as his hand got closer to her arm, the skin liquifying, a white bone rising up through her arm.

"Dad!" Jarren moved before Treadon registered the whole scene. The glass walls reflected the haunting light that flowed away from Ellie's body on the altar. The whole scene bounced back off the glass as Jarren ran at his dad, hitting him full force with his shoulder. There was a crack, rock hitting rock, as Jarren hit his father like a crash-test-dummy car hits a wall. Xander didn't move, the impact barely affecting him as Jarren slumped to the ground, holding his shoulder.

The only effect was a slight jerk as Xander's hand pulled away from Ellie's arm. The white bone jerked free and fell to the floor with a metallic clang. Ellie's body jerked with a seizure-like motion and then she lay still. It wasn't a bone. It was a long white dagger.

"Ellie." Treadon moved forward. Ellie lifted her head, looking at him. Instead of the pain he expected to see, he saw a deep determination.

Xander Calivan bent over, reaching for the dagger that had fallen. Treadon's mind cleared. Energy flooded through his body. It was the same way he'd felt in the locker room the day he fought Bridger Michaels. It was the way he felt when he thought of helping Ellie, of keeping her safe. His body and mind in complete alignment. One purpose.

The glowing lights swirled and shifted around Jarren. He rose to his hands and knees and dove for the dagger, knocking it from Xander Calivan's fingertips. Treadon tackled Xander from behind. He buried his shoulder into the midsection of Xander. The impact from Treadon threw Xander off his feet and the two of them slid across the floor away from Ellie. Xander pushed Treadon off with incredible force. Treadon managed to land on his feet. Xander rose to face him, seeming taller than a moment before. Even with the distorted wax features, pure rage shone through Xander's eyes. Treadon's stomach clenched, and fear closed his throat, his mouth as dry as a desert sand dune.

Jarren recovered the white dagger and made his way back to the altar. He cut the rope that held Ellie's wrist to the stone.

Treadon ducked as Xander swung a punch. Treadon returned the favor by burying his fist in Xander's rib cage. Xander curled into the force, and Treadon brought his other fist around in an uppercut, catching Xander in the jaw. A normal man would have been out for the count, a knock-out, but Xander only stumbled backward a few steps.

Xander looked at Treadon with bewilderment. He was confused, not injured. That didn't bode well. Xander reached out and put his hands around Treadon's neck, squeezing. Treadon's vision went blurry as he tried to pry Xander's fingers off. And then Jarren was there with Xander's office chair. He swung the chair and slammed it into the back of Xander's head.

Xander released his grip and stumbled back. Ellie had the dagger and was cutting her feet free. "You messed with his girlfriend. That's what happens when you make Treadon Nelson angry." Jarren was breathing hard, like the walk across the room had winded him. How could Jarren run five floors without a pause, but now seemed out of breath?

Xander shook his head. His eyes looked hungrily past them toward Ellie and the white dagger. He pulled both hands back and then shoved them forward. He wasn't close enough to touch them, but a force of wind hit them both in the chest and sent them hurtling backward. They slid across the floor and hit the altar where Ellie was still cutting herself free.

"He's as hard as a rock and as strong as a gorilla." Jarren rubbed his shoulder where he'd hit Xander.

"Are you okay, you're usually more creative with your similes."

"I'll give you some creative language." Jarren bent over his knees with a groan before he could show Treadon his more creative curse words. "This stupid headache feels like my skull is splitting in half. I guess that's not a huge concern if we're going to be dying in the next few minutes."

Treadon helped Jarren get to his feet. Ellie worked on the last rope holding her right hand. Xander regarded them like flies on the wall, as if the man was debating whether to swat them with a fly swatter or crush them with his bare hands. Xander's suit was crumpled, the white shirt hanging out, his breaths coming heavy, not from exertion, but a passionate rage.

Treadon felt like a David facing a Goliath, except Treadon didn't even have a stone to throw. Ellie had the dagger that had been ripped from her arm and she swung it up toward Xander as he approached them. The tip of the dagger cut a long gash across Xander's cheek. The cut turned black, a fowl-smelling smoke rising from the wound.

Xander shoved Treadon one way, Jarren the other way, and he caught Ellie's wrist, twisting the dagger from her grip. He held her arm down to the altar.

Treadon regained his balance and made eye contact with Jarren. They would have to do this together. Jarren and Treadon hit Xander from both sides, knocking Xander forward, the dagger slicing across Ellie's stomach, cutting through her shirt, and ripping into her skin. Blood pooled on the top of the altar.

Treadon hit the dagger's handle, knocking it out of Xander's hand, and sending it spinning across the floor. He grabbed Xander's outstretched arm and twisted it behind his back, kicking Xander in the knee. Treadon expected more resistance after Jarren and Ellie's reactions to Xander, but the arm bent, Xander went down to one knee with a grunt. The whites of Xander's eyes were not visible; the pupil expanded to cover the entire eye, so it looked like a dark black hole. An unearthly growl rose from Xander's throat.

"I can't stop the bleeding." Jarren had his hands on Ellie's stomach.

"Can you heal?" Treadon asked.

"I can't. I don't have the energy." Ellie's voice was weak, her breathing labored. Her face was pale, her color draining out with the blood. Jarren took off his shirt and pressed it against Ellie's stomach.

Xander struggled, but Treadon pushed him to the floor with his knee in Xander's back.

The door flew inward and four of the dog-like creatures stepped into the room growling and snapping.

"I think we're screwed." Jarren wasn't looking much better than Ellie. "I should have borrowed one of those swords from Conan."

Ellie rolled off the altar, Jarren supporting her, but the dogs blocked the door. Xander whipped around, catching Treadon off balance, and shoved his hand against Treadon's chest. Treadon flew backward, colliding with Jarren and Ellie. They all crashed to the floor and slid across the room. Stopping when they hit the far wall made of glass.

The creatures approached them. Ellie kept the shirt pressed against her stomach and raised one hand out toward the dogs. The room smelled of rot and burnt hair. The dogs slowed, shaking their heads against Ellie's attempt to influence their minds. Her hand shook in the air and the creatures seemed to be able to shake off her influence as they started forward again.

"Kill the Ordinaries but leave the Descendant. She still has the second dagger." Xander straightened his suitcoat. He climbed to his feet on the far side of the altar.

"I have some choice last words for you," Jarren said, somehow managing to still sound arrogant.

Four demon dogs flexed their haunches, leaning back, baring their teeth, preparing to pounce.

The creatures jumped. Ellie dove to the right. Treadon and Jarren dove to the left, landing behind Xander's huge oak desk. The creatures hit the glass with four solid thumps, followed by a squeaking sound as they slid down to the floor. It would only take a moment for them to recover, and the desk wasn't much cover from four demons with sharp claws and poisonous teeth.

Ellie yelped as Xander picked her up by her hair and dragged her back to the altar. Treadon clenched his fists. He had felt helpless before, but never like this, with Ellie so close and yet so impossible to reach.

The creatures' claws scratched and screeched on the marble floor as they scrambled back to their feet and turned their sniffing snouts to where Treadon and Jarren crouched behind the huge wooden desk.

Desperate for anything, Treadon opened a drawer on the desk and found a single pen.

"Not my weapon of choice." Jarren shook his head. "I'm sorry I got you into this. I should have listened to Gabe. We should have waited."

"We would have been too late."

"That's what I like about you. The kind of guy who wouldn't be tardy, even for his own demise."

"We can't just hide here while he kills her. We have to do something."

"You got a plan, Hero?" Jarren asked.

Treadon reflexively looked down at his arm where he kept his plays during a game. There was nothing there. No plan. No team. Too many enemies and not enough offense.

One of the creatures jumped on top of the desk, leering down at them. A drip of drool rolled down the creature's dangling tongue and landed on Treadon's forehead. The black slime burned his skin. He wiped it away.

The creature leaned down as a second jumped up and joined its companion.

Ellie yelled from across the room. Treadon could see that Xander had pinned her arm to the altar and had his hand hovering above it, the skin starting to boil. She kicked at Xander, but it looked like she contacted a concrete surface. Her leg crumpled against the force. Xander wasn't even phased.

Treadon gripped the pen in his hand. If Ellie was going to die, he wasn't going to watch it happen hiding behind a desk.

Forty-Four

GABRIEL TUOER

Gabe's last sense to go was his hearing. He waited for the sound of his own sword cutting through the air and slicing open his chest. Everything was black, his mind spinning, his body succumbing to the pressure. In the last moments of consciousness, Gabe thought he heard footsteps, feet shuffling across the concrete.

Bachman still stood over him, Gabe was sure, or else the pressure would have lost some of its crushing force. Then there was a sound Gabe couldn't place, or maybe it was the ringing in his ears. He thought he heard several small explosions.

The pressure disappeared. Gabe's lungs expanded as he gulped fresh air. His vision returned as he sucked in another breath, his body fighting to recover from the oxygen deprivation. He caught sight of Bachman, still standing within reach. Bachman's body jerked violently, his hands up, protecting his face. Something impaled Bachman's hand and he dropped Gabe's sword to the ground.

Gabe reached for his sword and wrapped his fingers around the hilt. At the same moment, Bachman let out a piercing yell of frustration and stumbled backward, his foot landing on the blade of the sword. Gabe's fingers were crushed as Bachman's foot pinned the sword to the concrete floor.

Bachman stumbled again, his face flashing through the dim light coming through the window. One of Bachman's eyes was pierced with something that had a small circular end. Clear and brown fluid flowed down Bachman's face from the demolished eye socket. Bachman's suit was riddled with similar punctures.

Something pierced the side of Bachman's skull as he looked down at Gabe. The thing sticking out of Bachman's head was a nail. Bachman let out an inhuman roar. The air whizzed with noise as nails continued to slam into Bachman's torso, arms, and head.

Gabe stayed on his back, pulling his hand free as Bachman's weight lifted off the sword. Bachman turned, several nails burying themselves into his back, and ran out of the warehouse through the gaping hole Gabe had created earlier. Gabe lifted his sword off the ground and pulled it toward him. He had only made it up to one knee when he heard footsteps approaching from the opposite direction.

He whipped his sword in front of him, the point touching the chest of an old man, fedora hat pulled down low over his face, long heavy trench coat sagging from his shoulders.

"Vox."

"Come on." Vox grabbed Gabe's arm and helped pull him to his feet. "That will only keep him busy for a minute."

Gabe let Vox pull him toward an interior wall. Gabe grabbed his second sword as they made their way across the floor. They reached the wall and crouched behind it.

"What was that?" Gabe asked.

Vox held up a framer's nail gun. "I personally modified a powder-actuated nail gun. This baby can shoot seven nails a second and can hit a target from over thirty yards away." Vox patted the gun tenderly.

"Thank you." The sentiment felt empty, but he couldn't think of anything else to say to the brother that had saved his life. "It's good to see you."

Vox smiled, the leathery skin of his face lining with deep wrinkles.

"I told you I'd be the one to save you someday. Just didn't think it would take me forty years to do it."

Gabe set a hand on Vox's shoulder. His younger brother had aged decades beyond him. It was sobering. He'd been given the gift of youth, but his brother would always be his hero.

They both leaned to the side so they could peer around the wall. A blinding pain shot from Gabe's side and he looked down to see a black shard of hematite protruding from his rib cage.

Vox reached into his heavy trench coat and pulled out a pair of dirty pliers. "Here. Let me help." Vox lifted Gabe's elbow and grabbed the end of the shard between the teeth of the pliers. He gave a sudden, sharp jerk, pulling the shard free. He held the hematite up, pinched in the plier's grip. Gabe felt a wave of dizziness, as if every ounce of energy he possessed had just been pulled from his body.

"What else have you got in that coat?" Gabe asked.

"A little surprise for our friend."

Footsteps echoed, crushing on the rubble from the building's destruction. The pattern was a step, drag, like one leg was dragging from an injury.

Gabe tightened his grip on his double-edged swords. Vox reached into the recesses of his overcoat. This was not a battle for an Ordinary.

"I'm grateful for what you did, but this isn't your fight. You've done enough."

They made eye contact, his brother's stubbornness in youth had stayed with him all these years.

Gabe listened for the tell-tale sign of Bachman's breathing. The footsteps stopped. He pulled both his swords next to his body and stood.

He swung around the corner, weaved around the anticipated rain of hematite shards, and jammed one end of his sword into the concrete. He used the handle to propel himself into the air and twist sideways. With his other sword he aimed for the pulsing jugular on Bachman's neck.

Bachman bent backward. Gabe's sword missed again, his body continuing forward, over the top of Bachman's head. Gabe twisted in the air, bringing his feet under him. Bachman turned to face him.

"You get chances to redeem yourself, to taste revenge, but you keep falling short," Bachman said. "It's time to give up."

Gabe clenched his jaw. He no longer cared if he lived or died. He just wanted one shot.

Glass shattered followed by a splash of liquid.

Bachman's entire body burst into flame.

In the flickering light, Gabe could make out Vox standing beside the wall, wearing a satisfied smile. The remains of the shattered bottle at Bachman's feet smelled of gas. Vox had broken a bottle filled with gasoline over Bachman's head and ignited it in a single swipe.

Gabe was impressed.

Bachman batted at his chest and arms. The gasoline-soaked fabric of his suit was being consumed and Bachman's attempts to put out the fire were useless. Gabe felt a tug of dread as Bachman stood calmly amid the flames. There was a sudden change in pressure. His ears popped. Air rushed past him. The flames disappeared as quickly as they had ignited.

Bachman stood in front of Gabe, his body still smoking, glowing red spots remained from the fire. A bone-chilling laugh emanated from Bachman's smoldering form.

"The pathetic use of Ordinary knowledge. We have the knowledge of creation itself and you think you can stop me with fire."

Bachman turned, moving faster than Gabe could track. He was by Vox before Gabe could let out a warning. Bachman grabbed Vox by the neck and threw him across the room. Gabe moved fast enough to catch Vox's coat and stop him before he smashed into the far wall.

Vox's breath came in ragged gasps. Gabe felt a warm trickle of blood run over his hand from Vox's neck.

"He isn't your average demon-possessed soul, is he?" Vox said.

Bachman had an energy Gabe had never seen before, a knowledge of controlling things that only Descendants had access to. When fighting Possessed, the goal was to destroy the body and the demon would have to move on, find a new soul to feast on. Bachman wasn't following that generalization. The body he possessed was beyond ruined, but the demon remained, more powerful than ever.

Bachman took a step forward and a small amount of light from the night sky illuminated his disfigured face. His missing eye still drained fluid that ran down his now red and blistered face. His suit was melted in places, burned away, revealing burnt flesh. Bachman smiled, revealing blackened teeth through half melted lips.

"No. He's not." Gabe felt like he should have an explanation, but his mind was blank, the cold dread of death freezing his heart.

Bachman lifted his hand. Gabe prepared for the agonizing pressure that would follow. He accepted the futility of the fight. He stood tall, shoulders back, looking the Possessed in his one good eye.

Instead of being hit with a force, Vox was ripped from his hands, the frail form of his brother flying across the room, slamming into a column with a sickening crunch.

Forty-Five

TREADON NELSON

Blood dripped down the side of the altar, running onto the floor with the golden specks in the hematite. Ellie struggled, pulling her wrist free from Xander's grasp and rolling away, but he caught her by the back of the shirt and slammed her head down against the stone. Treadon felt the pain like it was his own, but it only fueled the rage rising inside him.

The two creatures growled above them, crouching down as the other two circled around opposite sides of the desk, surrounding them.

"No way I'm going down curled up in a ball." Jarren jumped to his feet, fists in front of his face. One of the creatures lunged, but Treadon stood and slammed the ink pen into the creature's eye. It stopped, turning its head almost all the way around so it could look at Treadon with its good eye.

The door slammed open.

Rachel and Abigail stepped into Xander's office, pulling the attention of all four creatures and Xander away from their current battles.

Treadon took advantage of the creature's distraction and pulled the pen from its eye. The creature lunged again and Treadon shoved the pen into the creature's mouth, jamming the point up through the pallet, crunching through bone. The creature's teeth sank into his forearm. Treadon fell back against the wall, pain shooting through his arm. The creature disintegrated before it could close its mouth all the way.

Treadon dropped the pen. There was a puncture wound between the two bones of his arm. It wasn't bleeding. The hole oozed a dark substance, and his skin turned a rotting black.

Abigail held a mace in each hand. Green stones tipped the sharp points protruding from the metal balls at the top. She wore a red chain mail vest, thick leather pants, and black boots that looked like they could punt a football to the moon.

"Mom?"

"Rachel?" Jarren echoed Treadon's disbelief.

Rachel looked like a warrior from a comic book. Her long, dark hair was pulled back in a ponytail with shards of green rock clipped to the ends of her hair like tiny, pointed daggers. She held a short sword in one hand and a three-pronged weapon in the other.

The three creatures charged at the two women. Rachel spun, catching the creature across the jaw with the end of her ponytail, following the strike with a stab to the creature's rib cage. It disintegrated to dust.

With a battle cry, Abigail swung the mace and crushed a creature's skull. Before it had completely disappeared, she pulled a bag from a pocket and tossed red dust at the last creature. It sneezed, then began convulsing, the skin growing sores and oozing where it contacted the red dust. Rachel brought her sword around, cutting off the creature's head.

Xander had to cover his face as a small amount of red dust reached him, but he didn't lose his grip on Ellie. He held her down with one hand around her neck.

Jarren ran across the room to Rachel. "What are you doing here and where did you get a sai? You know Raphael was my favorite turtle." He shook his head and grabbed her shoulders, dropping the wall, flipping the switch. "If you're here and I'm about to die, that means I can't protect you. That means I can't keep you safe."

Treadon stepped closer to Xander, but Xander only tightened his grip on Ellie's neck, her fingers scraping uselessly against his hand. She couldn't breathe. Treadon stopped as Xander put his hand up, calling more of those creatures from the ground. Treadon didn't know how many there were. Maybe an endless amount. They could fight these dogs all night while Ellie died.

He tested his grip. The pain in his arm was intense, but he focused on Ellie, on the fight going on around him.

The growls and barks sounded from the hallway. Abigail turned toward the door. She stood tall and straight, confidence Treadon had never seen in her, but realized had always been there. She was herself with the weapons in her hand and the smear of black creature remains across her forehead.

Rachel leaned in and pressed her lips to Jarren's, her weapons held to the side.

"Have you stopped to consider the fact that I'm meant to protect you?" She stepped back into the hall. "We'll keep these guys busy. You get Ellie."

They turned to face the creatures. Xander growled and lifted Ellie up by the neck, her feet kicking in the air. Treadon launched himself forward and wrapped his arms around Xander, pinning Xander's arms to his side and forcing him backward. Xander lost his grip on Ellie's neck, and she fell back to the altar.

Treadon pulled Xander away, stumbling to the center of the room. All he had to do was hang on until Ellie and Jarren could get out of the room.

Abigail and Rachel were slicing, dicing, and crushing the dog-like creatures out in the lobby, but when one creature disintegrated, another took its place. They were being pushed back from the hallway toward the office. There was only a small space for them to escape through the door.

Jarren was by Ellie's side, helping her off the altar. Xander twisted, trying to knock Treadon off like a mechanical bull. Their feet kicked the white dagger that had dropped to the floor earlier, and it skidded to Jarren's feet. He picked it up. He and Ellie headed toward the door.

"I'm not finished." Xander spoke through gritted teeth. He burst free of Treadon's hold with a strength that defied reality. Treadon fell to the ground, holding his wounded arm and rolling back and forth as his vision blackened around the edges.

Jarren turned and threw the dagger at Xander's throat. His aim was dead center, but the knife slowed in the air. Xander lifted one arm straight and shoved it toward the knife. All Xander's energy seemed focused on slowing the dagger in the air. It stopped an inch from his throat. Xander's hands were shaking, beads of sweat popping out on his forehead, concentration causing a small wrinkle in the wax features. The knife turned in the air.

The tip pointed at Jarren's heart. Jarren didn't flinch, didn't move out of the way. He stared at his dad as if daring him to kill his own son.

Xander showed no remorse as his hands pulled back like they were preparing to shove the dagger through the air.

Treadon was out of time. He pushed himself up, grabbing Xander again. This time, when he pinned Xander's hands to his side, the dagger clattered to the ground. Treadon squeezed as hard as he could and struggled to hang on. His hold was loosening. He didn't understand what was happening until he realized his feet were no longer touching the floor. Xander was growing. His body was larger than Treadon's arms could encircle. Xander grew taller and wider until his head hit the ten-foot ceiling. Treadon's grip failed. He slipped and started to fall, but Xander's gigantic hand shot out and caught Treadon by the throat.

The hand was large enough for the fingers to encircle his neck, and he felt the pressure as Xander began to squeeze.

Treadon twisted helplessly, his feet dangling. Xander's face had ballooned out, his nose pulling flat, his jaw stretching forward. Xander's eyes bulged from his head. The beast that used to be Xander Calivan roared in anger, shaking Treadon's body like a rag doll, shooting spittle across the room. Treadon could barely grip Xander's wrists with both hands as he fought to get free.

Then Jarren was there, jumping off the ground, grabbing Xander's massive forearm. Jarren opened his mouth and bit into the flesh of Xander's arm, clenching his teeth and pulling his head back sharply. A large chunk of distorted skin and muscle ripped from Xander's arm, and the monster released Treadon as he threw his head back and let out a blood-curdling roar.

Treadon fell to the floor.

Xander lifted his arm in the air, Jarren still dangling, going back in for another bite. Xander swung his arm down like a man attacking a fly with a newspaper. The arm came down on top of Jarren, slamming him to the floor with the snap of a bone. Jarren yelled, his leg twisted and bent at an unnatural angle.

"Jarren!" Rachel screamed. She watched him fall, but another creature attacked her before she could move.

Abigail fought next to her, hair escaping her tight bun, flying around her head like angry snakes. More dog-like creatures blocked the entrance into the office. Ellie leaned against the far wall, unable to get to the door, her strength seeping out of her as she slipped down to the floor.

He was going to fail. Treadon could feel the chances of success slipping away. The momentum was gone. Their offense was out of plays. The other team was ahead. Their loss was assured. The fear gripped him around the neck, sat on his chest, and made his legs feel weak.

Xander's body was shaped more like a giant ape than a man. He raised his arm again, fist curled into a ball like a hammer ready to fall.

Treadon crawled backward and his hand hit the white dagger that had fallen to the floor. The blade seemed short compared to the giant of a man in front of him, from hilt to point, the dagger was as long as Ellie's forearm. It felt like trying to fend off a giant with a needle. But it was all he had.

Xander swung his arm, appearing to put all his force into his fist aimed at Jarren. Treadon threw himself between Xander and Jarren, using his whole body to thrust the dagger up and into Xander's chest. The entire weight of Xander's colossal body fell on the point of the upturned knife. The dagger buried itself into Xander's chest, a black smoke erupting from the wound, smelling of rotten eggs and burning plastic.

Treadon's fingers sunk into the enlarged muscles of Xander's chest, and he had to let go of the dagger to pull his hands free, a black gore covered his fingers. There was a hissing sound, like air escaping through a hole in a balloon.

Xander staggered back, stretching to his full height, knocking chunks of the ceiling to the floor. His head thrashed back and forth as an inhuman scream escaped his mouth. Treadon watched in horror as skin fell from Xander's face and hands, like small grains of sand pulling away from his body. As more of Xander fell away, the tiny pieces began to spin as if caught in some whirlwind.

The grains of sand bit into Treadon's face and he raised one hand for protection. He crawled along the floor, finding Jarren. He helped Jarren to the wall where Ellie sat with her arms crossed over her stomach. The intensity of the sand increased. The three of them huddled together, trying to protect their faces against the wind. The wind blew the door shut. Abigail and Rachel stuck on the outside.

The sand pulled at his clothes and bit into his exposed skin. The sand hit the glass windows and scraped along the marble floor with an awful grating noise. The pressure in the room increased until Treadon felt like his eardrums might explode.

There was a deafening crack. The entire wall of glass windows shattered outward as the sand escaped. The pressure reduced and the whirlwind of sand lessened, escaping into the night. Treadon opened his mouth to flex his jaw, popping his ears. He peeked over his arm that was wrapped protectively around Jarren and Ellie.

The real Xander lay on the floor in the middle of the room, the white dagger sticking out of his chest.

Forty-Six

GABRIEL TUOER

The crumpled form of Vox's body didn't move. Gabe turned back, Bachman's working eye staring at him.

"See the fruits of your labors? The first of the weak Ordinaries you've led to their death. The first to suffer and die because of you. But not the last."

Gabe gripped his swords and ran forward. He had no plan this time, no anticipation or goal to get out of the way. He had one target. He would not miss. Bachman raised his hands and five more shards shot from his fingertips. Gabe didn't flinch or dodge. He ran right into them.

He focused only on Bachman. The shards sunk into his arm, upper thigh, and stomach. His vision shrunk, a black circle closing in, the only thing visible in the very center was Bachman.

Gabe swung his sword.

The distant sound of shattering glass reverberated in his ears.

The sword hit its target.

He felt the resistance as the sword went into Bachman's side and continued up through the first two ribs. He jerked the sword out of Bachman's torso with satisfaction and prepared to swing again.

Bachman didn't react as Gabe stabbed his sword directly into Bachman's belly. Bachman's face was turned up, away from Gabe. It might as well have been a mosquito bite for all the reaction Bachman had to the sword in his gut. He stared out one of the high windows in the building. The outline of the top floor of XC Energy was visible through the gap.

There was still a light on the top floor, but it was dim, almost like a shadow had moved between them and the building.

"No," Bachman whispered. "Impossible."

The shadow grew darker, larger. Something was coming closer. Gabe dove to the floor and covered his head as a whirlwind of biting dust slammed into the building, entering through every hole and crack, swirling around them.

The whirlwind centered around Bachman in a funnel. Bachman extended one hand as if trying to catch a few pieces. Bachman's features were unreadable, but his movements were slow, careful, like someone tending to a wounded cat. He looked down, noticing that his torso was nearly severed in half. He placed one hand on the wound as if trying to hold himself together. He leaned back, face to the whirlwind.

"Pravus." The word was a mournful scream. "After thousands of years, you will never return. My old friend. My strongest servant. Goodbye."

He stepped forward, focusing on Gabe. His body jerked, unsteady, not as a man suffering from pain, but like a malfunctioning machine. One arm hung useless, the other wrapped around the wound in his side. "You haven't won. This is only the last breath of hope before consuming darkness."

The black whirlwind grew in its intensity, pulling together, focusing around Bachman's body, swirling in closer, tighter, until Gabe could only see a column of swirling black sand. The spinning column exploded.

Gabe covered his head for protection as the sand burst outward in all directions and then settled, lifeless, to the ground.

When Gabe looked up, Bachman was gone.

Silence reigned.

Gabe could just make out the sound of ragged breathing. Vox.

Gabe tried to stand, but he could feel the darts in him, draining him of hope and energy. He resigned himself to crawling across the floor to reach Vox's side.

Vox lay face down in a widening pool of blood. Gabe gently pulled on Vox's shoulder and turned him onto his back. He swallowed hard. Vox's chest cavity was crushed in, broken ribs visible through the skin.

"Vox."

Vox's eyes fluttered.

"I did it." Vox's voice was nothing more than a garbled whisper. "All I ever wanted to do was to die fighting that man."

"You did more than fight him. You beat him. You saved me." Gabe swallowed the lump in his throat. He tried to separate Vox's saturated shirt from his body.

Vox reached up and grabbed Gabe's wrist. His fingers were cold and there was no strength in the grip. Gabe stopped. Vox's head shook once, minutely.

"Go," Vox said between short breaths.

"Stay with me," whispered Gabe, grasping Vox's hand as if to force him.

"Go save your boy." Vox said the last two words in one drawn-out exhale. The corners of Vox's mouth turned up as he stared over Gabe's shoulder. His eyes glazed over.

Gabe gritted his teeth and let go of Vox's hand. He brushed Vox's eyelids down, hand hovering over his face.

"Farewell, brother. May the Angels reward you for your courage and guide you to eternal rest."

He didn't want to move. He had nothing left. No energy. No hope. He could close his eyes and let everything slip away.

Vox's last words echoed through his mind. Vox's boys were gone, but there was another boy. A boy he would happily call his son: Treadon. And Abigail. Sweet, patient Abigail. If he slipped away, let the darkness take him, they would be left to face the consequences alone. As much as he wished for death, he couldn't leave them.

Not yet.

Not like this.

He reached into Vox's trench coat and found the pliers. He locked them onto the sliver in his arm and yanked. Gabe was grateful he was already on the ground as the dizziness from the pain nearly knocked him unconscious. He waited for his head to clear and then yanked the second one from his leg. Each time he said their names.

Abigail.

Treadon.

He lifted his shirt to find the shard that had penetrated his stomach. Only a small black dot revealed its location. There was no time. He could feel the blackness sucking his energy into the last shard. The little reasoning left in Gabe's weakening mind was that Treadon must not have done as he was told, must have gone into the building and faced an enemy without him.

He searched through Vox's coat again. He found the nail gun, a hammer, nail strips, some miniature saw blades, and a meat cleaver. A coat full of weapons. A man fighting for revenge with every resource he could find. Vox was a hero in a way Gabe had never been.

Finally, Gabe found a utility knife and slid the blade out. He took a deep breath and sliced across the spot where the black shard had disappeared. He sucked in air through his teeth as he pushed the pliers in, felt the resistance, and positioned the pliers around the end of the shard.

The strength to pull it out was gone. He had one thing left to live for.

As he pulled, squeezing the pliers, he yelled her name.

"Adura." His Angel. His lost Descendant. Caden Bachman said she was alive. And his Guardian instinct kicked in. The pliers came out dripping with blood, pinching the last black shard of hematite.

He tossed the pliers to the side. The relief was immense, but not complete. The slice on his belly was healing, but slowly. There was more, something else was wrong, but at least he could stand and stumble out of the building toward the light.

Forty-Seven

Jarren Calivan

The whirlwind disappeared into the darkness. Jarren rolled away from Treadon and Ellie. The pain in his leg had ebbed away into shock. His breathing was labored and his heartbeat was too fast.

He kept his eyes averted from the body in the center of the floor, not sure if he'd see a monster or his father. His entire life he'd wanted the man's approval, his acceptance. A sharp pain of sorrow kept his arms wrapped around his chest.

Abigail and Rachel slammed their way through the door. Jarren switched his gaze to Rachel.

"They're gone," Rachel said. "The fenris disintegrated, kind of like the finger snap." She had a bleeding cut on her shoulder and a bruise on her cheek.

She looked amazing, tall and fierce and strong and everything he'd always feared he wasn't. He didn't deserve her, but he'd always pretended he was too good. He regretted that.

"What happened in here?" Rachel made her way to him as he pushed himself up into a sitting position.

"Is everyone okay?" Treadon asked, helping Ellie sit up. He kept his hand over the wound in his arm. Black tendrils were working their way up through his veins. Jarren could see the skin turning dark at Treadon's elbow.

"Just so you know, that's a really stupid question." Jarren grimaced when he tried to straighten his leg. His shin appeared misshapen through his khakis—a lump that could only be a bone.

"Good to see you're still you." Treadon slapped Jarren on the shoulder, but it was a half-hearted slap. Treadon kept his right arm tight against his side.

Jarren swore.

"We should get you to a hospital." Treadon tried to help him up.

"You need to get her to a hospital." Jarren pointed to Ellie.

Ellie lay on the floor, breath coming in shallow gasps, her eyes closed. Her color had leeched out of her face. Her lips were a strange shade of purple. Her chest rose and fell in a sporadic rhythm. One side of her face was red and scraped from the whirlwind.

"No," Abigail said. She stood in the doorway. "There would be too many questions we couldn't answer at a hospital. We'll take her to our house. Gabe can help her. Where is Gabe?"

Treadon and Jarren exchanged a glance. "He went to fight the other guy. There was an explosion."

"I'll go look for him. And I'll pull the car up to the front door." Abigail left.

"Why isn't she healing?" Treadon brushed a strand of hair away from Ellie's face. Jarren looked away from the intimate moment, feeling his friend's pain, knowing he didn't have a way to help. His gaze landed on his dad's body, and he felt like his chest was caving in on itself.

"I don't know, but the sooner we get out of here, the better we'll all feel."

"What about your leg?" Rachel asked. "Ellie's too sick to help herself. I don't think she can heal you."

"Treadon can fix it." Despite everything, Jarren reveled in the look of shock on Treadon's face. The guy needed to learn to fake confidence. It was a useful skill.

Treadon scooted closer to Jarren and placed a hand on his broken leg. Jarren couldn't keep the hiss of pain in.

"I don't know what to do," Treadon said.

"It's not rocket science." Jarren spoke through gritted teeth, either the shock was wearing off or the pain was getting worse. "Rachel will hold my hand and you'll shove it back where it's supposed to be. On the count of three. Ready?"

Treadon nodded and put both hands on Jarren's leg. For some reason, Jarren thought Treadon would fight harder, try to pass the job onto someone else, but the guy was really going to do it. Jarren squeezed Rachel's hand. She wrapped her other arm around his shoulders and put pressure on him, her strength holding him up, making him brave enough to start the count.

"One, two . . . Ow!"

Treadon didn't wait for three. His hands clamped on Jarren's leg, moving with a confidence Jarren hadn't expected, like he knew what he was doing, like putting a bone back into place had been written into his DNA.

The bone crunched back into place. Jarren had to curl up and close his eyes, rocking back and forth. Rachel placed a hand on his head, telling him it was going to be okay. But he could barely hear her, barely feel her through the pain.

He found the strength to open his eyes when he heard Treadon wretch all over the office floor. Jarren took a deep breath.

"You're such a wimp." He didn't know where Treadon's confidence had come from, but he was grateful for it. He could tell the bone was back in place, still broken, but at least not trying to break through the skin.

"Okay." Rachel stood and brushed the dust and fenris remnants from her hands like she'd finished cleaning the kitchen. "Let's get you out of here."

He reached up and grabbed Rachel's hand. She pulled and he put his weight on his good leg, hopping into her side, leaning into her body with unnecessary exaggeration.

"I said I'd protect you. And I'll always support you. But I'm not carrying you." Rachel pushed him so he balanced on his own.

He needed her. He wanted her. He had always wanted to be the strong one, the one who protected and took care of her, but he'd been wrong. They could take care of each other. He looked in her eyes. She reached up and touched his face.

It wasn't the right time, it never seemed like the right time, but life felt too unpredictable, too out of control to wait another second. Jarren leaned in and Rachel met him half-way, their lips pressing together. The cherry ChapStick took him back to an era he never lived in but had always loved.

A crashing sound came from behind them and both he and Rachel jumped. Jarren was aware enough to stumble back with small hops on his good leg, Rachel keeping him from falling over.

"What the hell?" Treadon had still been leaning over Ellie, trying to get her to respond. He ran to stand by them, his body tensed, ready for a fight.

He didn't have a weapon, not even a pen.

A creature was crawling into the room, gripping desperately to the edge of the broken windows, a hunched form that moved like a wounded animal.

"I thought you said the fenris ran away," Jarren said to Rachel.

"That's not a fenris."

"Gabe." Treadon was the first to recognize the form as a man. He darted forward and grasped Gabe's wrist before he lost his grip. The man looked like he'd survived a battle zone. Or a meat grinder. Blood dripped down one side of his head from a rip in his ear. His clothes were covered with a gray dust and the smell of smoke lingered on him. Treadon steadied Gabe as he wavered in the opening.

Gabe's eyes took in the scene. "What happened here?"

"That's a long story." Jarren couldn't resist. "Do want the cliff notes or the director's edition?"

Gabe stumbled forward when he saw Ellie slumped on the floor. The bleeding had slowed, but her wound still oozed.

"Get her off the floor," Gabe said. "It's black hematite. It's weakening her. Get her out of here now." Despite looking like a guy ready to collapse, he sure could give an order.

Treadon ran back across the room and lifted Ellie from the floor. The golden specks in the black, marble floor stilled, puddling around Treadon's feet. Ellie groaned with the movement but being pulled away from the floor seemed to make a difference as the bleeding in her stomach stopped.

Gabe hobbled over to Treadon's side. "Let's get her to my office. Tell me what happened on the way."

Treadon stepped out the door with Ellie in his arms. He held her like she was weightless. Gabe motioned for he and Rachel to go next, but as Jarren hopped toward the door, Gabe stumbled to the side, leaning on the wall for support.

"Help him," Jarren said, nodding to Rachel. "I can hop fine. I used to cheat at skipping when they graded us in kindergarten. I only ever used one leg."

"You're such a nerd." Rachel shook her head at him but slipped over and put Gabe's arm over her shoulder to help him out the door. Gabe and Rachel were in the doorway, Jarren just behind them when he heard his name.

"Jarren." It was barely a whisper.

He froze in the doorway. He hunched his shoulders, not knowing whether to hope or to scream.

The voice came again, a little stronger.

"Please, Jarren. I have to tell you something."

Jarren didn't know if it was paranoia, exhaustion, stupidity, or strength, but he wanted this. He needed this. And he needed to do it alone.

He reached forward and slipped his hand into Gabe's leather jacket pocket. He gripped the ring for the motorcycle key just as Gabe turned.

Jarren wished he could apologize. Hoped there would be time for apologies later. Then he balanced himself on his good leg and shoved Rachel and Gabe into the hall. They both stumbled, not expecting it. Recovering too slowly.

The sight of Rachel's face as he slammed the office door and flipped the lock into place was the scariest thing he'd faced all night.

She hated being locked out, especially when she knew he was in pain.

He hopped around until he was facing his father. Xander Calivan's head was lifted an inch off the floor, one hand stretched toward him, pleading.

Jarren hopped forward and stood over his father's dying body.

"I'm sorry," Xander said. "If you believe nothing else, please believe, I am sorry."

Jarren studied the wound in his dad's chest. The knife was buried halfway up the blade. Blood seeped out around the white blade, now stained with red fingerprints. A puddle of blood pooled around Jarren's foot, soaking his dad's usually pristine dress shirt.

If someone had asked him yesterday, he would have said his father had a lifetime of sins to ask forgiveness for. And he would have given that forgiveness in a heartbeat. If only his dad had asked him then.

Now, Jarren wasn't even sure what his dad was sorry for.

"Why?" There were so many ways to end that sentence Jarren couldn't go on.

"I wanted to protect you, but I was too late. I'd given them too much. I wanted to undo what they'd done to you. I was a coward. But I can give you what I have. Maybe you can help Vox finish what he started."

Jarren used his good leg to lower himself down next to his father. "But you're going to be okay. The dagger shoved the demon out of you. Gabe said that was the only way."

Rachel's pounding on the door was distant. He wanted to tell her to go away. He wanted to wrap him up in her arms.

"It's too late for me. I can't undo what I've done."

"What are you talking about?" Jarren looked at his dad's hand, still extended toward him. "You want to undo what you did to Ellie? To that poor girl?"

Xander's eyes followed Jarren's pointing finger to the stone pillar in the middle of the room. He squinted in confusion. "What girl?"

"Dad. Do you not remember the girl you just tortured on a stone altar and pulled that white dagger in your chest out of her arm?"

Xander's mouth formed an O and he looked back at Jarren. "He must have found her. The Descendant of Adeona. He'd been searching for lifetimes for the power she possessed."

"What are you talking about?"

Xander took a shuddering breath that was punctuated by the sound of liquid. Xander choked and sputtered. He turned his head to the side and spit blood onto the floor.

"I don't have time to explain. But you deserve to know two things. I see you now. I see you as my son."

The words didn't bring Jarren comfort. They made him angry. "I've always been your son."

"And your mother deserves to know. You need to find her."

"Let me get you out of here. I'll call an ambulance."

"It's too late for me. I can only hope that what I was able to do was enough to save you in the end."

"It's not too late. You're okay. It's not too late." Jarren couldn't stop the tears the slipped down his cheeks. He wiped at them angrily.

"My personal laptop is in a hidden compartment in my desk. Press the lower panel three times and turn the nob to the right. Your mother's information is under the file Salina. Find her."

"Dad."

"Get the computer."

The desk seemed a hundred miles away. Unreachable. His dad was right there. He could reach out and touch him. Jarren finally gripped his dad's outstretched hand. Squeezing. Xander squeezed back, shaking their grip up and down.

"I am proud of you. You have the power to do great things. I only wish I could be there to watch."

"Dad."

"Go grab it. I'll show you how to turn it on."

Jarren knew his dad. There would be no more discussion until he did what he was asked. Jarren balanced on one leg as he stood up. He hopped over to the desk and felt the paneling beneath the drawers. He followed his dad's instructions and a secret compartment opened. A laptop and power cord inside. That was it.

He pulled them out and lifted them up to show his dad.

Xander lay flat on his back in a pool of his own blood. His eyes were open. Both hands were on the handle of the white dagger.

"No!" Jarren screamed, throwing himself toward his dad, putting pressure on his broken leg. His strength gave out and he crashed to the floor, laptop clattering beside him.

Xander looked over at Jarren. "When you find her, will you tell her? Tell her I was wrong. Tell her I was sorry . . . in the end." Xander took one last gasp of air and pushed the knife farther into his chest.

Jarren watched in horror as his dad's body went rigid. His head dropped to the floor and his hands dropped from the dagger, sagging to the side. All the air was sucked from the room. Jarren lay on his belly staring at his dad's bloodied hands.

There was a splintering sound as Gabe joined Rachel's efforts to get into the room. He couldn't. Jarren couldn't face them right now. He grabbed the laptop and forced himself to his feet, gritting his teeth against the pain. He walked to the shattered windows.

Somehow, he knew the ground would catch him. The same way the mountain had caught the car. The same way the football field was his playground.

Jarren stepped to the edge and jumped.

Forty-Eight

TREADON NELSON

Ellie's head lay against his shoulder, her eyes closed, her breathing evening out the longer she was away from the black hematite. Treadon kept his arm around her shoulder, resisting the urge to touch her face, to trace her perfect lips. She was safe. That was all he'd wanted. She'd made her feelings clear, and he would respect that.

Abigail drove the Pontiac home in record time, flinching each time a sharp turn made Gabe groan. Gabe sat in the front seat, a hand over his stomach, his head against the window. He looked like he'd fought his way through Hell and back.

When Abigail pulled into the driveway and put the car in park, Ellie's eyes finally opened. She saw him.

"You came."

"Of course."

She sat up, her cheeks coloring as her hand paused against his chest. "Even after what I said, about never being able to choose you."

Treadon dropped his eyes. "Yes. I had to know you were safe. I was going to find your Guardian so they could help you. Finding you was worth letting you go."

He reached into his pocket and pulled out the necklace by the chain. She took it from his fingers. He pulled the journal out next and held it out to her.

Ellie reached for it, but stopped as she caught sight of his arm. "What happened?"

"Dog bite. I'll be okay."

Abigail looked over the back seat and gasped. "Why didn't you tell me you were bit. The fenris have poisoned fangs. Most Ordinaries would be dead already."

Treadon felt a little dizzy. He pulled his sleeve up and saw that the poison almost reached his armpit.

"You'll have to learn to take care of yourself without me." Ellie stayed calm, despite her drained color and her forearm burns barely starting to heal, she reached for his arm and touched her finger to the wound.

Treadon felt the cool pulse of her healing touch. He saw the extra drain on her and wanted to pull away, but she pressed his back against the door. Her grip was firm and determined. He never wanted her to let go.

He felt the poison drain, and the hole in his arm closed. Ellie sat back, closing her eyes for a moment as she squeezed the amulet.

"I'm glad you found my journal."

"It helped me ask the right questions."

"Did you read the whole thing?" She hadn't put her hand out to accept the journal.

"No. I only got to the part about how the amulet leads your Guardian to you."

Ellie pushed the journal back toward him. "I want you to finish reading. So that you understand." She opened the door and got out of the car.

Rachel studied her hands beside him. "He just disappeared, without saying anything. Why would he leave?"

They'd all heard the roar of Gabe's motorcycle engine as Jarren drove away.

"Where would he go?" Gabe asked.

"He probably needs some time to process. Alone." Rachel watched out the window, her eyebrows pulled down, sorrow tugging at the corner of her mouth. "Why does he have to try to be so strong? He knows he can ask for help. He knows I would do anything for him."

Treadon put a hand on Rachel's shoulder. "He knows. And that's what gives him strength."

Rachel blinked against the tears threatening to fall.

"Treadon, help me with Gabe." Abigail had walked around the car and was trying to get Gabe out of the passenger seat. Treadon climbed out of the car. Ellie stood at the end of the driveway, looking up at a full moon, the stars nearly invisible.

"Here." Treadon pulled one of Gabe's arms over his shoulder and helped lift him out of the car. "Are you coming in?" he called to Ellie. "I make a mean grilled cheese."

She nodded, following them through the front door. He helped lay Gabe on the futon in the office and then Abigail shoved him out, shutting the door in his face.

He turned and saw Rachel and Ellie staring at him. "Just go in," Rachel said. "They're so used to keeping you out they don't know how to invite you in. Show them you're serious. We'll make the sandwiches."

The door handle was locked, but it was just a door. He used to accept locks and rules and secrets, ignore them so he could pretend life was great, focus on football and normal life without facing things bigger than he was. He didn't want that anymore. He wanted to face things as they were, not as he wanted them to be.

He grabbed the handle with both hands and twisted with a determined jerk. The mechanism inside snapped and the door opened.

Gabe sat on the futon against the far wall, his torso was bare above the waist. Abigail sat next to him with a knife and tweezers. Abigail jumped as the door swung open. Gabe looked up. "Took you long enough."

"What happened?" Treadon asked.

"A hematite shard broke off in Gabe's stomach. It's sucking the life energy from his body and preventing him from healing. I don't know how he has any strength left."

Abigail's voice shook. The cut on her shoulder was still bleeding. Treadon leaned forward and placed his hand over her shaking fist. "Let me help. You should go see Ellie and let her heal you. I'll help Gabe."

"I'm all right." Abigail shook her head.

"Let me help," Treadon said. "You don't have to do this alone anymore."

Abigail dropped her head like she'd been handed a gift she'd never expected to receive. She was afraid but wanted this with every ounce of her soul.

"Let him help." Gabe's voice was rough and low. "You've done enough for today."

Treadon thought Gabe would reach up and touch her cheek, lift her gaze, but he just gripped his own knees tighter. "You were amazing. I didn't realize how good you'd gotten with the maces."

Abigail nodded. "I've had to work out a lot of anger over the years." She slapped him a little harder than necessary on his injured shoulder. And then stood up and left the room.

Gabe flinched. "I think she's mad."

"You deserve it."

The slight smile on Gabe's lips pulled at Treadon's heart with the deep sorrow and gratitude mixed on the stoic man's face. But it was wiped away as quickly as it appeared with a grimace of pain.

"Tell me what to do," Treadon said.

"Cut an incision," Gabe said. "Pull the piece of shard out."

Treadon hoped he didn't have anything left in his stomach after throwing up earlier. He swallowed hard and poked uncertainly at the small black hole in Gabe's stomach. The muscles were rock hard which made it easier to press the knife against Gabe's skin.

He hesitated.

"Confidence is the best way to overcome doubt." Despite the exhaustion in his voice, Treadon could hear a note of teasing.

"I don't need cheesy fortune cookie quotes right now." He set the knife against Gabe's skin, but his hand shook. He took a deep breath to calm himself.

"Press harder, like you mean it."

Treadon clenched his teeth together and pressed the knife down. The skin split and the cut filled with blood.

He grabbed the tweezers and a rag Abigail left behind. He pressed the rag into the wound and then pulled back. Using instincts he didn't know he had, he shoved the tweezers in, seeing a dot of black when he pulled the rag away. He felt the tweezers hit something hard and he squeezed, tugged. The piece of hematite shard came free. It was small. The tip of a sliver.

But the effect on Gabe was immediate.

His color returned. The wound started to stitch itself back together. Gabe didn't even wait for the wound to close. He stood up and pulled his dirty shirt back over his head.

"I need to talk to all of you in the kitchen."

Treadon leaned against the back of the futon. His legs felt like rubber; his hands shook. Black stains covered his fingers from shoving the dagger into Xander's chest. It was all so much, too much. He could feel the anxiety tightening around him. Ellie was safe. His family was home. Just when he should be feeling better, his body was rebelling against him.

He took a deep breath and shoved the tension deep inside. He felt like he was pressing a jack-in-the box spring into too small of a box. He followed Gabe into the kitchen and sat at the table. There was a pile of grilled cheese sandwiches in the middle of the table, but Treadon couldn't get himself to unfold his arms from across his chest.

Ellie sat down next to him and placed a hand on his arm. It helped. His muscles relaxed just enough for him to reach out and grab a sandwich cut in a triangle half. He nibbled on the end.

Rachel, Abigail, and Gabe sat down as well, a circle of faces looking at each other.

"What happened after I left?" Gabe asked.

"Jarren and I ran up the stairs and found Xander pulling a dagger from Ellie's arm." Treadon couldn't swallow the small bite of sandwich he'd taken.

"The white dagger."

Ellie nodded.

"You're the Descendant of Adeona. You have the twin daggers written into your DNA." Gabe's hands were pressed flat to the table like he was holding it down in case gravity reversed itself. "The Triune wanted the daggers and somehow they knew you were the key."

Ellie looked down at her hands. "I always thought it was just a story my mom used to tell me to get me to go to sleep. I started to realize that she was telling me history, but I never thought I had the daggers."

"Twin daggers?" Rachel asked. "I only saw one. The white one that killed Pravus." Rachel didn't meet Treadon's eyes when she said it.

"Xander was interrupted," said Gabe. "There's still the black dagger in her—the one the Triune really wants. It has the power to tear the Descendants apart so that their souls never die, but they're trapped in limbo like his own demons, living forever in a half-existence."

"That's awful." Rachel reached for Ellie, offering comfort as they took each other's hands across the table.

"What do we do now?" Ellie asked.

"We keep you safe, at all costs," Gabe said.

"What about finding her Guardian?" Treadon asked. "Maybe that will help keep her safe."

Gabe shook his head. "I have a place I can take her. She'll be protected there."

"More hiding." Ellie whispered the words.

"There are other Unguarded there. You won't be alone."

Ellie and Rachel moved to the couch. Abigail cleared the table and Gabe left through the front door. Without Ellie's touch, Treadon's panic rose to a whole new level. He slipped to his own room and curled up on his bed, his hand gripped around the journal. He couldn't close his eyes and he couldn't get his mind to stop swirling. He opened the book and stared at her handwriting. He found the place he'd left off and read.

He wasn't sure when the words blurred into nightmare, but the dream blossomed out of the darkness of Ellie's story. The boy. The blood. The park.

Treadon sat on a swing, the chains creaking as he rocked back and forth. It was night, the park deserted. The wind helping leaves play around the swing's poles. A broken teeter-totter lay half-buried in the bark of the playground area. Across the road from the park was a thick forest with tall trees that swayed, branches blocking the moon.

He didn't feel afraid. Despite having the small feet of a child instead of a towering athlete, he was waiting for something. He wouldn't be alone for long.

He heard the sobs of another child. Coming from the forest. From across the road. He wanted to help, wanted to be a hero like another person he knew. Gabe. He had wanted to be a hero like Gabe. The crying pulled at his heart, and despite his instructions to stay put, to not wander, Treadon moved toward the road, away from the park, the forest getting closer.

He thought he could see the other child, curled against a tree. He stepped onto the road, focused on the form. A girl. Her dark hair forming a silhouette against the lighter bark of the tree.

The car came out of nowhere, going way too fast for a twisty, two-lane road. He looked down to see his sneaker centered perfectly on the solid double lines. He looked up into the two bright lights and open his mouth. He didn't even have time to scream.

The dream shifted. The lights changed. They were no longer white headlights. They turned brown, shifting shapes, a pupil forming in the middle and long eyelashes framing the beautiful eyes. Ellie's eyes sparkled with humor as he felt the crushing pain shoving all the air from his lungs.

Forty-Nine

TREADON NELSON

A knocking sound pulled him up from drowning in her eyes. He gasped and looked down. He was on the last page of Ellie's journal, the handwriting shaky.

Whoever you are, however I hurt you, boy, I am sorry.

She'd left him. She'd erased his memory and left him in the forest. Her own Guardian.

As the knock sounded again, Treadon stood, drained, confused, but at the same time, completely sure.

Treadon cracked the door. Rachel stood with her fist up preparing to knock again. "Did I interrupt your workout?"

"No," Treadon said, grabbing the bottom of his shirt and wiping it across his forehead. The dream had left him sweaty, his face dripping with perspiration.

"I thought you'd want a chance to say goodbye before she leaves, give her a chance to say thank you."

Treadon was in a daze, not sure how to feel or what to do. He opened the door wider and started to step out.

Rachel put up a finger. "Throw on a new shirt. It never hurts to make a good impression."

"Now you sound like Jarren."

Rachel's face fell.

"I'm sorry. I'm sure he's okay. I'm sure he knows what he's doing."

Rachel nodded. "He'll find his way."

Treadon changed his shirt, stopping to look at his chest in the mirror. There were no scars, no signs of the wound he imagined . . . remembered . . . having.

He pulled on the shirt and stepped out into the living room. Ellie stood like a soldier in front of the couch.

"I know your story." Treadon's voice didn't hold any emotion. He had to keep it flat because he wasn't sure where to put the inflection. "I finished reading the journal." The book was in his hands. He must have grabbed it as he walked out of the room.

She nodded, her eyes filling with tears. "I never should have used my powers without training. I wish I had never run away from my fate."

"Why don't you want to look for him?"

"Because it wouldn't be fair. It wouldn't be fair to him. It wouldn't be fair to me. The connection was never completed. If I found him now, he would be pulled toward me, but we would never know if it was real, if it was his choice."

Treadon swallowed. "So, you don't want to know. You don't want to give him a chance."

"It's more complicated than that," Gabe said, placing a mug of warm tea on the table. "We don't know the implications of an incomplete bond and at such a young age. And with Ellie's DNA still containing the dagger that can slay an angel, we couldn't take a chance on an untrained, unvetted Guardian. I may not agree with everything the Veil does, but they do prepare Guardians for the life they'll have to lead. We have no idea what kind of person Ellie Bonded with or what state they are in today. Even if we gave them a choice, it might be a bad idea."

The words twisted Treadon's gut. Ellie did deserve the best. What did he have to offer? He wasn't even sure he should reveal what he knew, but he couldn't let her leave not knowing.

Ellie looked down at her arms, one wrapped with gauze where the white dagger had been ripped from her bones. The left arm had a burn scar from Xander's attempt to get the second dagger.

"If we could find out who it was, would you give him a chance?" Treadon kept his hands clasped as he leaned against the kitchen counter. His heel bounced as he waited nervously for the answer. The question was directed at both Ellie and Gabe.

Ellie held perfectly still. He could see her running through the possibilities. "It would be too much to ask. If he managed to have a normal life after what I did, I would be asking him to give up everything, risk his life for a life he didn't choose."

Abigail and Gabe stood by the door. Treadon saw their glance, heard their communication. They had both given up so much, lost so much, but in that moment they both silently agreed they would do it again.

"If we could find him, there would have to be a series of tests," Gabe said. "There would be a chance he would be rejected, even if he did choose to be a Guardian. What you've just experienced is only the beginning. Things will only get harder. Caden may lie low for a little bit while he recovers from this setback, but he will come again. He will come for the dagger."

Ellie shook her head. "How could I ask anyone to face that without any understanding or experience? I couldn't."

"What if I want it," Treadon said, reaching out and taking Ellie's hand. "What if I chose to face what was coming? What if I chose to stand by you?"

Ellie shook her head. "It's not you. I'm already broken . . . I mean Bonded."

"What if it is?" Treadon could hardly breathe. "What if it's me? Would you choose me again?" Treadon's chest felt like he had a vice tightening down on him. She could reject him and where would that leave him? Still, he had to try.

Abigail took a step forward, putting a hand to her mouth. "Why would you say that? Treadon, why would you volunteer to be her Guardian when you know she's already chosen someone else."

Treadon looked at Gabe. "I'm ready for the first test."

"I don't understand," Gabe said. His back was straight, his muscles tense.

Treadon put out his hand. "Let me see the compass. Gabe said they were connected to the Guardian's DNA."

Ellie hesitated and then set her jaw. She didn't believe it. Not yet. She lifted the chain over her head, pulling the amulet away from her chest. The movement looked like it ripped out part of her soul. There was a mixture of terror and hope in her face. The terror of allowing herself to hope.

She set the necklace in Treadon's open palm.

For a moment, nothing happened. Treadon's heart dipped, his stomach flipped. Could he be wrong? The amulet had spun before, but never pointed in a direction. If he was right, it was because Xander had been blocking her aura. If he was right, it would point at her. If he was wrong, he really would lose her.

A strange tingle worked its way up his arm. The chain shifted as the amulet rose off his palm and started to spin. The amulet made three full rotations, the spheres twisting around the circles, rising, falling, lining up. The amulet slowed and stopped, still floating above Treadon's hand. The yellow jewel stopped in the center, the other spheres aligning to point at Ellie's nose.

She sagged to the couch. Abigail stepped forward.

"It's impossible." Abigail turned to Gabe, shaking her head. "Tell him it's impossible."

"The compass is connected to Treadon like my compass is to me," Gabe said, "but I have never heard of this happening. An incomplete bond. A connection formed so young. There is no precedence for it."

"Gabe," Abigail said, approaching Gabe like he could undo the situation. "Tell him it can't be him. I would know. You would know. When would this even have happened?"

"You left me at a park." Treadon wanted to sit down next to Ellie, look into her face and read exactly what she was feeling, but he was afraid of what he'd see. Disappointment. Rejection. What if she didn't want him to be her Guardian? He suddenly understood why Ellie hadn't wanted to go looking. He kept his eyes on Gabe and Abigail, building up his courage before looking at Ellie.

"Alone. Never." Abigail shook her head. "I mean, maybe when you were older, but we were always close by."

"I was seven or eight. There were a lot of trees and a road."

"Why didn't you tell us before?" Abigail asked.

"Because I didn't remember." He yelled the words, anger coming up from nowhere. The last few years coming back. The nightmares. The fear of cars. Seeing people differently. Being different. Always feeling like he was hiding. The frustration rose in him. "I didn't remember any of it. Just in my nightmares."

Abigail's mouth gaped open. "The nightmares. I remember when they started."

"I erased his memory." Ellie spoke softly. The sound sent chills through Treadon. They were as cold and flat as his voice had been when he'd first stepped into the living room. She hadn't decided. She hadn't decided if this was good or bad. Treadon's throat tightened. "He had been hit by a car and was dying. I didn't want to let him die. And then I tried to cover up the mistake with a bad decision. I was young and scared. I'm sorry."

"Where did this happen?" Gabe asked.

"A small tourist town," Ellie said quietly. She was so good at keeping her voice even. Treadon couldn't get a read on her without looking at her and he didn't want to look. Not yet. "My mom liked to meet a lot of different kinds of people outside the city atmosphere. She loved it there."

"Where?" Gabe's voice was a stone dropped in a lake.

"Coos Bay. We lived there for two years before they found us."

Abigail gasped. Gabe's breathing stopped, a muscle flexing in his neck.

"You were there." Treadon saw the guilt on his mom's face.

"You've never been hit by a car." Abigail's head was shaking in denial like there was an annoying fly buzzing around her head.

"Are you sure?" Gabe asked Abigail.

"Of course. I would know if my son had almost died."

Gabe came across the room and sat on the coffee table across from Ellie. "You are the daughter of Vita and Curtis. We thought you died that night, when the fenris came."

Treadon couldn't help it. He looked. Ellie wasn't thinking about him now. Gabe's words had taken her back to the last time she'd seen her parents.

"I ran back to the house." Ellie dropped her head into her hands so that her voice barely carried. "I thought I could tell my mom, get her help, but they were gone, there was nothing left. No bodies. Only the floor covered in a swirling black dust." Ellie took a breath and sat up straight, dropping her hands to her lap and looking Gabe in the face like she was ready for the judgement and execution. "The pulse created when I Bonded must have destroyed them. Just another thing I didn't mean to do."

Gabe leaned back; his hands squeezed into fists. "You've thought this whole time that it was your fault your family was gone?"

"I saw the dust. The house was empty." Tears slipped from Ellie's eyes, but she held her head high. "I've been hiding from my mistake for way too long. I'm glad someone finally knows, no matter what my consequences will be."

Treadon half-expected Ellie to put her wrists out for Gabe to cuff her and drag her off to some kind of Descendant prison. Treadon stiffened, ready to fight Gabe off to give Ellie a chance to run. But she wouldn't. She was turning herself in.

"I think there are some things about that night you need to know." Abigail came around the coffee table, her fingers brushing Gabe's shoulder with the slightest touch. Then she sat down next to Ellie and put an arm around her.

"I know that a man came to take me away," Ellie said. "He wanted to keep me safe, but I didn't want to go. I was scared."

Gabe nodded. "That man was me. I'm the one who told your parents about the Vision of Adura."

Ellie shook her head. "I never heard the vision, only that I would have to leave."

"That makes sense," Abigail said. "I was there, too. This was before the Unguarded started disappearing. I helped Gabe deliver messages, but that was the last night I traveled with him."

"Why?" Treadon asked. He remembered traveling with Gabe. He hadn't known what they were doing, but they'd felt like vacations.

Abigail shuddered. "Because of what happened that night. And I don't mean the car accident. I didn't even know about that."

Gabe nodded and then continued the story. "Your parents went into the bedroom to wake you and your brother, but at that moment we were attacked. A dozen fenris broke through the windows, slammed through the back door, and ripped through the roof. Abigail had to use a fire poker to defend herself. Vita, Curtis, and I fought with our weapons. Even their son fought. But we could all tell it wasn't going to be enough. Abigail was backed into a corner where the fenris swiped at her face. It's where she got that scar on her forehead. Vita and Curtis were overwhelmed and the fenris pulled them through the window. I was protecting the boy, barely able to keep the fenris at bay, when there was a pulse. The fenris vanished, disintegrated before our eyes. I thought Vita had done something to get rid of the fenris, but she never came back. I never knew what happened, but now I know. You've got it all wrong, Ellie. You didn't destroy your family. You saved us."

Ellie's hands pressed to either side of her head. "You were there?" Realization stole across her face. "You were the messenger at the door that was going to take me away?"

"Yes." Gabe swallowed. "But your parents were taken."

"And then you just left?" Ellie said, looking away. "You left me?"

"The bedroom was empty," Abigail said. "We looked for you, but we thought the fenris had taken you with your parents. We had no idea you'd run away, nor that you would come back. We had to get the boy to safety, and I was panicking about Treadon, that we'd left him. But when we got back to the park, he was fine. I never traveled with Gabe again. I wasn't willing to put Treadon in that kind of danger."

"That's when my nightmares started," Treadon said.

"Yes." Abigail shrugged. The pieces fit together, but the result was the same. Treadon had an incomplete Bond with Ellie. Ellie's family was still gone.

But now they knew.

"What about the other kid?" Rachel asked. Treadon had almost forgotten she was there. She leaned against the counter on the far side of the fridge, arms folded. "What happened to Ellie's brother?"

"I took him to a safe place."

Ellie was as stiff as a statue, almost like if she moved, she would break the spell. "My brother's alive?"

"Yes." Gabe stood and offered Ellie a hand to help her up. "I can take you to him and you'll be with other Unguarded in a safe place. We can protect the dagger and make sure Caden never finds you again."

Ellie looked at Gabe's hand and then looked at Treadon. He sat next to her. Her eyes were open wide, her lips parted slightly. A war on her face between what she wanted and what was right.

Treadon reached out to touch the scars on her forearms. The partial bond she'd created with him had changed him, had created this pressing desire to protect her, to be near her. But Gabe had said that Guardians needed to be trained, prepared. Ellie was one of the most wanted Descendants on planet earth. They wanted the dagger that could kill Descendants and Treadon had almost watched them take it. He'd only been able to stop them with the help of Jarren, Rachel, and his mom. Maybe he wasn't the right person to be her Guardian. She needed to be safe.

"You should go to be safe," Treadon said, the words feeling like he was ripping a piece of duct tape off his heart.

Ellie swallowed, her fingers tightening into fists. "I could see my brother. I should do what I didn't do ten years ago."

Treadon nodded, opening his hand to reveal the compass. Ellie put her hand over the compass, holding her hand against his, their skin touching the cool metal of the amulet. She pulled away, taking the amulet into her fingers.

"What about you?" Ellie asked. "What will you do?"

Abigail shifted, her mouth opening and one hand coming out toward him. Treadon could sense Gabe's tension as well. They doubted he was the right person to be Ellie's Guardian.

"I don't know if I can be the Guardian you need. I'm not even sure

I'm the Guardian you would choose, but I would choose you. I would be your Guardian."

Ellie's head dropped. "Not a full Guardian, and I have no idea what that means for you. You could be following me into danger that you don't have the full abilities to face. I would be asking you to risk your life for a girl you hardly know. To give up everything like your mom."

Her last words caught in Treadon's soul. His mom's misery. Her sorrow. His own desire to break her free of the life she was living. And here he was, offering to do the same thing.

He paused too long.

"But I'm not ready to do that to you." Ellie reached out and took Gabe's hand, standing and leaving Treadon feeling like he'd been hit by a blast of frigid air. "I'm ready to go. I'm ready to stop running."

"We'll leave first thing in the morning," Gabe said.

"You'd better get some sleep." Abigail let out a long sigh. "One thing you'll learn about this life is that you have to keep on doing everyday things even while it feels like the world is falling apart. You've got five hours before school."

"School?" Treadon asked.

Fifty

Treadon Nelson

Treadon stared at the blank paper on his desk. He thought his mom had been joking, but she'd been nothing but serious.

He'd gone to bed without another word, spent the rest of the early morning hours tossing and turning. In the end, he was grateful that he had an excuse to get up and move. Laying there felt like torture.

A hand landed on his shoulder. He was surprised when he looked up into the face of Mr. Ashcroft.

"Don't let it get you down. Losing a football game isn't the end of the world." He spoke with sincerity.

"Football?" Treadon's mind struggled to break out of its foggy stupor.

"I know it's hard to see right now, but it's just one game. You've got your whole life ahead of you. And, with what I've seen of your work ethic, you have the potential for great things. You know what you want and how to work hard to get it. Don't give up. You can do anything you want."

"Anything I want?" Treadon tilted his head.

"Sure," Mr. Ashcroft said, motioning toward the windows. "The sky's the limit. If you see something you want, you've got to keep at it until you achieve it. You'll always have setbacks. The person who comes out on top is the one who gets up after a loss and sets his sights on the next game. I've seen that persistence in you. You've got a bright future, Mr. Nelson."

Mr. Ashcroft returned to the front of the room and wrote an equation on the board.

Treadon stood up.

Mr. Ashcroft turned around and nearly dropped his smart pen.

"Is everything okay?" Mr. Ashcroft asked.

"You're right," Treadon said, his chest feeling lighter. "Thanks, Mr. Ashcroft." He picked up his bag and walked out of class.

He moved down the hall, decision feeling as good as a full night's sleep. He had something he wanted: Ellie. He just had to go after her. Let her know his choice.

Treadon was halfway across the parking lot when something caught his eye.

A familiar Harley leaned on its kickstand near the entrance to the football field in the middle of the sidewalk. Treadon changed directions and headed up the side street between the gym and the football field. He thought he'd check the locker rooms, but then he saw a lone figure on the bleachers.

"Jarren?" Treadon crossed through the gates onto the track. He ran up to Jarren from the other side of the waist-high fence. "Dude, what happened to you? You jumped out of a five-story window and just disappeared. Rachel's going crazy. And I'm sorry about your dad. Are you okay?"

Jarren sat on the bottom level of the bleachers, staring at the field with a blank expression. His leg was propped up, balanced on the bench in front of him. The deep lines across his forehead were the only sign of sorrow Jarren let slip through his façade.

"Aren't you supposed to be in class?" Jarren raised an accusing eyebrow. "Were you seriously about to skip without me?"

"I don't need your permission to skip class. Just because I never would have done it alone before, doesn't mean a guy can't change. I've grown up."

Jarren smiled. "About time. So where are you headed now that you're all grown up?"

"I'm going to find Ellie."

"She's missing again?"

"No." Treadon looked down, wishing he had a better answer. "She's leaving."

"And you didn't catch the hint? I thought you were good at reading people."

"It wasn't a hint." Treadon wanted to hit something. He wished he'd reacted faster last night. "I waited too long. I hesitated."

"The death of fools."

Treadon sighed. Abigail still saw him as a child. Gabe didn't believe he was strong enough. Even Jarren could see his weaknesses. He had hesitated. He had anxiety. And if he was honest, he feared facing those monsters again. But he would do it for her. "Gabe doesn't think I'm the right person for her, and she's not sure I'm willing to do what it takes. But I'm ready to prove them all wrong."

"This is the most intense game of playing hard-to-get I've ever seen." Jarren kept a stoic face of disinterest.

"That's the understatement of the year."

There was a lull in their conversation, and Jarren's attention went somewhere else. His eyes raked the football field.

"Seriously, man," Treadon said, wanting to reach out to his friend, but reading his need for space. He stayed on the other side of the fence, leaning closer. "What happened to you? How can you even explain what happened last night?"

"I can't," Jarren said. He took a deep breath like he was trying to bench press his max. "I can't explain anything. All I know is that I need some answers."

"You're leaving too." Reading Jarren's emotions left an empty space inside Treadon's chest.

"Don't sound so heartbroken. You've always known I'm straight. It never would have worked out between us."

"I'm serious. Where are you going?"

Jarren looked at a laptop setting next to him on the bleachers. "I've got some things to figure out."

Treadon saw the answer in Jarren's eyes—the hunger, the curiosity.

"You know where to find your mom."

"Will you cut that out?" Jarren squinted into the sun. "Yeah. I want to see my mom."

"Don't you want to wait until graduation?"

"Nah. Graduation is for unimportant people who don't have fathers who were rich, evil supervillains. I'm set for life." Jarren flipped Gabe's keys around his finger.

"I'll give you a ride," Treadon said. "Gabe will hunt you down and skin you alive if you take his bike."

A car approached the back of the school. Probably Coach bringing in the equipment for practice. He ignored the slam of a car door.

Jarren rocked his head back and forth. "Being seen in your mom's Pontiac or being hunted by a Guardian?" He lifted one hand and the other like he was testing the two ideas on a scale. "I'll take my chances with the bike. Gabe's a cuddly teddy bear on the inside."

"Uh, I wouldn't let him catch you saying that." Treadon shivered, thinking of Gabe's scowl of disappointment last night.

"Say what?" Jarren said. "That he's a soft, squishy man wearing a muscle suit that wishes he was as cool as me." Jarren jutted his chin forward, his eyes looked past Treadon.

Treadon had been too focused on Jarren to notice the footsteps weren't headed out to the football field. Several people were approaching them from behind.

Treadon whirled.

Gabe stopped a few feet from them, eyebrows raised at Jarren's insults. And behind him—Ellie. Rachel and Abigail came forward and sat on the bleachers behind Jarren like they were ready to watch the game. Rachel put her arms around Jarren, and he leaned into her shoulder.

Treadon only had eyes for Ellie. The breath rushed from his lungs. She hadn't left, yet. "I thought you'd already be gone."

Ellie shrugged as she passed Gabe and stood directly across the fence from Treadon, hands behind her like a sergeant doing an inspection. "Do you remember how I said we'd make a good team?"

"Yes." Treadon could barely find the air to push the word out.

"I think we'll be stronger together, even with the incomplete Bond." Ellie took a breath. This was a test and Treadon wanted to pass with every fiber of his being. "I don't want to run anymore. I ran away when I was eight and I've never stopped running. Going with Gabe now, leaving to hide, feels like doing the same thing. This time I want to stand and fight."

"Fight?" Treadon asked. The impulse to protect her flared up in his chest. He was her Guardian, and his job was to keep her safe. But that wasn't what she wanted anymore. "How are you going to do that?"

"I don't know, yet" Ellie said. "But I want to start with my foster family. Get them back together. Find Jake. And then we'll go after the Triune. Stop them from doing what they've been planning. You already know it will be dangerous. You've already seen what that looks like."

"What about the dagger?" Treadon asked.

"That's only part of Caden Bachman's plan," Rachel said. "From what I've found out about XC Energy, we've only broke the surface of what is really going on."

"I want to do more than run." Ellie dropped her eyes. "And I want to choose a Guardian who wants to fight alongside me, not protect me."

Jarren groaned behind them. "I'm so glad I'm leaving. I do not want to be around to see the two of you make out." He pushed away from Rachel. She didn't try to hold him back. He tried to stand, but grimaced.

"Your leg," Ellie said, moving over to Jarren. "I can help you now."

Ellie slipped her hand into Jarren's. Jarren's hands clasped hers. His eyes opened wide, and he sucked air in through his teeth. Treadon could see the relief on Jarren's face.

"That was incredible." He put his full weight on the leg and smiled. "Perfect."

"Wait," Ellie said, reaching out and pulling Jarren down to sit on the bleachers again. "There's something in your head."

"I had brain surgery when I was a kid, but they said they fixed whatever was wrong. They never actually told me what they took out. A tumor or something."

"Has it been hurting?" Ellie asked.

"Headaches," Jarren nodded, "but it's probably from stress."

Ellie reached up and touched Jarren's cheek. Jarren closed his eyes and leaned into her hand. His mouth opened. A small sigh of relief escaped his lips.

Ellie's face went pale. A red gash on her cheek opened like a fresh wound.

Gabe let out a cry of warning. Treadon jumped over the fence and caught Ellie as she started to collapse. Abigail helped Treadon lower her to the bleacher. Her hand fell away from Jarren's face. Her color returned almost immediately, the cut closing on its own.

"What happened?" Jarren asked.

Treadon stood up and shoved Jarren. "What do you mean what happened? What did you do to her?"

"Nothing." Jarren put his hands up in surrender, but his eyes examined his fingers like he was seeing them for the first time. "I don't know what happened, but she—she did something. I haven't felt this good for a long time." Jarren exhaled out his mouth, lifting his chin. "Almost like I can breathe again." He closed his eyes. "Like I had been wearing earplugs, but now I can hear." He tilted his head to the side. "Do you feel that?"

"Jarren don't—" Gabe said.

Abigail put a hand to her mouth, staring at Jarren with wide eyes.

Jarren didn't seem to be listening to them; he listened to something far away or deep underground. He put his hands out to the side. The ground started to shake—a loud rumbling filled the air. Car alarms went off in the parking lot. Some of the stadium lights shattered.

He dropped his arms. Everything stopped shaking.

Gabe looked at Abigail and Abigail nodded. Treadon looked between them and then down at Ellie. It couldn't be. He'd known Jarren for over two years.

"I can help you," Gabe nodded, reaching out in a gesture of peace, "if you come with me."

"Nah, I've got a date with my old lady. But we'll meet again." Jarren pursed his lips together, widening his stance.

Gabe pulled keys out of his pocket and stepped to the side, gesturing toward the parking lot. The Aston Martin gleamed in the sunlight. "New tires." Gabe tilted his head toward the car. "It'll take you where you need to go." He turned back to face Jarren. "But I want my keys back."

They tossed keys at the same time, both wanting what the other had.

Jarren looked at Rachel. "I'll be back." He jogged over to his car and jumped in.

He left two long tire streaks as he pulled out of the school parking lot.

"What just happened?" Treadon asked, Ellie standing by his side.

"Whatever Ellie did to Jarren's mind, she changed something." Abigail squeezed Treadon's arm. "He has a white aura now. He's glowing."

"What does that mean?" Treadon asked, arm wrapped around Ellie's shoulder, ready to face the hordes of Hell to prove he could be her Guardian.

Gabe answered without taking his eyes off the disappearing car. "Jarren is a Descendant. He's an Unguarded."

Acknowledgments

Every person who has entered my life has left an impression on my heart. I have been changed, challenged, cared for, criticized, comforted, and encouraged. Thank you to every person who has touched my life and given me the strength and confidence to finish this book.

Thank you to my editor, Katie Lewis, to my beta readers, Michelle, Amanda, Jeneane, Joy, and of course, my wonderful mother who has read as many versions of this book as there are stars in the sky.

I wouldn't be the writer I am today without my amazing writing friends. The Hot Mess Writing Group has been with me through dozens of manuscripts, both good and bad. I will be forever grateful for the help and support of these wonderful people who need to be named, Valerie Doll, Jordan Wright, Jessica Flory, Dave Munk, Patrice Carey, and Heidi Rogers. There have been dozens of other authors who have supported me and helped me improve my writing.

My family has eaten plenty of burnt dinners due to my writer's brain, but always stood beside me. They are my inspiration for life. My husband, Philip, and my kids, Evan, Jacob, and Katelynn. Thank you for being with me through the ups and downs. Life is beautiful with all of you. And thank you to my sisters and nieces and nephews. Some of my earliest fans!

Finally, thank you! The reader who made it to the end of the book. I love that you have shared this journey with me. We will be forever connected.

About the Author

Tracy Daley wrote her first book in fifth grade and will forever be grateful for amazing teachers who encourage and empower their students. She spent ten years working in the publishing industry and has developed her love of storytelling through reviewing, acquiring, and reading every great book she could get her hands on. She is the author of a middle grade historical fiction, *If the Fire Comes,* and a YA Contemporary, *The Wrong Side of the Setting Sun.* She now owns her own publishing company, Night Nook Publishing, where she publishes her own stories and is working to support other writers in the future. She loves skiing, eating, and traveling with her family.

For news about future stories, information about supporting authors, and Night Nook Publishing products, sign up for the newsletter.

www.nightnookpublishing.com

Also by Tracy Daley

Descendants of Angels Series
Loss of the Unguarded

Fall of the Guardian - Available February 2023

Rise of the Captive - Available April 2023

Paranormal Short Stories
Demon Confessions of Sansa Plath

Contemporary YA
The Wrong Side of the Setting Sun

Middle Grade Historical Fiction
If the Fire Comes

Made in the USA
Monee, IL
17 April 2024